A SHILLING FOR A WIFE

A SHILLING FOR A WIFE

EMMA HORNBY

TRANSWORLD PUBLISHERS
61–63 Uxbridge Road, London W5 5SA
www.penguin.co.uk

Transworld is part of the Penguin Random House group of companies
whose addresses can be found at global.penguinrandomhouse.com

First published in Great Britain in 2016 by Bantam Press
an imprint of Transworld Publishers
Corgi edition published 2017

A CIP catalogue record for this book
is available from the British Library.

ISBN 9780552173230

Typeset in 11/13.25pt New Baskerville by Thomson Digital Pvt Ltd,
Noida, Delhi.

Printed and bound in Great Britain by Clays Ltd, Elcograf S.p.A.

Penguin Random House is committed to a sustainable future
for our business, our readers and our planet. This book is made
from Forest Stewardship Council® certified paper.

For those whose belief in me never waned, especially Mark and Mum, thank you. Without your support and encouragement, this book would not have seen the light of day. And my ABC, always x

I think people really marry far too much; it is such a lottery after all, and for a poor woman a very doubtful happiness.

Queen Victoria

Chapter 1
Mid-October 1853

THE AIR IN the dank kitchen was thick with desperation.

'Please, I have no idea what you're talking about!'

'Liar! I know you're lying, you whore. Tell me the truth or by God, I'll beat it from thee!' As he roared the threat into Sally's face, Joseph Goden drew back his huge arm, fist more than ready to strike.

'Joseph, please. I need help.' Her voice a strangled whisper, she screwed up her face in dreaded anticipation of the blow. She knew only too well the world would explode into sharp bursts of light and blinding pain.

Yet despite her terror and the agony tearing through her back and stomach, determination not to crack burned fiercer. She wouldn't tell him. She wouldn't!

Her eyes flickered to the sofa; if she hadn't been in the latter stages of labour, she'd have bolted behind it. Not that it made a difference. Her instinct to hide when he lifted his fists offered no protection. He'd laugh in grim satisfaction as she cowered and, more often than not, wet herself with fear waiting for his next move.

Sometimes, he'd simply grow bored with torturing her and bellow, 'Clean up your filth, whore!' He'd then resume his terrorisation as, cheeks flaming with humiliation, she scrubbed the floor, kicking out at her and sending her sprawling across the wet flags.

Otherwise, he'd reach behind the sofa, grab her hair and lift her clean over the top. Then he'd beat her so badly, she'd be unconscious for hours. Or, dear God, he'd drag her to bed, which was like visiting hell itself . . .

Even if she'd been physically able, the thought of running into the row and screaming for help didn't enter her mind. She'd find no sanctuary there. He'd seen to that.

Upon their arrival at Spring Row to begin wedded life, he'd gripped her by the throat and whispered into her face, 'Now you listen to me, my girl, for I'll only say this once. You ever blab your mouth off to anyone outside of this here cottage and I'll snap your scrawny neck. D'you understand?'

Five years of abominable marriage later, she understood, all right. She didn't disbelieve his threat for a second.

He'll do it this time. Oh, how could I have been so foolish? she thought now, trembling on all fours, awaiting the torrent of blows that always came when he'd had a bellyful of porter.

His drinking had worsened considerably of late, his weekly visits to Ma Thompson's for a jug of her strong, home-brewed ale now a nightly occurrence. Little went into Sally's hand for the housekeeping. Though she'd had to be frugal since the beginning with what he allowed her from his wages, lately it was a constant battle putting a meal of sorts on the table and making the impossible amount of coal she could afford last.

Of course, Joseph fared better at mealtimes. She survived on almost nothing, to prevent his wrath if his meals were insufficient. No amount of imploring would see him tip up another farthing. He blamed her for not being careful with what he gave her.

'I'll give thee summat in a minute, all right, but it'll not be brass,' he'd snarl, raising his hand, if she dared beg for more.

So far, somehow, she'd managed. Now, it seemed all her hard work and careful planning were for nothing.

Hearing him lumber from their bed several hours ago, still half-drunk from last night, she'd stuffed the ball of cheap wool and knitting needles into the dresser drawer and hurried to the fire to heat the kettle. Even with her back to the staircase, she'd sensed his foul mood as he stomped down to the kitchen. Minutes passed in silence as she brewed tea and cut the loaf, while he sat nursing his aching head in his hands. Then, placing his breakfast before him, her world had crumbled around her.

Grabbing her wrist, he'd stared at her hard, head cocked, and asked, 'What's that?'

Ignoring the pain caused by his dirty nails, she'd frowned. 'Bread and drip—' He'd cut her off with a backhanded slap to her mouth.

'Not the grub. That.'

Nursing stinging lips, she'd followed his gaze to a length of pale wool dangling from the drawer. She'd felt blood drain from her face.

'Please, Joseph, I cannot manage on what you give me. It's not enough to make ends meet,' he'd whined mockingly, grip tightening. 'Yet you can manage to buy wool, you lying bitch, yer. No one steals from me! What else has tha bought without me knowing about, eh? What else has tha been frittering my brass on?'

'It's for the infant. It will need clothing when it's here. The wool only cost—' To her horror, searing pains ripped across her middle before she could finish. They, and Joseph's threats, had only intensified with the hours.

Now, her work-reddened hands flew protectively to her stomach. Relentless beatings had snuffed out all previous life to grow in her womb. She'd fight to the last breath to protect this one. This child was a fighter. The risks she'd secretly, patiently, carried out for years were for this: the child to survive its father's abuse.

On cue, Joseph's fist struck out. It flew by her head, missing her by inches. Gasping, she forced herself to look at her husband.

Dark eyes glinting, he released a bark of laughter. 'Fricken you, then, did I? That were a warning but next 'un won't be if you don't tell me the truth, you sneaky, thieving young slut.'

She didn't know how much more she could bear on top of the waves of pain threatening to split her in two. Asking him to fetch help was pointless. Being Sunday, the row's residents would be at the Meadow Lane Chapel and besides, her husband wouldn't want anyone seeing the rainbow of colours covering her face from his last attack.

Another contraction ripped through her, making her scream out. 'Joseph, p–please. The child is coming. It's coming now!' The last word ended on a torturous wail and in desperation she fumbled for the hand squeezing her upper arm. To her astonishment, his grip loosened.

Her eyes widened as he smoothed her drenched hair from her brow with the coal-dust-ingrained hand poised to strike moments before. 'Oh, Joseph, help me,' she whispered on a sob, taking advantage of this tenderness she'd never known from him. 'It hurts so much. Please . . . I don't know what to do.'

He ground out his reply. 'Are you going to tell me what you've been up to?'

She closed her eyes, heart sinking. She'd have to confess. Any chance of receiving help rested on it. *But if I do, it will all have been for nothing. Dear Lord, what do I do?* she agonised.

Mind consumed with hopeless options, she didn't notice that the hand stroking her hair had slid, until it clamped her breast. Her eyes sprang open and her heart banged at his leering grin.

Mother of God, surely not! The thought exploded through her brain. 'Joseph . . . ? What are you *doing*?'

'Tell me the truth or I'll force it from thee the hard way.'

Her dress had ridden to her hips with her writhing; her heaving breasts, glistening with perspiration, spilled over the top. Eyes raking over her, his breathing quickened.

She stared around wildly. Surely to God he wouldn't – couldn't – take her as she was about to give birth? How could he contemplate something so disgusting? She knew from experience he was capable of anything, but not *that*, surely? He was bluffing. He had to be!

'You wouldn't,' she forced herself to whisper.

His grin deepened. 'Oh believe me, my girl, I would.'

Panting through another contraction, she glared up in complete disgust, fear giving way to uncontrollable anger at his expression of enjoyment. 'You've gone too far this time. Mary, Mother of God, how could you think to do that while I'm in agony bearing your child? That is sick beyond belief, even for you.'

'The truth, then!' he bellowed, but she saw him waver and, to her sheer relief, he grunted, gave her breast a last, hard squeeze then released it.

As she stared in repulsion at the face she loathed, twisted with evil, words dripping with long-suppressed hatred poured from her. 'Lord above, I detest you. I wish you were dead, do you hear, *dead*. You make me sick to my stomach, you despicable bastard.'

After a moment of stunned silence, his eyes bulged and with a roar he threw back his arm. 'You midden-mouthed whore, I'll murder thee!'

His arm swung and she whimpered, her bravado vanishing at the sight of the fist heading for her face. 'Please, no!'

A furious voice from the cottage door pierced the air, reverberating like a gunshot:

'Don't you fret, my lass. He wouldn't dare!'

As the congregation spilled from the recently built, sandstone edifice of the Wesleyan Chapel, Arthur Morgan shielded his eyes and squinted at the chattering worshippers making their way homeward. The brisk breeze soothed his bewhiskered face after the muggy chapel and he breathed it in gratefully. Humming along to the faint strains of the organ at his back, he scanned the women's bobbing heads for his wife's fawn-coloured bonnet, but couldn't see it.

Where the heck has she got to? he wondered in bemusement before strolling down the stone steps and on for Meadow Lane towards home.

Earlier, seeing the preacher bringing out the collection tin, Ivy had hissed in his ear, 'Eeh, I've forgot my bleedin' purse!'

He'd left his precious coppers at home. Each Saturday, he ungrudgingly handed Ivy his full wage and she'd then give back several coins for him to do with as he pleased. It wasn't much, enough for a few pots of ale and a twist of tobacco, but it suited him. She had a hard task making ends meet but was a thrifty housewife; she had a knack of stretching a farthing to tuppence.

Kicking a stone across the lane, he smiled, recalling the disapproving frowns at the colourful words she'd dared speak in the Lord's house. A chuckle gurgled in his throat remembering her response.

'Youse lot mind your own, for I've a fair few words what would shock you more than that.' At her growled warning, the listeners, aware of her fierce temper, had looked away. However, the braver ones turned again when she muttered, 'I'll have to go home and fetch the bugger.' But at her hard look as she slipped from the pew, their heads had soon snapped back to the front.

By, she's a rum 'un, he thought fondly, turning into Spring Row.

Some ten years old, the cluster of cottages nestled in a fold between the Wesleyan Chapel – or the Meadow Lane Chapel, as locals referred to it – and the Coach and Horses public house. Though idyllic-sounding, Spring Row was deceptive in its name, as pleasing to the eye it wasn't.

The two-up, two-downs, with back bedrooms open to the staircase, were damp and alive with vermin, the shared privy middens in the back lane foul and stinking. Despite most residents' dogged attempts to keep them tolerable, the sight and smell were sickening, especially in fine weather.

However, the rent was manageable and with the cottages facing south towards Bury Road, the occupants were compensated by rich fields stretching for miles behind, Breightmet Bleach Works at Red Bridge the only blot spoiling the beautiful view.

Aye, but it's not so bad, he mused. There were worse places. His and Ivy's last dwelling, one of a mound of hovels by aptly named Rough Close, near the Old Hare and Hounds public house, sprang to mind. He shuddered at the memories. Yet as his home came into view, all thought melted at the unbelievable sight that met him.

Joseph Goden was hammering at Arthur's door with both fists, bellowing, like a crazed bull, threats and insults to Ivy within.

White-hot fury surged through Arthur. When he reached his wicket gate, grim-faced neighbours stepped aside but his fellow miner didn't notice until he gripped his shoulders and spun him around. Joseph grunted angrily but the normally placid Arthur's rage-filled state visibly threw him.

'What in the name of God d'you think you're doing, Goden?' he roared incredulously. Though older and not as powerfully built, he was none the less solid-muscled, more than capable of standing up to him.

'Your interfering bloody wife's got my Sally in there,' Joseph blustered, thrusting a thumb. 'Come barging into my bloody home without being invited, she did. She wants putting in her place. By God, she does!'

Arthur's advancing fist paused as Martha Smith from two doors down shouted, 'Aye, what, like your wife, you mean? The lass has started with the babby and yon Ivy's took her into yours to aid her, like,' she added to Arthur. 'Covered in bruises her poor face were, an' all.' Swinging her ample frame forward, she spat to Joseph in disgust, 'You want stringing up treating that lass as you do, you bully yer.'

A red hue crept up his neck and she laughed derisively. 'D'you think I don't know how tha treats that young wife of yourn? You can tell a mile you lead her a dog's life. Flits to the privy and to and from Percy's shop like a frightened rabbit, she does, and them's the only times we see her leave yon cottage. She don't speak a word to nobody. You make sure of that, don't you?'

The silence was deafening; then followed other bystanders' murmurs of agreement.

Arthur shook his head. 'You snidy, evil . . . You hid your colours, all right, didn't you? Well, the game's up, now, Goden. In nowt but seconds, I could round up half a dozen fellas with a click of my fingers to give you the going over you deserve; aye, happen I should.' He nodded and the neighbours jeered their support.

Joseph's Adam's apple bobbed as he glanced around. He licked his lips. Then puffing out his chest, he lifted his chin. 'And what of it, anyroad? A fella's entitled to discipline his wife if need be. Pity others don't follow my example,' he added, looking pointedly at him.

'You bullying swine, yer!' Arthur swung his fist but Joseph swerved and hurried down the rutted path. A chorus of angry voices, thick with threat, mingled with the sound of his clogs as he ran down the lane.

'You should've given the divil what for, speaking ill of yon Ivy like that,' Martha muttered disappointedly when he disappeared from view.

'Ay, don't fret, wench. I'll have my day with him.'

Arthur spoke quietly but the steely edge pacified her enough for her to say, 'Aye, tha will that.' As her words died away, a piercing scream from his cottage filled the air.

Sally's baby was born.

Chapter 2

OPENING A BLEARY eye, Ivy frowned as the wispy mew sounded again. It took a moment for her tired brain to register it and she smiled as recognition dawned. She heaved her thin body from the straw mattress, still spiky and itchy despite the two blankets, and lifted her shawl from the foot of the bed.

She tried in vain to stem a shiver. The early morning breeze still found a way through the draughty window, despite the rags stuffed around the edges, and it seeped through the threadbare shirt of Arthur's she wore for bed.

By, I bet the babby's freezing, she fretted, wrapping the matted shawl around her shoulders.

She slipped out of bed, careful not to wake her husband who would have to be up soon enough for the pithead at Breightmet Colliery; its two pits provided employment for many locals. After padding to the makeshift cot – the bottom drawer from the kitchen dresser which, lined with a ragged blanket, had served all eight of hers – she lifted the scrap of life, swaddled in old clothing, and headed for the door.

It was still pitch black behind the lengths of worn sacking that served as curtains. Cradling the baby in the crook of one arm, she held out the other as a guide. She could have lit the stub of candle on the chipped saucer by the bed, but was loath to. Brass was tight with but two children at home and Arthur's meagre wages.

Granted, they were better off than some and she counted her blessings daily for what they had but still, life was a constant struggle. After rent, food and coal, little remained for luxuries.

Jonathan whimpered and she shushed him quietly. 'All right, my little lad, all right. Let's get you a drop of milk afore you waken the men. Oh, did he waken thee?' she added guiltily as Arthur stirred. He'd allowed her since the start to have the child in with them so she could care for him during the night to let Sally rest.

'Nay, wench, it's all right,' he answered on a yawn. 'What's the hour?'

'I'll go and see. Stop in bed while I light the fire and make breakfast.' She lifted her bottle-green weekday dress from a chair and descended the stairs.

Gasping as her bare feet met the kitchen's cold flagged floor, she hurried to the fire and laid the baby upon the colourful rag rug before it. Squatting beside him, she raked out the dead ashes then built a small pyramid of twigs and dried moss on the faintly glowing cinders.

When it crackled and smoked, she added lumps of coal from a pail and watched in satisfaction as they turned crimson, bathing the room in a cosy glow. She then filled an iron kettle from another pail, hooked it on the bar and swung it over the fire.

She chuckled as the baby stared up at her intently, quieter now warmth radiated through the bars. Noticing his napkin was sopping, she poured the warmed water into a tin dish, stripped him, cleaned him with a scrap of cloth and dressed him in a woollen vest from a string line above the fire, cooing and smiling as she worked.

She removed her shawl, wrapped him in it and returned him to the rug. She then washed herself with the remainder of the water in the dish and slipped into her dress.

Her mouth curved in a smile as she glanced at the clock ticking quietly on the mantel. Her husband and sons still had half an hour's luxury of staying in bed before another day's grafting on the coalface began. The perilous work was gruelling; they needed all the sleep they could snatch.

She brushed a kiss across the child's fuzzy hair. 'Come on, my little love, let's get your belly filled.' Opening the door to the front room of the cottage, she allowed her eyes to become accustomed to the gloom before making for the narrow, iron-framed bed.

Sally lay on her back, covers pulled to her chin. Even sleep couldn't lift her troubled expression, Ivy noticed sadly. The bruises were now myriad faint yellows and blues and the near fortnight in her care had put some much-needed flesh on the young bones. But body and mind were exhausted.

When she roused from the slumbers that consumed her each day, Sally's tearful apologies at being such a burden brought a lump to Ivy's throat. She'd assured the pathetically grateful woman that she and her child were welcome for as long as needs be.

Anger bubbled inside her at the thought of Joseph. 'What's he done to thee?' she whispered to the broken girl. Sighing, she shook her gently. 'Lass, Jonathan wants feeding again.'

Sally struggled into a sitting position. 'What time is it?'

'It's early yet. Latch him on and go back to sleep. I'll keep an eye to him.'

The young woman slipped her shift from her shoulders. Her son, blue eyes wide, nudged at her open-mouthed, and laughing softly, she guided him to her. 'He's perfect, isn't he, Mrs Morgan?'

Emotion rose in Ivy at the sight of mother and child. 'Aye, he is that. Now, are you for kipping or stopping up? If it's the latter, you fill his belly and I'll fetch summat to fill yours.'

The smile slipped from Sally's face. 'Wait a moment until he's had his fill and I'll help you. It's not right you waiting on me; let me mash the tea at least.'

Halfway to the door, Ivy turned. Despite the offer, her eyelids were drooping. 'It's all right, lass. You rest with your babby.'

Sighing, Sally snuggled against him. 'Thank you, Mrs Morgan. Thank you.'

When the door clicked shut, Sally smiled softly with gratitude. The sounds of suckling and faint clinking of crockery from the kitchen were comforting, safe; blissful feelings she'd thought she'd never again encounter.

She still couldn't quite believe she was here. It had taken days to comprehend that, after all these years, she'd finally escaped. It seemed like a lovely dream, and that any moment she'd wake to find herself back in the nightmare she'd suffered so very long. She ran a hand through her hair and sighed. What was she to do? She couldn't stay here for ever, however much she'd like.

That these strangers had taken in her and her child without hesitation, showing nothing but kindness and understanding, still amazed her. She wished she'd told of the abuse years ago and Ivy had scolded her gently, saying the same.

Why didn't I knock when he was at the inn or pit and beg Ivy's help? she asked herself again. The answer was always the same. It was easy in hindsight to berate herself but quite another thing when in the thick of it, with seemingly no way out.

All those wasted years. All those beatings and poor babies born too soon. But this miracle child, thanks to Ivy, survived. He was her gift, her reason to fight. She could never repay this family. They had given not only her child but herself a chance at life.

Within days of her marriage, she'd begun planning her escape. Yet though she hated to admit it, even to herself, she wasn't sure she'd have ever found the strength. His hold had been so extreme that, but for Ivy, she'd probably still be next door.

She peered down at the baby. *Born from a monster's seed.* The thought flitted often, but this child wouldn't grow to be like *him. He* may have created this life with her but that was all he could lay claim to. Shaking her head to dispel the painful thoughts, she lifted the baby's tiny hand and kissed it. Her son, *her* son, would be a decent man and a good husband, she'd make sure of it. She had to stop thinking of the past and concentrate on the future, however uncertain.

She'd been terrified of Joseph turning up but knew now that as long as she was here, she was safe; Ivy had told of his running away when Arthur challenged him. A smile touched her lips. For once, he'd have known how it was to be scared. No, he wouldn't return. For now, she and her child were free from harm.

Movement from the floor above pulled her from her thoughts and she smiled again. She'd become used to the cottage's routine, knew that it was Arthur rising for work. His sons would be down shortly and the family would have breakfast.

She liked this time of day most. Each morning, she'd lie here listening to these people in wonder. The easy chatter, the banter, the elder son's deep, infectious laugh . . . The cottage exuded warmth and happiness and she drew strength from it, soaking it up like a thirsty flower in a downpour. This was how a home should be.

A surge of anger towards Joseph and the home he'd created caused her chest to constrict and she closed her eyes, revelling in it. She'd become so used to being afraid for so long, she'd almost forgotten how it was to feel anything else. Pride flowed through her as she remembered venting her fury that day and the astonishment on his face. She was glad she'd spoken her mind. And she'd meant every word. She did detest him and did wish he were dead.

She'd also managed, despite everything, to hold fast about the money.

Maybe the old Sally *was* inside somewhere, she thought with a smile, slipping back into a peaceful sleep.

Pushing and shoving one another down the well-scrubbed stairs, the Morgan sons halted, their laughter dying, as Ivy hissed, ''Ere, youse two, the lass and babby are akip in there.' Hands on hips, she scowled. 'By, you're a pair of noisy swines.'

Shaun raked a hand through his mop of light-brown curls. 'Sorry, Mam. I didn't think.'

'Aye, sorry, Mam. Not used to having a babby in t' house. Nor a bonny lass, eh, Shaun?' Tommy winked slowly then laughed as he dodged a swipe from his red-faced brother.

'Aye, you can stop that sort of talk right now, my lad.'

'I'm only jesting, Mam. Our Shaunie boy's hardly noticed her. Have you?' Draping an arm across his brother's shoulders, Tommy gave another exaggerated wink and Shaun shrugged it off and stalked to the table. 'Ay, come on, Shaunie boy. I'm only jesting with thee.' Grinning, he chucked him under the chin.

Taking another swipe, and missing again, Shaun glowered. 'Well, it's not funny. And stop calling me Shaunie boy.'

'Right, youse two, give over,' Ivy said over Tommy's laughter. 'You're not too big forra clout and you'll not dodge mine as fast, Tommy lad.'

'Aye, and hers will hurt a damn sight more.' Arthur crossed the small space and joined his sons at the table, smiling fondly at her. 'Gorra reet belting left hook, has your mam.'

'Don't talk daft, Arth— Oi, you, mucky hands!' Placing a smoke-blackened pan on the table, she clicked her tongue when Tommy scooped out a dollop of porridge. She rapped his knuckles with a wooden ladle and he grinned then popped his finger into his mouth. And despite her best efforts, she couldn't help smiling back.

Nineteen-year-old Tommy was strikingly handsome and the apple of her eye. Though she'd have never admitted to having a favourite, he was hers. With floppy hair as black as the coal he'd mined for nigh on ten years and sweeping eyelashes any woman would be proud of, framing grey-blue eyes that crinkled at the corners when he smiled, and a strong, square jaw – not to mention his muscular physique – he cut a fine figure.

It's not his looks, mind, she mused as she spooned porridge into three bowls and sprinkled on the last of the sugar. *It's his way with folk.*

The joker of the family, nothing got him down; not even working the pit, which Shaun hated with a passion. There was nothing to dislike about Tommy and she was proud to call him her son. Her surviving children were precious, all five, but he brought her that little more joy. Ashamed as she was of this, she couldn't change her feelings.

With a small shake of her head, she pushed away the guilty thoughts, reached for the cream, pockmarked teapot and poured weak tea into four handleless cups. After passing them around, she lifted her own and took a hesitant sip.

I'll have to see if Percy will let me have a few more bits on tick, later, she thought, grimacing at the unsweetened brew and noticing Arthur and the lads doing likewise.

The old man, who had converted the front room of his cottage into a shop, allowed Spring Row's women to make purchases 'on the slate', clearing their debts on Saturdays when their menfolk were paid.

As she was busy mentally listing what she needed, a loud bark made Ivy jump. She cursed as tea sploshed from her cup, settling in the grooves of the table.

'I'll throttle that scraggy pest. I'm bleedin' sick of it.' She craned her neck to the window for a glimpse of the black dog that had hung around the lane for months. 'Some bugger must be feeding it; just wait till I find out who.

'Now come on, you three, afore you're late,' she added, mopping at the table with her coarse apron. 'The hooter will be sounding if you're not careful. You know they'll tolerate no excuses for bad time-keeping; you'll finish up having your wages docked. Or losing your places.' She shuddered. No family could risk that.

Shaun, as usual, dragged his feet as he made for the door with his father and brother.

''Ere, lad.' Her tone softened as she handed him his bait tin containing a hunk of the bread baked last night, smeared thinly with pork dripping, for his midday meal. Arthur's and Tommy's contained the same, though her husband's was marginally thicker.

Shaun took the battered box and immediately checked inside for the stub of candle he insisted on carrying, 'just in case'. His logic behind this, she neither knew nor asked. If the grubby block of wax brought the lad comfort, made his working life more bearable, it was fine by her.

His young face relaxed a little to see it, which pierced her heart, but as all pit wives and mothers must, she hardened herself to it. She had to; what choice was there? For men of their class, uneducated and unskilled in everything but lifting a pickaxe, it was the pit or starve. It was that simple.

She'd have given her right arm – both legs, too – for the lads to have the chance of bettering themselves, as their father hadn't. But her determination that they would avoid the inevitable direction of the pit came to nothing. Hopes and dreams she'd fiercely held while lovingly cradling her children had been just that: pointless hopes and shattered dreams.

Reality had proved very different. Their daughters, married with children of their own, made counterpanes in a cotton factory, as did many of Breightmet Fold's residents; their husbands worked at the bleach works. Their eldest son, who toiled alongside his father and brothers, lived with his new wife in a tiny, wood-built house on Red Lane, a short distance from Spring Row.

The township of Breightmet, where she'd dwelled her whole life, lay on the east side of the Parish of Bolton, in Lancashire, between Bradshaw Brook to the west and Blackshaw Brook to the east. Harwood straddled its northern boundary. Its name literally meant 'Bright Meadow'; views from its upper ridge revealed a landscape dominated by hills.

The jumble of scattered homesteads housed a relatively small population. Though most were pitifully poor, the sprawling greenness, dotted with springs and babbling brooks, seemed to hold them in a hypnotic trap; leaving was, to many, incomprehensible. However, three of her and Arthur's younger children had left. And dear God, how they missed them.

An outbreak of cholera had raged throughout the town in '48 and stolen them, ravaging their little bodies until she, their own mother, prayed for their deaths and an end to their suffering. Thankful as she was that it spared her others, memories haunted her day and night.

Now, seeing Shaun, her baby, his freckled face etched in misery no fourteen-year-old should know, soul-corroding grief and cruel injustice bubbled like a cauldron set to explode.

On impulse, she drew him to her flat bosom. Silence filled the kitchen. Though not a cold wife or mother, open shows of affection were not in her nature.

Arthur touched her shoulder. 'Me and our Tommy and James allus keep an eye to the lad. He's gorra get used to it, as do we all, and should've by now,' he said gruffly.

She sniffed, nodded and gently pushed Shaun from her. *But he's not like most lads*, she wanted to protest. *He's sensitive, unhappy, scared.* Yet she didn't. What was the point? It wouldn't make a scrap of difference. Instead, she wiped tears from his flushed cheeks and cleared her throat. 'Aye, they'll keep an eye to thee.'

'Aye.' Tommy flashed a smile that didn't reach his eyes. 'We'll allus have your back, Shaunie b— Shaun.'

The amendment didn't go unnoticed. Shaun smiled ruefully. 'Don't be telling all the fellas I've been bawling on Mam's shoulder, our Tommy. I just hate it down there.'

For once, Tommy made no joke or quip, nor laughed his hearty laugh. He didn't even smile. 'No fear, lad.'

Back to her brusque self, she shooed them through the door into the row, where a slight drizzle fell from a slate-grey sky. The men pulled their jacket collars around their chins and, heads lowered, trudged down the path.

Standing in the doorway, she wrapped her arms in the folds of her apron against the cold and, when Arthur turned, called, 'Aye, I'll not forget.'

Satisfied, he swung through the gate and fell into step between his sons, merging with others on their way to work, the nails in their pit boots ringing in the misty dawn.

Reaching on tiptoe then stooping, she bolted the door. No one had seen nor heard a word of Joseph Goden, but he'd be back. They knew that for sure.

As she cleared the table, her brow creased. He was an evil swine capable of anything, as that Sunday proved. His rage-filled face, as he'd towered over his wife, had shocked her to the core.

When she'd heard Sally's cries when passing their cottage to retrieve her purse, her first thought was she'd gone into labour and was having a difficult birth. Knocking several times and getting no reply, she'd opened her neighbours' door, the offer of assistance on her lips. The sight that met her had rendered her speechless.

After pouring hot water into a ceramic basin, she now put in the breakfast dishes and attacked them with a cloth as the memories ran on. He'd been about to beat his defenceless wife. That in itself was bad enough but by God, the lass was in labour. What make of man would do such a thing? *That's just it*, she thought, nodding grimly. *He's not a bleedin' man. He's a dirty great coward.*

Despite her anger, she couldn't suppress a smile as she recalled striding forward and delivering an ear-splitting slap to his cheek, sending him stumbling into the wall. He'd stood slack-mouthed for a good half a minute as astonishment, slowly followed by rage, passed over his face. In that time, she'd managed to half carry, half drag Sally out.

They were barely in the safety of her cottage when, his shock seemingly having worn off, Joseph's barrage of abuse began outside her door. She was just thankful Arthur arrived when he did.

She plucked a huckaback cloth from a rope line beneath the window and, muttering to herself, dried the assortment of dishes and placed them on the rack. From the old bruising and what little she'd gleaned from Sally, that wasn't the first time he'd raised his fists. Yet in all the years living next door, she'd seen no indication he was leading Sally a dog's life; not a sound penetrated the stone separating them.

Aye, he's a snidy one, all right. He'd have known he could fair do as he liked without anyone hearing, she thought angrily. And whenever she'd glimpsed Sally in the row, she had her shawl drawn low, obscuring her face. No doubt to hide her many bruises.

Easing into a chair, Ivy shook her greying head and poured herself the stewed dregs from the pot. He wasn't the friendliest of neighbours, granted, but discovering he treated the lass as he did came as a huge shock. The rage Sally's escape evoked must have chased all caution of revealing his true self. Others had voiced their suspicions but – she felt ashamed admitting it, now – she'd thought it nothing but idle gossip. She'd even gone as far as defending Joseph, when Martha Smith questioned her in Percy's one afternoon.

'Surely you must know, Ivy, dwelling next door, like. You heard owt untoward?'

Folding her arms, she'd stared back fixedly. If there was one thing she couldn't abide, it was gossip. 'You want to be careful flinging mud like that about, Martha, for some might stick. I've neither seen nor heard owt amiss from yon Godens' cottage and unless you have, you ought to keep your opinions to yourself.'

'Well, there's summat queer about that fella, if you ask me. And that young wife of his is like a frightened rabbit. Never given no one the time of day, they've not, since moving here.'

'Aye, well. You just mind your own and let others mind theirs,' she'd retorted, convinced that Martha's problem was there were people in the row she knew nothing about; Martha made it her business to know everyone else's.

Ivy and the Godens had never spoken except for a cursory 'hello'. Some folk were like that, preferred keeping themselves to themselves; she hadn't given it a second thought. She should have listened to Martha's concerns. If she'd pressed for an explanation, could they have avoided this?

Tongues will be wagging now, all right. Gossip must be rife, she thought with a sigh. She crossed the room and lifted her outdoor shawl from a nail in the wall. Imagining Martha's gloating face when their paths next crossed, she heaved another sigh. She wasn't relishing the 'I told you so' speech Martha had undoubtedly rehearsed.

A stab of unease pricked as she dragged the bars across. Arthur wouldn't like it if he knew she'd left the door unbolted but she had to get the evening meal in, not to mention sugar for a decent brew. Sally usually locked it behind her but she was reluctant to disturb her. The poor girl needed all the rest she could get.

Percy's was only five doors down and being early, it shouldn't be busy. She'd be no longer than a minute or two, she reasoned. She drew the shawl across her shoulders, knotted the ends beneath her breasts and picked up her basket.

Thankful the rain had stopped, she stepped into the weak sunshine. But glancing left to Sally's cottage, apprehension ran down her spine.

Frowning, she dithered a moment longer. Then pulling the door shut, she hurried down the path.

'And how's the lass fettling?' Lifting Ivy's requests from various shelves, Percy Flint smiled over his shoulder.

'She's bearing up, Percy.'

She heard sadness cloud her voice and knew the old man had, too; he tactfully changed the subject. A weeping woman in his shop was the last thing he'd want. Though he knew she wasn't the soft sort, clearly he wasn't taking any chances.

'Right, Ivy love. Milk, sugar, ham shank, tatties and a screw of tea. Owt else, lass?' Squinting through rheumy eyes, he grinned across the dust-speckled counter, revealing shiny pink gums beyond his sunken mouth.

Remembering all the bread had gone into the men's bait tins, she nodded. 'Can I have a stone of flour and a quarter of yeast, please, Percy? I'll clear up with you the morrow when Arthur and the lads get home.'

'I know you will, lass, you allus does. Not like some I could mention.' Despite her being the only customer present, he lowered his voice. 'It's rich they must think I am. They gets stuff on t' tick then come up with all the excuses under the sun come payday. But for folk like your good self, my belly would be meeting my backbone by now.'

Placing her purchases into her basket, she chuckled. 'Now you know Nancy wouldn't see that happen. Thinks the world of thee, that lass does.'

His only child called twice daily with his midday and evening meal. Her mother had succumbed to pneumonia the year before and Ivy knew he relied on the visits and hearty meals more than he'd admit. His wife's passing broke his heart but, fiercely independent, he'd declined Nancy's offer of her and her brood joining his lonely but comfortable abode.

Despite his grumbles of customers' shortcomings, his convenient little shop, which sold all manner of foodstuff and more, was, Ivy suspected, a lucrative business. And shrewd Nancy likely knew it, too.

Running a gnarled hand through his shock of white hair, Percy smiled impishly. 'Aye, she keeps me in grub, don't see me clemmed, but it's not out of the goodness of her heart, let me tell you. She's got her sights set on this place when I've kicked the bucket; that's all what's dragging her arse here!'

'She's a long wait if them's her intentions, eh? Fit as a new fiddle, you are. You'll outlive us all.'

'Well, we'll see about that, Ivy, for it wouldn't surprise me if she were adding summat to them dinners she fetches,' he mused, stroking his whiskery chin.

She hooted with laughter. 'Don't talk so bleedin' daft!' Lifting her laden basket and resting the handle in the crook of her arm, she headed for the door. 'I'll be seeing thee, Percy love, and thanks.'

Having written her purchases in a leather-bound ledger, he returned it to a shelf beneath the counter. 'Aye, lass, I'll be seeing thee. I'll be seeing our Nancy shortly, an' all.' Licking his lips, he winked. 'Mmm, arsenic stew. I can't wait!'

She was still smiling as she walked the short distance home. He was a canny sod. The sharp-tongued Nancy might be a grabbing article but looked after him well enough.

Turning through her gate, her breath caught in her chest, thoughts of Percy vanishing, when she saw the half-open door. A deep voice from within spilled into the row and she marched up the path and shoved the door, sending it crashing against the wall. The scene sent fury through her veins.

The man towering over Sally turned sharply. Dropping her basket, she met his equally hostile stare. 'What the divil's going on here?'

Chapter 3

FROM A FLAWLESS teapot garlanded with pale-blue forget-me-nots, Ivy poured tea into three delicate cups and placed a matching plate on the lace-edged cloth. 'Barley cake, sir?' she proffered stiffly.

Oliver Bailey ran a finger beneath his stiff collar. 'Thank you, Mrs Morgan.'

Sipping their tea, she and Sally watched him warily as he took large bites of the generous slice.

He popped the last piece into his mouth, swallowed and cleared his throat. 'Well, now. Isn't it pleasant to sit, have tea and discuss matters amiably?'

Ivy stared back blankly.

Unperturbed, he continued. 'Firstly, allow me to make one thing quite clear. I did not come here to in any way *bully* Mrs Goden, as you so slanderously put it, into anything whatsoever. Neither, madam, will I be spoken to in such a disrespectful fashion. Do we understand one another?'

Hostility thickened the air. She placed her cup in its saucer and folded her arms. The local preacher was a formidable man, widely feared by his parishioners, which, she suspected, he knew and relished only too well. He put the fear of God, literally, into most but she – all seven stones of her – was afraid of no one.

'For what reason are you here? You were shouting at the lass summat shocking just now and I for one didn't like the tone of your voice.'

'Madam! I—'

'Please, both of you, enough.'

Ivy and the preacher turned in surprise.

'He wants me to return home to my husband.' Sally lifted a hand as Ivy made to respond. 'Please, Mrs Morgan, let me finish.'

Ivy stared in open-mouthed admiration at her sudden change.

Steely-eyed, Sally addressed the preacher. 'Sir, I will never, *never* again dwell with my husband. I don't intend burdening Mrs Morgan much longer – though I'll be eternally grateful to you and your family for treating my child and me as you have. You've been wonderful,' she added to Ivy, squeezing her hand.

'Mrs Goden, may I remind you that you are a married woman and that your rightful place is by your husband's hearth—'

'No, sir! No more! That man has beat me since the day we wed. He's done things to me, terrible things, treated me in ways I cannot bring myself to mention; things you wouldn't believe. He stripped away everything I was and for years, I sat back and allowed him. Well, no more.' She swiped away angry tears with the back of her hand. 'I will never return. It's finished, sir, finished. Nothing and no one on God's green earth will ever change my mind.'

Sitting back, he brushed an imaginary crumb from his black garb and Ivy stifled a grin. She could almost hear his cogs of thought turning – this wasn't going as he'd obviously planned!

'Our good Lord weeps at such talk,' the preacher cried passionately, piercing eyes gleaming with religious zeal. 'He wept to see I had to browbeat you and your husband to attend chapel when you moved here. He weeps still that He does not see you as regularly as He should. An ocean of holy tears! You, madam, are under my jurisdiction. Trouble amongst my parishioners, I will not tolerate.'

'Nothing and no one will change my mind,' Sally repeated.

A slight smile touched his mouth. 'Nothing, Mrs Goden?' he asked slowly, almost deliberately. 'Not even your child?'

Ivy's eyes narrowed. ''Ere, hang on—'

'My . . . child?'

He blinked, his face a picture of innocence. 'Surely you are aware that a man has full claim to his children, even over the mother? Your husband would be well within his rights to walk in here at this very moment if he so wished and take his child from you. That is not what you want, is it? I'm sure matters are not nearly as bad as they seem. All marriages have their difficulties but they can be resolved. Now, your husband—'

'He's sent you here to threaten me, hasn't he? Hasn't he? He has, hasn't he!'

'Madam, control yourself! Your husband is residing with his sister – a Mrs Russell, I believe – on Deansgate and indeed, he has asked me to visit to remind you of your wifely duties. He feels coming himself would not be wise owing to Mr Morgan's threatening behaviour—'

Ivy's angry gasp interrupted him but he continued before she could protest.

'He wants you home, madam, and rightly so. The poor man has not even seen his child. Now, as your confinement is over, I suggest you collect your belongings at once and I will escort you home.' Seemingly blind to their horrified expressions, he drained his cup. 'Have you given thought to the baptism? I shall be free tomorrow evening if you and your husband would care to discuss the matter.'

Smiling, he rose. 'Thank you for your hospitality, Mrs Morgan,' he drawled with barely suppressed sarcasm, 'and for taking such good care of Mrs Goden and the child.' To Sally, he added firmly, 'Come along. Let's get you home where you belong.'

Ivy was speechless. The snidy, slippery old . . . However, Sally stunned her further by rising from the table. 'You've never let him talk you into returning to that lunatic?'

'Mrs Morgan, I have warned you already. You will respect my authority.'

'Oh, authority tripe! I'm not frickened of you, you bullying owd tyrant, yer.'

'How dare you!'

'It's all right, Mrs Morgan.'

Their furious exchange ended abruptly when Sally opened the door.

The preacher smiled smugly and strode forward. 'Ah, sensible girl! Fetch the child, come alon—' The last word rattled in his throat as Sally gripped his collar and shook him hard.

Yanking him close until his startled face was inches from hers, she murmured, 'Tell my husband he will never set eyes on *my* son so long as I breathe. And,' she added, pulling him closer, 'if you know what's good for you, *you* will stay away from us, too.' She flung him through the door and slammed it shut. Sagging against it, she closed her eyes, her breathing ragged.

'Oh, love. That were . . . That were bleedin' brilliant!'

A dazed Sally dropped into a chair. Beside her, pressing her apron to her mouth, Ivy bent double with mirth.

For several minutes, the cottage rang with their stunned laughter.

'Oh, Mrs Morgan, what on earth possessed me? I threw a clergyman through the door and spoke to him like muck. He simply enraged me speaking of Joseph as though he were the victim. As for threatening me with my son, I wasn't standing for that. I . . . snapped. He won't let this slide; as if I need further enemies.'

'Love, it'll be all right. Owd Bailey won't do owt. He'd not dare; not after that, anyroad!' Chuckling when Sally moaned and covered her face with her hands, Ivy put her arm around her shoulders. 'Look, I can fair understand why you did what you did, and if you hadn't of thrown that owd sod out on his ear, I would've.

'He pushed you to it and no one round here will blame you; they'll bleedin' well shake your hand, lass. It's my fault, anyroad. I should never have gone out without telling thee. Leaving the door open like that, what were I thinking?'

'You weren't to know. I heard knocking and was not about to open the door, naturally, but he walked in, bold as you like. I got the shock of my life, I can tell you. For a moment, I thought it was Joseph.' Sally shuddered. 'At least it was the preacher and not *him*.'

'He just come marching in? Well, of all the . . . He's a bullying owd swine if ever there were one. Now come on,' she added with a smile as tears welled in Sally's eyes, 'dry up, lass, and see to the babby. There's no use upsetting yourself, for what's done is done.' Nodding, Sally made to leave but Ivy clasped her hand. 'I don't think you've owt to fret about with him, love, but I promise, whatever happens – with him or Joseph – I'm here for thee. Just you remember that.'

Avoiding Sally's face, she cleared her throat, embarrassed at revealing the extent of her feelings. She felt protective of this lass as if she were one of her own.

Tears spilling, Sally sank to her knees and rested her head in Ivy's lap. Choking back tears herself, Ivy stroked her thick, chestnut-coloured hair.

'You've been so good to me. I'm sorry I was such a nuisance lying in bed all day while you waited on me hand and foot. I'll make it up to you, I promise. Please, Mrs Morgan, you *have* been good to me, all of you,' Sally insisted when Ivy clicked her tongue. 'All you've done . . . for Jonathan also – you and Mr Morgan must be exhausted with the broken sleep. Even your sons made sacrifices, giving up a bed for me and having to share.

'You've rescued me, given me back my life. No one could be as good a friend as you. In fact, you've been more like a mother. Thank you, so very much.'

Looking into blue eyes brimming with tears of gratitude, bright and brilliant in her heart-shaped face, it struck Ivy how attractive Sally was. She frowned curiously. 'What age are you, love?'

Sally smiled, revealing pearl-like teeth framed by full lips, transforming her face into one of even more beauty. 'Twenty-one.' Slowly, her eyebrows drew together. 'Twenty-one . . . I feel much older, Mrs Morgan.'

'I knew you were young, but . . . By God, what age did you wed that husband of yourn?'

'Sixteen, just.'

'How did you meet, lass? It's just you don't sound like you're from these parts; talk reet nice, you do.'

Sally's smile returned. 'I had a very dear friend who spoke ever so nicely. We were fascinated by each other's accents, would roll around laughing for hours asking one another to say certain words.' Her eyes filled with longing. 'I began speaking as she did. I worshipped her, wanted to be just like her, and she loved teaching me.

'She was my complete opposite – soft and gentle, whereas I was loud and quick-tempered.' She laughed when Ivy's eyebrows rose. 'Oh, believe me, I wasn't always a pushover. I miss Dicksy so very much.'

Recalling the incident with Oliver Bailey, Ivy nodded. 'Aye, thinking on it, I can fair believe that. You're a dark horse beneath. And Dicksy? There's a queer name if ever I heard one.'

'Isobella Dickinson,' she murmured. 'We never addressed one another by our given names.' She smiled softly. 'To me she was Dicksy and I was Silly Sally.'

'And Joseph?'

Sally released a long sigh. Eyes vacant, she stared into the depths of the fire. 'He bought me, Mrs Morgan. He bought me.'

After a moment of stunned silence, her gasp pierced the air. 'He *what*?'

As though lost in the hypnotic flames, Sally continued in an emotionless tone. 'I grew up in the workhouse. I knew he was evil the second I laid eyes on him, I just knew, but didn't believe anything could be worse than living in that place, not after Dicksy left.' A hollow laugh caught in her throat. 'How wrong I was.'

'Mother of God. What's the world coming to?'

'Girls were usually sent into service upon reaching fourteen. I believe that's what happened with Dicksy. The master summoned her to his office one day and I never saw her again. What she was doing in that place, I have no idea. It was clear she was of good breeding. She cried a great deal in the beginning but never spoke of her family, and I didn't ask. I hated speaking of my own, it hurt too much, and understood she felt the same.

'The parting broke my heart. I thought I'd be stuck in that hellhole the remainder of my days. The master said no employer would want me, that I was too pretty. He said ladies insist upon having unattractive girls working for them so their husbands and sons are less inclined to try something they shouldn't.

'He sold me to Joseph, instead. It happened often. If the price was right, of course,' Sally finished bitterly. She rose and crossed to the window. She folded her arms, and her tearful gaze swept the hills. 'How much do you think he paid, Mrs Morgan?'

'Lass, you don't have to—'

'A shilling. He bought me for the princely sum of one shilling.'

Ivy cringed with pity.

'I was sold like cattle at the market for a single shilling. And my God, he never let me forget it.'

'Ay, lass.' As she made to rise, Sally gave a soft smile.

'Oh, it's all right, really. That part of my life is finished, as is my marriage. All he wanted the day he came searching for a wife was a servant he didn't have to pay. Someone to keep his home clean and bed warm. Someone like me. A workhouse rat with no one to care where I was or how I fared. For years, he enjoyed that power, but he won't any more. It was the final nail in the coffin, what he threatened before you walked in—' She clamped her mouth shut.

Seeing revulsion ripple through her, Ivy shook her head. 'Dear Lord, he never did . . .'

'But it's all right, now, it will be all right,' Sally continued passionately. 'I have my son and never will I let anything happen to him. I'm not giving Joseph the opportunity to hurt me again. He'll take my child from me given the chance, believe me, he will. But he shall have to find us first. Monday, we'll go to Manchester.'

'Manchester?'

'My mother's sister dwells there – Ancoats. I've dreamed of finding her for years. The preacher's words made up my mind; I must try. I remember visiting as a child, before my father passed away. Afterwards, my mother couldn't make ends meet. She tried. My God, how she tried. But she was weak, in mind and body. It was either throw herself and her daughter upon the workhouse's mercy or starve.

'She died the following month, though no one bothered to inform me until I kicked up hell and refused to leave her the day Joseph parted with his coin. They separated families upon admission, you see, parted husbands from wives, took children from parents. According to the official policy, infants under seven could remain with their mothers in the women's quarter but, as in our case, they often overlooked this. Ten years, Mrs Morgan. Ten whole years my mother had been rotting in some paupers' pit and I had no idea.'

Wrapping her arms around the sobbing woman, Ivy rocked her. 'Oh, love. Shhh, shhh.'

A gusty cry sounded from the next room as they drew apart.

Glancing down at her earth-coloured dress and the wet patches over each breast, Sally blushed. 'I think he's hungry.'

Ivy smiled, but her mind spun from the shocking revelations. 'See to him, lass,' she murmured. 'I'll brew us some sweet tea.'

*

Later that day, the baby was asleep in his drawer. Sally had placed it beside the fire while she helped Ivy prepare the evening meal and as they worked, they discussed the upcoming departure.

'We shall be away Monday at first light. The sooner I put some distance between us and Joseph, the safer we'll be.' Glancing at her son, she felt the strongest urge to pluck him from his bed, hold his little body close and never let go.

Never will that monster get his hands on you. I'll kill him first. I'll protect you with my life, my darling, I promise. As she made the silent vow, he smiled in his sleep, as though sensing her devotion, and overwhelming love coursed through her. Blinking back tears, she returned her attention to the bread dough.

'That ham shank's smelling good.' Ivy sniffed appreciatively at the mouth-watering aroma pervading the stuffy kitchen. Reaching for a black-bottomed pan hanging by the fire, she sighed as she too glanced at the child. 'Eeh, I'll miss you and the babby, aye. But I support your decision.' She threw in potatoes, added hot water and a little salt then placed the pot by a pan of cabbage to cook. 'Set that dough to baking, lass, and we'll have a sup afore the men get home. Unless you'd rather lie down?'

'No,' Sally answered determinedly. 'It's time I pushed through this lethargy.'

'Summat's nagging me,' said Ivy as they drank their tea. 'What if your mam's sister don't dwell there any more?'

Sighing, she placed her off-white mug on the clothless table.

Ivy had returned the attractive tea service and snow-white cloth to the dresser upon the preacher's departure. She'd revealed they were wedding gifts and her pride and joy, used only on high days and holidays or when a visitor called. Whether she liked the caller or not, she'd have never poured them tea from a pock-marked teapot into chipped, handleless mugs!

'I don't mean to put a damper on things but if your aunt's upped and moved, you and the babby will be stranded. And by God, that's one place you'd not want to be alone. I've heard it ain't half grim. There's folk up there what would sell their own granny forra shill—' Ivy slapped a hand to her mouth. 'Bleedin' hell, sorry, lass. Eeh, I could chew this tongue off at times. I'm a brainless, daft owd—'

Sally laughed softly. 'It's all right, Mrs Morgan. And I share your concerns, but I have no one else to turn to. There's also the risk of passing Deansgate . . . But I must try.' Her mouth curved with fondness. 'She's a kind soul, Aunt Grace, from what I remember; happy, always smiling. She wouldn't recognise me, now. And whether I'll be welcome is another worry.' She forced a reassuring smile when Ivy frowned. 'I'm sure it will be fine. It's just that she and my mother quarrelled shortly after my father died and never spoke again.'

Ivy's frown deepened. 'The falling out must've been a bad 'un if your mam chose to knock on t' workhouse door over her own sister's.'

'I agree, but this is my only option. Besides, there is an advantage: Joseph doesn't know she exists.'

The bubbling vegetables and crackling fire were the only sounds as the woman fell silent, immersed, Sally was certain, in the same thoughts. Had Grace moved? And if not, would she be prepared to help her desperate niece?

Chapter 4

HAROLD RUSSELL RAISED tired eyes to where his wife banged dollops of mashed potato on to a row of mismatched plates – clanging and clattering that had dragged him from his sleep. She glanced back and her scowl turned into a contemptuous snarl.

He heaved himself from his fireside chair with a grunt and crossing to sit at the table, smiled faintly at his children, huddled on a filthy pallet.

With a flick of her wrist, Alice threw the lumpy mess on to another plate. 'Well? Were you taken on anywhere?'

He met her icy glare with a sigh. 'Not now, woman.'

The crash, as she slammed the pan down, made him jump several inches from his seat. The smaller children whimpered, covered their ears with grubby hands and pressed against their older siblings.

As he peered into her ugly face – the only way to describe the filthy, scab-dotted skin framed by straggly hair stiff with grease – a flush of fury rose up his neck to meet a muscle pulsating in his jaw. With a roar that surprised himself, he grabbed the steaming pan and hurled it at the wall with such force that it chipped the brickwork then clattered across the room, splattering the cowering children with its grey-coloured contents.

In heavy silence, he and his wife glared at each other across the table. And this was the scene his brother-in-law met with as he stumbled through the back door.

Joseph kicked the door shut, dragged an arm from his coarse jacket and, with one eye, took in the adults' stiff faces, the children frantically licking potato from their arms and hands, then the pan sitting on the flagstones as though it belonged there. He hiccuped twice and grinned. 'All right?'

Neither Alice nor Harold responded.

Still grinning, he yanked his other arm from his jacket. This sent him staggering and he made a grab for the table's edge, almost knocking off a plate. 'All right?' he slurred again in Alice's face.

She grimaced. 'Skenning drunk again? Though why I bother asking, I don't know. Anyone with half a nostril can tell you've spent the day with yours at the bottom of a tankard.' He hiccuped again and she shook her head in disdain. 'Sit down, you drunken fool, afore you fall down.'

Holding out both arms, he dropped on to a stool. Alice stomped across the room and snatched up the pan, and he nodded. 'Let's have it, then. I'm fair clemmed.'

'Oh!' Scraping out the dregs, her lips stretched against the blackened stumps remaining in her otherwise empty mouth. 'And why didn't you get a meal at Nellie's? I take it that's where you've been all day again?' She shook the spoon under his nose. 'Nay, but you'll not, will you? Too busy wasting brass you've not got on ale to buy grub, ain't you? Well, I'm warning you, brother or no, you'd best start getting your hand fast in that pocket of yourn or you'll be out on your ear.'

Pushing a plate towards him then slamming another in front of her husband, her voice dripped with scorn.

'There you are. Must feed the hard-working men, mustn't we?' She slapped her forehead. 'Eeh, I forget. Youse *don't* bloody work, do you!'

Harold's head snapped back. 'There's nowt about, woman. I've tramped the length and breadth of Bolton forra day's graft, from dawn till dusk, for nigh on a month. Folk won't take me on at my age, not when they can employ someone younger – or Irish – for less wages.' He looked at his plate with a hollow laugh. 'Them Irish should spend a night beneath this roof; they'd soon know the real meaning of famine.'

She ignored him and turned back to Joseph. 'And *you'll* not find work sitting on your arse in that inn. You leave a steady job and don't bother looking for another. Then there's that cottage of yourn lying empty. And as for that workhouse whore you call a wife—' She stepped back as he thumped the tabletop, sending the plates rattling in protest.

'I told thee, she'll come begging me to take her back once the preacher's put her straight. You'll see, I'll be back at Spring Row come the new week. And by God will she pay for forcing me from my own home.'

'You've likely lost that cottage by now, you bleedin' fool.'

'Nay. Them there cottages have nowt to do with the mine. De Mathers don't own them so losing my job don't mean I've lost my home,' he told her, referring to the owner of several Bolton pits who resided at Breightmet Hall, a centuries-old mansion with sprawling grounds and gardens situated on a peak of land overlooking the town. Lord de Mathers provided dwellings for his miners but the dilapidated hovels were a last resort if no alternative was available.

'Regardless, you've not kept the rent up.'

Folding his arms, he grinned. 'That's being taken care of.'

Alice jerked her head to the children. When the bundles of rags scuttled back to the mattress with their plates, she cupped her chin and frowned. 'What d'you mean, the rent's taken care of? Who's paying it, then?' She shook her head when his smile broadened. 'By God. That gullible whore's dafter than I thought.'

'You don't know the half of it.'

Alice and even Harold, his curiosity roused, stared at him in confusion. Laughing, he lumbered to his jacket and rummaged in a pocket. The children, cheeks bulging with potato, gawped as, like a conjuror at a magic show, he pulled out a string of fat sausages with both hands. He whipped out the remainder with a flourish. 'Ta-dah!'

Alice rose slowly, eyes like saucers. 'Eeh, Joseph . . . Meat? We've not had meat in bleedin' weeks.' She snatched it from him, held it to her nose and sniffed. 'Fresh, an' all!' she marvelled.

'That's not all.' He extracted a paper-wrapped parcel from another pocket which revealed, when Alice tore it open, a large pork chop.

Harold shook his head in wonder. 'She give you them?'

'Aye.'

'And she's paying your cottage's rent while you're here?'

'Aye.'

'Well.' He blew through puckered lips. 'You're a rum bugger, Joseph, you are. That wench must be besotted, poor cow.'

As Alice bustled around the fire with the frying pan, he eased into Harold's chair with a sly smile. He could still feel the fleshy folds of the woman he'd fondled in Nellie's, and her smell lingered on his hands.

She'd simpered over him, as she always did, and handed over the stolen meat with a seductive wink. She'd also paid for his ale all day and, in the dim recess where they always sat, willingly lifted her long skirts, letting his fingers probe roughly. He'd exposed breasts that glistened in the golden glow of the open fire, could still hear in his mind her groans of pleasure and pain as he sucked and bit her ruby-red nipples.

Nellie had ambled by at one point collecting empty tankards, murky eyes the colour of dirty dishwater lingering on them as she passed. He'd caught her eye and a smirk touched her lips. As she was often heard saying, her customers could do as they pleased so long as they lined her pockets in the process.

Establishments like hers, where hardened criminals and drunkards spent the majority of their waking hours, were the environments where he felt most comfortable. Home was merely somewhere to lay your head, have a meal and have your wife at your beck and call – in the bedroom as much as anywhere. *Or at least it had been,* he thought, jaw tightening.

He'd go to Bailey on Monday, see how his threat went down concerning the brat; the preacher put the wind up most people. Pity for him he couldn't spot a good liar when he saw one, Joseph reflected, his grin returning.

He'd been at the end of his tether, wondering how he could return to Spring Row without getting his skull kicked in, when by sheer luck, he'd spotted the preacher in Bolton town the day before. He'd laid it on by the shovel-load and the old man swallowed every word. Sally would have got it both barrels. She'd come crawling through that door before too long.

He didn't care a fig for the child, but *she* was his. He owned her. And when the time came and he tired of her, he'd sell her on. She'd fetch more than a shilling in the right places. He'd only got her at such a bargain price because the devil who ran the workhouse owed him. He could make a tidy profit on her in the future, even rent her out for a while first . . .

His smug smile turned to pure evil at the thought of the Morgans. 'Youse will pay, an' all, humiliating me and harbouring that whore,' he hissed. 'Aye, by God, you'll pay.'

Chapter 5

'DEAR GOD, HELP me!'

The fast-approaching footsteps grew louder. Sally hitched up the baby, her boots slapping the uneven cobbles as she pushed on through the foul-smelling alley, her every nerve and sinew urging her on. Joseph was drawing closer. Closer . . .

Pain scorched as he made a grab for her hair and wrenched her backwards, almost tearing it from her scalp.

'Please, no!' Her tortured plea rebounded off the damp bricks and his laughter swallowed it.

A blow to her temple forced her to her knees, but the pain in her heart seared far more when he snatched the baby from her. Skidding to her feet, she clawed at his jacket. A howl ripped from her throat as he bolted, Jonathan's screams ringing in her ears as they disappeared into the frosty night . . .

Sally sat bolt upright in bed with a loud gasp. Her chest throbbed from her heart's heavy beating, the wind whistling through the eaves icy as it met her sweat-slicked skin. Bile rose as the hellish nightmare flooded back. With a trembling hand, she felt for the drawer, almost not daring to check. Her fingers brushed her son's velvety cheek and she sagged.

Though now wide awake and aware they were in the safety of the Morgans', her thoughts remained tumultuous. Would that dream become reality? Was it a premonition? Could they really escape in a few short hours, start a new life in Manchester? Slowly, her every muscle tautened with determination and a love only a mother could understand streamed through her veins like new lifeblood.

Sudden visions from her childhood assaulted her mind. She used to be tough; her abominable upbringing in the workhouse had forced her to be. Any chance of surviving such a place required a quick mind and a hard heart. Constant hunger, beatings, complete lack of love and utter hopelessness, for years on end, could break the strongest person. For a girl of six, it was soul-destroying.

To enter the workhouse was to surrender your prior existence, freedom, relationships; many would sooner die in the gutter than knock at the poorhouse door.

Life before her father's death was far from idyllic. She'd regularly gone to bed with an empty stomach if he was out of work which, not from want of trying, he often was. But at least she'd felt safe, loved, *alive.* In the workhouse, you were not a person but an inmate. You ceased being human the moment you stepped over the threshold of that grey world.

Slipping an arm out of the covers, she fingered the crescent-shaped scar at the base of her temple. The overwhelming workload had taken its toll one particularly arduous day and she'd fallen asleep during her duties scrubbing the laundry-room floor. The matron's unforgiving hand, wielding a hot flat-iron, remedied that. The force of the blow had lifted her bare feet clean off the ground.

And that was the day the change in herself took root, she realised now. Something inside died and her heart hardened. The expression of shock – and slight admiration – on the matron's face, when she'd staggered to her feet and resumed her work without a word or tear, had jolted her from her coma-like existence. She'd felt alive – which she hadn't in a long time.

That new-found strength, that hardness, was her crutch throughout the years before Dicksy's arrival, when she'd ached for the warmth of a hug, a kind word, a smile. The only physical contact they were sure of receiving were beatings. And for some poor individuals, the horror of the master's flabby, sour-smelling body invading their innocent flesh at night. She'd sworn that day that no one would break her, as so many had been broken.

Yet *he* had.

Her nails dug into her palms as her fists tightened. He'd bent her, slowly, slowly, until eventually – she couldn't even recall when Joseph began winning his battle over her – she submitted to his will. Well, no more. The nightmare of him taking her baby had awakened what she'd believed long dead but had in fact been slumbering deep within: strength and a fierce determination to survive.

The realisation was like a rebirth. From this day onward, she'd never be the same. This was where her life changed for the better.

'You won't win, Joseph,' she whispered into the darkness. 'I'll stick a knife between your ribs if I must but I swear to God, so long as I have breath in my lungs, you won't win.'

Today was the beginning of the rest of her life. Soon, she must leave Spring Row and forge a new existence for herself and her son. Thoughts of returning to her birth town of Manchester evoked both longing and sadness.

Despite the hardships, the old weaver's cottage she was born in held comforting memories, still vivid in her mind. But her loving parents were no longer there. Her father, overworked and undernourished, had gone years before. And her poor, gentle mother . . . But Aunt Grace was there. *Dear God, please let Aunt Grace be there.* That her hope and saviour might no longer be where she remembered was a thought she forced away before panic could swamp her.

She caressed her son's hand. 'It's just you and me.' This conjured up a range of emotions. She'd soon have to leave these people for whom she'd come to care a great deal.

She felt humbled by how fortunate she'd been. Ivy's kindness had known no bounds; she'd even sat through several nights and knitted Jonathan an assortment of clothing from an unpicked jumper of Arthur's. Sally wished there was a way, however small, to repay them. And her mouth curved as an idea, a way to help Ivy this morning at least, formed.

The wind had eased and rain drummed steadily against the window as she slipped out of bed. Tensing her jaw to stop her teeth chattering, she hurried to a side table where her clothes lay neatly folded and tugged them on with hands already stiffening with cold. Journeying in weather this bitter, with a newborn in tow, wasn't something she was relishing. *But needs must when the Devil drives.*

She padded to the door.

She felt refreshed, despite the hour, and knew it was early as no movement sounded behind the door or from above. No Ivy lighting the fire in the kitchen and preparing breakfast, no Arthur dressing for work. Last night, for the first time, she'd had the baby in with her. Despite Ivy's assurance that it had been no hardship, she knew the older woman would have been glad of the uninterrupted sleep.

She'll have an easy morning, too, Sally thought, smiling, as she entered the kitchen.

She dropped to her knees before the near-dead fire and in no time it was crackling nicely. Reaching for a pan beside the hearth, she brightened further at the prospect of Ivy coming down to a warm kitchen and porridge bubbling away. Yet as she turned from the fire, her breath caught and the room swayed.

'Joseph . . .'

The name froze on her lips. Her legs buckled and she fell to the floor in a dead faint when, from the gloom, a figure rose from the table.

The tender hold was comforting. Sally snuggled into the broad chest, lips parting when they brushed his neck. A voice murmured her name, told her everything would be all right and in her half-conscious state, she felt completely at ease. It was as though she was supposed to be in these arms, as though she'd been away for a long time and was back where she belonged. Like she'd come home.

'There, now, that's it. Open your eyes.' A coarse, though not unpleasant, hand stroking her hair accompanied the soothing words. He laid her down gently.

She instantly missed his touch, was about to reach out in search of it when the world came into focus.

The figure stood motionless by the table. He'd lit a candle and the flickering flame illuminated his silhouette. She eased herself into a sitting position. The dim room swayed and, groaning, she flopped back against the chair.

Tommy was at Sally's side in seconds. Without a word, he carried her to the front room. She curled into him and the swell of her breasts pressed against his chest. His heart jerked beneath the soft mounds and it took him aback when a flame ignited in the pit of his stomach. His surprise mounted at the overwhelming urge to take the globes in his hands.

Frowning, he laid her on the bed and knelt before her. A sliver of moonlight fell across her face and he waited, watching, the only sound the rain pattering against the panes.

This was the first time he'd looked at his neighbour properly. He'd seen her occasionally over the years in the row as she scurried by, head down, and at several mealtimes since she'd been here, when she felt up to it. They had shared the odd smile and word, it was true. However, he'd not *seen* her, not really. Not like this . . . Until now.

The Sunday she came began like any other. His mother and father had gone to chapel, Shaun was out with friends and he himself was meeting Dolly Jenkins for their weekly stroll by the river.

Not particularly religious, his parents attended chapel most weeks more through habit than anything; it allowed them to catch up with friends and broke their monotonous routine for a few hours. They didn't mind that he and Shaun rarely attended service. They understood their need for fresh air and sunshine on their precious day off after working underground all week.

He'd been shocked, therefore, upon his return, his cheery whistle dying mid-tune, to discover Sally asleep in the front room, having just given birth to the squawking bundle in his mother's arms.

He knew the gist of why she was here. His mother had disclosed enough to quell her sons' curiosity, gain their understanding that Sally needed peace and plenty of rest, and warn of Joseph's likely return.

That madman wants his head testing, he thought now, drinking in her delicate features. Again, that flare sparked low within him. His eyes travelled down and he glimpsed old bruises streaking the creamy skin of her neck. His hands bunched into fists. He wished that swine was next door. He'd do more than bruise *his* neck; he'd snap the thing.

Suddenly, Dolly's smiling face flitted through his mind but he pushed it away, realising with a jolt that for the first time, it wasn't a welcome image. What was wrong with him? The bewildering thought was forgotten when Sally stirred.

He watched intently as she licked her full lips. She opened her eyes and he smiled. 'Easy, now. Feeling better?'

Sally nodded. Her mind was clearing and a memory, a feeling . . . She glanced at Tommy's arms, chest, neck . . . the neck she'd pressed her lips to. She looked away quickly, confused, feeling redness creep over her face.

'I am sorry. I saw you come into the kitchen and go to the fire, but you had your back to me and I didn't want to startle you. I know you've had a hard time of it lately.' He looked away and cleared his throat. 'I'll fetch thee some tea.'

When his footsteps faded, she released a breath she hadn't realised she held. She covered her hot face with her hands. What happened? She remembered leaving this room, entering the kitchen, lighting the fire . . . *Joseph.* She'd turned to the table . . . Dear God, Joseph had risen from the gloom! The huge figure, its outline a hazy red from the glow of the fire, loomed and the floor had hurtled towards her.

Her fuddled brain screamed at her to run: *Joseph's here! He'll take the child! Run! Run!* Her body jerked involuntarily and she leapt from the bed. She absently scraped back a lock of hair – and her hand froze. Tommy . . . Tommy had stroked her hair, murmured softly, held her close. Strong arms, his smell, his heart beating against hers . . .

Bewildered, she shook her head recalling the emotions his touch evoked. To know these . . . from a man? How, in God's name, after everything . . . ? She brushed her lips with her fingertips. The warm skin of his throat still lingered. Joseph wasn't here. He didn't rise from the table, Tommy did. Tommy had held her in his arms, and she'd . . . A knot of shame twisted her stomach. What on earth was she thinking? What must *he* think of *her*?

Her brow furrowed in disappointment as her thoughts switched back to Joseph. She'd broken her vow. She'd believed she was growing stronger, was putting her fear of him behind her. Clearly, she'd been mistaken.

The clinking of crockery drifted through and with a jolt she remembered that Tommy was making tea. Heat returned to her face. He'd be back any moment. Here, in this room. With her.

She reached the door in a heartbeat.

He paused when her footsteps sounded, but didn't turn. He placed the teapot on the table. 'Are you well enough to be up, Mrs Goden?'

She flinched that he'd addressed her by that monster's name and before she could stop herself, said too sharply, 'My name is Sally. Goden is *his* name, not mine.'

Tommy blinked, nodded, then inclined his head to a steaming mug.

Ivy spoke of him highly and often; Sally felt she knew this man already, it was true. None the less, it struck her that she was alone with him and she felt a little afraid. She hesitated and his eyes creased in a look akin to pity.

'That babby of yourn's a real beauty, Sally. Reet bonny, he is.'

She sensed something behind the murmured words. Not in the statement itself, but the way he said it seemed to hold almost a whisper of reassurance, that she needn't fear his presence. That not all men were like Joseph Goden. Whether she imagined it, she didn't know, but it put her at ease. Smiling, she slipped into a chair.

'Thank you. Yes, he is.'

She stole a glance at Tommy's bowed head as she sipped her tea. Catching sight of his hands, which dwarfed the mug they held, her skin tingled at the memory of his touch. The ensuing silence was stifling. In desperation, she stammered, 'Couldn't you sleep? It's rather early to be up when you've a day's work to get through.'

He rubbed tired-looking eyes. 'I've matters on my mind. Our Shaun.' He motioned to the ceiling. 'He's miserable. It's fair cutting me apart inside – Mam, an' all – seeing the lad like that. I've got to do summat. I just don't know what.'

The depth of feeling in his tone touched her. 'If you don't mind my asking, what's wrong with him?'

He rose, crossed to the dresser and opened a drawer. She tilted her head but his broad back blocked her view. Eventually, he turned, arms piled with wooden objects. He placed them on the table and sat.

She gazed at the items as he arranged them in a line. Finely carved animals and people stared back. The intricate detailing took her breath away. She reached out to touch a rearing horse then drew back for fear of breaking the delicate structure.

'It's all right. Here.' Smiling, he pushed it towards her.

The mane curved along the horse's head and down its back in swirling lines. Sally ran a finger over it, shaking her head in wonder at the facial features. The body was accurate in every way, from the muscular shoulders and perfectly shaped legs and hooves to the flowing tail; it was exceptionally crafted.

She shook her head again at the others: a cow with calf alongside; a shorn sheep mid-bleat; a bird balanced on one leg, exquisitely detailed wings outstretched as though preparing for flight – the list seemed endless.

'Did you . . . ?'

'Our Shaun.'

Her eyebrows arched in surprise. He was little more than a boy – an extremely talented boy at that. She fingered a figure of Ivy, complete with flowing apron and shawl. It was an exact replica, down to the fine lines around her eyes and mouth. 'Tommy, these are unbelievably good. I've never seen anything like it.'

His handsome face shone with brotherly pride. 'This is what he were born to do. He can turn a lump of wood into a work of art in the blink of an eye. That lad shouldn't be down the mine. He's not cut out for it. I can see the light in his eyes dying and one day it'll go out altogether unless summat's done.'

'Couldn't he try for a place involving woodwork? Any carpenter in the land would give his right arm to apprentice someone with this level of talent, surely?'

'I've been thinking the same. D'you know, he's carved these with all sorts of odds and ends: an owd knife, a few rusty nails, even bits of sharpened stone. Think on what he could do with the right tools and a master carpenter to guide him. The only problem would be the loss of his wages, for as an apprentice, he'd get nowhere near what he earns now.

'We'd all feel the pinch but I'm willing to do all the overtime I can; I'll even get work on one of the farms at the weekend. I'm not sure what a master would ask where tools are concerned and the premium for taking him on. It's a crying shame, seeing him the way he is. I'm going to try my damnedest to do this for him.'

Excitement stirred. Sally had wanted a way to repay Ivy and her family. Maybe this could be it. Joseph's face flashed across her thoughts and she gulped at the memory of their last afternoon. She'd begged and pleaded – had lied through her teeth. He'd suspected her of stealing his money and he'd been right.

'I awoke early to surprise your mother. I was planning to prepare breakfast, save her the job for one morning. It was all I could think of to repay her—'

'And I spoiled it by scaring thee senseless. Sorry for that.'

'It's not your fault. My nerves are in ribbons at the moment. What I wanted to tell you, to ask you, is whether, well, whether you and your parents would let *me* help. With Shaun. With the money.'

'You? But Joseph doesn't . . . well . . .'

'Seem the type to allow his wife her own money? You're right, he isn't. But I found a way.'

'You mean you put brass aside forra rainy day, so to speak?' he asked with a wink.

'I'm not proud of myself. Stealing is stealing, whichever way you look at it, but I did it for my child. I buried a little away when I could and Joseph was none the wiser. However, I had to buy wool to clothe the baby and he discovered it. He was furious and wouldn't let up until I told him the truth. But I didn't. And shortly, I'll be able to get away, as I've planned for such a long time. I shall be free of him. We both will.' Now-familiar panic rose, forcing her to stop. *Let all go well, please . . .*

Tommy lowered his gaze. 'I'm sorry. I meant nowt by that, Mrs— Sally. And by no means are you a thief, by God, you're not. That swine no doubt owes thee a damn sight more than what you've took. But there's no way we'll take your money.'

She frowned in puzzlement. Had she insulted him, bruised his pride? She heard the tinge of hurt in her own voice. 'But why?'

'If you've worked as hard as you say for that brass, we'd not accept a farthing. Besides, you'll need it for you and the babby. Mam would never agree.'

Her face relaxed in a smile. She'd planned to do this on her way to the coaching house but now was as good a time as any. 'Would you keep an ear to Jonathan? I shan't be long.'

'Aye.'

She glanced to the clock, nodded, then made for the door.

'Where you going?'

'Next door.' She wasn't surprised her response wasn't 'home'. That place had never been one. It had been a prison and she thanked heaven her sentence was over.

'But you can't! Joseph . . . The babby will be all right. I'll come with you.'

Her stomach flipped at the concern in his eyes.

'He might be lying in wait, could have returned in t' dead of night any time during the last weeks. I . . . can't see you go alone.'

After some deliberation, she nodded and they stepped into the darkness of the row.

Squinting left and right through the drizzle, she slipped through the gate. Tommy was right behind. At her own, she studied the dark windows for signs of life. His nod spurred her on and she hurried down the path.

When they reached the door, she turned and headed for the side of the cottage.

'Where are you—?'

'You'll see,' she whispered.

She halted at the rear and peered up at the low roof. Then she stood on an upturned pail, lifted a loose chunk of moss-choked slate and felt beneath.

'I should've guessed. You couldn't have hidden it inside the cottage; Joseph would've stumbled upon it eventually.'

She felt a warm glow at the admiration in his voice but seconds later icy dread replaced it. 'No . . . The money's gone. It's *gone*!'

Before Tommy could respond, a snapping twig punctured the stillness. He whirled around, fists poised. A huge dog leapt at him, knocking the air from his lungs. Standing on its hind legs, it rested its front paws on his chest and licked his face frantically.

'Get down, you daft divil, yer!' he hissed.

A moment later, Sally's desperate fingers brushed damp cloth. She heaved a sigh then clicked her tongue. The dog jumped down instantly, trotted over and lay at her feet. She scratched its ear with one hand. With the other, she dangled a bulging pouch between thumb and forefinger and grinned.

Tommy returned the smile then scowled at the dog, its legs in the air and tongue lolling on the stubbly grass. 'That thing's a menace. Barking in t' lane at all hours, and now this. My heart fair left my chest, there. And that breath – smells like week-old cabbage water. Near floored me, that did.'

She stifled a giggle. 'I feel sorry for him. I've been giving him titbits over the months whenever I've seen him skulking around.'

She didn't mention they were leftovers from Joseph's plate, which she'd sneaked for herself. Despite her hunger, she'd shared whatever scraps she obtained with the dog, understanding the all-consuming need when your guts gnawed from lack of sustenance. However, she'd never been tempted to dip into her hoard. She'd have sooner starved. The hunger for freedom had been far more intense.

'Oh, Lord,' he said on a chuckle.

She smiled. 'What's wrong?'

'Nothing, nothing. I were just thinking on summat Mam said about the dog the other day.'

At the mention of Ivy, she nodded determinedly. 'Speaking of your mother . . . Come, let's get back inside. I need you to do something for me before she wakes.'

Chapter 6

'LASS, ARE YOU ready?' Ivy rubbed her eyes with her shawl. There was a break in her voice as she added, 'Eeh, I must be getting a cold.'

Sally didn't attempt to hide her tears; they ran freely. Her gaze swept the kitchen, drinking in the image, knowing she might never see it again. She wiped her face and nodded.

The rain had ceased and the dew-drenched meadows winked in the weak sunshine like a sea of crystals. A fresh but biting breeze from across the hills whistled through the row as, head lowered against it, Ivy ushered them down the path.

Sally didn't look at her cottage and hoped she never would again. She hadn't been over the threshold since Ivy helped her across the day she gave birth, and she had no intention of ever doing so.

Other than the money, she'd retrieved nothing before leaving because the sad truth was, not a thing belonged to her besides the ragged shawl she'd left behind. An ancient one of Ivy's which, much to Sally's gratitude, Ivy insisted she have, lay across her shoulders. It was thin and matted but warmer than nothing.

Her patched dress and boots, issued to her the day she left the workhouse, were all she possessed. Joseph hadn't spent a farthing on her throughout their marriage.

No, she'd *never* go back. Lifting her chin, she walked on.

As they passed through the row, she glanced at the tatty canvas bag in her hand and smiled tearfully. It held the baby's clothes and a paper-wrapped parcel. This contained two cold sausages, a slice of bread and dripping and a hunk of currant cake to, in Ivy's words, keep her going on her travels to 'That Manchester'. This consisted of the upcoming cart ride, the train, then the trek from the station in Manchester to Grace's district – a journey of some two hours, she surmised. And inside the bag there was another item she couldn't quite believe was there.

Earlier, when the men were leaving for work, she'd shaken their hands and thanked them for their kindness. Arthur wished her well, as did Tommy – though she'd imagined he held her hand a little longer than his father. Before leaving, Shaun had rummaged in the dresser drawer and thrust something into her hand.

She'd blinked at his bowed head then looked down. It was the beautifully carved horse Tommy had showed her hours before. She'd gasped and tried to return it, insisting she couldn't accept, but he'd stepped away mumbling, 'Take it, for the babby.'

She'd never known such kindness, felt humbled to her very soul.

The coaching house came into view and she breathed deeply. This was it. Would she depart from Bolton undetected? Would she remember how to locate Grace's home once in Manchester? Would she find her larger-than-life aunt there if she did?

Ivy's voice broke her thoughts. 'Oh, that's all we need.'

Following her gaze, Sally groaned inwardly.

'Good morning, Mrs Morgan, Mrs Goden.' The stiff greeting belied the smile accompanying it.

'Sir,' they mumbled.

Noticing Ivy's lips twitch, nervous laughter bubbled inside her. Clearing her throat, Sally met his steely glare. 'Sir, allow me to apologise for my behaviour Friday. I acted disgracefully, throwing . . . throwing you . . .' She paused as another wave of giggles threatened to escape. 'I had no right evicting you from Mrs Morgan's cottage. I hope I . . . didn't hurt you when I threw you down the path.'

Ivy turned her snort into a cough. 'Excuse me, sir. I've started with a shocking cowd this morning.'

The preacher's nostrils flared and one eye twitched rapidly. 'The Almighty has, I am certain, an appropriate punishment prepared for you come Judgement Day. However,' he added grimly, '*I'm* prepared to forget the incident if you heed my advice and return to your husband today.'

She stiffened in outrage but before she could deliver a retort, Ivy flashed him a disarming smile.

'We've spoken on that and realise you're right. Sally sees she's been hasty, that she should try and make her marriage work. She loves the bones of yon Joseph, despite their disagreements, and is on her way to catch the carrier's cart to Bolton town. Going to his sister's, she is, to beg his forgiveness. Aye, rest assured, she'll do her best to smooth out matters. Won't you, lass?' she added with the briefest of winks.

'Oh. Oh, yes. Indeed. It was wicked of me to tell such lies about him. I love my Joseph dearly.'

He looked at them in turn through narrowed eyes. After what seemed an age, he nodded. 'I knew you would see sense. Your husband will be most pleased, though as I am sure you know, you have a great deal of apologising to do, madam. However, Mr Goden is a just man. He shall forgive you eventually. You should count your blessings to be married to one such as him.'

'Yes, sir.'

'Excellent. Well, I shan't keep you.' With a half-bow, he bade them farewell and strode down the lane.

When he was a fair distance away, they broke into laughter.

'Come on,' Ivy spluttered, 'we'd best get on. You don't want to keep that saint of a husband waiting, d'you?'

'Thank you, Mrs Morgan, for your quick thinking. But what about you? He'll be furious when he discovers we lied.'

'Humph! Don't you fret over me, lass. I'm not frickened of him. He can rant and ask as many questions as he likes. All he'll get from me is a clog up his arse.'

Dissolving into laughter again, they hurried to the waiting cart which, according to the sign in the coaching house window, departed for Bolton each day bar Wednesdays and Sundays.

'Hello, Ivy! Lovely morning, in't it?'

Ivy frowned at the murky sky but smiled none the less. 'Aye, lovely morning, George.'

The carter, a thickset man with mutton-chop whiskers and a weathered face, grinned then turned his bleary gaze to Sally and tipped his cap. 'Morning, lass.'

She smiled warily. This man was clearly drunk. She'd seen enough with Joseph to know. Hugging the baby closer, she whispered, 'Mrs Morgan, I . . . believe he's . . .'

Ivy nodded and strode forward. 'George Turner, are you sozzled again? You're a danger to your passengers, you are, driving that cart of yourn in that bloody state. Yon Sally here wants a ride into town and she's gorra young 'un with her. You best mind how you go, or you'll have me to answer to. Bloody shocking, it is.' Hands on hips, she shook her head but a smile played at her mouth.

The waiting passengers chuckled when he threw back his head and roared with laughter.

'Now, wench, you rest easy. Never had no accident yet, I've not. I allus have a nip of summat to warm my owd bones but these here hosses do the work.' Brown eyes dancing, he gave the mares' necks an affectionate pat. 'Know the way closed-eyed, they would.'

Stretching to her full height, which barely reached his chest, Ivy wagged a finger under his nose. 'Aye, well. You've been warned.'

Sally watched the exchange in astonishment. Men turned nasty with ale, didn't they? They threatened you, hurt you in ways no one should be. Yet this one wasn't angry, wasn't snarling at anyone or threatening to thump them. He was smiling broadly and her lips stretched into one, too.

He swayed to the cart and hauled himself into his seat behind the horses' rumps. Ivy chuckled. 'Have no fear, lass, he's harmless. He knows Bolton like the back of his hand. You'll come to no harm with owd George.'

Sally tried to smile but her lips wobbled and with a sob she threw an arm around Ivy. 'Oh, Mrs Morgan, I'll miss you more than you'll ever know. Take care of yourself. And please, don't ever change.'

Ivy sniffed, coughed, sniffed again. 'No fear of that, love. I'd not change for no bugger, prince nor pauper.'

'Ready, lass?' asked the carter softly, and she nodded.

While she climbed aboard, Ivy held the baby. She gazed at him for a long moment then kissed his brow tenderly. 'Goodbye, fella. Look after your mam, there's a good lad.' Eyes bright, she laid him in Sally's arms. 'Take care, lass. And just you remember, I'm here if you need me. Always.'

With a 'Whey up, there!' from George, the cart jolted forward.

Sally laughed through her tears and the passengers grinned when Ivy called, 'Think on what I said, George. I'll flay thee alive if harm comes to that lass or her babby. Just you mind where you're going, you bugger.'

With a nod and a wink, he touched his cap. 'Goodbye, wench!'

Standing at her father's door, Nancy Skinner nodded a greeting to Ivy passing through the row. She received a watery smile in return and frowned curiously. That the older woman was upset about something was clear to see.

Turning back inside the shop, a thought occurred and her cheeks burned with excitement. Hiding her smile, she entered the back room and reached for a plate from the dresser.

She was right, she just knew it. She'd been awaiting this day for months and now, *finally*, things would go her way.

As she dished out leek-and-potato pie for her father's dinner later, her heart danced. 'Please, Lord, let it be true,' she murmured, her smile spreading into a grin of pure delight.

Sally sat mesmerised as they rolled through Breightmet. After living as a virtual prisoner, as a workhouse inmate and then as Joseph's wife, she couldn't tear her gaze away. The last time she'd passed through was en route to Spring Row shortly after her wedding but, consumed with fear and dread, she hadn't noticed her surroundings.

Gurgling streams meandered alongside fields snuggled by farmers' cottages, surrounded with thick trees and snow-white sheep, grazing peacefully. Closing her eyes, she drew in scented air. Despite everything, she'd miss this little community.

She'd prayed for years in the dead of night, as Joseph lay snoring beside her, to make her escape but knew it wasn't Spring Row she'd craved to leave. She consoled herself with hopes that, one day, she and her child might again live amongst these hills, happily.

'Eeh, he's a bonny young thing. Your first?'

The innocent question, from a woman in her middle years seated beside Sally, stabbed her heart. She'd never forget the poor souls born to her too soon, nor cease to wonder whom they might have grown to become, but in a way, this child *was* her first. The first to survive the Devil's evil.

'I'm not prying, lass, just making conversation. Passes the journey quicker, is all.'

The soft words snapped her from her reverie. 'I'm sorry. Yes, he's my first. And he's so good, hardly ever cries.'

The woman chuckled. 'Aye, well, enjoy it. Others will follow soon enough and peace will be nowt but a memory.'

She forced a smile. *If only you knew*, she thought bitterly, glancing to her left hand.

Ivy had stopped her wrenching the thin band from her finger this morning with the sage advice, 'Whatever that there ring represents, it'll bring thee respectability.

And when times are lean, it'll fetch a few bob at the pawnshop.'

Though the sight of it turned her stomach, she'd left it where it was for now.

As they neared the centre of town, fields petered away. Rich green turned to grey as they weaved through crooked streets flanked by houses, shops and inns. Huge chimneys, almost shrouded from view beneath an overhanging pall, dotted the skyline, belching out dense smoke, and her chest tightened.

From what she knew, Bolton, situated in a natural valley on a vast sweep of moorland, developed on the banks of the River Croal. The upsurge in textile manufacture saw it gradually spread out as more and more people arrived, seeking jobs in the cotton trade. Sally remembered the noxious smell of the factories from her childhood; Manchester, some ten miles south-east, was also a thriving manufacturing town, on an even larger scale.

'They're an eyesore, ain't they, lass?' murmured the woman. 'Mill Town, folk are calling us, and no wonder. Everywhere you look a fresh 'un's sprung; nigh on seventy, now, so says my husband. We'll not see our hands afore our faces in a few years, I'm sure.'

Nodding agreement, Sally covered her nose and mouth. Despite the rapid growth throughout many towns, Breightmet remained relatively untouched, and the clogged air wrapped around lungs now unaccustomed to it.

Her heartbeat quickened as they approached one of Bolton's oldest roads, where she and Joseph lodged before and shortly after their wedding: Deansgate. Dark and miserable, riddled with ruinous, one- and two-storey homes and shops leaning shoulder to shoulder with as many alehouses, the grinding poverty was tangible.

Beneath Alice's roof, she'd had the role of slave forced upon her immediately. She'd rebelled, yet quickly realised her error. The punishments Alice doled out for her insolence had known no bounds. Without mercy, she'd lash out with fists, feet, even teeth, while Joseph looked on in amusement.

Yet despite her loathing for Sally, Alice had told her brother in no uncertain terms to get a band on her finger. Whatever her faults – and they were plenty – she wouldn't condone the mortal act of living in sin, thus shackling them for life. For that alone, Sally reciprocated Alice's ill feelings tenfold.

The preacher said Joseph was dwelling here. What if he saw her and snatched the baby? Surprise brought a smile when her inner voice growled, 'Let him try it.'

Her emotions were up and down. One minute, she was drowning in rage and the next – proven this morning – a quivering wreck at the thought of seeing him. It was a terrifying notion but she was determined to leave the fear behind. Her old hardness was increasing steadily and she was glad of it. Nevertheless, when the cart passed her sister-in-law's street, she sighed in relief.

Hope and excitement stirred. Not long, now, and she'd be free of him.

'Whoa there, my bonny girls!' At the carter's command, the horses slowed to a walk.

The woman smiled as they rattled to a stop. 'Here we are, lass. Want a hand down with the babby?'

Sally couldn't speak. Since escaping, she'd revelled in new experiences: speaking and laughing with others; eating more than she ever had; being free of the beatings that were part and parcel of daily life – all a wonder. However, the sights, sounds and smells before her now were like nothing she'd encountered.

She gazed in awe towards New Market Place, which Ivy had spoken of once or twice. Situated on an area of land to the south side of Deansgate, it claimed to be the finest uncovered market in the country.

Shops bordered all sides, taking advantage of the customers who flocked each week: cloggers, grocers, butchers, beer-sellers and bakers huddled alongside pawnbrokers, drapers, haberdashers and hatters, all jostling for business around the bustling square.

Accepting the woman's help, she stepped from the cart. She barely heard her warm goodbye, returning it just in time. Alone, she looked about and smiled. All around stood carts and stalls piled high with produce mostly locally grown and made. Meat and poultry, bred on the surrounding homesteads; fruit and vegetables; confectionery; grain; seeds; hay; straw – the variety seemed endless.

She was wandering through the swell of people when a hand on her shoulder stopped her in her tracks. Spinning around, she almost cried out in relief to see George's beaming face.

'Eeh, sorry if I frightened thee, but you've left summat behind.'

She stared at the carter in puzzlement. The sleeping baby lay in her arm and she was clutching the canvas bag. She possessed nothing else. 'You must be mistaken, Mr Turner. I have everything I set out with.'

'Nay, lass. You're wrong there.'

She followed his gaze. What she saw at his feet astonished her. Panting heavily, tongue hanging from the side of its mouth, was the dog from Spring Row.

George chuckled and patted its back. 'This fella's followed us from Breightmet. Watched him all the way, I did, running alongside the cart. And d'you know summat, lass? He never once took his eyes off thee.'

'But he's not mine, Mr Turner! I have seen him around, but—'

'Well, I'd say you'll have a job getting shot. Took a shine to thee, he has. He's a bonny chap; bit on t' thin side, mind.' Eyeing an inn behind a stall, he licked his lips. 'Anyroad, I'm off forra jar afore I wither with thirst. Think on with that there dog. He's a big 'un if ever I saw one.' His eyes softened. 'He'd be sound protection for them as needs it.'

She smiled gently. 'Thank you.'

'Take care, lass. I'll be sure to tell Ivy you survived the journey!'

When he'd gone, she looked down. 'How about it, Dog? Do you fancy a trip to Manchester?' It answered with a shake of its tail. 'Come along, then. We need to take the train.' Following Ivy's directions, she turned for Trinity Street Station.

Stallholders' and customers' chatter, peppered with laughter as they haggled and indulged in banter, enveloped her as she passed, the dog close on her heels. Men predominated but bonneted women in long aprons also sold their wares and their shrill voices, as they urged the townsfolk to buy, carried further:

'Fresh produce, here, lovies. No better in t' whole of Bolton. Golden butter! Delicious cheese! Eggs not long left my hens' backsides, still warm!' one rang out, followed by another at the next stall, and the next.

'Three and six for three pounds of butter? A prime swindle, that is! Throw in a few of them eggs and you've gorra sale. And none of them shit-smeared 'uns, neither,' a customer cackled.

The stallholder roared with laughter but, hurrying on, Sally missed her reply. Alice's home was too close for comfort; she couldn't hang around.

Minutes later, however, she had to stop; Jonathan seemed to grow heavier by the second. She moved him into her other arm and flexed the aching one he'd vacated.

The man whose stall she'd halted by smiled sympathetically. 'Little things, babbies, but they're dead weights after a while, ain't they?'

'Indeed they are!'

'Strap a saddle on that big beggar and let the babby ride on its back.' He nodded to the dog and laughed. 'Travelling far today, lass?'

Her smile froze. No one could know where she was heading. For all she knew, this kindly looking man might know Joseph or Alice. 'Some distance, yes,' she answered cautiously.

'Aye, I thought as much. You don't talk like folk round here; speak reet nice, you do.' He rummaged around his stall, shoved aside boots, kitchenware and medicine bottles containing colourful liquids. 'Not like the nobs what sound like they've a hot poker up their backsides but still, you speak nice. Proper, like.' He moved other mismatched items then, grinning, held up a basket. 'Lay a blanket in here and the babby will be lovely and snug.' He produced one and placed it inside. 'Will that do thee?'

'Oh, yes. Thank you.' From Jonathan's coverings, she extracted the bundle of coins from the eaves. 'How much, please?'

His eyes widened. 'Oh, call it a crown, eh, lass? Good quality that there blanket is,' he stated, fingering the coarse material, 'and the basket's in sound health, an' all.'

She glanced at the numerous holes where the wicker had snapped through age and use, but nodded none the less and counted money into his hand. She didn't like to question the price, not when he'd been so kind and thoughtful and, besides, he was the trader, not she. He obviously knew best.

Suddenly, a child no older than five years appeared from nowhere. Her bare feet were filthy, as was her ragged dress, which was several sizes too small for her scrawny frame. Sally's eyes softened with pity but the stallholder's hardened.

Holding his gaze through long tendrils of hair the colour of rats' tails, the girl addressed him boldly. 'At it again, Bob?' She pulled a face at Sally's purchases. 'You're a robbing owd goat. Falling to bits, them are, and you're asking a crown? You've a cheek asking tuppence, you swindler, yer.'

His face turned puce. 'Bugger off, you young imp, afore I ram my boot up that raggedy arse of yourn.'

'Your crusty owd legs wouldn't catch me. Give the lady a fair deal. You're trying to swindle her and you know it.'

Sally turned to him, hurt, and he flushed further. He looked at the coins in his hand. Then he poured the majority into hers without a word.

The girl grinned, snatched up the basket and steered her to the edge of the market.

They halted by an ornate drinking fountain and after laying Jonathan inside the basket, Sally smiled wryly. This child, who clearly knew the ways of the world better than she, had saved her a fair amount of money and she was grateful, if not a little embarrassed. Her naivety would be her undoing unless she wised up, and fast. 'What's your name?'

The girl wiped an arm across her dripping nose. 'Folk call me all manner of things, missis, but my proper name's Lily.' A grin spread across her face when Sally laughed.

'Well, Lily, I think you deserve this for your help back there.'

'Bloomin' hell. Ta, missis!'

Her stomach knotted as she handed over a silver shilling. She hated those coins with a passion. 'You're very welcome.'

Watching her replace her purse beneath the baby's covers, Lily frowned. 'You want to watch that bag of brass, missis. Hide it under your skirt on a bit of string. It'll be safer there.'

'Do you know, you may be right? You are a clever little thing, aren't you?'

The child smiled in delight. 'Ta, missis. You're nice, you are. You don't half talk queer, mind. Where you from?'

'You don't miss a trick, do you?' Talking about Dicksy had brought back painful memories. Unwilling to relive them again, especially with a child, she said, 'I'm from Manchester. Have you heard of it?'

Lily snorted. 'Have I! Went with Father, I did, last year. My sister skivvied in a big house up there but let the nob's son get her in t' family way, silly cow. Slat her out, they did, and Father went and thumped the son, right on t' nose. My father made *his* father give our Lizzie some money and we fetched her home.'

'What happened then?' Sally asked, agog.

'She gorra belting off Mam for her loose ways and losing a steady wage, and ran off in t' night. We've not seen her since.' She wiped her nose again. 'Don't matter. There's too many children at home. Didn't want another there, anyroad.'

Sally bit her lip. Despite the indifferent tone, tears pooled in Lily's eyes. She extracted the parcel of food from the canvas bag and the young face brightened instantly as delicious aromas wafted from within. 'Are you hungry?'

The child smiled at what she clearly deemed a daft question. 'Do fishes have a fondness for water?'

Chuckling, Sally handed her a sausage and the hunk of currant cake. She gave the salivating dog the other sausage, re-wrapped the bread and dripping and returned it to the bag. She watched with pity as the girl devoured the food ravenously. 'Better?'

Lily ceased licking crumbs from her grubby fingers to pat her stomach. 'Aye. Ta, missis.'

'Well, I have a train to catch so I'm afraid I must be going. Look after yourself and thank you again for your help. Goodbye.' She made to turn but Lily gripped her shawl.

'Will you take me with you? Please? Mam won't mither. Let me come home with you, missis, *please.*'

The sheer desperation in her eyes brought a lump to Sally's throat. 'You cannot come with me. What about your family?'

'They'll not mind, honest. And Mam's an 'orrible pig; *she'd* be glad to see the back of me.'

'Oh, lass. I cannot just take you with me, much as I like you. I'm sorry.'

Fat tears rolled down Lily's cheeks but she nodded miserably.

Sally took the remainder of the food from her bag. 'Here, take it. Goodbye, Lily.'

She hurried for the station without looking back. Guilt and the memory of Lily's sad blue eyes followed her all the way.

The sooner she was out of Bolton, the better.

Chapter 7

LILY RUBBED AN arm across her face and turned reluctantly for home. She normally hung around the market all day; there was more chance of filling her belly there. Distracted stallholders didn't usually miss a swiped piece of fruit or bun but if they did, and her forced tears didn't work, her thin legs could outrun any of them. Today, though, she wasn't in the mood.

She hugged herself as the final day of October's harsh wind whipped her mottled skin but didn't quicken her pace. The longer she could avoid home, the better. The odd stone bit into her as she dragged her feet but as she'd never worn shoes, the skin was so coarse she barely noticed.

She paused at the entrance of Chapel Alley, debating whether to return to the market, but decided against it after glancing at the sky. She didn't like the rain. Due to the lice she couldn't recall not having, her head itched ferociously when wet and open sores on her scalp burned when she scratched.

Despite her foreboding as she neared her door, a smile stirred. She'd wolfed down the bread and dripping and was wonderfully full for once. That grub had been the best she'd ever tasted. She wished the lady had taken her with her. She'd been kind, had smiled and spoken to her softly. Not like her mam, who screeched at her and slapped her face for nothing.

She glanced around then unclenched her fist and grinned. A whole shilling! She smoothed a thumb over a young Victoria, feeling even richer than the pretty monarch. Saliva filled her mouth with thoughts of the food she could buy with the precious piece. Sighing happily, she slipped inside.

The stench of stale cooking and unwashed bodies enveloped her. Her mother was by the fire and after shooting a glance at her stiff back, Lily hurried to the corner. Damp from the rotten pallet seeped through her dress and she winced when straw poking through the thin fabric scratched her leg. Pressing against the wall, she wrapped her arms around her knees.

'And where have *you* been?'

Lily hugged her knees tighter. 'Market.'

Her mother stabbed the fire savagely with the poker. 'Well, don't get too comfy. That useless father of yourn won't have found work, you can bet your life on that, so you best get your arse back down that market later and see what you can scavenge. Bone idle, that's his trouble, the good-for-nowt wastrel.'

Lily's nails bit into her palms as the scathing voice rattled on. She didn't like it when she spoke of Father that way. He wasn't idle or useless, he was nice and kind. Nicer than *her*, anyroad. She hated being alone with *her*. Thankfully, her siblings would soon be home from work. Her father would follow, tired and miserable after another day tramping the streets in vain.

Her brow creased at the thought of her twin brothers. It was anyone's guess when they would be home; they were hardly ever in. At six years old, they were not yet in work but their pockets always held pennies or food. She didn't know where they found their spoils but *did* know their mother wasn't aware of it. She smiled inwardly. They were clever and she must be, too, if she was to hold on to her shilling.

She squeezed her hand, imagining the endless possibilities it afforded. She could buy a whole bag of fruit, apples, aye, or juicy plums, and stuff her face with the sticky treats; maybe a few cakes, too. Or later, she could sneak to the alehouse for a potato pie. She could buy two, even three—

'What the bugger have you to grin about?' her mother snapped, dragging her from her daydream. 'I'm sure you're a bit simple, you. 'Ere, make yourself useful forra change.'

Lily crossed the room and took the steaming mug held out to her.

'Take that in to your Uncle Joseph, and mind you don't spill it. It's about time he were from that pit of his. Go on, then, hurry up.'

Sticking out her tongue in concentration, Lily headed for the door. Watching the pale-brown liquid swishing back and forth with every step, she remembered the uneven flagstone too late. Her toe stubbed the jutting corner and she stared in horror as the mug and shilling flew from her hands.

The mug landed with a smash but she didn't react when hot tea splashed her bare legs. All her attention was on the coin. She watched, transfixed, as it spun in a circle then rattled to a stop.

'You silly bitch, yer! I told thee to be careful, you gormless young—' The outburst died at the sight of the shilling.

Lily whimpered but a slap silenced her.

Her mother snatched up the coin and waved it under her nose. 'You snidy, sly little bitch. Where the bugger did you get this?' She shook her shoulder hard. 'Shurrup bawling and answer me. Where did you get it?'

'A l–l–lady gave it m–me.' Lily's stuttered explanation earned her another slap.

'What lady, you bleedin' liar?'

'I'm not l–lying, honest!'

'What the hell's afoot, here?'

They turned to see Joseph standing in the doorway.

Running a hand through his hair, he scratched his bare chest and yawned. 'What's all the caterwauling? You can't get a wink of kip in this dump.'

Her mother shot Lily a contemptuous look. 'We've been sat here without a scrap of grub in t' house and this little bitch had a shilling and didn't say nowt. Said a lady give it her, lying cow.'

Joseph stepped over the shattered mug and lowered himself into the fireside chair. 'All that wailing for that? Bloody hell.'

'Listen 'ere, we can't live on fresh air, you know, and I don't see you handing over no brass. This lying swine should've give me this straight away but nay, were planning spending it on herself, no doubt. Selfish through and through, she is, just like her rotten father.'

Bunching her fists, Lily glared at her. 'I'm *norra* liar! A lady *did* give it me. She were from Manchester. I helped her buy a basket to carry her babby in, for the stallholder were trying to swindle her. She were going on a train and she said I were clever. Reet nice to me, she were.'

Her mother laughed scathingly. 'Clever? Thee? Huh!'

Joseph's dark eyes narrowed. He silenced his sister with a flap of his hand. 'Did she tell you her name?'

Lily shook her head. 'I never asked.'

'Take no notice, you fool, she's lying. I bet she's robbed it from somewhere, the little—'

'Alice, will you shurrup a minute, for God's sake?' Before his sister could respond, he turned back to Lily. 'What did she look like, this lady?'

Lily cocked her head in thought. 'She wore a brown dress and her hair were brown, an' all. And she spoke queer.' She reached up to touch her temple. 'Had a scar like a half-moon, she did, just here.'

He paled. 'And she had a babby with her?'

'Aye. Tiny, it were.'

With a roar, he leapt up and rushed from the room. He returned fully dressed, face now purple with rage. 'I'll kill her. I'll bloody well *kill* her!'

'You don't reckon it were Sally?' asked her mother.

'Course it bloody were, the scheming whore. I *knew* she'd been thieving off me; where else would she of got brass to throw about? Catching a bloody train, were she? Well, she'll not get far. By God, she'll not!' He snatched the shilling and bolted from the cottage.

Staring at the open door, Lily's mind whirled. She'd heard them talk about someone called Sally before but from what they had said, she sounded horrible. The lady at the market wasn't; she was lovely. It couldn't be her!

Eyes swimming with tears, she sloped to the corner and curled into a ball upon the mattress.

Jostled at every step, Sally, hugging the basket close, made her way across the crowded platform. Smartly dressed gentlemen, and ladies in beautiful dresses and hats, breezed towards the first-class carriage of the waiting train, porters scurrying behind with trunks and boxes. At other compartments, beshawled women, children, and men in rough clothing and caps dominated the entrances.

She looked around uncertainly. The bustling market had been noisy but the atmosphere jovial, relaxed. This was something else. Footsteps pounded the platform. Children's cries and laughter mingled with the hum of conversation. Porters' shouts rang, unintelligible amidst the throb of noise. Yet it was the train that was turning her legs to jelly.

Upon leaving the workhouse, she and Joseph had travelled to Bolton on an open cart. Never had she been on one of these huge, hissing beasts; the prospect filled her with panic.

She continued hesitantly when passengers in front began entering the carriages. However, as she reached the entrance, her resolve wavered and she turned, ready to bolt from the station. But she knew she had no choice – she *must* get on. Inwardly cursing Joseph to the bowels of hell, she turned back.

The dog had already leapt aboard and stood, head cocked, as though urging her on. With a deep breath, she stepped forward. She'd barely entered when a hand gripped her shoulder and hauled her back on to the platform.

'What d'you think *you're* playing at?'

Her legs almost buckled. Twisting around, she found herself facing a broad chest. Slowly, her eyes travelled up, not wanting to see the face she knew it was. She'd almost done it. By sheer misfortune,

Joseph had found her. Dear God, he'd kill her for sure, he'd—

'I asked thee a question. What d'you think you're playing at?'

She tried yanking free but he held on tight. 'Let me go! I won't go back with you, I won't! I'll scream this station to the ground if you don't *let me go*!' Her last words were indeed a scream and she shoved him hard in the stomach.

His grip loosened and, gasping, she made to jump aboard but the dog knocked her aside and leapt from the carriage. It landed on the man and passengers stared open-mouthed as he hit the platform.

The animal planted its huge paws on his chest and pressed its face close to his, snarling menacingly. She suspected it was only her cry of horror on realising he wasn't Joseph after all that stopped it sinking its teeth into the man's neck. It looked up, awaiting her instruction.

'What the . . . ? What the . . . ?' The stationmaster craned his neck slowly so as not to provoke the dog further. 'What's its name? Call it off, God damn it, call it off!'

'He hasn't got a name. I haven't given him one, yet.'

'Well, think of one and quick. It's crushing my bleedin' ribs, here!'

The dog watched her calmly as she approached. She laid a hand on its head. 'Off, Dog. It's all right, I'm all right. Off.'

The stationmaster gasped in relief when it obeyed. He staggered to his feet, eyes blazing, and pointed a quivering finger in her face. 'You . . . you swine, yer. I'll have you and that thing strung up! I only asked what you were playing at fetching that fiend on t' train. Animals ain't permitted in here.'

Sally lowered her eyes in mortification. 'I'm sorry, I am, really. You startled me. I thought you were someone else.'

'Sorry, is it? Tha bloody will be when—' A man stepped from the crowd, silencing him.

'You're the one who'll be sorry if you don't leave this lass alone. 'Tis a disgrace how you dragged her from the train; and her with a babe in arms, too. The dog acted admirably and *I'll* be the one knocking ye back down, so I will, if you don't back off.'

Sally gazed at him then touched the stationmaster's sleeve. 'Let the dog on the train. I've said sorry and I'll pay extra. Please?' He glared from her to the stranger uncertainly and she turned to the young Irishman who had defended her. 'Please, I'm quite all right. You're making matters worse.'

His green eyes danced in amusement and a slow smile spread across his handsome face. 'As you wish, acushla, as you wish.'

A shrill whistle rang out and she turned back to the stationmaster, face creasing in desperation. 'Please. I *must* catch this train.' She fumbled in the basket, drew out a handful of coins and held them up.

Catching the eye of the Irishman, who nodded, he flapped a hand. 'Oh, give me your fare. I've had a bloody bellyful. Go on, get gone.'

Sally almost cried out in relief. She handed over the money and she and the dog hurried aboard. Taking a seat on the wooden form, she heaved a sigh.

'I suppose the carter was right, Dog. You did well protecting me, there!'

It lay at her feet and rested its head on its paws. Patting the dog, she peered across the platform. She caught sight of the stationmaster and pulled back quickly, covering her mouth as laughter bubbled. Peeping back, she scanned the faces and frowned. The Irishman had gone.

She sat back and shrugged. It was no concern of hers. Besides, he'd had no right interfering. Nevertheless, as the train pulled away, she again glanced out but great clouds of steam obscured her view.

Sally shrugged once more, placed the basket next to her and closed her eyes. Her stomach fluttered with a range of emotions. She could scarcely believe she was leaving Bolton after all these years. And what would she face in Manchester? Her heart lurched, already aching for Ivy and her safe little cottage.

A tall, muscular man with floppy, coal-black hair and grey-blue eyes assaulted her mind's eye. Allowing herself to study him, she recalled the time they spent together in his cosy kitchen. She remembered how his shoulder muscles rippled through his shirt when he scraped back his hair, heard his smooth, deep laugh . . . She hugged herself, a smile caressing her lips.

As the train rattled along the tracks to her birthplace, she slipped into a light sleep.

The train was spluttering to a halt when a growl woke Sally. She was startled to see the dog staring beyond her shoulder and turned slowly.

'Lily?' As soon as she uttered the name, she knew she was mistaken. The child, though plainly dressed, was neat and clean and whilst her hair was the exact colour of the other girl's, it wasn't falling across her face in greasy tendrils but lay in tidy plaits.

'Begging your pardon, lass, but I heard you telling the stationmaster you were Manchester bound.'

She hadn't noticed a man standing behind the girl and jumped in surprise.

'You were out for the count and I didn't know whether to waken thee in case that big beggar took a chunk from me.' Flashing a wary glance at the dog, he laid a protective hand on the child's shoulder.

She smiled sheepishly. 'Are we in Manchester?'

'We are, lass.' He touched his cap then hastily guided the girl from the carriage.

Sally looked down and sighed. 'You're going to get me into trouble. I don't need shielding from everyone.' She nodded thoughtfully. 'That is an ideal name; I cannot continue calling you Dog. How about it? Shall we name you Shield?' He woofed softly and she smiled. 'Shield it is, then.'

She lifted the basket but looking inside her smile slipped. Jonathan was wide awake and sucking his bunched fist. 'Come, Shield, this fellow needs feeding.'

The long, single-storey building of Manchester Victoria Station milled with people. She made for an empty bench, lifted the grizzling child and after positioning her shawl around them, opened a few buttons on her dress.

Shield sat by her feet, scrutinising all who passed. Women glanced in their direction, smiled understandingly and looked away. But the lingering stares of some men had his hackles rising and she softened towards him further.

He clearly held a deep distrust of men; they had an affinity in that sense. Then the memory of him jumping up excitedly at Tommy swam across her mind and she smiled. Well, not all men. That was another connection they shared – they recognised a good one when they saw one.

The suckling ceased and after repositioning her clothing, she laid the baby in the basket and rose.

She'd done it. She'd escaped and Joseph was none the wiser. God willing, she'd soon be seeing her aunt. Her heart beat furiously with terror and excitement.

She took deep breaths. Then squaring her shoulders, she walked from the station.

Chapter 8

THE FIRST THING Sally noticed when she stepped from the station was the all-encompassing smell. Wrinkling her nose, she stared around and above. Soot-blackened buildings, their chimneys spewing thick smoke, greeted her mournfully.

The factory-building boom had transformed the Manchester she knew; it had expanded at an astonishing rate. The area she stood in looked densely populated and was much busier than she remembered. She'd have guessed there were well over three times the residents encased amidst these grimy surroundings than in those she'd just left.

She glanced right to the run-down tavern where Joseph had taken her upon leaving the workhouse and grimaced, remembering his leering face as he scrutinised her young body from top to toe. He'd drunk jar after jar of ale while she huddled in the corner, scared witless and aching with grief for her mother. They left for Bolton that night and she hadn't set foot in this town since.

She fought to keep her eyes from straying in the opposite direction. Yet she knew she had to see it, one last time. Maybe then, she could lay the past to rest. Slowly, she turned to the place of her nightmares.

Behind high walls, New Bridge Street Workhouse stood tall and intimidating on the hilltop, its black chimneys rising against the dull sky. Rectangular windows dotted the exterior, staring at a world most wretched inmates beyond the panes wouldn't again know.

She reeled back as though slapped by an invisible hand. Her mother's and Dicksy's faces assaulted her mind and she tore her gaze away with a sob.

Sensing her distress, Shield whined and pawed her leg. Swallowing her pain, she patted him. 'I'm all right, Shield.'

'You've given the fellow a name, then? Ah, Shield's grand. It suits him, to be sure.'

Whipping around, Sally raised her eyebrows then drew them together in a frown. 'What are *you* doing here?'

The Irishman grinned. However, it slipped from his face when her eyelids fluttered. She swayed drunkenly and he grabbed the basket's handle and caught her around the waist.

Her vision cleared; blinking in bewilderment, she pulled away. 'I'm sorry, I don't know what came over me. I'm quite well, now, thank you.'

Handing back the basket, he glanced to the workhouse and frowned. 'Are you sure? 'Tis mighty pale, your face, so it is.'

She nodded then breathed deeply when nausea swept through her.

'No, you're not, acushla. Come with me.' Taking her elbow, he guided her across the busy road.

She allowed him to lead her but when he halted at the familiar tavern, drew back sharply.

''Tis all right in here. You need a hot meal inside you, put some colour back into that pretty face of yours.' He took her arm again but she snatched it back.

'Thank you, but I'm quite well. I must go.'

'If you're sure . . . ?'

'Quite. Goodbye.'

'Wait, let me pay for a cab. You could have another turn and there may not be a handsome man around to catch you next time.'

At the teasing twinkle in his eyes, her lips twitched. 'You ought to save your money and buy yourself a larger cap.'

He laughed heartily. 'Come now, acushla. You don't believe you're the first to fall at my feet, do you?'

Rolling her eyes, she smiled lopsidedly. 'Very well, Mr . . . ?'

'Con Malloy, ma'am, at your service.'

'Very well, Con Malloy, I'll take a hansom. But I'm paying.'

She realised that, albeit a shocking extravagance, it was sensible. Many years had passed; she'd likely never locate Grace's home otherwise. She only remembered the street because it was her aunt's married name; Grace had often teased that she and her husband owned the road.

Con made to protest but when she raised an eyebrow, laughed in defeat. He whistled to a waiting cab, which was at their side in seconds, and swept an arm theatrically. 'Your carriage awaits, acushla.'

Hiding a smile, she stepped aboard.

'Well, Mrs . . . ?'

'Sally Swann. And it's Miss.' She'd decided this morning to revert to her maiden name and relished the familiarity on her tongue.

He glanced at Jonathan then to the band on her finger, but didn't comment. 'Well, *Miss* Swann, perhaps our paths will cross again. Goodbye.'

She frowned as a thought struck. 'You never answered my question. What *are* you doing here?'

'And why wouldn't I be?' He spread his arms wide. ''Tis my home, so it is.'

'But I looked— What I mean is, I didn't see you on the train.' Heat scorched her cheeks when he smiled slowly. 'Well, goodbye.' She inclined her head then tapped the cab. 'Boslam Street, please.'

Con watched her go, his smile deepening. Miss Sally Swann . . . Their paths would indeed cross again. Of that, he was certain.

As the hansom rattled through the streets, Shield running alongside, Sally's stomach churned. She'd assumed her dizzy spell to be exhaustion but now recalled hardly touching her porridge this morning, worry over the departure having chased away her appetite. And she hadn't eaten a scrap from Ivy's parcel. Maybe she did need a hot meal.

She frowned at the thought of the man she'd just left by the roadside. Who was he and why did he seem to appear when she needed help? His knowing smile, when she'd let slip about searching the platform, brought fire back to her cheeks. What must he think of her?

She told herself it didn't matter. She wouldn't see him again; not a third time, surely?

They turned down another cobblestoned road and the tumbling in her stomach intensified. They couldn't be far from Boslam Street, now.

Please, *please* let Aunt Grace be there, she prayed. And yet, what welcome would she receive? As Ivy pointed out, the reason behind the sisters' estrangement must be serious for her mother to have taken the desperate step of entering the workhouse. But Grace was her only relative. Whatever the outcome, she had to try.

Continuing through the maze of narrow streets of back-to-back houses, made more miserable by the drizzly weather, she breathed a sad sigh. Since leaving Victoria Station, she'd barely seen a speck of green.

Mills and multi-storey factories abounded as well as foundries, engineering factories, glassworks and more. Clearly, such high need of manual labour had brought droves of people to the district but she'd seen no parks, grounds or recreational facilities for this large population. It seemed every available space had been used for industry and housing.

Hastily built dwellings, to accommodate the influx, were painfully apparent; their quality and condition were dire. The majority of streets she'd passed were undrained and ran with human waste from the privies and ash pits at the rear of houses. The stink was overwhelming. She dreaded to imagine how poor souls living in unventilated cellars fared – they must swim during heavy downpours.

Watching young and old scuttling by or lounging in courts and streets, Sally ached for the rolling hills she'd taken for granted. The thought of raising her child in these dark surroundings filled her with horror. We *will* return to Breightmet some day, she vowed.

The cab finally halted and she alighted, nauseous and aching everywhere. Shield bounded around her. Stroking his damp fur, she peered about.

The rain had abated but the dull sun barely pierced the pewter clouds. Wind whipped her skirt and shawl, making her shiver. Glancing up and down, she tried to remember which house was her aunt's but it was useless: each was exactly like its neighbour. The basket rocked and as she looked inside, desperate tears pricked her eyes when Jonathan screwed up his face and wailed.

'All right, lass?'

Sally turned to see an elderly woman, craggy face creased in smile. 'I'm looking for my aunt's house.' She raised her eyebrows expectantly, adding, 'Grace Boslam?'

'Grace? Aye, I know her. But you'll not find her here. Not any more, anyroad.'

Her stomach lurched but the woman chuckled.

'No need to look so worried, lass, for she's not moved far.' She jabbed a finger to an entry between two houses. 'Go through the ginnel, there, and turn right. Grace's is the second-to-last house on t' end.'

'Oh, thank you. Thank you so much.'

She smiled and ambled away, soggy black skirts trailing in the filth behind her.

Sally made for the narrow passage. It gave entry to a row of terraced houses and she crossed the cobbles quickly, eyes fixed on one in particular. Halting before it, she sent up a prayer. In a moment, she'd know what the future held for her and her child.

Heart hammering, she knocked on the door.

Chapter 9

'AYE?'

Sally stared at the young man who had answered her knock. Did she have the wrong house? She stepped back, glanced left and right. No, this was it.

'Can I help you?'

'Yes, I'm sorry, I . . . A woman said my aunt dwells here. Grace Boslam?' She frowned when his face paled. He blinked and opened his mouth but uttered nothing. 'I'm sorry, are you all right? You see, she directed me here. She said that Grace's was the second-to-last—' His crushing hug smothered her speech.

Shield growled but the lad didn't seem to notice. He held her at arm's length. 'Sally Swann? Is it really thee?'

Before a stunned Sally could respond, a weary voice sounded within the house: 'Stan, who is it, lad? Don't leave them standing on t' step, it's perishing out there.'

Air erupted from Sally's lungs. She pushed past Stan into the house.

A cry escaped her. The ash-blonde hair, though bound as usual at the nape, was lank and flecked with grey, and she seemed smaller than Sally remembered. Rosy cheeks, which used to dimple when she smiled, were pasty, the lines around her eyes unfamiliar. But it was her aunt, all right!

'Aunt Grace? Oh, Aunt Grace, I cannot believe . . . After all these years!'

Grace rose slowly. Stan came to stand beside her and she gripped his arm. 'Is it . . . ? Really . . . ? Oh!' She threw herself at Sally and flung her arms around her neck.

Sally smiled at the faint scent of lavender she remembered so well. Burying her face in her aunt's shoulder, she heaved a long sigh.

A cry broke through their tearful laughter. Peering inside the basket, Grace covered her mouth.

'Our little Sally a mother? I don't believe it.' She stroked the baby's cheek then her niece's. 'Oh, where have you been all these years, lass?' She glanced to the door, as though searching for someone else, and her smile faded. 'How's your mam? How's our Rose?'

Fresh tears welled in Sally's eyes at the longing in her aunt's. How could she tell her?

'It's all right, I understand. She'll never forgive me, will she? I don't blame her, honest I don't, but I miss her . . . so very much. Norra day's passed that I've not thought of you both, you know. Norra single day.'

'Oh, Aunt Grace . . .'

'Tell me, lass, please; is she all right, our Rose? Is she well?'

Sally clung to her, heart breaking at what she must say. 'My mother's dead.'

Time seemed to stand still. Then the heavy silence was shattered when, bending double, Grace howled like an injured beast.

'Mam, come and sit down.' Stan led her, sobbing and shaking, to a fireside chair. 'I'll brew some tea.'

Sitting opposite, Sally clasped her hand. 'I'm so sorry, Aunt Grace, so very sorry.'

'I . . . can't . . . My lovely Rosie. And you. Oh, you poor girl.'

She lowered her head, Grace's devastation too painful to witness. She hadn't meant it to be like this. For years, she'd planned this meeting, intended to break the news gently, not blurt it out.

'What happened, lass? When did . . . ? Where have you *been* all these years? Did she ever talk about me? Did she ever forgive me? Did she—?'

'Easy, Mam.' Stan abandoned the teapot to wrap his arms around her, and she crumpled.

'She's been gone these fifteen years,' Sally choked. 'They didn't tell me, Aunt Grace. I had no idea and it near killed me when I heard. I don't even know what happened. It haunts me day and night imagining . . . I'd give anything to feel her arms around me again, anything.'

'Fif . . . fifteen years? How did you not know? What in God's name happened?'

A faint voice drifted from the gloom: 'Mam, where are you? It hurts. It . . . hurts, Mam.'

Grace jumped up and hurried to a narrow bed in the corner. Sally gazed across in surprise; she hadn't noticed anyone else present. Stan beckoned and she followed him outside. Shield was right behind her. He lay on the cobbles by the door, eyes never leaving her.

Stan closed the door to and sat on the step. 'Our Peggy took ill last week. The neighbours have been kindness itself, 'specially Mrs Knox next door. She fetches round a meal of sorts when she can, but her offers of relieving Mam of her bedside vigil are allus refused. Nowt will shift her from Peggy's side.'

'Oh, I am sorry.' Sally lowered herself beside him. 'I had no idea I had cousins. Your mother hadn't been married long when I saw her last. I remember attending the wedding.' She smiled at the memory. 'How is Uncle Ed?'

'He's all right.'

'He's a good man, your father.'

A look passed over Stan's face but was gone before she could determine its meaning. He smiled faintly and looked away.

'I remember him vividly. He would sit me on his shoulders and run up and down the street pretending to be a horse.'

This time, her cousin's smile was as warm as hers. 'He did that with Peggy when she were younger.'

'Is it just the two of you? How old are you both?'

'Aye, just us. I'll be sixteen next month, and Peggy . . .' His face darkened. He kicked the step with his heel. 'It's not fair. It's not *bloody* fair. Eleven year old . . . She's nowt but a babby.'

'Stan? What's wrong?'

His answer was barely above a whisper. 'She's dying. There's nowt can be done for her any more.'

'Oh my . . . ! I didn't realise—'

'You weren't to know. It's just not fair. It's killing Mam.'

'Is there really nothing that can be done?'

He stared at the sky through dull eyes, ran a hand through his dark-blond hair. 'Nay, not now. It's the consumption, but Mam won't believe it. She's convinced she'll get better. She used to get ill then rally but the last time, she coughed up blood.

'That's a sure sign, that is. I've seen it enough round here to know. There's nowt for you once that gets a grip of you.' He looked at Sally for a long moment. 'I'm glad to finally meet thee. I don't know what went on betwixt our mams, for she's never said, but she's allus spoke of you and Aunt Rose. She's missed youse summat awful. I don't know how she'll get over your mam, what with everything else . . .'

She squeezed his arm. 'I'll help whichever way I can. I'm here to stay if you'll have me. I'm so glad I've found your parents – and you and Peggy.'

He covered her hand with his. 'Aye. I'm glad, an' all. It's queer but d'you know, I feel as though I've known thee all my life.'

Sally smiled curiously. 'Do you know, I feel the same with you?'

She was so thankful Grace hadn't turned her away, as she'd often feared she might. Whatever had happened between the sisters, Grace clearly didn't hold it against her. It felt so good to be amongst family. Ivy and Arthur were wonderful but there was no real substitute for blood. For the first time in many, many years, Sally felt like she belonged.

At the thought of the Morgans, Tommy flashed through her mind but she pushed him away. It was time to nip those foolish imaginings in the bud; he'd been being kind, nothing more. She must put the past behind her, for she had a new future here, now. Her family needed her.

This brought a rush of happiness. She curled her fingers through Stan's. 'Let's get back inside and see if your mother's all right. We have a lot of talking to do. I cannot say I'm looking forward to it but she has a right to know.'

'I'll find a scrap of summat for the dog and dish up some broth for you and Father. He'll be home shortly.'

Her stomach rumbled at the mention of food and she smiled gratefully. She didn't want to swoon again, needed a clear head for the painful yet unavoidable conversation to come.

When they reached the kitchen door, Stan paused. A teasing smile played across his mouth. 'This talking what must be done, will it shed light on why you speak like the bloomin' gentry?'

She pushed him playfully. They were going to get along well, she just knew it. He already felt like the brother she'd never had.

The lamplighter's whistle broke through the quiet room. Sally wandered to the window and lifted the faded curtain's edge. Absently, she watched him extend his long pole, bring the gas lamp to life then continue on his rounds, leaving a misty pool of yellow-gold in his wake.

Leaning her forehead against the cold glass, she closed tired eyes. It had been a long day, and the dreaded conversation had been as painful as she'd anticipated. She and Grace held each other for hours and, slowly, the flowing words had eased Sally's shoulders of their long and heavy burden. From entering one hell to escaping the second, and everything between, she left out nothing.

Between sobs, Grace had repeated one question: 'Why didn't my Rosie come to me instead of the workhouse?' Unable to answer, Sally could only hold the broken woman. Grace had, however, managed a smile for the Morgans and blessed them for helping her escape 'that divilish bastard', as she venomously referred to Joseph.

Now, returning to her seat, Sally smiled softly at her aunt, who was asleep in the chair opposite. To have someone, be part of a family again – for Jonathan as much as herself – left a warm glow deep within. She bent to stroke Shield, stretched before the fire. She didn't know what life he'd led but suspected this would be his first home in a long time, too.

It had been a day of highs and lows. She smiled to herself, imagining Ivy's reaction when Tommy revealed her gift for Shaun. His handsome face swam in her mind but again she forced it away. Yes, quite an eventful day, she mused once more. Sorrow at leaving the Morgans, pleasure at gaining Shield, helplessness over little Lily, the stationmaster gazing up from the platform . . .

Her lips curved then bunched in rumination with thoughts of Con Malloy. Who was he? He'd appeared from nowhere in Bolton, then again in Manchester. She had to admit he seemed nice enough. He'd helped her both times without wanting anything in return.

The workhouse, she immediately banished. That building and all it stood for was in the past, she told herself firmly. She'd dwell upon it no more. Her mind switched instead to the reunion with her aunt and the surprising discovery of cousins. Their open-armed welcome was more wonderful than she ever could have envisaged.

She peered inside the basket at her slumbering son and stroked his cheek. 'We did it, little one. We got away.' This brought a surge of quiet jubilation. 'You lost, Joseph,' she murmured. 'You lost.'

Peggy's harsh cough pulled her from her thoughts. Admiration for her aunt filled her when, despite the deep sleep she appeared to be in, she instantly awoke and hurried to her daughter. A mother's love was a powerful thing.

Stan, dozing beside Peggy, stirred when his mother approached. He raised himself on an elbow. 'Is he home?'

Grace felt Peggy's forehead, crossed to a shelf and lifted a bottle of laudanum. 'Nay. He shouldn't be long, now.'

'Not long enough for me.'

She sighed. 'Not now, son.'

Sally frowned. What did Stan mean by that? And where *was* Uncle Ed? He must have finished work hours ago.

Peggy coughed again. Murmuring soothingly, Stan smoothed hair from her forehead. Grace watched with a soft smile then measured medicine from a dark bottle and added it to drops of laudanum in a cup. Stirring the mixture, she glanced across the room. Sally smiled.

'Oh, I thought you were sleeping, lass. Come say hello to your cousin while she's up, for she'll be asleep again soon. She'll be that pleased to see thee.'

'She can hear you,' Stan told Sally as she neared. 'Say summat, tell her who you are.'

Purple eyelids flickered when she covered a small hand with hers. 'Hello, Peggy. I'm Sally, your cousin. It's lovely to meet you.'

Soft brown pools rested on her face. The girl gave a half-smile and said laboriously, 'Ah . . . in't she . . . bonny, Mam?'

Grace and Stan nodded, eyes misty, and tears pricked Sally's.

'Not as pretty as you, Peggy, not by a mile,' she whispered.

Peggy managed another smile and closed her eyes. She nodded when Grace asked was she in pain then squinted up again. 'Nice to . . . meet thee, Sally.'

Too choked to speak, she kissed Peggy's hand then moved aside while her aunt administered the medicine. Stan put his arm around her shoulders and led her away and they had just sat down by the fire when the sound of the front door opening rattled through the house. Moments later, Ed entered.

Grace made no mention of his absence. 'Look who's here, Ed. Our Sally's come home.' She smiled when her husband gasped and embraced Sally warmly.

'Eeh, I don't believe it! Where have you been hiding, lass?'

Sally knew instantly where *he'd* been; the smell of porter was unmistakable. Yet as with George Turner the carter, she now realised not all men were violent brutes she must avoid at all costs when they had taken a sup.

'Oh, Uncle Ed, it's lovely to see you.'

He hugged her again then eased into a chair, almost stepping on Shield's tail. 'Is this big divil yours?' When she laughed and nodded, he cocked his head, eyes thoughtful. 'By, you're the image of your mam, lass, you are that.' Shooting a glance at his wife, his smile vanished. 'Is she here, your mam?'

Sally shook her head.

'Nay, don't suppose she would be, and who could blame her?'

'Ed, please, you don't understand,' whispered Grace. 'Rose . . . My Rosie's dead.'

He blinked at her bowed head then turned to Sally. 'I'm sorry to hear that, lass, I am really. I thought . . . She were a sound wench, your mam, a sound wench.'

Sally suppressed a frown. What was behind her aunt and mother's falling out? From the little she'd gleaned, Grace seemed to be in the wrong. She determined to ask her aunt, but not yet. They had shed enough tears this night. Right now, she wanted to enjoy her family.

'There's someone I'd like you to meet, Uncle Ed.' Stooping by his chair, she lifted the basket. 'My son,

Jonathan. The moment I held him, I knew what to name him. And if he turns out to be half the man my father was, I'll be the proudest mother on earth.'

He stared at the infant for a long moment, smiled faintly and looked away.

'Stan, is that tea ready, lad?' Grace asked, cutting through the silence. 'And warm the rest of that mutton broth for your father.'

'Aye, hurry up. And when you've done that, you can run to the Blue Bell and fetch us all a penny pie. Our Sally's back and what better way to celebrate than with one of Betty's meat and tatties?'

Stan's back stiffened at Ed's tone, but his eyes remained fixed on the table. He poured tea into a large mug and passed it across.

'And the grub?'

'It's warming.'

'Aye, well, take yourself to the inn while you're waiting, boy.'

Stan's jaw tensed as he took coppers from Ed. When the front door slammed, Sally caught Grace's eye and the older woman lowered her gaze.

Ed stared at the door and breathed deeply. Then he rose and crossed to the bed. He gazed at his daughter. 'How's she been?' he asked. The edge to his voice when he'd spoken to Stan had gone.

'No better, no worse. She managed a drop of broth earlier.' Grace smoothed dark hair from Peggy's brow. 'My poor lass.'

He stared down at her bowed head. When he lifted a hand to her shoulder, Sally made to look away from the private moment between husband and wife. She was confused, however, when he flexed his fingers inches from her aunt then let his arm fall to his side.

She bit her lip. Something was wrong with her family; she could have reached out and touched the strained atmosphere. She wondered whether it was simply the stress of Peggy's condition, but discarded this. The child's illness was obviously distressing for everyone but something else was afoot here that she couldn't put her finger on.

Lost in thought, she jumped when the front door clattered. Stan entered and, smiling, she took the steaming parcel from him. 'Allow me. You warm yourself by the fire.'

He thanked her and held his hands to the leaping flames. 'It's beyond cowd out there. I reckon we'll have snow afore the night's out.'

Returning to his chair, Ed nudged him aside. 'Don't talk daft. It's not *that* bloody cowd.'

Stan didn't respond and as she unwrapped pies and dished out broth for her uncle, Sally kept her head lowered. These exchanges were uncomfortable to witness. Doubt snaked down her spine. Had she done the right thing coming here? It seemed her family had enough troubles without her adding to them.

Ed rubbed his hands as she approached with a delicious-smelling pie, hunk of bread and bowl of broth. 'Eeh, that smells good.'

After passing Stan a pie, she turned to her aunt. 'Aunt Grace, will you eat this now?'

'Nay, I'm not hungry.'

'Come and get some grub down you, wench, while it's hot,' Ed murmured without looking up. 'It'll do you good.'

The whisper of a smile lifted the corners of Grace's mouth. 'Aye. Aye, all right.'

When his wife sat, he began to eat. He didn't see the eyebrow Stan raised at him – or the curling of his lip – but Sally did.

Lowering her head again to hide her frown, she nibbled her pie without tasting it. Tomorrow, she'd have that word with her aunt. Something wasn't right here and she was determined to find out what.

Dodging a pile of manure, Nancy Skinner hurried across the frosty cobbles. Her heart fluttered in anticipation of the meeting to come and she smiled, glad she'd made the extra effort.

She'd donned her best dress, a revealing item in deep maroon, which clung to her curves and accentuated her large breasts. Her hair she'd brushed until it crackled and the soft tresses fell across her shoulders like burnished copper.

Along the length of the street, laughter and bawdy singing poured from alehouses when doors opened to admit or eject a customer. Before they could swing shut, sickly streaks of light from within sliced across the cobbles, revealing the silhouettes of rats scuttling by. Watching her step, she lowered her shawl and turned left.

Across the street, a group of rough-looking men peered at her as she passed and she tossed her hair, knowing the gas lamp would highlight the amber-flecked locks she was so proud of.

'How much, love?' Leering laughter followed and the speaker grinned at his friends.

Eyes narrowing, she looked him up and down. 'Trust me, fella, you couldn't afford it. And I'm fair certain you'd not know what to do with *that.*' She inclined her head to his crotch and smirked when his friends roared with laughter.

His face darkened. 'Trust *me*, whore, after I'd finished with you, you'd not be able to sit forra week. Come over here if you want proof; though you might find this here wall a bit rough on your face, for I could only stomach doing thee from behind.' His friends snorted and patted his back, and now he wore a smug expression. Yet it slipped from his face when she crossed the road.

Halting, her barely covered chest almost touching his, she gazed up from beneath her lashes. 'That right, lad? You saying I've gorra face like the back end of a horse?'

The group fell silent, mouths dropping open when she cocked an eyebrow at their friend then eased down the neck of her dress. Each emitted a whistle – including the man before her. She cupped his quickly swelling crotch, smiling inwardly when he groaned low in his throat.

'Still prefer doing me from behind, would you?' She drew his eager hands to her breasts. 'You'd not like to press your face into these, then, nay?'

Seemingly oblivious of his grinning friends, he squeezed and tweaked her nipples, his breathing heavy. 'Nay, lass, I didn't mean what I said. You're a fine figure of a woman. By God, you are that.'

She smiled in satisfaction at his simpering tone. Men were such fools. They didn't understand the power women had over them, didn't know when they were being played once their pricks took over. She rubbed his solid member, smile deepening at his gruff moan. Then in one sharp movement, she closed her hand and squeezed hard. The man yelped, eyes widening in pain and confusion.

'For your information, I'm norra streetwalker, you shovel of shit. Give me one good reason why I shouldn't rip this sorry excuse forra prick off.'

The stunned group loomed, faces twisting in anger, but when she tightened her grip and the man whimpered to them to back off, they stepped away.

'Now, then, lovey, what d'you say? One little word and tha might still be able to use it. Otherwise . . .' She squeezed again and grinned when he squealed.

'Sorry! I'm bleedin' sorry! Leave go!'

She released him and he fell to his knees. As his friends crowded around him, she readjusted her dress and walked away. Within seconds, she'd dissolved into the misty night. She smiled as the men's heavy footsteps, shouts and curses filled the air. The maze of dark alleys and passageways swallowed a body in the blink of an eye; they wouldn't get to exact revenge for their friend.

Her lip curled in distaste. No one disrespected her and got away with it. No one. That sorry excuse she'd left snivelling in the gutter, and many she'd encountered over the years, didn't have a clue. They didn't know how to treat a woman, nor satisfy one. Not like the man she was meeting. Now *he* knew how to show a lass a good time. Her skin tingled in anticipation. No man would ever match up to him.

Turning into Deansgate, she quickened her step. She patted the package beneath the folds of her skirts and smiled, knowing he'd be pleased. It was getting harder to sneak away the gifts but she'd continue to. Keeping her man happy was all that mattered. For him, she'd do anything.

Upon reaching the familiar meeting place, she smoothed her hair with shaking hands. Then, taking a deep breath, she slipped inside Nellie's inn.

Her gaze immediately went to the dim recess and at the sight of the slumped figure, her heart leapt. She sat on the hard bench with a giggle. 'By, I've missed thee summat rotten.'

Nursing a tankard, eyebrows knotted in a black frown, Joseph ignored the hand she tried to place in his and downed the rest of his ale. He slammed the tankard on to the plain-topped table and she jumped to her feet.

'I'll fetch you another.'

As she reached for the empty jar, he grabbed her wrist. 'Leave that and sit down.'

'But I want one meself. I'll not be—'

'I said leave the bugger!'

Flinching, she lowered herself beside him. 'What's wrong? Is it summat I've done? Did I keep thee waiting? Sorry if I did, lad. It were that daft daughter of my neighbour's again. Seven sharp, I told her to come round to keep an eye on t' children but she—'

'You don't half bore the liver out of me at times. No wonder that husband of yourn snuffed it years ago; you probably bored the bugger to death. Shut tha mouth for one minute and listen. There's summat I want you to do.'

Swallowing the pain his words brought, she produced the package, desperate to please him. 'I've fetched you this, love, and I paid your rent.' She placed the meat on the table then ran a hand up his chest. 'Now, what d'you want my help with? Just say the word, lad. I'll do owt you want, you know that.'

'Shift your hand, for Christ's sake. You're like a bitch on heat.'

The sharp slap brought tears to her eyes. She held up her hands. 'All right, I'm sorry.'

'Don't try me, girl, for I'm not in no mood for it. I've had a bellyful today. Just sit there and shut your trap.'

She lowered her eyes to the earth-packed floor.

'How long have we been meeting, now?'

His question surprised her. 'Three or four months, in't it, love? Aye, 'bout that, yeah.' She nodded slowly, as though contemplating her answer, but knew exactly how long, down to the day. Their meetings were precious. As far as she was concerned, life held little meaning before them.

She'd first caught his eye at Ma Thompson's when fetching a jug of ale for her father; she'd seen him once or twice in the row but they hadn't spoken until that night. He'd remarked on her hair's lovely colour and she'd blushed in delight, instantly drawn to the rugged miner.

Ten minutes later, she'd been on her hands and knees in a field with her skirts over her head. When Joseph, trousers around his ankles, collapsed across her back, she'd known he was the man for her. She'd never felt so wanted, fulfilled.

Their meetings continued at Nellie's following the trouble at Spring Row, but she didn't mind the tramp to Deansgate. She'd walk to earth's ends to be with him.

'Aye. Suppose it is a few months.' He shot her a sidelong glance. 'You said you'd do owt I wanted just now, didn't you?' At her eager nod, he added, 'I've had a right day of it. Our Alice's lass spotted Sally this morning in t' market.'

Her stomach lurched. She knew it! Ivy's face, earlier, had said it all; she *knew* she'd been right! She also knew, however, that Joseph couldn't know. If he discovered she'd suspected Sally of leaving hours ago and did nothing, he'd . . . Well, Lord knew. She wasn't taking any chances.

'That right, lad?'

'Well, the lass fair described her exactly but . . . Oh, I don't know.' His tankard rattled as he banged the tabletop. 'Either that gormless cow's mistaken or Sally's cleverer than I thought.'

'Why, were it not her, then?'

'I don't know, do I? That's what I'm trying to tell you,' he snapped. 'I pelted down to the train station and questioned the master, and he said he'd had a run-in with someone what sounded like her, but—'

'Station? I thought the young 'un saw her in t' market?' Her words melted when he turned slowly to face her. 'I'm sorry, I didn't mean to interrupt. Ignore me, love.'

Nostrils flared, he ground out, 'He said it sounded like her but that she'd had a ruddy great dog with her; attacked him, it did, by all accounts. We've never had no mutt.

'I were all for forgetting the whole thing till I spoke to Bailey, earlier. Said he'd seen her not long since with that owd bitch from next door to us, on her way to catch the carrier's cart. She told him some cock and bull tale of how she were going to our Alice's to beg my forgiveness.'

Nancy's excitement mounted but she kept her voice even. 'Did you ask him if it were right? George Turner, I mean.'

'Well, of course I did. The varmint looked me straight in t' eye and swore blind he'd not seen hide nor hair of her.' He rubbed his stubbled chin. 'I don't know what's afoot, if she's still at Spring Row or no, but believe me, I'll find out.'

When he lapsed into silence, she stared into the depths of the open fire beside them. If Sally *had* gone – *and pray God she has,* she inwardly pleaded – Joseph would be hers. She didn't know his wife but from what he'd said, she sounded like a right uppity little bitch. He clearly didn't care a fig for her – he'd proven that by asking Nancy back to his cottage on their first meeting, even though his wife was home, she recalled with amusement.

Though tempted, she'd suggested the nearest farmer's field. Her father's cottage had been too close for comfort. The old man might get on her nerves at times but when all was said and done, she loved the bugger and wouldn't do anything to bring shame upon him if she could help it.

Nancy picked her words carefully. 'Would it matter if she has scarpered, for you said yourself she means nowt to thee? Lord, the bitch had been thieving off you, hadn't she? Aye, from what you've told me, you're well shot of her.'

Why he'd even married the girl was a mystery. She'd questioned him months ago but he'd become angry and told her to keep her snout out.

It didn't matter, now, she thought happily. *With her out of the picture, he'll finally be mine for the taking.*

When he didn't respond, she ran tentative fingers along his strong jaw and down his neck. Emboldened when he didn't slap her away, she slipped her hand inside his shirt and stroked his thick chest hair.

'So long as you have me, you'll never need another woman,' she purred. She leaned in, pressed her breasts against him and circled his earlobe with her tongue. Her heart swelled when her skirts lifted. He squeezed the inside of her thigh and she moaned.

'I'll kill her when I get my hands on her. *They'll* get what's coming to them, an' all. Harbouring that whore's going to cost them,' he growled against her lips.

'Who, the Morgans?'

'Aye.' Wrenching down her dress, he buried his face in her breasts. He drew an erect nipple into his mouth then rolled and flicked his tongue over the glistening peak. When he raised his head, his next words were thick with menace: 'And you're going to help me.'

Chapter 10

IT WASN'T UNTIL the following Monday that Sally managed to get Grace to herself. She'd tried to find a moment to have a private word with her but there was never the right time. Due to inclement weather, Ed and Stan had hardly moved from home. When on occasion they did, Grace was either catching up on much-needed sleep or attending to Peggy.

The strained atmosphere between father and son hadn't intensified over the week but neither had it abated. There had been a particularly uncomfortable incident when, despite the temperature, only wind and rainfall accompanied it; Ed's prediction that it wouldn't snow proved correct.

He'd seemed to revel in mocking Stan, and she'd ached for her cousin as Ed's scathing remarks rang all morning. Stan's silence paid off; eventually, Ed had stopped, much to her relief. The misery in her cousin's eyes was painful to witness and she'd been on the brink of telling her uncle to leave him alone.

Throughout, Grace sighed several times but, to Sally's bewilderment, said nothing. When Ed left the room, the look Stan threw – first at the door then at his mother – scared her. It held what she could only describe as utter contempt.

Now, sitting with Grace at the table and Shield, as usual, sprawled by her feet, she knew this was her chance. The men had left for work and Peggy was sleeping. Monday was washday and Grace would soon be too busy; she'd asked if Sally would help with washing Peggy's sheets a moment ago.

Having just fed the baby, she rubbed his back and breathed deeply. She'd rehearsed what to ask yet now the time had come, didn't know where to begin. To her surprise, Grace did it for her.

'So, how you liking it back in Manchester, love?'

'It's still rather strange but I'm very happy. Since being a child, I always prayed I'd see you again one day.'

'Ah, lass.'

She smiled when Grace leaned across and patted her knee, then continued hesitantly, 'Aunt Grace, may I ask you something?'

Nodding, her aunt reached for the teapot. Refilling their cups, she glanced up. 'Go on, lass. What's on your mind?'

'I wondered whether, well, whether I'm in the way. I don't want you to feel you must have me here because I'm your niece.' When Grace made to protest, she added, 'Perhaps you all have enough worries without the burden of a runaway wife and newborn adding to them.'

'You've noticed, then?' She sighed when Sally lowered her gaze. 'Aye, course you have. You'd have to be blind not.'

'Aunt Grace, I—'

'Don't be embarrassed, lass, it's not your fault. Ed and Stan . . .' Raising dull eyes to the damp-patched ceiling, she shook her head. 'Eeh, where do I start?'

'What's wrong, Aunt Grace? Why are they so . . . cold towards one another?'

'Our Stan, poor lad. He don't bother no more, not like when he were younger, and who could blame him? All his life he's strived for Ed's love. I think he accepted . . . well, that it weren't to be. But it's not Ed's fault, it's not, lass. It's hard for him, an' all. He tried in t' beginning but . . .'

She fell silent and foreboding filled Sally. Something unpleasant was coming, she could feel it. Moments later, Grace proved her right.

'You see, I'm the cause, what I did . . . And Ed, he loved me so vowed to try and forget. Course, he couldn't. It were a constant reminder when I began to show.'

Sally reached for her hand. 'Are you saying Uncle Ed isn't Stan's father? Is that what you're trying to say?'

'I . . . I were expecting afore we married.' Her words were barely audible and Sally had to lean in. 'He's a good man, your uncle, a good man. I don't deserve him. My actions ruined him – ruined our marriage afore it began.

'You could've knocked me down with a feather last week when he invited me to join him in that pie supper. The way he spoke . . . it's the nicest I've heard forra long, long time. Whether it were because you were there, or because he felt sorry for me after hearing of Rose, I don't know. Either way, it were lovely.'

Sally laid the baby in the basket and knelt beside Grace. 'Oh, please don't cry.' As she wrapped her arms around her aunt, her mind spun.

Whatever she'd expected, this certainly wasn't it; although it made everything clear. What on earth she was to do, she didn't know. She'd sworn to herself that whatever the problem, she'd do her best to help. How in the world could she, with something as deeply rooted as this?

'I'm sorry, love, I shouldn't have told thee. What must you think of me?'

'Please, don't think that. You don't have to explain yourself to me. I'd never judge you, never. You're my aunt and I love you. I love all of you.'

'He don't know, lass. Our Stan don't know. He's asked me time and again why Ed's the way he is with him, but I can't tell him. He can't know the truth, he can't. Please, don't say owt to him. He'd hate me.'

'I'd never say anything if you didn't want me to. It's not my place.' She frowned as a thought occurred. 'Did this cause your rift with my mother? Was she . . . ashamed of you?'

Grace answered with a moan, and Sally sighed. She *knew* the cause must have been serious.

She'd longed to know the truth, yet now felt nothing but heavy sadness. All those wasted years! All she and her mother suffered in that awful place because of one woman's mistake and another's inability to forgive.

Her aunt, too, had suffered, that was clear. She also understood her uncle's pain. Then there was poor, sweet Stan. Through no fault of his, what had he gone through all his life? What an utter waste. It was all so sad.

'I'm sorry, for both you and my mother, that you were unable to be reconciled. She must have felt very strongly about your actions. However, I don't. Your past doesn't change my feelings for you. You're the nearest thing I have to a mother, now, and I promise, if there is anything I can do to help, I will.'

Grace's shoulders heaved with sobs. 'Oh, lass, you don't understand. What I did . . . It were wicked, *wicked*!'

'I do. I understand you made a mistake. No one is perfect; we all do things we later regret. Don't torture yourself any longer. It's the future that matters. I don't want to lose you a second time. We have the rest of our lives to get to know each other again, to be there for one another. Please, wipe your tears. I hate seeing you upset.'

For an age, Grace stared back through pain-filled eyes, then nodded. 'I don't deserve your kindness, nor deserve you for a niece. By, I don't that.' She caressed her cheek. 'Eeh, I do love you, lass.'

Sally kissed her brow. 'And I you. Now, let's have that tea.' After passing Grace her cup, she took a sip from her own. 'Aye, we'll have a sup then get on with that washing,' she informed her in perfect imitation of her strong Lancashire accent. 'Them sheets won't wash their rotten selfs.'

Her aunt spluttered on her tea, chuckling, and Sally smiled, relieved that the tension had passed. She'd do her best to help heal her lovely family. How, she had no idea, but she had plenty of time to try. She wasn't going anywhere. These were her only relations in the world. She wanted a different childhood for her son, filled with people who loved him. She'd sooner die than have him suffer a second of what she had as a child.

Her mother's smile swam across her mind. *Why, Mam?* she pondered. *Was it impossible to forgive the sister you adored one mistake? Was the shame of an illegitimate child really too much to bear?* She pushed the upsetting thoughts away. As she'd told Grace, there was no point dwelling on the past. The future mattered and she was determined to make it a happy one.

Peering at the band on her finger, she was thankful Ivy had persuaded her to keep it. The money from the eaves wouldn't last for ever. She'd given a fair chunk towards Shaun's carpentry and had enough to pay her keep for several weeks, but what then? She couldn't live here on charity; her family were barely scraping by as it was.

To remain and help them, as she desperately wanted, there was but one solution. She'd have to find employment.

Several hours later, the washing was billowing in the wind in the tiny backyard. Having brewed fresh tea, Grace placed a plate of bread on the table. A pot of jam, which Sally treated her to yesterday, stood alongside. Backs and arms aching, they sat gratefully.

'Aunt Grace, where could I secure a position? My money won't last for ever.'

Grace popped bread in her mouth and licked raspberry stickiness from her fingers. Since the revelation, her whole demeanour had changed. Her eyes were less haunted, face smoother, as though the worry lines had melted. It seemed the sheets were not all Sally had helped wash; she'd cleansed Grace's tortured mind of bad memories, too.

'Depends, lass. What were you thinking of?'

Sally thought for a moment. Along with the workhouse girls, she'd learned female duties such as sewing but not much else. She'd have to take whatever was available.

'I'll do anything, scrub floors if I must. I'm not proud.'

'I dare say you'll find summat if you're that willing. Course, there's the mills. I'll bet they're allus looking for spinners and such. Jonathan will be all right. I'll gladly watch him if you get taken on.' She smiled at him. 'He's good as gold and I'm in all day with our Peggy, anyroad.

All you'd need do is call in your dinner break and give him his feed.'

Sally brightened. 'Yes, that would work. Are you certain you wouldn't be taking too much on, what with caring for Peggy?'

'Nay, love, it'll give me summat to do. The lass sleeps a lot. I'm only rattling round fretting about her all day. The babby would take my mind off it.'

'Well, if you're sure, I'll look around. I must admit, I'm nervous. I've never had a job. What if I find I'm not good at anything?'

'What, a clever lass like thee? Whatever you find, you'll take to it like a fish to water. Now, finish your tea and go look. Flash one of them bonny smiles of yourn, be polite, and they'll snap you up. You'd best leave the dog here, mind. He might put folk off.'

Filled with hope at Grace's encouragement, she donned her shawl and set off.

The streets were quiet; those lucky to be in employment were toiling in the many factories. Mainly, she encountered beshawled housewives buying in the evening meal, and sullen-faced men on street corners, another morning's search for work having proved futile.

Other men squatted on pavements tossing coppers, their angry curses when their gambling didn't go in their favour ringing through the frosty November air. Occasionally, a policeman appeared up ahead and the groups would scoop coins into flat caps and quickly disperse, only to re-form in the next street.

Her small smile never wavered as she passed along. Since arriving, her fears had diminished considerably. No one knew of her whereabouts besides Ivy, and she knew hell would freeze before her friend revealed them. Feeling worry-free, sure that Joseph wouldn't suddenly appear as she'd often feared since escaping, was wonderful.

An enormous, seven-storey cotton mill came into view as she turned into Bradford Road. Glancing skyward at the columns of smoke streaming from its tall chimneys, she shuddered. Confinement within those sweltering death traps filled her with dread, but she needed money. Thousands upon thousands endured it to feed their families and keep a roof over their heads. She must try.

Approaching the gates, she read the sign and nodded determinedly. Brunswick Mill. With luck, she'd be an employee before the day was through.

'Get off me, you swine! Get *off* me!'

Sally heard the furious voice before seeing the speaker. Squinting towards the mill, she frowned when two figures emerged. One held the other by the scruff of the neck and as they drew nearer, she gasped to see that the shorter was a young woman. The man towering above dragged her, kicking and cursing, to the gates.

'You sod, yer! Make you feel big, does it, bullying lasses?'

His face twisted in a snarl and Sally stepped hastily aside when he hauled open the gates. With an almighty shove, he sent the woman flying into the gutter by Sally's feet and slammed the gates shut.

'Now bugger off, you idle bitch. There's wenches aplenty what will fill your place – hard-working wenches at that.'

The woman's eyes blazed. 'Idle? *Idle?* I'm one of the best spinners in that place and you know it. You've lied through your rotten teeth to get me out 'cause I told you where to go when you tried it on, you dirty swine, yer. Can't keep your filthy hands to yourself, can you?

Aye, well, you can shove your job where the sun don't reach! I'd sooner starve in t' gutter than you touch me.'

Sally, already horrified by the brutal treatment, could hold back no longer. She shook her head at the smirking man in disgust. 'Is this true? You've dismissed this woman for *that*?'

With a curl of his lip, he looked her up and down. 'And what the bugger's it to do with thee? Go on, clear off the pair of you, afore I fetch a constable.' He threw the last words over his shoulder and strode away.

She watched his retreating back in disbelief then turned to the woman, a pretty thing with dark hair and an elfin face, sitting on the flagstones. 'Disgraceful! He cannot get away with that, surely?'

Chuckling, she allowed Sally to assist her up. 'By gum, lass, you don't know the way of things reet well, d'you? Course he'll get a-bloody-way with it. Anyroad, I'm not mithered. I'm glad to be free of that place; least I'll not have that sod's roving hands to fight off any more.'

Sally helped her brush dirt from her skirt and shawl, thankful she'd witnessed the incident before enquiring for a position. She certainly didn't want to work in environments like that, with people like him.

'I came seeking employment. I'm glad I didn't get the chance, now. Are you all right?' she asked when the woman winced and rubbed the arm that had taken the brunt of the fall.

'Aye, tough as owd leather, me. Ta for speaking out for me. What's your name?'

'Sally Swann. You?'

The woman shook the proffered hand warmly. 'Maggie Benson. Nice to meet thee, lass.'

A sigh chased away Sally's smile. 'I don't know what I'm to do. I'd pinned my hopes on finding work there.'

She frowned, realising Maggie was now in the same position. 'What about you? Will you find alternative employment?'

Maggie bit her lip. 'I hope so. I'm a widow with two young 'uns to feed. Mam helps out but we'll not manage with no wage coming in.' She glanced up and down the street. 'I'd best get looking. Take care, Sally, and good luck to you, lass. I hope you find summat. 'Ere, if you're ever passing, I live at Davies Street, number thirty-two. You'd be welcome any time.'

'Thank you, Maggie, that's very kind. Good luck.'

She watched her hurry down the road and hoped fervently that Maggie would find something soon. She didn't deserve dismissal because that awful man couldn't keep his hands to himself. Life was so unfair.

She turned and retraced her steps. She'd walked no further than a hundred yards when snow began to fall. Her first thought was Stan. He'd been right, after all – albeit a few days out. Drawing her threadbare shawl over her head, Sally trudged on.

She glanced in every shop window for the small cards placed when staff were needed, but each proved empty. Halting at the end of the street, she shivered and peered about uncertainly. People rushed in all directions, heads lowered against the flakes spiralling from the yellow-tinged sky, footsteps muffled as flags and cobbles disappeared beneath a blanket of white.

Maybe she should call it a day, she thought reluctantly, heart heavy with disappointment. She couldn't stay out in this much longer. Her face was stinging, fingers and toes numb. She'd have to try tomorrow. And the day after, and the day after that if necessary. No matter what, she *would* find work.

The promise of hot tea and a hearty fire urging her, she turned for Grace's. As she crossed the road, a girl by a string of shops caught her eye. Drawing level, Sally watched curiously as she continued to peer through a pawnbroker's window. However, she wasn't admiring the array of goods on sale but staring at a white card.

Her stomach lurched. They must have a position, yet she'd spotted it too late. This girl, no older than fifteen, would surely leap at the chance of shop-work rather than a mill.

The girl squinted at the scrawled words a moment longer. Then to Sally's surprise, she snorted, muttered, 'Aye, not bloomin' likely!' and walked away.

Frowning, she hurried to the sign. Her workhouse education was limited, to say the least, but she could read a little. She traced a finger across the cold glass:

Seeking companion for elderly lady
Must have lots of patience
Apply within to Miss Sharp

Sally read it again. After the third attempt, she still hadn't deciphered what she must have 'lots of'. Dicksy had taught her many big words, whose spoken meaning she understood. Reading them was another matter.

She read the tricky word out loud, prodding each letter: 'P–a–t–i–e–n–c–e.' Still none the wiser, she shrugged, excitement stirring. Miss Sharp would surely tell her what she required.

She lifted her face to the snow-filled sky. 'Please, Lord, let me get this position,' she whispered. Pushing the girl's words from her mind, she turned the brass knob.

A bell tinkled as she entered and a willowy figure, mousy-brown hair bound in a neat bun, emerged through a door behind the counter. Her disarming smile immediately put Sally at ease. Lowering her damp shawl, she stepped forward.

'May I help you, dear?'

Sally fought the urge to raise an eyebrow. The articulate tone contrasted sharply with how the majority of Manchester's inhabitants spoke. 'Are you Miss Sharp?'

'I'm Pru Sharp, yes.'

'The card in the window said apply within. Is the position still vacant?'

Pru's eyes widened. 'Indeed. Do you wish to apply?'

What was it Aunt Grace said? she thought quickly. *Flash a smile and be polite, that was it.*

'I'd be most grateful to be considered for the position, Miss Sharp, and believe that, given the opportunity, I would be a worthy employee. I would not cut corners or shirk my responsibilities. My full attention would be on the job in hand at all times. You'd receive complete dedication from me, I assure you. You have my word and my honour.'

Pru's lips twitched. 'Well. That was a mighty fine speech, Mrs . . . ?'

Sally flushed. Had she ruined her chances? Her tongue had run away with itself in her desperation to make a good impression. 'Swann. Sally Swann.'

'Well, Sally, you certainly have a way with words. You're not from around here, I presume?'

'I was born here. I have recently returned and am residing with my aunt—'

'And in order to pay your way, you're seeking employment?'

'Yes.'

'Agnes, my mother, requires constant care. However, the shop needs running and I cannot be in two places at once. She is bed-bound and hasn't left her room in many years.' Brow furrowing, Pru looked Sally up and down. 'The position would require lifting, to bathe and dress her and suchlike. Do you believe you are up to it? She's small but can be somewhat difficult when she chooses. You would need a lot of patience.'

Patience! *That* was what she'd need lots of. Her shoulders relaxed. Putting up with Joseph all those years was proof she had the patience of a saint. 'I'm very patient, Miss Sharp, and stronger than I look.'

'The position has been open for some time. That was how I knew you were not from these parts. You would not have enquired if you were.'

The girl in the street's scathing comment came back to Sally. She frowned curiously. 'I don't understand.'

Pru glanced to the ceiling. 'I'll be honest with you, Sally. My mother can be rather . . . fractious. Another young woman used to care for her. There was . . . an incident, shall we say, and afterwards . . . Well, I can see why people are reluctant to take the position.'

'Incident? What kind of incident?'

Dull banging sounded. They looked up in unison.

'What incident, Miss Sharp?' she repeated.

'Prudence? Prudence!'

At the gravelly voice from above, desperation flickered in Pru's eyes. 'I must see what she wants. So, dear? Are you up for the job?'

After a brief hesitation, Sally nodded. What choice had she? She needed the money. Besides, how bad could the old woman be?

'Good! That is good! I will see you tomorrow morning, nine o'clock sharp.' Hurrying out from behind the counter, Pru ushered her to the door. 'Goodbye, dear.'

'Wait, what about payment? What of my hours?'

'Prudence Sharp! Do you hear me?'

Her smile slipping as she glanced to the ceiling, Pru flapped a hand. 'Oh, we shall discuss the necessary details tomorrow. Now, I really must go.' She turned on her heel and disappeared inside the shop.

Sally stared in bewilderment at the closed door then turned for home. Her emotions were conflicting. On the one hand, she was elated to find work so quickly, yet a worm of doubt was growing. What had occurred between the elderly lady and her previous employee? She'd ask Grace. Miss Sharp said most knew of the 'incident'; surely her aunt had heard?

By the time she reached the entry, she'd all but dismissed her misgivings. Whatever had happened, she wouldn't let it put her off. She was just thankful she'd soon be bringing in a wage. Besides, at least she wouldn't be working in the factories, fighting off the advances of men like him at Brunswick Mill.

She said a private prayer that Maggie Benson would manage to find another position. She'd ask Grace for directions to Davies Street and visit her on her first day off. Perhaps they could become friends.

Feeling brighter about the future than she had in a long time, Sally hurried across the snow-covered cobbles with a happy sigh.

She couldn't wait to tell her aunt the good news.

Ivy Morgan flopped into a chair and wiped her brow with the back of her hand. Peering at the wooden rack above the fire festooned with sheets and clothes, she pulled a face and reached for the teapot. She hated

Mondays with a passion. The scrubbing, wringing and heavy lifting played havoc with her ageing bones.

She glanced at the clock, swore under her breath and gulped down her tea. The men would be home shortly and here she was sitting on her backside, with the tin bath to fill and evening meal to prepare.

After filling at the well and boiling on the fire pan after pan of water for the bath, she dragged herself to a cupboard, selected vegetables and returned to the table, collecting a knife on the way. Deft hands peeled and chopped and in no time the veg was bubbling away, adding to the steam from the drying clothes and bath.

The stuffy room became too much. She refilled her cup, opened the cottage door and, leaning against the frame, let the breeze soothe her flushed cheeks.

Snow had at last ceased and the pure white landscape was breathtaking. Bright domes of hills looked magical, like summer clouds that had fallen from the sky. It had even transformed the row from grubby to beautiful.

'Bugger it! God-awful snow.'

Ivy glanced to her left and watched Martha Smith, slipping and sliding, in amusement. ''Ere, Martha. Watch your bleedin' step, wench. Don't you go falling and showing the row your dimples.'

Martha's head shot up, making her wobble dangerously. Round face beetroot-red, she stretched out her arms to steady herself then shook a beefy fist. 'You swine, yer! Nearly went arse over elbow, then.'

Ivy burst out laughing and Martha, grinning, shuffled on her way.

Ivy had been dreading seeing her but Martha had been surprisingly understanding yesterday. She'd tried making eye contact several times at chapel but Ivy had looked away. When service was over, she'd made a beeline for her outside but Ivy quickly struck up conversation with another neighbour, and Martha hadn't approached. However, Ivy had arrived home to find her waiting at the gate.

Martha's expression, soft with friendliness, had thrown her, and when she invited Ivy to her cottage for a sup of tea, she had been unable to refuse.

She was glad she hadn't. The hour spent in Martha's spotless kitchen was pleasant. Over tea, they had a good natter. Conversation had eventually swung to the Godens and though Ivy didn't disclose anything Sally told her in confidence, she did admit guilt at not noticing what was going on – even after Martha voiced her concerns.

Martha had told her not to be daft. 'You don't expect it on your own doorstep, wench. Least she's out of it, now, thanks to thee. You gave her the means and strength to leave the divil.'

Curious, Ivy had asked how she'd guessed the poor woman's plight when she herself had had no idea. Martha confided that she had suffered like Sally during her first marriage.

'My Reg's my second husband,' she'd revealed of the local mole catcher. 'Wed thirty-odd year we've been and I couldn't be happier, but me first 'un . . . He were an evil blighter like yon Joseph,' she'd murmured. 'I noticed the signs, for I'd been in t' same boat meself.'

It's queer how folk look in a different light, Ivy mused now, returning to the kitchen. Since their chat, they were like old friends.

The door opening pulled her from her thoughts and she smiled at Arthur, Tommy and Shaun. Weary faces smiled back, coal-blackened skin glistening in the firelight.

'Get washed while I see to the grub,' she instructed.

Behind a length of curtain, the bath stood waiting. Arthur trooped off first to scrub his tired body and she dished out the meal. Her hand stilled, however, when she glimpsed Tommy's drawn face as he headed for the stairs.

Her son wasn't himself. Usually he lit up a room. Even after a full shift he'd return with a cheery smile, would chase her around the kitchen for a kiss while she shouted at him to 'Bugger off covered in that muck!' But for days he'd been subdued, as though the worries of the world were on his mind.

Midway through the meal, she tackled him. 'You all right, Tommy lad?'

'Aye, Mam.'

'You've been morose these past days. You crossed swords with Dolly, or summat?'

Frowning, he lowered his gaze. 'Nay, why?'

'Well, when you meet her of a Sunday, you're usually out all day but you were gone no more than an hour yesterday. Frightened the bloody life from me, tha did, when I returned from Martha's and found you sat here.'

'Dolly were snuffly. We cut our walk short so her cowd didn't worsen.'

He speared a potato with his fork and resumed his meal and she let the matter drop. Maybe she was reading into things that were not there. She'd had a niggling suspicion what – or more to the point, who – had caused this sudden change in him and had tried dismissing it, hoping to God she was wrong.

Her mind drifted to the morning Sally left. After waking, she'd headed for the kitchen but halfway down the stairs was taken aback to see Sally and Tommy at the table.

He'd smiled like he did as a child when caught doing something he shouldn't. Ivy asked why he was up so early and he'd said he couldn't sleep. Sally explained she'd wanted to repay Ivy's kindness, had motioned to the pan of porridge, and their explanations placated her. However, her unease returned when she'd mentioned Sally's upcoming departure.

Tommy's head had shot up. 'You're leaving today?' At Sally's nod, his smile quickly returned.

Ivy had watched the exchange through narrowed eyes. She knew her son too well, especially when he smiled like that. Forced. *What went on before I wakened?* she'd wondered. She'd sensed something between them, some . . . spark. And if she was honest, she didn't like it.

She did feel a lot for Sally, and the cottage seemed empty without her and the child. Nevertheless, Sally was a married woman. She didn't want her Tommy mixed up in something like that; particularly when the other man was as unstable as Joseph Goden.

Absently pushing food around her plate, she felt, for the first time, relief that Sally had left. But it was tinged with guilt and she offered up yet another silent prayer that she was safe and well. The lass deserved happiness, by God she did. She just hoped that aunt of hers was looking after them.

Sighing, Ivy pushed the youngsters from her mind. Sally was gone. It was pointless fretting over what might be her imagination.

After mopping up gravy with a hunk of crust then popping it into his mouth, Arthur pushed away his plate and burped appreciatively. 'Eeh. Lovely, that were.'

She reached for the teapot. 'Bugger these pots, I'll wash them later. You want another sup?'

'Aye.' He moved to his fireside chair and reached for his clay pipe on the mantel. After pressing paper-thin slices from a stick of tobacco into the bowl, he held the slender stem between his lips, took a spill from a pot by the hearth and lit it. As he puffed, he glanced at her. Despite her smile, his brow furrowed. 'You still fretting over that lass?'

She passed him his cup. 'Aye, summat like that.'

'Wench, she's shot of Goden. He's never showed his face again at Spring Row and you said yourself, he don't know she even has an aunt, so she's no worries there. And she promised to return if she had no joy in Ancoats, didn't she, so stop fretting.

'Anyroad, anyone what can stand up to the preacher as you said she did can more than take care of theirself! I bet the owd swine got the shock of his life.'

Shaun joined in his laughter. 'Aye, good on her! I dread crossing his path. He's allus saying I'm destined for hell for not attending chapel.'

Ivy flashed him a crooked smile then glanced at Tommy. He looked away, and unease gnawed again. Whenever anyone mentioned Sally, he reacted the same way. She *knew* she'd been right; it was written all over his face. Well, this needed nipping in the bud. 'Tommy, why don't you call on Dolly the morrow after work, ask her to come for her dinner on Saturday?'

Every face showed surprise. All knew she wasn't keen when Tommy began walking out with the dairymaid last year. She'd voiced often that the lass was too flighty for her liking; she smiled too much; her laugh set Ivy's teeth on edge . . .

Ivy and her son stared at each other. After a long moment, he nodded. Then he rose and left the room.

Tommy threw himself on to his bed. His father's bemused voice, asking Ivy what was wrong with their son, drifted up and when she answered that he was probably just tired, heat crept over Tommy's face.

She knew exactly what ailed him. He'd seen it in her eyes – that same knowing look when she found him and Sally alone. Any grain of hope she *didn't* suspect, she'd shattered when suggesting he ask Dolly to dinner. She'd never encouraged their courtship, had certainly not invited her round before.

He squeezed his eyes shut. His father's question was a good one – what *was* wrong with him? He didn't know himself. It was like a ten-ton weight bearing down on his chest, the ache inside like an itch he couldn't scratch. A yearning for . . . something . . . wouldn't leave him but he couldn't grasp what it was or how to make it better or go away.

He peered at his calloused palms and, as he'd done a hundred times, thought back to when they held Sally. The ache intensified; he could almost feel her softness. He scrambled from the bed. He needed to get out of this stifling cottage before he went raving mad.

When he bounded downstairs, everyone looked up in surprise. Averting his eyes, he snatched up his jacket and threw it on.

'Where's tha going at this time, and in this weather? It's bleedin' perishing out there.'

'Out. I need some air.' Before his mother could question him further, he swung the door shut behind him.

Stars peppered the blue-black sky and the row held a stillness that soothed his jumbled mind. Golden fire and candlelight from cottage windows slowly faded as he walked on through the deserted night.

A low stone wall stood out against the darkness. He brushed off snow with his sleeve and sat down. Silence enveloped him and digging his hands into his trouser pockets, he closed his eyes. Sharp air burned with each breath but he relished it; it was a welcome relief to the pain in his heart.

What had come over him? What switch had been triggered in his brain to turn him from the happy-go-lucky chap into this snappy, distracted one who could think of nothing but the married woman no longer here? At the thought of her, his stomach bounced and he sighed in frustration. This wasn't like him. No woman had ever had this effect upon him – not even Dolly, he admitted.

An open face framed by corn-coloured hair floated across his mind. He smiled sadly. A fine-looking, lovable woman, was his Dolly. Creamy skin with its dusting of freckles lent her an almost childlike appearance. But her plump body, from what he'd felt, was definitely that of a woman.

He allowed his thoughts to wander. Her soft buttocks, which she sometimes let him squeeze when they were alone by the river, and her hips, which swayed when she walked, made his hands itch for her. Then there was her generous bust, like overripe melons awaiting discovery, which pressed against him when they kissed. And yet . . .

He heaved a sigh. Despite his carnal desire, despite her cheery disposition and saucy laughter, he'd never felt that . . . *something*, that special spark. The spark that hit him like a thunderbolt the other night when gazing upon Sally in the moonlight.

He hadn't realised something was missing until he felt it with Sally. Never had his heart jolted so violently. Never had his loins burned with a desire that engulfed him. Never had anyone so completely, hopelessly, consumed him.

He wasn't a vain man but was aware what impact he had on the opposite sex. He'd had his pick of

Breightmet's lasses but Dolly's sunny personality and cheeky ways hooked him. She was full of life, a breath of fresh air to be around after being holed in the ground's inky confines with sweaty men all week.

His mind drifted to the day before and their usual weekly stroll by the river. *The first afternoon with her he'd had to drag himself to.* He hadn't lied to his mother; Dolly *had* been snuffly. But she'd insisted she was fine, that nothing would keep her from seeing him. He'd used her slight cold, however, as a means of cutting the meeting short.

Picturing her blue eyes deep with hurt at his words, he cringed. Hardly able to keep the edge from his voice, he'd told her she'd be better off going home, had almost sighed in relief when she eventually agreed. Conversation was stilted on the walk back, and when they reached her door his lips barely touched her cheek before he strode away.

Shaking his head to dispel the guilty thoughts, he rose and paced up and down, unseeing. He was a simple fellow, always had been. As long as he had a meal in his belly and clothes on his back, he was happy. All he wanted in life was for he and his loved ones to be content and one day to raise a healthy family of his own. He'd had his future mapped out but now, his whole world had turned on its head.

What was he to do? How could he visit Dolly tomorrow, sit with her at dinner on Saturday, make small talk, act like all was well? How could he pretend nothing had changed, that one day, as they both thought inevitable, they would wed? How could he sign away his life to someone who stood beside him in the flesh yet came second to the one in his heart?

He couldn't do it. Marriage was for ever and he wouldn't live a lie. He didn't deserve to spend the rest of his days unhappy and, more importantly, neither did Dolly.

That he was considering this! Dolly, his Dolly . . . He'd never imagined his feelings could so rapidly change because of another woman – one he'd spent just a few hours alone with, at that. And what of Sally? She was miles away, bound for life to a husband a few cows short of a herd. And for all he knew, she might have already forgotten him.

Chest constricting at the possibility, he slapped the wall. She'd shown no indication she felt anything for him, except for pressing against him when she fainted. She'd clung to him, reached out when he laid her in the chair. But that was the workings of her fuddled mind, he realised with a jolt.

Say he did call it off with Dolly; what then? Track Sally down and declare his love? She'd either laugh in his face or ask when he was due back at the asylum.

He sat down and covered his face with his hands. How in God's name could he imagine she might feel the same?

Tightness in his chest returned at the prospect of never seeing her again, but with great effort he ignored it. For days, he'd pined for someone he could never have. He'd been so damn *foolish.* Relentless thoughts of her were even affecting work; he'd been yelled at down the pit today for not paying attention. He knew hardly anything about her, yet couldn't rid his mind of her.

She was like no one he'd ever met. He was constantly going over every word she'd uttered in that well-spoken voice, every little smile, how she'd looked up at him from beneath her lashes . . .

He rose and turned for home. This had to stop. He was acting like a lunatic. She'd flitted in and out of his life without knowing the impact she'd left on him and she never would. He *must* forget her.

Nearing Spring Row, his thoughts switched to the money beneath his mattress. He'd been flattered when she asked his help, had hidden it before the house stirred. It had felt like their little secret, something they shared that was just theirs, and he hadn't wanted anyone taking that away. Well, this fantasy ended now. Tomorrow, he'd inform his family of the generous gift.

Despite his inner turmoil, his mouth curved, picturing Shaun's face when he discovered he could finally shake off the pit's shackles. The lad had been born with a talent few people were lucky to have. He had no doubts he'd make a fine carpenter.

His heart swelled with brotherly pride. He might jest with Shaun but, deep down, loved him dearly. Recalling teasing him over taking a fancy to Sally, he smiled ruefully. He'd known the lad hadn't, was simply of an age where the mere mention of a lass had him blushing to the roots of his hair. The irony was almost laughable.

'Tommy Morgan? That you, lad?'

Peering through the darkness, he saw Ma Thompson at her cottage door. 'Aye, it's me. Everything all right?'

'Eeh, lad, am I glad to see thee. I thought I'd be stuck with him the night. Will you lend a favour to an owd woman and help him home? He come forra jug of ale, supped it in one then fell asleep and for the life of me, I can't waken the swine!'

'Who is it?'

'George Turner, lad. It's not the first time he's done this, nay it's not, but I were worried sending him on his way in this snow. With the state he's in, he'll finish up breaking his skull. He were fair skenning when he arrived. I'm buggered if I know how he managed to get here at all.'

In the kitchen, the inebriated customer sat sprawled across the tabletop, snoring loudly.

'George Turner, wake up, you bugger,' she called in his ear.

The carter moved not a muscle and Tommy smiled when the old woman turned red and shook the shoulder harder.

'I know tha hears me. Come on, gerrup. I want my bed.' She jumped when, suddenly, George sat bolt upright.

'Eeh, wench, that's the best offer I've had all year,' he slurred, snaking an arm around her waist.

Tommy burst out laughing and George grinned across at him.

'Get out of it, you bleeder, yer!' she shouted, swatting his hand. 'You might be sloshed but I'm not. Come on, out!'

'Come on, Mr Turner, I'll see you home.'

Chuckling, George lumbered to his feet and blew Ma Thompson a kiss. 'Goodnight, God bless, my lovely.'

'Oh, go on with you.' Clicking her tongue, she shooed him from the cottage. 'You will see him right inside, won't you, lad?' she asked Tommy as he took the carter's elbow and led him down the path.

'Aye. Goodnight.'

With a grateful smile, she bade him goodnight, rolled her eyes at George and closed the door.

Tommy steered him into the row. 'You had a lucky escape, there, Mr Turner. I thought she'd go at thee with the poker.'

'She's a feisty one. Just my kind of wench, lad, just my kind of wench. D'you know, I'd marry her the morrow if she'd let me. She'd make a fine wife.'

Tommy hid a smile, suspecting her greatest asset to the carter was her ale-brewing abilities.

After zigzagging to George's home, he helped him inside and lowered him into his fireside chair. 'Will you be all right, now, Mr Turner?'

'Aye, lad, aye. Eeh, you're a good 'un, Tommy.'

'It were no bother. Goodnight.'

'Goodnight, God bless. 'Ere, give a message to your mam, tell her I got the young Goden lass to Bolton in one piece, will you?' He peered up through one eye. 'Said she'd have my guts for garters if I didn't look after her. By, she's a fine woman, your mam, she is that.'

At the mention of Sally, Tommy swallowed hard. 'I'll tell her.'

'Aye, the lass will be all right with that big bugger she's took on. No one will try owt with him by her side.'

Halfway over the threshold, he turned. 'What's that?'

'Ruddy great mutt followed us on t' cart; took a shine to her, it had. She took it with her for protection, like.'

'Big black 'un?'

'Aye.'

He smiled. 'I don't believe it. Well, I'm glad to hear that. It did seem fond of her.'

'Aye, lad. And I hope that if it ever gets a grip of that divil, Goden, it rips his rotten throat out. Gorra grip of *me* Monday night last, he did, snarling like a rabid dog, wanting to know if I'd given the lass a lift. Aye, well, he went off with a flea in his ear, for I told him I'd not seen hide nor hair of her. Bloody fuming, he were. But he got nowt from me, he didn't that.'

As the grinning carter closed his eye, Tommy gripped the door frame. 'Joseph? He's been back to Spring Row?'

'I were on my way home from the Old Hare and Hounds – been forra jar to warm my bones – and he cornered me in t' lane.'

'But he can't . . . How did he find out so soon?' Without waiting for a reply, he mumbled goodbye and left the cottage.

Sprinting through the snow towards home, his mind raced. How in hell had that madman found out so quickly? What if he discovered where she'd gone? It didn't bear thinking about. Was Sally aware he was on the prowl? Tommy very much doubted it; she probably felt safe, now. But if what George Turner said was right, she was anything but. She needed warning.

He couldn't just forget her. He couldn't switch off his feelings, had been foolish to think it. She'd possessed his very soul. He'd do anything to protect her.

No one would harm her again. Not if he could prevent it.

Chapter 11

PEERING THROUGH A speckled sliver of mirror propped on the mantel, Sally smoothed her hands over her hair. Deep-blue eyes stared back, her apprehension visible.

Soon, she would meet the old woman she was to care for. The old woman whose company she'd be in for most of each day. *The old woman who had struck her previous employee around the head with the poker, sending her hurtling into the open fire . . .*

She squared her shoulders. She wouldn't allow anyone to bully her, not again. Whatever the old woman tried, she'd put her in her place right away. No one would treat her as muck beneath their boot, man or woman. Those days were over.

'Eeh, I don't know whether you're brave or barmy. You'd not get me within ten feet of that vicious owd swine. You should take the dog; he could savage the blighter if she tried owt.'

Sally looked to Shield, stretched beside Peggy's bed. As though sensing it, he lifted his head and peered at her with one eye, and she smiled. 'He's taken a shine to Peggy, hasn't he?'

'Aye. He did nowt but whine when you went searching for work yesterday; nowt I said would shut him up. But our Peggy began coughing and no word of a lie, he stopped like that,' Grace marvelled, clicking her fingers. 'He lay by her bed and went to sleep. I couldn't believe it.'

'He's a good dog. I'm so glad I brought him along.'

Grace's smile mirrored hers, but it soon vanished. 'Are you sure you'll be all right, lass?'

'I'll be fine. I'll not deny that what you told me hasn't shocked me, and I can understand why no one applied for the position, but I need this job, Aunt Grace. Miss Sharp seemed amiable; she'll be there should I require assistance. I simply cannot believe a lady of that age could be so . . . well, so—'

'Ruddy wicked? Well do. That owd 'un might be knocking ninety but she ain't nobody's fool. Her legs are useless but her mind's as sharp as her tongue from what I've heard. And that's nowt on t' slaps she's not shy of dishing out. Aye, her legs are neither use nor ornament but there's nowt wrong with her arms. The lass what worked there last would vouch for that, I'm sure.'

'What do you think became of her?'

'Lord alone knows. As I said last night, after what that nasty swine did that day, the lass apparently flew from that shop like hell's hounds were at her heels. If you are sure about this, you be careful. Keep your eyes on her. If she does try owt, you get out of there, and fast.'

Sally heaved a sigh. She'd been so pleased to find work but upon relaying the news to Grace, her happiness had rapidly diminished. All evening, Grace had tried talking her out of it. Even Ed and Stan, when informed, frowned disapprovingly. But she was determined and told them so. Whatever this job entailed, she'd stick at it. If she could endure what she had at Joseph's hands, she could cope with anything.

At the thought of her uncle and Stan, hope stirred. Ed had rushed in from work the previous evening yelling, 'Rotten snow, I'm frozzen!' A smile touched Stan's lips and, catching his eye, Ed had looked away. Yet as he hurried to the fire, she'd spotted, much to her delight, the hint of a wry smile as he glanced once more at Stan.

It was a good sign, surely? she mused again. He hadn't conceded but neither did he berate the lad about his 'I told you so' smile.

'Now, you sure you're sure about this?'

She couldn't help chuckling. 'Yes, Aunt Grace, I'm sure.' She looked from the baby to the deathly pale girl in the bed. 'Are you sure *you'll* be all right managing with Peggy *and* Jonathan?'

'Course, lass. And this little lad will be sound; the feed he's just had will see him through to dinnertime. Anyroad, never mind fretting over us. Just you look after yourself today.'

It was lovely knowing people held concern for her welfare. She'd worried that her aunt's confession might cause awkwardness, but instead it had strengthened their bond. A woman's love and guidance were what she'd missed and she was so thankful to have found it in not only Ivy, but her aunt.

Grace and Ivy were much alike. They shared those motherly qualities; one felt cosseted by them. In other ways, they were oceans apart. Her aunt was soft, mild-mannered – the opposite of direct and self-assured Ivy. Yet Sally loved both wholeheartedly, knowing that she couldn't have chosen two kinder women to look to.

Her mother's and now Ivy's absence was gut-wrenching, but bearable thanks to Grace. On impulse, she kissed her cheek.

'Ay, lass, what were that in aid of?'

'For being you. I miss my mother and Mrs Morgan terribly but having you makes up for it. Thank you.'

'Our Rosie . . .' Grace had shed enough tears over the weekend to fill the River Irwell. Still, her bottom lip trembled. 'Eeh, you'll have me blubbing like a babby in a minute. Now go on, you'd best get going. See you at dinner, lass.'

Sally kissed her fingertips and brushed them down Jonathan's cheek. Eyes the exact colour as hers stared back from the haven of Grace's arms and she felt a pang at leaving him. Her touch lingered, then, bidding her aunt goodbye, she set off.

Pru's welcoming smile was a mixture of astonishment and relief.

'Sally, how lovely to see you! Come, sit down, dear. Would you like a cup of tea?'

'Good morning, Miss Sharp. Yes, thank you.' She removed her shawl and when Pru patted the stool beside hers, joined her behind the counter. 'How is your mother today?'

'Fine, dear, fine. I must admit, I didn't think I would see you today. You have surely heard by now . . . ?' Pru raised her eyes to the ceiling.

'Yes, but I need the money,' she answered honestly. 'I do so want to get along with your mother. I hope we can become friends.'

'I feel wretched for her previous employee. And despite what people believe, so does my mother. You are probably wondering what happened. The truth is, I really don't know. My mother said she suspected the woman of stealing, admitted lashing out but insisted the fall was not caused by her hand, that the poor woman tripped on the rug by the fire. I had no chance to ask or even help; she left in such a hurry and I have neither seen nor heard from her since.

'My mother gets angry, you see, stuck in her room day and night. She . . . loses her temper sometimes. However, I'm not defending her actions. No, no, I'm not. What happened was terrible, simply terrible.' Pru massaged her temples with her fingertips. 'You may have wondered why the position advertised was not for assistance in the shop; after all, why should one residing with their daughter require a companion?

'The truth is . . . It's difficult, Sally. I'm the only soul she has in the world. She's my mother and I love her, yet sometimes . . . sometimes, I cannot stand the sight of her.' Her eyes widened with guilt. 'Does that make me wicked?'

'No, no.'

'Thank you, truly. It is nice having someone to talk to. I get so very lonely at times. Look, after what you have heard . . . if you've changed your mind, I will understand and—' A thud from above cut short her speech.

Sally placed her cup on the counter. 'May I meet her now, Miss Sharp?'

'Yes, yes, of course. Thank you. You have no idea how grateful I am, dear.'

She followed Pru up the narrow stairs, heart thumping. Should she have bolted when she had the chance? What on earth was she walking into?

Pru paused at a closed door, whispering, 'You'll be fine.'

Following, Sally entered the musty-smelling room. Dust motes swirled in splinters of sunlight filtering through partially closed curtains. She glanced through the gloom to the unlit fire then looked away quickly. Yet at the sight of the poker propped by the bedside, her stomach turned. Mrs Sharp must use that to summon her daughter. *And as a handy weapon when the mood takes her . . .*

'Well, well, well. What have we here, Prudence?'

Sally froze, and saw Pru's back stiffen.

'Mother, this is Sally. She is here to—'

'I know why she is here. Oh, yes. I know why she is here, all right.'

'Mother, Sally is extremely nice. I'm sure once you get to know her—'

'I will be the judge of that. Go, get downstairs,' ordered the old woman with a jerk of her head. 'The shop will not run itself.'

Pru lowered her gaze. 'I shall leave you to it, Sally. Bang on the floor if you require anything.'

Sally had to fight the urge to grab her arm, beg her not to leave her with this acid-tongued woman. When the door clicked shut and Pru's footsteps faded, she raised her head.

Swamped in a tawny-coloured nightgown buttoned to the throat, Agnes Sharp sat propped against a mound of pillows. Despite the half-dozen thick blankets, Sally could see she was painfully thin; her small frame barely made an impression beneath. Tufts of snowy hair sprang in all directions and a crimson birthmark stained one side of her forehead, finishing below her temple.

Yet it was the piercing, almond-shaped eyes she couldn't tear her gaze from. They were the deepest, most vibrant green; so out of place in her face. Her sunken mouth, long thin nose and withered skin seemed to have dried up and died years ago, but those eyes . . . They burned with vitality.

'Are you a mute, girl?'

The question threw her. 'Am I . . . ? No, Mrs Sharp.'

'Are you dim-witted? A touch simple-minded?'

'I am not,' she answered indignantly. 'Are you?' The last words were out before she could stop them. 'Oh! I'm sorry, Mrs Sharp, I don't know why I said that!'

Agnes's mouth curled at the corners. 'Witty, very witty. Tell me, do you make a habit of being an insolent little bitch?'

Her mouth dropped open, anger flooding through her. She'd suffered enough intimidation in the past. She wouldn't stand for it again. Lifting her chin, she looked the old woman in the eye. 'No, Mrs Sharp, not always. Only when spoken to the same way, by people who ought to have been around long enough to have learned some manners.'

Agnes arched an eyebrow, mouth curving once more.

After a full minute of silence, Sally's fight drained away. Grace, and even Pru, had warned her; they'd told her what this horrible woman was like, yet she'd ruined everything by stooping to her level. She'd have to try the mills. She'd learned her lesson today, would keep her mouth closed if fortunate enough to find another position.

Meeting Agnes's cold stare, she asked flatly, 'Shall I just go?'

'Yes, yes, I think you *should* just go.'

She inclined her head and walked away. At the door, Agnes's voice stopped her.

'Go and make me a cup of tea, that is. Make haste, girl. No dawdling.'

Turning in surprise, she swallowed a sigh of relief. 'Yes, Mrs Sharp.'

Pru appeared before she was halfway downstairs. 'You're not leaving already? What has she said? What did she—'

'Miss Sharp, I'm not leaving. Your mother wants tea.'

'Oh, thank goodness. Come through, dear.'

'I'd better hurry. She said no dawdling and I don't want to annoy her further. We've had . . . words already.'

Pru spun around, teapot in hand. 'So soon? What has she said?'

'To be perfectly honest, it's more what I said. I'm afraid I lost my temper and . . . said some things I shouldn't have. I'm sorry, Miss Sharp. It won't happen again.'

'I don't believe . . . What did you say?' Pru breathed, hand fluttering to her throat.

'Well, first I implied she was dim-witted then I accused her of lacking manners.'

'Good Lord. And she still wants you here? I really don't . . . What happened?'

Sally glanced towards the stairs. 'Could we talk later, Miss Sharp? I'm hanging on by the skin of my teeth. I must get back.'

'Yes, yes, you're right. Here's the tea, you run along. We will have a cup later and you can tell me all about it.' Her eyes shone with admiration. 'I'm glad you're here, Sally. I have a feeling you are going to cope just fine.'

After flashing Pru a less-than-confident smile, she mounted the stairs. Pausing at the old woman's door, she resolved to treat this entrance as a fresh start. She'd be polite, wouldn't under any circumstances rise to the bait. She nodded determinedly and entered.

'You took your time.'

Lowering her gaze, she placed the tea on the bedside table. 'Do you require anything else, Mrs Sharp?'

'Yes.'

She waited but when Agnes remained silent, glanced up. She was staring at her intently and Sally had to fight the urge to look away. Those eyes . . . It was as though they were looking into her soul, as though they could see exactly what she was thinking, feeling.

'Can you read, girl?'

Heat crept over her face when Agnes fumbled beneath her pillows and produced a small black book. 'Not very well,' she admitted. 'Did you want me to read to you? I'll try but as I said—'

'No matter, you'll learn.'

Sally took the book and crossed to a chair by the window. The weak sun peeping through the thick curtains offered little light. She squinted at the title. 'May I open the curtains, Mrs Sharp? I cannot see the words properly.'

'No. Sunlight annoys me. Light the candle if you must.'

For over an hour, she stumbled and stuttered over the hardly visible, strange new words. She was on the brink of screaming in frustration and hurling the book through the window when Agnes held up a hand.

'That will do. Extinguish that flame, it is giving me a headache.'

She closed the book and blew out the candle. 'Do you require anything else? Another cup of tea?'

Agnes shifted beneath the mountain of covers. 'You can bathe me, now. I'm sticky and this nightgown is starting to smell.'

The rest of the morning passed in a blur, with Sally performing her duties in silence. As she'd resolved, she'd kept her head down and only opened her mouth when spoken to. And with a tangible air of irritation, Agnes was tolerating her presence.

She'd bathed and clothed her employer. Then Agnes ordered her to brush her hair. She'd stroked the heavy brush over the rough tufts until her arms ached. Finally, eyes drooping, the old woman had indicated with a flap of her bony hand that she could stop. Those tasks were all she'd asked of her.

Long periods, she'd spent on the hard chair, awaiting the next demand, and her mind filled the inactivity with worrying thoughts of Jonathan and whether Grace was coping.

None the less, before she knew it, Pru's voice drifted up, informing her she could take her dinner. Hurrying downstairs, Sally smiled proudly. She'd survived the morning at least. What the afternoon held, however, remained to be seen.

Entering the shop, she saw through the window snow falling in earnest. 'Oh, I didn't know it had started again. The curtains upstairs are almost drawn.'

'Yes, I'm afraid so.' Pru bade a customer goodbye then asked eagerly, 'How are you getting on, dear?'

'All right, I think. I'm sorry, Miss Sharp, but I must go. My aunt is minding my child and I promised to call in to give him his feed.'

'Of course, dear, of course. We shall talk later when work is through.'

Thoughts of Jonathan screaming for her milk and the burning need to see him propelled her through the streets and in no time, she was at Grace's door.

'I've found you at last. I knew I would eventually.'

Sally whipped around to see a tall figure, almost shrouded from view in the fast-falling snow. She blinked flakes from her lashes and squinted harder, heart hammering.

He stepped closer and she shook her head in astonishment. 'What are *you* doing here?'

Chapter 12

GRACE SMILED AT the man seated at the table. 'More tea?'

'You're an angel from heaven, to be sure. Isn't she an angel?' he asked Sally.

She glared at him then cast her aunt a tight smile.

'Oh, go on with you.' Grace laughed, flapping a hand. 'You Irish. Charm the birds from the trees, you would.'

''Tis both a blessing and a curse, Mrs Boslam.'

Grace laughed again and Sally rolled her eyes. For fifteen minutes, she'd had to force smiles and make small talk with this man. What he was doing here, she didn't know. He had no right turning up like this.

Initially, the accent didn't register and she'd been petrified, believing Joseph had tracked her down. Before she could ask what in the world he was doing here and how he'd found her, her aunt appeared at the door. Grace had taken an instant shine to Con Malloy; his easy smile and charming ways made it difficult not to. When he explained that he and her niece were friends, she'd invited him inside for a sup to 'thaw him out', much to Sally's exasperation.

Grace had been anxious to hear how her morning had gone but, unwilling to discuss her business in front of a near stranger, she'd said they would talk later. While Grace brewed tea, she'd taken the baby into the next room to feed him but not before throwing Con an angry look. He, however, had merely smiled.

Her annoyance grew when his deep brogue drifted through, telling her aunt of their previous meetings. Grace's responses showed she was suitably impressed and by the time Sally rejoined them, the smooth-talking Irishman had well and truly won her over.

Now, as Grace made to refill his cup again, she'd had enough.

'Aunt Grace, I think it's time Con was leaving. I must get back to work.' To him, she added stiffly, 'I'm sure you have business to be getting on with. Please, don't let us keep you.'

His slow smile appeared. Taking Grace's hand, he kissed it soundly. ''Twas a pleasure meeting such a grand woman as yourself, Mrs Boslam.'

'And you, lad. You're welcome any time. A friend of my Sally's is a friend of mine.'

Sally dropped a kiss on to Jonathan's head and passed him to Grace. Then taking Con's elbow, she steered him to the door.

'Your aunt's a sound woman, so she is. Was the colleen in the bed your cousin? I didn't like to say inside but she looked mighty poorly.'

She remained silent until they reached the entry, where she halted and glared up at him.

'What the hell do you think you're playing at? What are you doing here? How did you find me?' He answered with his slow smile and her anger rose. 'What is it you find amusing? That you twisted my aunt around your finger? That you managed to track down a woman, for God alone knows what reason, whom you barely know? Look, I'm grateful for your assistance last week but—'

'You're even more beautiful when you're angry, acushla.'

'I am not your acushla! I don't know what your intentions are but I can assure you—' He wrapped his arms around her and kissed her hard, smothering her rant. She was so shocked, she couldn't move. However, he drew her closer and her senses returned like a thunderbolt. She sprang back as though he'd scorched her. 'How *dare* you!'

He ran a hand through his hair, his breathing heavy. 'I shouldn't have done that. Forgive me. I just . . . I don't know what it is about you. From the moment I saw you standing on the platform in Bolton, looking so lost, so vulnerable, I felt something in here.' He tapped his chest. 'I always did have a soft spot for a damsel in distress.'

His smile stirred but when her face remained stony, it died. 'I remembered you telling the cab driver to take you to Boslam Street. I asked around but no one had heard of you. I was about to give up when I caught sight of ye rushing through this here entry. I wanted to get to know you, find out more about you. I hoped that seeing me again, you'd—'

'I'd what? What did you expect I'd do, Con? Throw myself at your feet? I certainly wasn't wrong when suggesting you need a bigger cap.'

'No, Sally, I—'

'We spoke no more than several words last week. I never expected to see you again. Then today, I find you lurking in the shadows. It's all a little . . . odd. I don't know a thing about you.'

He reached out tentatively and took her hand. 'Give me a chance. Get to know me, as I want to get to know you. I'm nothing special, Sally, 'tis true, but . . . Please, can't we at least be friends?'

She sighed. Hope creased his eyes and Sally found herself softening. Despite her experience of men, she felt no fear with this one, feeling comfortable in his presence from the moment they met. 'Well, maybe we *could* be friends . . .' she heard herself say.

His face spread in a grin. 'I'd like that, Sally. I'd like that very much.'

'Let's forget today and start afresh, shall we? If you're free, you may call again on Sunday. Now, I really must get to work. I only started this morning; it won't look good if I'm late back. Oh, and Con?' she added over her shoulder.

'Aye?'

'Don't ever creep up on me again. I don't like it.'

Still smiling, he nodded, and she set off.

Hurrying through the streets, uncertainty tugged at her. She touched her lips. Would agreeing to be friends give him the wrong idea? He was nice, and there was no denying he was handsome, but after Joseph . . . She could never feel *that* way for any male. He'd warped her perception of men for ever.

One with floppy black hair and grey-blue eyes flashed in her mind and she realised that this wasn't entirely true. She *had* felt something, with him.

She still did.

Three pairs of eyes gazed from Tommy to the table.

'Eeh, the silly girl. The silly, *silly* girl. Why the bloody hell didn't she keep it for herself and the babby?'

'She insisted, Mam.'

'But how did she get away with taking all this? How did Joseph not notice?'

'She didn't tell me the ins and outs, just said she buried coppers away over the years.'

His father ran a hand over the mound of coins. 'I can't fathom it. If she worked so hard saving this up, why leave it here, with thee?'

Tommy pulled out a chair and sat down. Excitement flowed through him when Shaun traced a finger over a shiny penny. God willing, this would change his life. 'This here brass is for you,' he murmured. 'Every penny, every copper coin, it's all for you.'

'Aye, very funny, our Tommy.'

Grinning, he turned to his mother. 'You remember the morning Sally left, when you came down and we were already up?' Her lips tightened into a thin line and he continued quickly, 'I said, didn't I, that I couldn't sleep? It were because I had matters on my mind.'

'What matters?'

'Our Shaun. It's no secret he loathes the pit, Mam. I were sitting here racking me brains forra way to help him. Sally came in and . . . well, we got talking. She wanted to repay thee for taking her in. When I told her of our Shaun's talent, that I were going to try and secure him an apprenticeship, she offered to help. As tha knows, they might require a premium, then there's his tools—'

'You wanted to do that?' Shaun cut in, brown eyes shining. 'You *both* wanted to do that? For me?'

'Aye.'

Ivy covered her mouth, her own eyes bright. 'That lass. What an angel. She got one over on that divil, all right. Eeh, the clever girl.' She shook her head. 'All that morning . . . over breakfast, on our way to catch the carrier's cart, she never said a word.

'Mind, now I think back . . . Assuming she were potless, I gave her a few coins for her fare and there were a definite twinkle in her eye as she took them. Why the bugger didn't she say owt?'

'She knew you'd not accept. We planned how she'd let you pay the cart so you'd not suspect,' Tommy admitted, winking. 'She said to tell thee to take the fare, and whatever it's cost for her stay, out of this.'

'Eeh, you pair of sneaky swines. Well, nowt needs taking for her stay. She hardly cost us a thing; she had the appetite of a swallow.' Her face was suddenly serious. ''Ere, she kept some aside for herself, didn't she? This ain't all the money she had, is it?'

'Nay. Don't fret, Mam.'

As she squeezed his hand, her voice was tender. 'You're a good lad, son.'

His smile came with deep guilt. This had quelled her suspicions regarding him and Sally, he could see it in her eyes. How wrong she was. He wanted her more than ever.

'Can you believe this, Shaun? God willing, we'll get thee apprenticed somewhere, eh?'

Face set like stone, Shaun pulled from her embrace.

'Lad?'

'This is a dream, in't it? I'll waken in a minute and it'll be morning, time for work down that bloody pit. Things like this don't happen, not to folk like me.'

'Oh, lad.' She took his face in her hands. 'Now you listen to me. Thanks to that lovely lass, you're getting out of that pit and you're going to make summat of yourself, d'you hear? It's real, lad. It's *real*.'

Shaun laughed brokenly. Then he jumped up and punched the air.

As the trio chattered excitedly about the future, Tommy smiled. It warmed his heart something lovely to see them happy. And it was all down to Sally. *Sweet, beautiful Sally*. George Turner's words returned to haunt him. He glanced at his mother, debating whether to tell her, but decided against it. This was Shaun's moment and he wanted him to enjoy it. He wouldn't wipe the joy from their faces.

Dolly assaulted his mind but he hastily pushed her out. He couldn't think of her; the guilt was unbearable. Earlier, he'd lingered by her cottage for an age but couldn't bring himself to knock at her door. When he returned home, his mother had asked if she'd agreed to come to dinner and though he'd felt terrible lying to her, the tale concocted on the way back slipped easily from his tongue.

He'd told her Dolly couldn't come, she was needed at the dairy. To his relief and shame, Ivy believed him.

It would have been torture; he'd have been unable to pretend all was well. Yet there was another reason he hadn't invited Dolly – he wouldn't be here. When he finished work on Saturday, he was going to Manchester.

He didn't have a clue where in Ancoats Sally's aunt lived, but he'd find out. He'd have gone this very second, walked if he must, but it was impossible. He couldn't miss work. His family's reliance upon his wage was too great.

What excuse he'd use, he didn't know, but he was going. He had to warn Sally. He *had* to see her. Nothing, no one, would stop him.

Chapter 13

WEDNESDAY AND THURSDAY passed similarly to Sally's first day. Routine remained the same and Agnes had seemingly resigned herself to the fact she wasn't going anywhere. There had been no further altercations and Sally was certain if she continued speaking only when spoken to and kept her head down, things would be fine.

Today was Friday and as Agnes handed her the tattered book, her heart sank. The daily torture was taking its toll. It was ridiculous straining to see when opening the curtains a touch more would solve it. How did sunlight annoy one, anyway? She had to say something. What use would a blind mother be to her son?

'Mrs Sharp, I know we've spoken about this but could I open the curtains just a little more? The light in here is incredibly weak. I'm worried that my eyesight—'

'You have the candle, do you not?'

'Well yes, but—'

'Then cease your whining and read the damn book, girl.'

She breathed deeply. 'Mrs Sharp, the candle is insufficient. My eyes have become painful since working here. Opening the curtains would help enormously and would make such a difference in here, too.'

Pru's long hours in the shop, and reluctance to spend time with her cantankerous mother, had resulted in a dreadfully neglected room. Dirt and dust covered every surface. Ancient cobwebs drooped from the ceiling and a musty smell pervaded the air, adding to the morose feel. A good clean and sunlight would cheer it up no end. Maybe the old woman would be happier in less dismal surroundings.

Agnes's eyes narrowed. 'Difference?'

'Well,' she began hesitantly, 'perhaps I could do some cleaning. The dust cannot be good for you, surely. It wouldn't take long. Then there's the light. Opening the curtains would brighten everything and I could open the window and . . .' Her speech died, her enthusiasm with it, as Agnes shook her head. However, when the old woman spoke, she pleasantly surprised her.

'You're persistent, girl, I'll give you that. I suppose you will drone on and on if I refuse?' Annoyance tinged her guttural voice but a hint of amusement glimmered behind her eyes.

Sally's lips twitched. 'I simply believe the change would be most beneficial, as much to you as to me.' She clasped her hands to her chest. 'Do I have your permission, Mrs Sharp?'

'All right, girl. I'm willing to humour your silly whim. But I warn you, if I do not like the changes you decide upon, you will put back everything exactly as it was, however hard you've worked. Do I make myself clear?'

Sally had a sneaking suspicion she'd decide this just to be difficult, but had to try. 'Yes, Mrs Sharp. Do you require anything before I begin?'

A whisper of a smile played across her shrivelled mouth. 'No, no. You go ahead.'

Beaming, Sally headed straight for the window.

Besides rushing home to feed Jonathan and fulfilling Agnes's occasional request, she worked non-stop. By late afternoon, her body screamed for rest and she was terribly grubby, but it had been worth it. Hands on hips, she blew her hair from her face and gazed around.

Every piece of furniture she'd pulled out and cleaned thoroughly. She'd swept and scrubbed the floor and skirting boards, and stripped the walls and ceilings of the many cobwebs. Most importantly, the curtains, which she'd taken down, shaken well then rehung, were open wide, as was the gleaming window.

The difference was unbelievable. Sunlight uncovered things the gloom had disguised. Wallpaper, though faded, revealed swirling sprigs of pale-green flowers. The large rug, after she'd shaken out years of muck, showed traces of the vibrant colours it once held. Paintings that had hung limply – from cavalry charging across a battlefield to a countryside complete with rushing stream – were now vivid depictions.

She glanced to the old woman, who was snoring softly. All day, she'd been aware of Agnes watching her. It was unnerving having her every move silently scrutinised and she'd sighed in relief when she'd fallen asleep. Now, however, Sally pondered whether to waken her. The bed was the only thing she hadn't touched; she itched to give behind it a good clean.

Taking another look around, she smiled proudly. Everywhere sparkled; the smell was gone. Surely Mrs Sharp would like it?

After closing the window and drawing the curtains, she knelt before the cleaned and blackleaded fireplace. Within minutes, flames danced up the chimney. As she rose, the door opened and a smiling Pru appeared.

'I've brought you both a cup— Oh! What an absolutely wonderful job you've done!' She placed the tea tray on the bedside table then traced her fingers over the walls and furniture. 'I'd forgotten how this room once looked. I cannot believe the difference you have made, dear.'

Sally smiled in delight. Pru had ventured up several times to see how it was progressing but she'd been told she couldn't see until it was completed. Chuckling, Pru had sidled back downstairs. Sally was glad she'd made her wait; her reaction was proof she'd done well.

'Has she seen it?'

'Not yet. I do hope she likes it, Miss Sharp.'

'I think she just may. I still cannot believe she gave permission. You must think me a dreadful slattern. I . . . couldn't . . . Life is much easier if I keep my distance. She finds my very presence irksome. I don't know what it is about you but she has accepted you as she never has anyone else.'

'I believe an unspoken truce was made when I stood up to her.'

Pru's gaze flicked to the poker propped against the wall. 'Just remain watchful, dear. Don't let your guard down for a moment. Promise me, Sally. Promise me you'll be careful.'

She sensed more behind the whispered warning. 'This isn't only about her last employee, is it, Miss Sharp? Has your mother used that blasted poker on you, too?'

'Of course, dear. Many times. But I don't want anyone else getting hurt, not again.'

As the shocking admission hung in the air, anger gripped Sally's chest. How could anyone treat their own child like that – particularly one so sweet and kind? She glared at Agnes in disgust. Why did some people behave this way? What pleasure did they derive from causing others misery?

'Miss Sharp, I suffered a bully's hand for years. He beat me into submission for no other reason than that he could. A dear friend helped put a stop to my torment.' She marched forward and snatched up the poker. 'Now it's my turn to help another.'

'What are you doing?' hissed Pru.

'Something which should have been done a long time ago.' She wrenched the curtain aside, opened the window and threw the poker out. It struck the cobbles with a loud clang and she nodded in grim satisfaction.

'You're still here? What time is it?'

Whipping around, Sally found Agnes staring at her, green eyes mere slits. Sally was about to give her a piece of her mind when Pru's pleading gaze caught her eye.

'I think you *are* a mute, girl, after all. I asked you a question. What's the wretched time?' Suddenly, peering around, Agnes's lips twisted in a smirk. 'Well, well, well. I see you've been busy.'

'Isn't it wonderful, Mother?' Ashen-faced, Pru wrung her hands. 'I brought tea. It is on the table, there.'

Agnes ignored her and turned back to Sally. 'We had an agreement, did we not? I stated quite clearly that if I did not like it, I wanted it putting back exactly as you found it.'

'Let me guess. You don't.'

'Actually, it is rather pleasant. You've done well, girl.'

Sally and Pru glanced at each other in shared surprise and distrust.

'There is just one question I would like you to answer,' Agnes murmured, bony fingers gripping the bedclothes. 'What do you propose we now use for the fire?'

Under the intense stare, Sally felt colour stain her cheeks. But glancing to a terrified-looking Pru, anger lifted her chin. 'That poker hasn't been used for what it was intended for, for a long time, Mrs Sharp, and you know it.'

A range of emotions flitted across the lined face. When a scratchy laugh leaked from her mouth, her expression told it was as much a shock to her ears as theirs.

'You are without doubt the most insolent, hard-faced little bitch I have ever encountered,' she spluttered. She threw her head back and laughed harder at Sally's outraged frown. 'Oh, put your face straight, girl. I mean that as a compliment. If only this useless chit had an ounce of your gumption. She's brought me nothing but disappointment. What he saw in her, I will never know—'

Pru's harsh gasp sliced through her words. 'Don't you *dare* talk about that. I have warned you before; never, ever talk about that! I made a mistake, Mother. One mistake. Am I to suffer it the rest of my days?' A solitary tear slipped down her cheek. 'Haven't I suffered enough?'

Sally looked on in confusion. Her perplexity grew when Agnes's eyes deepened with what she could only interpret as guilt. Pru's ragged breaths were the only sound until, softer than she'd ever heard, Agnes spoke.

'Pull yourself together and fetch the poker before some scoundrel pilfers it.' She nodded once. 'Go on, Prudence.'

Pru left the room. Moments later, without a word, she returned the poker to its home by the bedside.

'As for you . . .' murmured Agnes to Sally. 'Ever behave in such a foolhardy manner again and you will be dismissed faster than you can blink. I like spirit but I will break yours if you attempt to push me too far.

Remember your place, girl. Now, go on home. Your child will be wanting your milk.'

Too bewildered to argue, she stole a last look at Pru and headed for the door.

'Girl?'

Her hand stilled on the knob.

'Thank you.'

Sally glanced around the space she'd worked so hard on then slipped from the room.

Chapter 14

SATURDAY DAWNED BRIGHT and clear. The snow had finally exhausted itself and Sally's walk to work was through a sea of grey-black slush. Carts crawled along the patchwork of icy cobbles; the horses' safety was paramount. A slip of a hoof could, she knew, claim not only the beast's life but a driver's family when no work meant no food and coal.

In biting temperatures, with dwellings often as cold as the streets, inhabitants clung to life grimly, praying for spring. Many, particularly the young, old and infirm, wouldn't see this spell through.

'Spare a penny, missis?'

This, delivered through a beggar boy's chattering teeth, no longer shocked her as it had when she first arrived in this town.

Children fortunate to own clogs had enjoyed the white blanket that encompassed their world; the lanes had rung with screeching laughter. Others, who worked the streets trading everything from their bodies to kindling – and those like this bundle of bones shivering beneath old newspaper in a doorway, bare feet probably plagued by burning chilblains – no doubt hadn't shared the fascination.

'Ha'penny, then?'

Yesterday's performance with the Sharps had wrapped around her a veil of dejection. She'd lain awake all night, dreading returning. Why was nothing ever simple? Why had she always suffered so? Why were a select few born into a life of privilege and ease while others were clawing for survival upon leaving the womb?

The morose thoughts had swamped her yet now, looking at these people around her, skin blue, eyes utterly void of hope in sallow faces, Sally felt ashamed.

'Missis, please. My guts ain't known grub since Thursday.'

Lord, what had she to gripe about? Her clothes and boots, though thin and patched, dulled the edge of the cold. She'd suffered the workhouse then as Joseph's wife, but was free of both. Countless children were lost but she had Jonathan. Evil drove her from Spring Row but she now had a safe home. Her parents had passed away but she had Aunt Grace, Uncle Ed, cousins. Dicksy had gone but she had solid friends in Ivy and her family, and potential ones in Con and Maggie Benson.

And she had her job. Though it wasn't the most enjoyable, nor safest, many would give their eye teeth to be earning an honest crust. No, things were never as bad as they seemed.

She pressed a coin into the beggar's hand and continued on her way.

Tomorrow, her day off, she was determined to make the most of. She'd visit Maggie. She couldn't wait to see her and hoped she'd found another position. She'd take Jonathan. Spending time with him would be lovely and Grace deserved a break.

Also, Con was calling. She was rather looking forward to that, was glad she'd decided to try his friendship. There were things she didn't know about him but then, there were things he didn't know about her. However, he was a decent man who deserved a chance.

Entering the shop, she found Pru busy behind the counter. When she closed the door and Pru didn't turn, she bit her lip. She usually greeted Sally warmly; was she cross about last night? She should never have slung the poker through the window or spoken to the old woman as she did. From where had that spark of courage come? It seemed the old Sally, that feisty, defiant girl who, mindless of the consequences, thought nothing of standing up to the workhouse matron – master, too – with bunched fists and eyes, and tongue spitting venom, was slowly but surely resurfacing, whether she liked it or not.

Nevertheless, what went on with mother and daughter was between them. From now on, unless Pru asked for her help, she'd keep out of their affairs.

'Miss Sharp, my conduct last night . . . I'm so very sorry. I simply loathe one suffering at another's hand, for I know how it feels. It will never happen again.'

Still, Pru didn't turn.

Sally lowered her head. Would she dismiss her?

'Don't apologise, dear. You have nothing to be sorry for.'

Her head jerked up. She sighed in relief. 'I'm truly sorry, Miss Sharp, I— Oh!' The word ripped from her throat as Pru turned.

'I'm quite all right. It looks worse than it is,' Pru murmured, hands fluttering to her face.

Sally covered her mouth in horror. Pru's face was badly swollen. Her gentle eyes peeped through puffy slits and dark bruises streaked the skin in livid patches.

'Can I get you a cup of tea, dear?'

'A cup . . . ? Miss Sharp, what on earth has *happened* to you?' She shook her head slowly. 'That wicked old woman did this, didn't she? What is *wrong* with her? She could have killed you!'

Pru's split lips parted but whatever she'd been about to say remained unspoken.

Glaring at the ceiling, Sally was consumed with fury. Moments later, she was sprinting upstairs. She burst into Agnes's room, strode to the bed and stared in disgust at the sleeping form.

'Sally, please.'

Glancing to the doorway, her face softened. Pru was wringing her hands furiously, eyes wide in desperation.

'If you question her, you'll make matters worse for me. Please, dear.'

She shot Agnes a last look then followed Pru downstairs. 'I'm sorry, Miss Sharp,' she said when they reached the shop. 'Of course I don't want to make things more difficult for you. It's just . . . She cannot get away with treating people like this!'

Pru patted the stool beside hers. 'Come, sit down. We shouldn't be disturbed. No one will be in to redeem possessions until they receive their wages, later.'

'Is this about last night? Did she take it out on you because of my actions?'

'No, no, dear. Don't blame yourself. It's entirely my fault. I foolishly continued the argument after you left. You would think I'd have learned by now, wouldn't you?'

Recalling their exchange, she frowned. 'Miss Sharp, I couldn't fail to hear what your mother said regarding . . . a man? It's none of my business but if you ever want to talk . . .'

'Thank you, dear. She hasn't mentioned . . . that, in a while. She brings it up now and then to hurt me. And Lord, her words *do* hurt. Far more than the feel of that poker. She believes it a necessary measure; spare the rod, spoil the child, so to speak.' A small sigh escaped. 'I'm able to ignore most of what she says, but not that.

'It's the one thing she knows will garner a reaction. And I fall for it every time.' She patted Sally's hand. 'You're a lovely person. I appreciate your concern, truly. One day, I may take up your kind offer and release my demons. But not yet. The memories are very raw, dear.'

Sally covered her hand with hers. 'I understand, Miss Sharp.'

'Mother will shortly be awake. Go on up and I shall bring you both some tea. And Sally, please don't mention this, will you?' Pru entreated, pointing to her face.

Sally sighed inwardly. How was she to bear that woman's company? She'd love nothing more than to shake her awake, give her a piece of her mind, leave and never return. But she couldn't. She needed this job, and Pru needed her.

'I won't, you have my word. But Miss Sharp, what will you do?' she couldn't help asking. 'You cannot continue living in fear of her beating you whenever the mood strikes. I lived that way for a long time and it near killed me.'

'It shan't happen again, dear. If she ever mentions . . . I'm determined not to rise to it. I have no choice. She has no one in the world but me. I must simply grit my teeth and get on with it.'

Heart heavy with pity, Sally reluctantly headed upstairs.

The level of poverty in Manchester was like nothing Tommy had encountered. Since he'd stepped from the train and met the abjectness of Sally's new home, an ache had taken root in his chest. Settling back in the hansom hailed outside the station, he prayed Ancoats wasn't as bad as the parts he'd already seen.

He didn't have a clue how he'd find her. Unsure where to begin, he'd simply instructed the driver to drop him 'somewhere in Ancoats'. The man had scratched his head and stared at him as if he were mad. But when Tommy raised an eyebrow and jingled coins in his pocket, he'd shrugged and told him to hop aboard.

Rattling through the streets, Tommy kept his eyes peeled. It was a long shot but he might just spot her; she could be anywhere, after all. His breathing quickened at the prospect. The urge to see her was like coiled rope in his stomach, tightening, tightening. He felt like a man possessed. Nothing would stop him until he found her.

His mother's smile returned to haunt him and he gripped the seat. He'd lied to her again; only this time, he'd gone further – he'd used Dolly as an alibi.

Unable to think up an excuse, he'd informed her he was off to see the dairymaid. Then, remembering his previous lie, that she couldn't come to dinner because she was needed at the dairy, he amended his words, adding he'd wait at Dolly's until she returned from work. His mother hadn't suspected a thing. How he'd kept his tone even, his fixed smile in place, he didn't know.

What he *did* know was that he hated himself for it. Lately, the lies flowed and it worried him. Being deceitful wasn't in his nature. Yet where Sally was concerned, he couldn't help himself.

They turned into a road teeming with carts and people. Reasoning the busier the place, the better the chance of someone having heard of her, he tapped the cab, alighted and stared about.

The sheer magnitude of his task slammed home. He hadn't thought this through at all. After working a half-day then travelling here, the day was almost through. If he had no joy, he'd seek a lodging house and try tomorrow, he resolved.

As for his overnight absence, he'd tell his parents that after leaving Dolly, he'd met a pit lad at a tavern and, after too many jars, was unable to make it home and had bedded down at his cottage. His mother wouldn't be best pleased but he'd face her tongue when the time came. Right now, all he could think of was finding Sally.

Questions tumbled over themselves in his mind, each more worrying than the last. Was she even here? Perhaps, unable to locate her aunt, she'd moved on.

As he turned from the roadside, a hand brushed his buttocks and hot breath fanned his neck. Jerking around, he saw a woman of indeterminate age, gaudily painted face fixed in a seductive smile.

'By gum, lad, you're easy on t' eye. You looking for some fun?'

He peeled her arms from his waist, his colour rising. That she was a streetwalker didn't surprise or embarrass him; he'd seen plenty in Bolton in his time. It was being propositioned in broad daylight that rendered him speechless. Prostitutes usually loitered in back lanes, attainable yet concealed. And this clearly wasn't a random act; people passing barely batted an eyelid.

'I know somewhere warm and dry we could go.' Her simpering tone held the desperation in her eyes when he'd removed her hands. 'I'll do owt you've a fancy for, lad.'

Taking stock of her, he sighed. She wasn't a woman at all. Behind the painted eyes, lips and cheeks, her pinched face was that of someone no older than fourteen or fifteen.

He extracted coppers from his pocket, took her icy hand and pressed them into her palm. Then he put his lips to her ear. 'Go home, lass.'

Tears filled eyes old long before their time. Standing on tiptoe, she kissed his cheek and walked away.

Watching her scuttle through the throng of bodies, his guts lurched. What if Sally was in the same desperate situation . . . ? No. He wouldn't, *couldn't*, think that. She was safe, well. She had to be.

A deep voice cut through his thoughts. Across the road, he saw a tall, good-looking man catch a beshawled woman around the waist. Smiling down, he guided her inside a pie shop, and Tommy swallowed a pang of envy. Would he one day be that happy? Would he ever hold Sally again?

As he peered around, a lump formed in his throat at the hopelessness of it all. He was never going to find her.

'You see, 'tis to be there when you need rescuing I was put on this earth, acushla.'

Meeting the Irishman's laughing eyes, Sally couldn't help smiling. 'Con, this is serious. I don't think I can return. How I held my tongue today, I do not know.'

'Hush, now, and start from the beginning. Sure, 'twas a stroke of luck I spotted ye leaving.'

She took a sip of her tea. 'I'm glad you did. I couldn't have allowed Aunt Grace to see me like this. She didn't want me taking the position in the first place. Whenever she asks how I'm faring, I say all is fine. She'd only fret if she knew the truth.' She placed her cup on the table and closed her eyes. 'Oh Con, she is wicked, *wicked*. Miss Sharp's face . . .

'My anger as I ran up those stairs . . . *I* could have taken the poker to *her*.' A man at the next table glanced over and she lowered her voice. 'She believes it's for her daughter's good, that if she didn't remind her of the feel of the poker, it would only be a matter of time before she sinned again. Can you believe that?'

'What sin has she committed before?'

'I don't know. Miss Sharp seems the last person to do anything immoral; a more decent and generous soul you couldn't wish to meet. However, Mrs Sharp said something about a man, that she didn't know what he'd seen in her daughter.'

Con leaned forward, his slow smile surfacing. 'It sounds like your Miss Sharp is a touch *too* generous.'

'Whatever her past, it doesn't excuse her mother's actions. Nothing can justify what she's done to her poor face – has done many times.'

'What will ye do?'

She stared absently through the window. 'I honestly do not know. I need this job but am not sure I can be around such evil. The way she was today . . . she must have known I'd seen her daughter's injuries, yet she showed not a flicker of shame.

'Do you know something else? Yesterday, I broke my back cleaning her room. I thought she'd announce she didn't like it, to be awkward, but surprisingly, she said I'd done well.'

'That's grand, isn't it?'

'No, Con, I don't think it is. I believe she intended to dislike the room before I even began but, when she noticed Miss Sharp there, saw it as a perfect opportunity to belittle her. She merely sang my praises to hurt her. How could she derive enjoyment from her child's misery?'

He took her hand, the pleasure in his eyes when she didn't shy away, clear. 'When are you next in?'

'Monday.'

'And will ye go? Can you brave this out or will you look for something else?'

'If I do stay, it will be for Miss Sharp. I doubt she'd find anyone to fill my position and the duty would fall to her. She'd be at that monstrous woman's mercy completely.'

Stroking her fingers, he smiled. 'You're a grand woman. You're gentle and caring, yet you've a feistiness I find irresistible. You intrigue me.'

His hand strayed up her arm and she pulled back, cheeks flushing.

'Sally, I'm sorry, I—'

'I'm sorry, too, Con. I don't feel for you as you do for me.' She glanced at him and sighed. 'You're handsome, you make me laugh, I feel safe in your company . . . but we cannot be more than friends.'

'Because of this?' He tapped her wedding band. 'Whatever the reason your marriage broke down, who and where your husband is, it doesn't bother me. I don't care about your past. I just want to be part of your future. 'Twas fate, us meeting as we did. And whenever you're in need, I always seem to be close by, to help and look after you. 'Tis like it's meant to be, acushla.'

His heartfelt words touched her and when she spoke, there was a catch in her voice. 'Aunt Grace was right about you Irish. You *could* charm the birds from the trees with your blarney.'

He flashed a weak smile. 'But . . . ?'

'There's no future for us, not like that.'

'Is your heart already claimed by another?' he asked suddenly. 'Was your wistful smile on the train for him?'

Her cheeks burned but she tossed her head. 'Con Malloy, I don't know what you're talking about. I harbour feelings for no man.'

He grinned. 'I don't believe you.'

'Believe what you will,' she said mildly. 'Furthermore, there are several questions *I* would like to ask *you*.'

'Such as?'

Her lips twitched when his infectious smile grew. 'Why were you in Bolton that day? What do you do for a living? Where and with whom do you reside?'

'We have a lot to discuss, to be sure. And you know what that means?' He winked, his grin returning. 'I get to spend more time with ye.'

Rolling her eyes, she laughed. 'You're incorrigible. Now, I'm afraid I must go as Jonathan will be needing me. You're welcome to walk with me if you're going my way.'

'Feeling better?' he asked when they exited the pie shop.

Sally linked her arm in his. 'How could I not with a friend like you to cheer me up?'

He nudged her playfully and, laughing, she hurried him along the street.

Chapter 15

JOSEPH SQUINTED THROUGH the gloom. His mouth was parchment dry, his head thumping.

'Bloody thick heads grow worse as I get owder,' he muttered, hauling himself up in the lumpy bed.

A leg wrapped around his, making him jump. Wrenching back the covers, he frowned, trying to cast his mind back to the night before, but the pounding in his skull pushed out all thought.

Nancy lay on her side, arms entwined above her head, hair streaming across the pillow. He shoved her hard.

''Ere, what—?'

'What the hell's tha doing here?' he cut in harshly. 'Get up, get dressed and get gone afore our Alice wakens.'

Stretching like a lazy cat in the sun, she smiled sleepily. 'You asked me back last night, you daft beggar. We had a nice fumble in Nellie's as usual, but when we went into the back lane like normally at kicking-out time, I said I were sick of lifting my skirt for thee outside and you fetched me here.' She dropped kisses on to his chest. 'You not remember?'

'Nay, I bloody well don't.' He dragged a hand through his hair. 'I must've had a reet skinful.'

She pouted. 'Oh, ta very much.'

'Listen, you daft sow, if our Alice finds out I've had thee here, I'll be out quicker than that,' he growled, clicking his fingers. 'Reet funny, she is, 'bout things like that. Get moving.'

Arching in another stretch, she laughed when his glare flicked to her bare breasts, which had risen invitingly. 'We've a few minutes, ain't we? It's early yet. Look.' She motioned to the window. 'It's only just gone light.'

Irritation sparked but he didn't object.

'Good lad. You lie back and enjoy.'

His eyes narrowed with desire as she straddled him. 'You're a bitch. My head's splitting.'

Hips moving rhythmically, Nancy smiled. 'And that's what you like about me, in't it?'

Ivy couldn't keep the smile from her face. Her husband and sons donned jackets and caps and her stomach fluttered in excitement.

'Wish us luck, Mam.' Shaun bent and kissed her cheek. Making for the door, he checked the cloth bag's contents for the dozenth time.

'Good luck, son. You got the money?'

Tommy patted his pocket. 'I've got it, Mam.'

'You got them carvings?'

Shaun held up the bag. 'Aye.'

She nodded, then frowned at Arthur. 'You got that package I made up for your dinners?'

'Aye, wench, stop your fussing.' He rolled his eyes at his grinning sons. 'Let's get moving afore the day's gone.'

She watched them pass down the lane. When they reached the end of the row, Tommy lifted an arm in farewell and she smiled. She returned to the kitchen and, reaching for the teapot, clicked her tongue at her trembling hands.

'Be calm, Ivy,' she told herself. 'What will be, will be.'

They had barely slept last night – indeed, no one had much since Tommy had poured the money on to the table. Anticipation had stroked the cottage; she couldn't believe the day was here. It seemed they had waited weeks for Sunday to crawl around.

Naturally, Shaun felt it more. Dragging himself to the pit was difficult before – having to do so with that money sitting here had been unbearable. She just prayed to God he was taken on today.

She smiled as her musings switched to Tommy. Whatever had ailed him wasn't a sickening for Sally, she was now certain. He'd simply been fretting over Shaun's future and she felt terrible about her suspicions. She was even thankful that Sally had left, she remembered shamefully. Why had she harboured such foolish notions? Sally was a lovely lass, her Tommy a good lad smitten with the Jenkins one.

At the thought of Dolly, she sighed. She'd shot herself in the foot, there; her daft imaginings even saw her encouraging the courtship. She didn't know what it was about the dairymaid, couldn't put her finger on it. There was something about her she couldn't take to.

That there *wasn't* anything wrong with Dolly, that merely, in her eyes, no one was good enough for her Tommy, niggled, and she sighed again. She just loved the lad, wanted him to be happy, that was all.

With a yawn and a stretch, she settled into Arthur's chair. Closing tired eyes, her mind remained on Tommy. If that Jenkins lass was who he wanted, she'd have to accept it. He wasn't getting any younger. It was time he thought about settling down.

A sudden thought struck and her eyes sprang open. 'I wonder . . . ?' she murmured to the empty room.

He only met Dolly on Sundays yet yesterday, Saturday, he visited her cottage. He was gone all day and, now Ivy thought about it, preoccupied on his return. Had her inviting Dolly to dinner spurred him into taking things further? Would her apparent support bolster him to propose? With effort, she told herself that, whatever occurred, she'd keep her opinions private. It was his life, his decision.

Nights of shattered sleep, coupled with the fire, took effect. Before Ivy drifted to sleep, a young woman appeared in her mind. However, it wasn't Dolly, but Sally. And she realised, if circumstances were different, there was no one she'd want more for a daughter-in-law.

His lust spent, Joseph pushed Nancy off and climbed from the bed.

''Ere, I weren't finished. What's the rush? Tha getting bored of me, or summat?'

He turned sharply and grabbed her by the throat. His grip tightened and he forced himself to stop. He could happily beat her to a pulp; her whining was really getting to him, lately. But it would raise questions. That father of hers would surely notice and want to know what had happened.

She held up her hands. 'I'm sorry. I'm a grumpy cow of a morning. Leave go, eh, lad? I'll get dressed quick and be out of your hair.'

With a curl of his lip, he slung her away, sending her sprawling across the bed. He watched with increasing anger as she scrambled up, rubbing her neck.

He'd have to get shot of her. She was a convenient tool to sate his carnal needs, and the stuff she thieved from her father's shop placated Alice, but the urge to hurt her – and the struggle not to – mounted with each meeting.

That's where he'd been clever with Sally. He'd had plenty of flings before her but none lasted. When they got on his nerves and he'd used his fist to shut their gobs, they scarpered. But not Sally. She couldn't, with no one and nowhere to run to.

As he pulled on his trousers, admiration filled him for the workhouse master. He was on to something, there, all right. He knew plenty of men would pay well for women who did as they told them. Women with no ties, to use however you wanted without fear of their fathers or brothers giving you a good hiding. He'd had it until that interfering old bitch next door stuck her nose in. And by God, he'd have it again.

Snarling at Nancy's smile, he flung on shirt and jacket. Aye, this whore had to go soon, before he lost his rag. It was coming, there was no doubt about it. He wasn't prepared to dangle at the end of a rope for her, however tempting. Once he'd used her to find Sally and get back at the Morgans, he'd get rid of her.

Amusement bubbled. She was still paying his rent, probably hoping he'd move her in. Silly bitch. He couldn't return, with them next door, not without getting a round of clogs to his head. Even if he did, this dried-up sow certainly wouldn't be in tow. Sally would.

His jaw tightened in fury. Had she left Bolton? He'd told Nancy to keep her ears open for shop gossip but so far, customers hadn't mentioned her. *Was* it her who Alice's girl and the stationmaster had met? If so, why would she return to Manchester? She had nothing there, no roots to lay claim to besides the workhouse.

His hand stilled on the button he was fastening. Had she somehow discovered . . . ? No, she couldn't have. The master assured him she never would.

'Did you hear me, love?'

At Nancy's sickly-sweet tone, he longed to knock her teeth down her throat. 'What you on about now?'

'I were saying, my kiddies will be all right with my neighbour a while longer; d'you want to get summat to eat and drink afore I make for Breightmet? I could murder a sup. Nellie will find us some grub so long as we've the brass; I've a few coppers, here. You want to, love?' she finished, soft-eyed with expectancy.

He shrugged. He might as well. He wouldn't get anything here, that was for sure. They hadn't had a scrap in for days. Dragging on his cap, he headed for the door.

As they slipped to the kitchen, he was grateful it was early. Alice would have a fit if she knew he'd had a woman back. He couldn't risk her slinging him out. It might be a hovel but it kept the chill from his bones and rain off his head.

Glancing at the sleeping children in the corner, he smirked in satisfaction then pushed Nancy into the muck-strewn alley.

'Shaun, mind out!' Tommy hauled him from a cart's path. 'Christ, wake up, will thee? An inch closer and you'd have been under their hooves.'

Shaun's smile, a fixture since waking, didn't waver. He scanned the length of Deansgate. 'Are there any round here?'

Their father scratched his chin. 'Aye, I've seen one up this end afore, I'm sure.'

As they continued in search of a carpenter, Tommy fell behind. He smiled when Arthur pulled the distracted Shaun from a pile of horse manure, glad he'd accompanied them. It not only offered an excuse not to meet Dolly but a much-needed diversion. Dear God, what he'd witnessed yesterday . . .

A low moan escaped when the vision returned to torture him. He didn't believe his eyes when she emerged from that pie shop, had laughed aloud, convinced he was the luckiest devil on the face of the earth. His sweet Sally had appeared, right there in front of him. *As had the good-looking man she'd clung to.*

He winced at the image now forever burned in his memory. Why was he foolish enough to hope she felt something, too? Rancour for the man she'd smiled up at, face alight with – was it love? – scorched his veins. Who the hell was he? Where and when did they meet? She'd left Spring Row not a fortnight ago!

If she'd rebuffed his declaration, of course, she'd have devastated him. But another man? That was too much; his heart had wilted. Staggering back to Victoria Station, he'd been thankful for the emptiness inside, considering the pain he knew would come once the shock wore off.

Throughout that day, she'd consumed his thoughts yet, surprisingly, sleep claimed him when his head met his pillow. But his dreams tormented him more than consciousness ever could.

He shook his head to dispel the cruel trick his mind played last night. He dreamed he and Sally were married. They were in bed, entwined in each other's arms. He stroked the dawn rays playing across her bare shoulders and she smiled. Yet when he made to kiss her, she turned away. And the man from the pie shop had entered, swept her up and carried her off . . .

Tommy quickened his pace to catch up with his father and brother. He was safe with others, felt forced to suppress his anguish. He wanted nothing more than to kneel by the roadside and howl his throat raw, but he couldn't. He *couldn't.* All he could do was try to forget her.

'All right, son?'

Wrenched back to the present, Tommy blinked back tears he hadn't realised had formed. 'Aye.'

His father frowned but before he could enquire further, Shaun spoke in his ear:

'Look. Over the road, there. It's Mr Goden.'

As they glanced around, the thickset man turned.

Then all hell broke loose.

Chapter 16

MONDAY ARRIVED SOONER than Sally would have liked. Yesterday, she'd spent a lovely afternoon with Maggie Benson, her mother and small twins. She'd taken along Jonathan and Shield. Flo and Harry had squealed in delight over the dog and played with him all day. The gentle beast would make Jonathan a fine friend when he was older.

Passing through the dreary streets to work, she smiled, recalling the warm welcome. Ellen had thanked her for defending her daughter, railed over the mill overlooker and his filthy ways and bemoaned that Maggie hadn't found further employment. Yet despite their problems, Maggie and Ellen were great company, had her in fits of laughter.

When leaving, Sally had promised to keep eyes and ears open for a position for her new friend. Along Davies Street, into Ridgeway Street, past St Philip's Church and on down Butler Street towards home, she'd racked her brains for a solution to the family's dilemma. And as she reached the corner of Bradford Street and Bradford Road, an idea had formed.

Now, hurrying on, she crossed her fingers that Pru would agree. There was no harm in asking – nothing gained, nothing lost.

Entering the shop, she gave her Pru best smile. 'Good morning, Miss Sharp.'

'Ah, Sally, good morning.' As had become habit, she patted the empty stool. 'You're in high spirits, dear.'

'I am, though I'm afraid you may deem the reason impudent.'

'Impudent? I'm intrigued.'

She took a deep breath. 'Miss Sharp, I have a friend in desperate need of work. Her name is Maggie Benson and until recently she was an employee of Brunswick Mill. Through no fault of hers, the overlooker dismissed her; she spurned his advances, nothing more. She's widowed with twins, and I, I wondered—'

'Whether I had a position for her?'

'She's trustworthy and hard-working. She'd prove most helpful in the shop. Just several hours a week would ease her financial woes.'

Pru frowned in contemplation. 'I must admit it is difficult managing this place alone. Naturally, some days are busier than others – Mondays and Saturdays are somewhat arduous. I don't suppose it would take long to train her . . .'

'Oh, it wouldn't,' Sally readily agreed. 'She's a lovely woman. You'll like her, Miss Sharp.'

Pru tapped a finger against her lips, eyes thoughtful. 'I don't doubt it, if you recommend her. I respect your judgement. It *would* be nice to have company in here . . . Very well. She may help out Mondays and Saturdays for the time being and if she proves satisfactory, I shall increase her hours. There will be a fortnight's trial period, you understand?'

Grinning, Sally nodded. 'Yes, Miss Sharp. Thank you.'

'Inform her that she starts on Saturday. We'll discuss wages and so forth then. Now, we'd better get to work.

The shop will be filling soon and Mother will be awake shortly.'

At the mention of Agnes, Sally's happiness dipped. 'How was she over the weekend? She wasn't . . . hasn't . . . ?'

'No, dear, no. She was no more difficult than usual.'

Sally couldn't contain a small sigh. 'I'm glad to hear that, Miss Sharp.'

Pru filled two cups. 'Here. Tea for you and Mother when she wakes.'

Another day with the pernicious old woman stretching before her, Sally squared her shoulders, needing all the resolve she could muster.

'Please don't mention Maggie to Mother. I shall tell her myself, soon.'

Smiling sadly in understanding, Sally climbed the stairs.

'The bastards! The rotten, stinking bastards!' Nancy fumed. She shifted the hot pie dish in her arms. 'You should've let me at them, lad. Cowards, that's what they are. Bleedin' cowards!'

Joseph stared ahead, mind clearly on the upcoming task.

'Who do they think they are, anyroad? And that young 'un what flew at thee, well, you can see he takes after his mam. She can be a vicious bitch at times, can Ivy. Then there's Arthur: why drag his son off you then thump you one hisself ?'

'For the love of Christ, will you shut that gob of yourn? Tha knows why. That bitch must of told them a pack of lies about me.'

She shook her head in disgust. 'Well, after what they did to you yesterday, I'd happily swing for the lot of them.' As she gazed at his bruised face, her heart contracted. 'It were reet thoughtful of you to push me into Nellie's when you spotted them. They'd have shouted their mouths to my father about us seeing each other. I do love thee, you know that, but I can't bring shame upon him.

'Once you've dealt with Sally, we can be together proper, can't we? Then you'll not have to stop at that filthy cottage of your sister's; we can live together. Aye, not long now and I can shout my love for thee, to anyone who'll listen, from the bloody rooftops.'

She ignored the usual prickle of unease when wondering what he planned for Sally. All she knew was he wanted rid of her for good. And more than anything, so did she. With her out of the way, they could be together for ever. She just didn't like dwelling on how he'd achieve it.

Skirting a small stream, Joseph continued through the field. He began to laugh and she smiled.

''Ere, what's tickled you?'

'Is that what you thought I did, pushed you out of sight for your reputation's sake?' Her smile slipped and he laughed harder. 'You're a stupid bitch at times, you are really. Aye, I didn't want them knowing you've been messing with me, you're right there. But it weren't for you, you daft sow.

'I did it because if all that lot you've thieved from your father's shop comes out, I don't want my name dragged into it. Folk will know you swiped it for me. That's why I did it, you silly bitch.' Snorting with mirth, he quickened his pace. 'Now move it, for God's sake. I've been waiting for this. I'm going to get so much pleasure from wrapping my hands round that scraggy throat.'

Gulping heartache, Nancy hurried after him. Yet doubt, for the first time, tugged at her. Staring at his broad back as he scaled a wall and dropped behind Spring Row, she bit her lip until she tasted blood. *He does love me. He does. He doesn't mean to be cruel, it's just his way,* she told herself firmly. She rested the pie dish on the wall and hauled herself up.

Joseph hopped from foot to foot. 'Hurry up and jump afore someone spots us. 'Ere, give me your hand.'

His large one closed around hers and she melted. 'Ta, love.'

When she stood beside him in the deserted back lane, he placed his hands on her shoulders and grinned. 'By God, I'm going to enjoy this.'

She pressed her lips to his. He pushed her against the wall and her body relaxed. She knew she'd been right; he did love her. Feeling him harden, she smiled inwardly. The thrill of danger turned him on something rotten and she knew just how to stoke the flames.

Crushing Nancy closer, Joseph sucked and bit her neck. But, returning his lips to hers, he gasped and stumbled back. For a split second the face before him had been Sally's.

'Love?'

He shook his head. What in hell had just happened?

'You all right? You've gone a shocking colour.'

'Eh? Aye. Get that dish and get moving.'

Rage made his blood boil. That bitch was sending him mad. She was constantly on his mind. He had to find her. And when he did, she'd suffer more than she could imagine.

'I'll be away, then.'

He nodded. 'You sure you know what to do?'

'Aye. Serve Father his meal then keep an eye out from the shop door.'

'And?'

'And if I see anyone making for Ivy's, sing as loud as I can to get your attention.'

'Are you certain that father of yourn won't think it queer you squalling all of a sudden?'

'Nay, I'm allus bursting into song. Love singing, I do. It sends him barmy, mind.' She smiled at the admission. 'I'll not let you down, love.'

'You'd better not. Mess this up and you'll regret it, girl.' Glancing to the cottage, his spine tingled. 'The owd bitch won't be so brave this time.'

'Scare the liver from her, lad. She'll soon talk. And don't fret, I'll be ready if I see anyone coming.'

When she'd rounded the corner, he looked left and right then sprinted to the Morgans'.

Pressing against the stone wall, he craned his neck to steal a glance through the kitchen window. He grinned to see that Ivy had her back to him, peeling vegetables by the fire. Silently, he eased open the door.

His fists tightened in hatred. She'd suffer for her meddling, his humiliation, for slapping his face. She'd suffer for harbouring Sally. And she'd suffer for her husband's and son's blows.

Baring his teeth, he crept across the flagged floor.

Midday seemed to take an age to arrive and Sally sent up a thank-you when Pru's voice drifted upstairs. She was home in no time and after feeding Jonathan, cuddled him tenderly. She treasured these snatched minutes before she had to leave him again.

Grace pushed a cup across and motioned to a plate of bread and butter. 'Eat up, lass.'

As she ate, Sally told her of Pru's decision. 'I cannot wait to tell Maggie the good news. I'm so glad Miss Sharp agreed.'

A mischievous smile played at Grace's mouth. 'So Con was right. He said no one could deny you, didn't he?'

She laughed softly. 'You can look at me like that all you like. I'm sure he'll make some woman very happy but—'

'It'll not be thee. Aye, you've said. Eeh, you want your bumps feeling, lass. He's a good 'un, he is, and thinks the world of thee; you can see it a mile off. Ed and Stan got on with him yesterday evening, didn't they? And you know I approve. Just don't rule him out altogether. I know you're still married but you don't know what the future holds. Tha might be a free woman one day—'

'And I'll remain one,' she murmured, all trace of laughter gone. 'I couldn't be with any man . . . like that . . . again.'

The memory of Con's kiss brought back a small smile. It was a good thing Grace didn't know of that; she'd plan to have the banns read!

'You still fret over that divilish bastard, don't you?' Sally lowered her gaze and Grace sighed. 'You're rid of him, love. He'll not hurt thee again. You've your family, here, now. You're not his to do with as he pleases, with no one to question him, not any more.

'Anyroad, you said yourself he don't know you're here. And if your Mrs Morgan don't tell him, he ain't likely to find out. It's time to start living, lass, to lay the demons to rest and look to the future – for that babby's sake as well as yours.'

Tears pricked her eyes. Sally wanted desperately to agree but couldn't. The horrors he'd put her through haunted her. Him finding her, snatching Jonathan – even killing her – were very real possibilities.

'Aunt Grace, I'm in heaven, now. Life before was hardly worth fighting for.' She stroked Jonathan's cheek. 'It is, now, and I've this one to thank. However, I cannot deny I'm terrified that fiend will find me. He'll be trying, you can be sure of that. I pray daily, until I run out of words, he doesn't succeed.'

Grace's eyes flashed with protective love. 'I half hope he does turn up, for he'd get his comeuppance, have no fear of that. Your uncle would thump his warped head in. Raging, Ed were, when I told him how that swine treated thee over the years. I'll say that for him, in all the years of our marriage, he's never once lifted a finger to me. Though by God, I've give him cause to many a time.' She chuckled. 'Aye, he's been a fair husband.

'I only wish things were better betwixt him and our Stan, but you can't have it all, can you, lass? Maybe in t' future . . . ? What I'm getting at is I want that for thee, to know the love of a good man. And as far as I'm concerned, you'll not find it with no one nicer than Con Malloy.'

Peggy's hacking cough saved Sally from responding. As Grace murmured over the skeletal figure, Sally pondered over Con. Could she take a chance on love? As Grace pointed out, she might indeed be a free woman one day. Would she rue it if she let him slip through her fingers?

The more she saw of him, the more she found to like, it was true. He'd revealed he ran a clothing stall at nearby Smithfield Market. The day they met, he'd been visiting Bolton market as he was considering opening a stall there, too, which his cousin would run. She knew if this cousin was anything like Con, it would be a roaring success.

Con had a way with both women and men; he'd had Ed and Stan in his palm last night. Grace's opinion of him also strengthened when he'd sat by Peggy's bedside and, with real tenderness, told her what a big brave colleen she was and promised to buy her a pretty ribbon for her hair.

And yet . . . She sighed. *Was* it her experience with Joseph or for an altogether different reason that she'd rebuffed his attentions?

'Oh! Sally, help me, lass!'

Thoughts of Tommy melted. She placed Jonathan in his basket and hurried to the bed. Peggy's mouth, nightdress and sheet were stained crimson. She grabbed a rag and dabbed at blood still trickling between the grey lips, while Grace rushed for a clean nightdress.

When the flow ceased, she lifted a small hand and kissed it. 'Rest, now, good girl. Shall I fetch Thunder?'

At Peggy's weak nod, she lifted Shaun's carving from the shelf. Though too frail for play, the girl found comfort in the wooden beast she'd lovingly named, would tuck it in beside her.

Sally watched the chest rise and fall laboriously. To see her withering away pained her dearly. She and Stan sat by her bedside each night, talking to her, holding her hand. Sally just wished she'd met her sooner, that she had memories of her before this hideous disease.

When Peggy was sleeping, she went in search of her aunt. As she passed Shield he looked up dolefully, as though sensing the child's plight, and she stroked his ear. She found Grace in the backyard, slumped against the mangle, Peggy's nightdress pressed to her mouth. Her muffled sobs tore at Sally. She wrapped her arms around her aunt with a sigh of despair, wishing she could take away her pain.

'She's dying, i'nt she? There's no use denying it any longer. My little girl's dying.'

There was nothing she could say. She held Grace tighter, her own heart breaking.

After throwing carrots into a pan by her feet, Ivy reached for the cabbage. Her back muscles twinged and she sighed, knowing she had a pile of clothes and sheets in steep to see to once she finished here.

When she felt the searing pain around her neck, her reaction was to scream but the pressure restricted it. She tried twisting around; the grip tightened and light spurted behind her eyes. She clawed the hands choking her but the world was fading . . .

Suddenly, they released her. Rearing back, she took an almighty breath and whirled around, but her streaming eyes blurred the room. When the voice cut through her splutters she didn't need to see to know to whom it belonged.

'That's just for starters, Poison Ivy.'

Bending double, she fetched up a stream of bile. She spotted the dropped cabbage and knife beneath her chair but moments later, his large hand snatched up the latter.

She drew a trembling hand across her mouth. 'How . . . I thought I'd locked . . . ?'

Sitting down at the table, Joseph smiled. He ran the blade's tip under his nail and wiped the dirt on his trousers. 'Tha needn't fret on that. It's what I'm to do now I'm in what's important.'

'You demented bastard, yer. I ain't scared of thee.' Glancing at the knife, Ivy's mouth ran dry but she lifted her chin. 'I'm warning you, Joseph. Get from my cottage and Spring Row on your two feet or I swear on all that's holy, you'll leave in a box.'

He threw his head back and laughed. 'I've gorra better idea. Tell me where that slut of mine is and I might let *you* live to see the morrow. I could've snapped your worthless neck just now and believe me, I'll not stop squeezing next time if you don't start talking. Where is she?'

'Out of your evil reach, that's where.' Despite her fear, she stepped closer. 'You'll not harm her again. Threaten me all you want. I'd sooner you gut me like a fish than tell you where she is.'

With a roar, he leapt up, grabbed the front of her dress and lifted her off her feet. 'Tell me!'

'Never! You don't frighten me, you bastard,' she bluffed. 'I ain't no slip of a lass and I don't bully easy. Go on, do your worst. You'll not get far. My Arthur and the lads will be home any minute.' She ran her gaze over his bruises. 'Did a right number on you, didn't they? They'll finish the job, mind, when they find you here.'

Grinning, he tossed her to the floor. 'Did you really think I'd swallow that, you stupid owd bitch? They're at the pit, will be for hours.' She looked away and he laughed. 'You see, I've been racking my brains forra way to get youse back. I were thinking on burning yon cottage to the ground while you slept, kill four birds with one stone, but that's not my style.

'You'll suffer, all right, but I want to see the terror on your faces while I do it. I'll pick you off one by one, torture the lot of you till you're begging me to put you out of your misery. I were going to bide my time but your husband and son, jumping me yesterday like the cowards they are, put paid to that. The time for waiting's over.'

Her blood ran cold at the eerily soft words but the threat to her family sparked fresh bravado. Lunging, she landed a punch to his mouth. He staggered back and she leapt forward and snatched the abandoned knife from the table.

Panting with pure fury, he charged. She jabbed the blade at his face. Lightning fast, he grabbed her wrist and twisted. She fought like a raging bull but the pain of the bone close to snapping was too intense. To her horror, the knife clattered to the floor.

Joseph threw his hands around Ivy's neck, bent her over the table and squeezed with all his might.

'You're first to go but don't fret,' he hissed, pressing his face to hers, 'your family will be joining you shortly. I'll find Sally without your help. And when I do, I'll watch the life drain from *her* worthless body, an' all.'

As her flailing limbs stilled, singing rang out from the row.

His mouth fell open. He flung Ivy's inert body aside and bolted. Knocking at the front door sounded as he reached the back one. He scrambled through into the lane.

Sprinting away, he smiled jubilantly as the scream of Ivy's visitor filled the air.

Chapter 17

AGNES WAS IN a foul mood. For two hours, she'd lain silently, facing the wall. She'd refused a bathing, rejected breakfast, and the tea Sally brought up upon her arrival sat untouched by the bedside.

Itching with boredom, Sally shifted on the hard chair. Though tempted to ask what ailed Agnes, her expression deterred her.

She'd wondered whether she'd annoyed her by returning late yesterday, Peggy's incident having prolonged her break, but dismissed this. Agnes wasn't one to hold back; she'd have made her feelings known immediately. That perhaps she knew about Maggie, she also rejected; Pru hadn't mentioned anything earlier, was her quietly cheerful self.

Glancing for the hundredth time at the clock, she sighed inwardly. Lunchtime was a while away and this inactivity would only prolong the delay until its arrival. Her eyes flicked to the bed. Agnes wasn't talkative at the best of times but this brooding silence was unnerving. In desperation, she tried again.

'Would you like some fresh tea, Mrs Sharp?'

Agnes grunted refusal.

'I could read to you, if you'd like?' Sally persisted. 'Or perhaps fetch you a bite—?'

'How much does your child mean to you, girl?'

The unexpected question, and its nature, took Sally by surprise. 'Why, he means the world to me, Mrs Sharp. He's my entire reason for living.'

'When you are parted, do you pine for him?'

'Indeed. I know he's well cared for, but still—'

'You're bereft in his absence?'

'Yes, yes, I am.' She waited. Silence. Curiosity got the better of her. She crossed to the bed. 'Is something wrong, Mrs Sharp? You seem somewhat—'

'She was such a tiny baby. Such a delicate scrap of life. I didn't think she'd survive the night but she proved me wrong.' Agnes turned and her eyes were unusually soft. 'Did you have a difficult time bearing your child?'

A smile touched Sally's lips. 'I did. But I had the most wonderful help at hand that anyone could wish.'

'I shall remember it until my dying breath. The weather was atrocious; it fitted the occasion perfectly. Never in my life had I prayed as fervently as that night. Never had I begged the Almighty's help, nor needed it as much. I waited, waited, watching that chest rise and fall. And as the new day dawned, I knew He would not claim her. My pleading had come to nothing.' Sighing deeply, the old woman closed her eyes.

She gazed at her, aghast. 'Why, Mrs Sharp? Why would you wish such a wicked thing?'

The answer was like a whisper on the breeze. 'It matters not. None of it matters, now.' Suddenly, her features returned to normal, the maudlin look leaving her eyes. From beneath the bedclothes, she extracted an envelope sealed with a black wax stamp. 'Would you deliver this when you leave at lunchtime? The address is not far: number forty, Great Ancoats Street.'

'Yes, Mrs Sharp.'

Agnes handed it over with a curt nod. 'Now, I think I shall have that tea. Make haste, girl. No dawdling.'

On the walk home, Sally still reeled from the confession. She'd heard and seen enough the past week to gauge her employer – today's behaviour was out of character.

To spare Pru's feelings, she didn't mention the conversation and had carried out her mother's request with barely a word. When she'd returned to the room, Agnes's expression held no trace of remembrance, and Sally's bewilderment grew. The rest of the morning passed as usual, and now she half wondered whether she'd imagined the incident.

Then there was the letter. As instructed, she'd delivered it before heading home. A maid had received it without a word. What it contained, who the recipient was, she didn't know; the envelope lacked an addressee. The oddness of it all made her head ache.

Grace and her close friend and neighbour, Winnie Knox, greeted her warmly. After feeding Jonathan, she joined them at the table. She inclined her head to Peggy's bed. 'How is she, Aunt Grace?'

Grace raised her hands in a helpless motion. 'Like I've just been telling Winnie, no better, no worse. She's peaceful, and for that I'm grateful.'

Sally smiled at the rotund woman beside her. 'It's nice to see you, Mrs Knox.'

'Aye, lass, and thee.' Leaning in, Winnie added in a loud whisper, 'How's things going with owd Sharp? She not tried clouting you one, yet?'

'Winnie!' spluttered Grace.

'What? I'm only asking.' She folded her arms beneath her mountainous bust. 'Queer pair, them two. I don't know how tha stomachs it. I'd be frightened to death alone with them all day.'

Pushing the morning's event from her mind, Sally smiled. She liked Winnie a great deal. She'd been a pillar of support to the family since Peggy became ill.

'It's going well, Mrs Knox. My friend starts work in the shop on Saturday, too.' She smiled again, recalling Maggie's delight yesterday upon hearing the news. 'Mrs Sharp doesn't seem so bad.' The blatant lie tasted bitter, but she had no choice. Troubles aplenty plagued her aunt as it was.

Winnie's chins wobbled as she nodded. 'Aye, well, just mind her, lass. If she does try owt, thump the bugger and run straight home.'

Grace hooted with laughter. 'Run straight . . . ? She's norra babby, Winnie. Eeh, I don't know, the things you come out with. *You're* bloomin' barmy, never mind them two.'

'Well, you know what I mean. Anyroad, she'd do well to, regardless, with that madman on t' loose.'

They fell silent, expressions sober, and Sally's smile died. 'Madman?'

'It's awful, lass, awful. I don't know what this world's coming to. It's a good job you left when you did.' Grace turned to Winnie, who nodded gravely. 'I said to you when you told me, didn't I, said it's a good job our Sally came here? It don't bear thinking in, does it?'

'It don't, Grace.'

Sally's face creased in bemusement. 'I'm sorry, has something happened in Bolton?'

'Eeh, it's terrible, lass. A wench were strangled yesterday – in her own kitchen, by all accounts, while her family were out at work. What if the swine what's done it makes his way up here? I hope they catch whoever's responsible, quick, and make him swing. Shocking, it is.'

'Goodness, that's terrible!'

'Our Fanny's husband were saying when he arrived home this morning,' Winnie continued. 'His mam dwells in Bolton and he were visiting her forra few days, for she's not long for this world, poor wench. He said the attack's on everyone's lips; no news travels faster than bad.

'He don't know the ins and outs, like, but whatever's gone on, it's shocking.' Frowning, she drummed the table with podgy fingers. 'Where did I say it occurred, Grace? Summer . . . summat or other?'

'Nay, not Summer, Spring. Spring Row.'

'*No . . .*' Sally reared back, mouth stretched in a silent scream.

Grace and Winnie's confused cries rang in her ears, then blackness consumed her.

'Now what d'you think you're about?' Brows knitted, Martha jerked her head to the fireside. 'Get your arse in that chair, Ivy Morgan, and stay put. I told thee last night, I said don't be doing nowt, that I'd do whatever were needed this afternoon.'

Ivy suppressed a sigh. Though aware that her friend was trying to help, Martha was beginning to get on her nerves. If not so weary, she'd have told her – nicely but firmly – to bugger off home. She couldn't stand this idleness, however much everyone insisted.

Martha raised Ivy's chin and peered at the angry welts. 'I'll give them another bathe in a minute. They still sore?'

'Aye,' she admitted, 'but don't tell Arthur or the lads I said. They fret as it is.'

Sitting at the table, Martha took over peeling the vegetables. 'D'you know, the day all this began, yon Arthur flew at that bugger, Goden, outside this here cottage. The coward scarpered but he swore to me, Arthur did, he'd have his day with him. Now, I know you're worried, wench, but it's been coming, has this.'

'He'll not let this go; it's gone too far for that. He blames hisself, you know, said if him and our Tommy hadn't thumped Joseph Sunday, this mightn't have happened. I don't believe that. It'd been brewing since Sally came. I knew he'd be back. He's not someone to walk away. He wanted revenge and got it.'

'Aye, and Arthur will get his the night. Tommy still set on going with him?'

'Oh, is he. I've never seen the lad as he were last night. Well, you saw yourself. I thought he'd explode with rage.'

Reaching for another potato, Martha nodded. 'I were bubbling, an' all, wench. The state that Jenkins lass were in, I thought he'd done for thee. It's a bloody good job she called when she did. It don't bear thinking on what would've happened if she hadn't interrupted the swine.' At Ivy's frown, she clicked her tongue. 'I'm sorry. I don't mean to be maudlin.'

'Nay, you're right. I owe my life to that lass. And to think . . .' Colour touched her cheeks. 'I've allus believed she weren't good enough for my Tommy, foolish sod that I am.'

'Well, I'd say you're stuck with her, Ivy. Anyone with half an eye can see she's fair smitten. She don't seem a bad lass.'

They lapsed into companionable silence. Gazing across the hills through the window, Ivy's frown returned as she recalled Dolly's words yesterday. The lass said she'd had to come, was worried as she hadn't seen Tommy in a while. What was going on? He clearly hadn't invited her to dinner, nor met her Saturday. Why lie? Where on earth *had* he been?

Her hand drifted to her neck. That bastard. What would follow? He'd said he'd pick them off. Was Arthur next? Her sons? Meeting those hate-filled eyes yesterday, the world slipping, she really thought it was the end. She'd woken, in more pain than she'd ever known, to Martha and Dolly cradling her, faces awash with tears.

She smiled, couldn't deny Martha had been an angel. She'd refused to let them send for the doctor so, with gentle care, Martha tended Ivy herself. Her friend had also calmed down Dolly, tidied the room and prepared a meal for the men. She'd known food would be the last thing on their minds, but Martha had meant well. She was deeply grateful for her support.

'That's the veg done. Shall I brew some tea?'

Ivy nodded. As Martha bustled around the fire, her thoughts returned to last night. Pandemonium erupted upon her husband and sons' return. Their anguish and fury were a terrible sight. Arthur made back for the door, intent on finding Joseph and smashing his head to a pulp, but Martha had stopped him, pointing out that his wife needed him.

He'd relented but insisted no one inform the police. He'd dole out Joseph's punishment. And it would be harsher than what any court in the land could decree.

'I want to say again how grateful I am to thee for stopping Arthur,' Ivy murmured as Martha poured tea. 'There's no telling what would've happened with the rage he were in.'

'He'll still give him the beating of his life when he finds him, Ivy – yon Tommy, an' all. He near murdered his mam, wench. You can't blame him for wanting to go with Arthur.'

She heaved a sigh. 'I'm frightened to death of what will happen. Don't get me wrong, that bastard deserves all he gets; I'd have gutted him meself given the chance. But if they finish up doing for him . . . They'll not swing for him,' she ground out. 'I were glad upon hearing they'd given him a thumping, but this . . . this is different. The murder in their eyes last night . . . I'm frightened, Martha.'

'I know. Were it my Reg and our lads, I'd feel the same. But they need to do this, their way. As Arthur said, there's no use going to the police, for that swine will no doubt have an alibi. It'd be your word against his. When all's said and done, you were the only one to see him. You have to let your men do what they need to. You've no choice, not with this.'

'They'll be home from the pit, soon. Mother of God, I pray they don't go too far. Happiness filled this cottage when that carpenter took our Shaun on. Over the bloody moon, we were; I didn't think owt could dampen my mood. Goden's ruined that. He's put a black cloud over my family, and after this night it'll only darken.'

'Eeh, wench, now don't you cry,' Martha chided softly when tears welled in her eyes. 'This ain't the Ivy I know. Don't you let him crush that spirit of yourn, don't you dare. Once he's got his, later, it'll be over.

'You've much to be happy about, and not just with young Shaun. There'll be a wedding to look forward to soon, you mark my words; all what's occurred will no doubt bring Tommy and that Jenkins lass closer. This time next year, there might be the patter of little feet, just think on that. All this, it'll be long forgotten.'

With effort, Ivy smiled. There *was* much to look forward to. Shaun started his carpentry work shortly, and Tommy . . . Would he and Dolly wed? From what the dairymaid said, something was afoot. When this business with Joseph blew over, she'd sit him down for a good talk, she determined.

'*I'll find Sally without your help. And when I do, I'll watch the life drain from her worthless body, an' all.*'

The haunting threat continued to plague her. She just prayed Sally would stay in Manchester, where she was safe. If she ever returned and he discovered her . . .

The consequences didn't bear thinking about.

'Sally, this is madness! Ed, will you tell her it's madness?'

Her uncle reached for his pipe. 'I agree, but it's her decision.'

Grace clicked her tongue and turned back to Sally. 'Please, lass, don't go. It mightn't be Mrs Morgan or owt to do with that husband of yourn. Whoever she is, she survived, so there's no need for you to go. Tha can't just up and leave. What about work? The babby?'

Sally's chin lifted: her mind was made up. 'Aunt Grace, I'm going. I understand your fears but I must. Mrs Morgan saved my life. I *must* make sure it's not her. I have Miss Sharp's consent to take tomorrow off work and, as you know, Mrs Knox shall ask Fanny to wet-nurse Jonathan.' Glancing at Ed's and Stan's worried frowns, she sighed. 'I have to do this.'

Grace turned away in frustration. 'You'll be like a lamb to the slaughter, don't you see? If this is his revenge for them helping thee, who d'you think he'll be on t' prowl for now? Please, don't go. I'll not lose you again.'

Sally forced herself not to rush to comfort her; Grace would only up her pleas until she conceded. She couldn't risk that. She must return to Breightmet. If Ivy had almost lost her life for saving hers and Jonathan's . . . Dear God, she'd never forgive herself. That woman was her saviour. She'd never live in peace until she knew.

Quiet weeping filled the kitchen and her heart ached with contrition. She hated seeing Grace upset – more so, knowing she'd caused it. She'd inadvertently sparked another row, too. Unwilling to risk taking Jonathan, she'd been grateful for Winnie's suggestion that Fanny feed him, but Grace was appalled and had blasted her friend for encouraging the 'bloody senseless plan'.

Grace wiped her face with her apron, eyes suddenly bright. 'If you must go, take Con. He seems the handy sort if you do cross paths with that husband of yourn.'

She was aghast. 'I cannot do that!'

'He'd agree if you asked, I'm sure.'

'Aunt Grace, I cannot journey with Con unchaperoned. What on earth would people say?'

'Take Ed, then. He'd give the divil a good hiding if you did see him. Will you, Ed? Will you go with her? Please?'

Her uncle opened his mouth but Sally got in first. 'Uncle Ed has work in the morning. He couldn't possibly take time off and I wouldn't let him.' Sighing, she wrapped her arms around Grace. 'I know you're worried and I hate myself for putting you through this but please, please don't make this harder for me than it is already.

'I don't expect you to understand but for my peace of mind I must do this, and do it alone. This is my and Joseph's mess and I'm damned if anyone else will suffer for it.'

'But Sally—'

'I'll take Shield. He's all the protection I could need,' she cut in gently. 'You have my word, Aunt Grace. As soon as I see with my own two eyes that Mrs Morgan's well, I shall come straight back.' She turned to her uncle and cousin. 'Do either of you know anyone with a cart who would take me in the morning? The train scared the life from me last time; I couldn't bear it again. I've money to pay them.'

Stan shook his head but Ed, avoiding Grace's eye, nodded. 'Aye. I'll call on him when I've had some grub.' His gaze softened. 'You watch yourself the morrow, d'you hear? I'd accompany thee if I could, you know that, don't you? I can't shirk work, lass, not with our Peggy's medicine to buy on top of everything else.'

'Oh, of course, I understand. Thank you.'

Admitting defeat, Grace trudged to the fire to begin the evening meal.

Sally strove to calm her thumping heart. Would Joseph discover her? Pure loathing consumed her at the thought of him. Would Shield be adequate protection? Should she heed her aunt's advice, send Con a message?

Fear of inciting gossip *had* been good reason to reject the suggestion. But deep down, as much as she hated admitting it, she knew her reluctance to have the Irishman accompany her was due to Tommy. She didn't want him believing she and Con . . . Not that he'd care, but still . . .

Heat flooded her face. However hard she fought the memory of him, of her body's response to his touch, it crept to mind often, filling her with longing and shame.

Now, as well as the terror of Joseph discovering her, of Ivy having suffered at his hands, a different one took root – fear of being unable to conceal her feelings for the man she could never have.

It hadn't taken Tommy and his father long to discover where Alice Russell dwelled.

They received information at the first inn at which they enquired. Whether folk disliked Joseph as much in Deansgate as in Breightmet, or the shillings slackened the tongues, they neither knew nor cared. They had the address. That's what mattered.

Passing down the ruinous street to Chapel Alley, they garnered mixed reactions. Prostitutes and customers, preoccupied in doorways, paid them little attention. Some doorways appeared empty but as they neared, wan-faced women sidled out, touting for business.

Bands of savage-looking men peered from the shadows, likely deliberating whether these strangers' pockets contained anything worth stealing. But Tommy knew their murderous expressions – if his was anything like his father's – coupled with their thick muscles, would deter them from trying. Plenty of ale-soaked sots spilling from inns, later, would make easier targets.

Scouring the decrepit cottages for number thirteen, he clenched his fists. Lying awake last night, he'd thought long and hard what he'd do to Joseph. He'd make him pay for what he'd done. Fury like no other engulfed him – interwoven with crippling guilt. He could have prevented this. If he'd told his family what George Turner had revealed, they would have been prepared. Too wrapped up in Sally, he hadn't thought of their safety.

Because of him, his mother had almost died. And to top it all, he'd failed Sally, too. His own wants overshadowed the purpose of his trip to Manchester. Was she next? Would Joseph do to her as he'd done to his mother?

His step faltered. The need for her, to love her, protect her, burned just as brightly, until he truly suspected he was going mad.

When his father pointed to a door, Tommy cleared his mind. He must remain focused. Sunday proved Joseph to be the devil they knew he was. He was damned if he'd let him off as lightly this time. This beating would be for his mother, who had never harmed anyone in her life, who had nurtured and cared for him always. Who had nearly died at the hands of the bastard behind this door.

He wanted revenge for her. And he wanted it for Sally. Whatever happened this night, he'd gladly face the consequences.

'Right, lad, remember what I said. Give him the beating of his life but don't lose it. He's not worth dancing at the end of a rope.'

Nodding, Tommy made to thump the door but Arthur stopped him.

'I'm serious, here. You need to keep a level head. Last Sunday . . . I've never seen thee like that.' A curious frown appeared. 'The venom in your eyes when you looked upon him fair shocked me, it did.'

Tommy was unable to meet his gaze. Seeing the man legally bound to the woman *he* loved more than life, a ferocious mist had descended. His feet had taken on a life of their own and propelled him across the road.

He still remembered the feel of Joseph's face meeting his fist. He'd landed a blow to his cheekbone, another to his mouth. If his father hadn't dragged him off, he wouldn't have stopped until the cobbles ran red, so extreme was the swell of loathing.

'Look, I know you were angry, lad; I bloody were, an' all,' his father added. 'After dragging you off, I were willing to leave it, figured he'd got what he deserved.

But when he started spewing insults about your mam, well, that's why he gorra thump off me, an' all. It's a good job he scarpered when he did.

'What I'm saying is this: that bastard knows how to rile us. We must play it different the night. He'll suffer, all right, and tha can have the pleasure of delivering the first blow, but we must keep our calm. Understand?'

'Aye.'

Arthur continued staring at him. Slowly, his eyes widened with a mixture of surprise and horror. 'You're in love with that lass, ain't you?'

Tommy could only blink.

'Your reaction to Goden . . . I *knew* there were more to it than met the eye. That's where your mind's been at for weeks, in't it?'

'I . . .' Words failed him. It was pointless denying it.

'We'll talk about this later. Let's get on with what we came to do. Now, remember what I said. Keep your calm.'

Glaring at Alice's door through tears of shame and despair, Tommy lifted a fist and thumped hard.

The smell emitted when it creaked open brought grimaces to them both. They pushed past the slovenly-looking woman without a word.

''Ere, what the divil's your game? Who d'you think youse are, barging in here?'

Ignoring her, they peered about. With no fire in the grate and only the guttering light from a single candle on the table, it took them a moment to become accustomed to the gloom. A man rose from the fireside chair and Tommy lunged. Grabbing his throat, he slammed him against the wall.

'What the—!'

'Shut your *stinking* trap. Did you really think you'd get away with it? Did you?' he shouted, grip tightening.

The woman screeched and rushed forward but Arthur blocked her path. 'What's *he* done?' she squalled, trying to claw past.

'What's he done? I'll tell thee what he's—'

'It's not him.'

'Son?'

'It's not him.'

Squinting at the figure, Arthur swore under his breath. 'Where is he?'

'Who?'

'Don't try me, woman. Where's that bastard, Goden?' He turned to the coughing man, who was clutching his throat. 'We know he's dwelling here. Tell us where he is or by God, you'll have more than a sore neck.'

'Listen 'ere, youse two. I don't know what's afoot but if it's our Joseph you're after, you're out of luck. We've seen nowt of him for days. You ask my husband. We ain't seen him, have we, Harold?'

Harold glanced at them in turn then shook his head.

Disgust filled Tommy. He'd noticed the warning glint in the wife's eye. How could they protect the evil swine?

'Well? What you still doing here? Clear off afore you get the poker across your skulls. He ain't here so you'll have to try elsewhere, won't you?' She swung the door wide. 'Go on, bugger off.'

Tommy brought his palms down on the littered table. 'How can you harbour that bastard after what he's done?'

'Son . . . Christ's sake.'

He followed his father's gaze. On a pallet, shapes shifted. Candlelight danced across small faces, white with fear. A child rose, skittered across and wrapped her arms around Harold's legs.

''Ere, sit your arse back down, you.'

Ignoring her mother, she gazed up. 'My uncle ain't here, mister, honest. Please, don't hurt Father again.'

Tommy drew a hand across his mouth then turned to Arthur, who nodded.

'This ain't the place, lad. He'll get what's coming to him but not here, not like this.'

'That's it, go on, get from my home,' Joseph's sister jeered as they pushed past.

'You'd best start praying for that foulness you call a brother. Me and my lad, we'll find him.'

Her smirk slipped at the sheer venom in Arthur's tone. Then she slammed the door in their faces.

'What now?' Tommy ground out as they turned back into Deansgate. 'He can't get away with this!'

'And he won't. I swore weeks ago I'd have my day with him and have it I will. He can't hide for ever.'

'They gone?'

Alice let the scrap of curtain fall. 'Aye.'

'What the hell were that about?'

Reaching the bottom of the stairs, Joseph shrugged at his brother-in-law. He eased into his chair and rested his feet on the hearth. 'How should I know?'

'How . . . how should *you* know? They were here for thee; course you must bloody well know!'

'That bitch Sally's told them a pack of lies, ain't she?' He turned to the window and grinned. 'You told them good and proper, our Alice.'

It was her turn to shrug. 'You're my brother. Bastards, who do they think they are, barging in like that? I *would've* wrapped that poker round their brains, an' all.' Her eyes narrowed when Harold shook his head. 'What's wrong with thee?'

'What's wrong with me? *What's wrong with me?* I near had the liver kicked out of me because of him. I reckon they would've, an' all, but for our Lily. You want to wise up, you do. He's up to summat, he is. Folk don't come baying for your blood for nowt.'

Joseph laughed and it grew in pitch when Alice stormed to her husband.

'Look at the poor bugger's face. He's already black and blue.' She tapped her temple. 'That pair ain't full shillings. What did you want me to do, let him get another thumping for what his whore of a wife's been spouting? He's my brother—'

'And I'm your husband! I'm telling you, summat's afoot, here. And what in hell's there to laugh at, Joseph? Kin or no, I'll not have you fetching trouble to my door, d'you hear? Whatever you've done, you sort it – and quick.'

Joseph grinned at his sister. 'He's as barmy as that pair.'

'Aye. Happen I should've let them give him a pasting. It might've knocked some sense into him.'

Harold gazed at them, snatched up his jacket and cap and slammed from the cottage.

Joseph settled deeper in the lumpy seat. 'Ah, ignore him, he'll calm down. He's right about one thing, mind. The lass did well, there. I reckon they'd not have let it lie but for her.'

Alice lumbered to the chair opposite. 'First thing she's done right in her life, silly bitch.' She picked at a stump of black tooth, her eyes turning thoughtful. 'D'you think they'll be back?'

Fear lurked in his voice, belying his nonchalant shrug. 'They'll not find me.'

'I'm surprised Harold didn't put two and two together. Folk are talking, you know. It's spread from row to street to bloody village, by all accounts. You're certain the owd 'un's well?'

'Aye, Nancy said last night.'

'Right, well, keep your head low. Bide your time. You'll find the bitch, somehow.'

His knuckles turned white as he imagined slamming them into Sally's face. Where *was* she? Obviously, Ivy knew, but he'd get no joy from that quarter, now. He couldn't risk returning, not with Arthur and that son thirsty for his blood. Frustration burned in him. He closed his eyes.

Keep running, whore. Keep running, he inwardly seethed. *You'll slip up eventually and I'll find you.*

Alice frowned when his eyes sprang open. 'What's up?'

'I'm wondering if it'd be worth me going to Manchester. Happen the workhouse master . . . ?' His enthusiasm died with his words.

'What about him?'

Stroking week-old stubble, he sighed. 'It's unlikely . . . Maybe, just maybe, he's seen her. If yon lass did see her at the market, she'll not have returned to Manchester without good reason.'

'What, you reckon she's found out about—?'

'The master assured me she'd not, but . . . If she *has*, she'd have been back to Manchester like a shot.' Excitement stirred again. 'You think it's worth me going?'

'You'll lose nowt from trying. When will you leave?'

As her uncle discussed his scheme with her mother, Lily shoved her fingers in her ears to block out their cackles. She snuggled closer to the twins and, for the hundredth time, wished the lady on the market had taken her with her.

Chapter 18

TWO INCIDENTS WERE to scupper Sally's plans.

The first occurred during the early hours. The strained atmosphere the night before worsened after the evening meal when, true to his word, Ed secured a cart. Upon his return, the household fell into uneasy silence. The lamplighter had barely passed when, unable to bear it another moment, she'd feigned a headache and escaped to the next room.

She was still awake when sounds of the family retiring filtered through. Long afterwards, sleep was no nearer; the impending journey made it impossible.

When a whimper reached her, her exhausted brain hardly registered it. At the second, her senses awoke. She slipped from the horsehair sofa, padded to the kitchen and squinted about. All was still. Believing her sleep-deprived mind was playing tricks, she was about to turn when a black form shifted by Peggy's bed.

Thinking it was her aunt, she made to tiptoe back next door. She froze when the doleful moan, more insistent now, echoed again.

As Sally approached, another noise replaced it – rattling gasps she hadn't heard across the room.

Surprise halted her step and she saw the figure wasn't Grace, but Shield. He whined again and, shushing him, she peered at the bed. The jagged breaths were coming from her cousin.

She rushed to the chair and shook her aunt's shoulder. 'Aunt Grace, wake up. Peggy . . .'

Grace's eyes opened instantly. When she crossed to the bed and dropped to her knees, Shield sloped to the corner, soft brown eyes never leaving Peggy.

'I'm sorry, I didn't hear you, I— Oh my . . . Peggy, can you hear me? Where does it hurt? Speak to me, lass.' Her daughter answered with a racking cough and she clutched Sally's arm. 'Waken our Ed and Stan, tell them to come quick.' Sobs burst forth but she gulped them back. 'Go, Sally. Go now.'

Nodding blindly, Sally darted from the room.

Within seconds, four figures huddled around the bed. Ed and Stan's murmurs to Peggy mingled with the breaths bubbling in her tortured lungs, and Grace's crying.

Sally brought down Thunder and laid it beside her cousin. She swallowed hard, desperate to stem her own grief for her family's sake, but it was useless. She burst into tears.

Below purple-shadowed eyes, twin spots of colour burned high on Peggy's cheeks and despite her shivers, beads of perspiration glistened on her forehead. She grew weaker, each breath shallower than the last.

Ten minutes later, she died in her mother's arms.

After a moment of stunned silence, a cacophony of noise erupted. Anguished shrieks punctured the dawn, Shield adding to them as he howled at the ceiling.

Sally threw her arms around Grace's neck and hugged the screaming woman tightly. Stan bent double with sobs. Without hesitation, Ed pulled him into his arms.

The following hours were a fog of grief-hazed activity. Neighbours, alerted by the cries, flitted in to pay their respects, Sally brewed endless pots of tea, and the hum of subdued voices and quiet weeping permeated the house.

The sun was high above the grey rooftops when Winnie arrived. Sally saw her slip into the kitchen, red-rimmed eyes tinged with uncertainty – probably owing to Grace's tirade yesterday. Over her aunt's head, she beckoned her across.

Still clutching Peggy, Grace rocked back and forth, dry-eyed, staring at nothing.

Winnie touched her shoulder. 'Oh, wench . . . I'm so sorry.'

Grace frowned down. She traced a finger along her daughter's marble-white cheek. 'I want to die. Help me, Winnie. Make this pain go away.' She started to shake, then a torturous cry ripped from her.

Swallowing her own tears, Sally moved aside and Winnie took her place. As the friends hugged and wept, she peered around. As was customary, they had left the curtains drawn and though several candles flickered, it was difficult to see through the gloom.

She spotted Stan by the window, two neighbours comforting him. Her gaze swept the opposite side. Hunched against the door frame, her uncle stood alone, arms wrapped around himself. She could almost feel his devastation as he watched his wife. His eyes were deep with longing, as though he'd give anything to be the one holding her. They then rested on Stan and she sensed the same burning urge.

Before Sally could reach him, he took a last look at Stan and slipped from the room.

*

After pouring out her grief to Winnie, Grace rallied. She'd finally released her daughter and when the neighbours trickled home, she and Sally laid her out. Tears flowing, they washed her emaciated body and dressed her in a clean nightdress. Afterwards, Grace whispered she was in a better place, free from pain. This seemed to bring her some comfort.

Evening was drawing in. Sally cradled Jonathan by the dead fire, which they wouldn't light before laying Peggy to rest. She glanced at Shield by her feet. He seemed to feel her passing, too. It was as though he'd sensed the child's life ebbing. If not for his cries, she might have died alone.

Bending to scratch his ear, Sally sighed, mind and body exhausted.

'Would you throw a meal of sorts together, lass?' murmured Stan. 'None of us feel like eating but it'll be there if we do.'

'Of course.'

'I'll take Jonathan.' As he held him, Stan's eyes clouded. 'I'm scared,' he whispered. 'My family's disappearing around me. First our Peggy, and you'll be making other plans for Bolton. I've a feeling you'll not come back, that you'll send for Jonathan and we'll not see you again.

'Things ain't so bad since you came. Mam's been happier than I've seen her in a long time. I couldn't bear you leaving, now, never seeing you both again.'

'Oh, Stan.' Dropping into a chair, Sally rested her cheek against his. 'That will never happen. This is my home. Here, with my family.'

'You mean you're not going to Bolton?'

She chose her words carefully so as not to upset him. 'I still need to make a visit, but that's all it shall be. I know you all think I'm mad but I must. They were so good to me.' She glanced at Grace by the bed, stroking Peggy's hand. 'However, I cannot leave Aunt Grace, yet.'

Also watching, Stan dashed away a tear. 'I hate the thought of leaving her alone the morrow.'

Sally nodded. She'd harboured the same concern.

'My master understood when I called in t' baker's, earlier, gave me a stale loaf to fetch home and the day off but I've to be in the morrow. Father's won't allow him time, the sod. I'll not be surprised if he gets the push for not showing today. You due in the morrow, an' all?'

'Yes. There's Jonathan, too. I cannot burden Aunt Grace with him, now. Perhaps Mrs Knox would sit in—?'

'I'll be all right.'

They blushed at Grace overhearing them.

'You'll leave the babby with me, as you allus do, and I'll not hear another word.' She looked around and frowned. 'Where's Ed?'

'I saw him leave earlier, Aunt Grace. Maybe he needed to be alone a while.'

'Aye, mebbe.'

Sally crossed to a cupboard, took out a half-loaf and began on the meal. She was cutting it into thin slices when the front door rattled. She turned, but her gentle smile froze at the sight of her uncle.

Swaying in the doorway, he glared at them in turn and her stomach tightened. Something unpleasant was coming. After years of experience, her intuition was razor sharp; it hadn't proved wrong yet.

Ed ambled to the bed, dropped to his knees and covered his face with his hands. His sobs filled the kitchen and Grace rushed to him. She put her arms around him but he shrugged them off savagely.

'Leave me be, woman.'

'Ed—'

'Leave me be!'

Her face crumpled and Sally bit her lip. Stan passed Jonathan to her and rose. She caught his sleeve. 'No, Stan—'

'It's all right, Sally.'

She held her breath when he laid a hand on her uncle's shoulder. Ed's back stiffened and from the dread in Grace's eyes, it was clear she shared her concerns. He could barely contain his bitterness for Stan at the best of times – consumed with grief and drink, he was capable of doing, and saying, anything.

Suddenly, Ed leapt up, lip curled in a snarl, and Stan stepped back in surprise. 'Father?'

'Don't you call me that. *Never* call me that, not ever again, d'you hear? Only one child in this house had that right and she's laying cowd in that bed.'

Grace's gasp shattered the silence. She gripped the hair at her temples. 'Nay . . . What have you *done*?'

Stan whimpered, and anger burst through Sally. She placed Jonathan in the basket and ran to him. Devastation screamed from his eyes and her fury, which she'd always struggled to contain when witnessing injustice, erupted.

'I never had you down as a bad man, Uncle Ed, but that . . . How could you be so cruel?' she cried. 'My heart is breaking for your loss. To imagine what you're going through . . . However, people make mistakes. Aunt Grace shall suffer hers the rest of her days, but Stan? What sin has he committed? From the moment he was born, he was your son. He's *your* son, Uncle Ed, in every way that matters.'

'You . . . *you* knew?'

Breath caught in her throat. She turned slowly. 'Stan, I'm so sorry. I gave my word—'

'Nay!' Wild-eyed, he turned to Grace. 'Tell me they're lying. Please, Mam!'

The fight left Ed. Like Shield, earlier, he lifted his face and howled. 'Stan . . . Lord, what have I done?'

Her cousin's expression turned empty. Sally fumbled for his hand but he snatched it away.

'Everything makes sense. The way you've allus treated me . . . All my life, I've tried to make you proud, make you love me.'

'I do love thee! I loved thee the moment tha were born. But I can see him. I *allus* see *him* when I look at you. And you,' Ed added to Grace. 'I watched youse earlier, breaking your hearts in front of me, and I couldn't . . .' He ground his fist into his chest. 'It hurts too much in here. Our Peggy kept this family together. She gave me right to be here. What have I, now, eh?'

'Oh, Ed.' Grace reached out, gasping when Stan knocked away her hand. 'Stan—'

'Get away from him. This is your fault.' He embraced Ed, a small cry escaping him when Ed returned it. 'All these years . . . Who was it?'

'Stan, love, I never meant—'

'Tell me!'

Sally put her arm around Grace's shoulders. 'Stan, please—'

'As for you.' His features contorted in disgust. 'You're no longer family to me, d'you hear? I thought . . . we'd become friends. And all the time . . . I wish you'd never come.'

'No, Stan, we *are*, we—'

'You lied to me! You're as bad as her.'

'No, please.' She reached out to him but her aunt, face oddly calm, pulled her back.

'This ain't Sally's fault. I begged her not to tell. This has gone on long enough. I can't do it any more.' Grace paused. 'Sally's more involved than you think.'

Ed's head jerked up. 'Grace, you don't have to—'

'Aye, Ed, I do. It's time I paid for my wickedness. I should've told this long afore this night.'

'Aunt Grace? Aunt Grace, you're scaring me. What should you have told?'

'Think on this,' Ed pressed. 'There'll be no going back.'

Slowly, tentatively, Grace caressed her husband's cheek. He closed his eyes and she sighed. 'Stan, Sally. I love you more than you'll ever know. Whatever changes by the telling of this, please, allus remember that.'

'Aunt Grace?'

Grace squeezed her eyes shut. When she uttered what she'd clearly hoped she never would, her tone was flat.

'Jonathan Swann was father to you both. You're brother and sister.'

Chapter 19

'WILL YOUSE TWO leave that dog be and sit down? Mithered to death, he is, poor blighter.'

Sally heard Maggie's twins, Flo and Harry, cross the room, bare feet slapping the floorboards. It was the knocking of wood on wood, as they rocked on rickety chairs, which fully roused her.

Those initial seconds were blissfully memory-free. Too soon, recollection slammed home, bringing pain so acute that nausea rose. She'd have given anything to fall back to sleep, forget. She didn't want to feel, think, imagine . . . How, in the name of *God*, would she get through this?

'Granny, we've ate our porridge. Can we play with Shield, now?'

Ellen, her back to them at the fire, flapped a hand and they scooted across the kitchen. Gradually, their giggles grew and, despite her misery, Sally couldn't help smiling when their grandmother addressed them.

'Right, get your clogs on and take your games outside. You're giving me a thundering headache. Go on, afore I tan your backsides.'

Though they scrambled up, it was evident they had never felt her hand – they hooted with laughter. 'Can we take Shield?'

'Aye, go on. Just mind for carts and don't be bothering folk.'

As they skipped out, Shield bounding between, Sally closed her eyes. But memories trickled back and she knew she must get up. If sleep wouldn't release her, she'd have to hold them at bay by keeping busy. Allowing them free rein would send her stark, staring mad. For the first time, thoughts of work brought blessed relief.

'Morning, lass. Our Maggie's out; she'll not be long. There's a pot on t' table not long since brewed.'

Spying awkwardness in Ellen's eyes, she sighed inwardly. Who could blame her? 'Thank you for last night. I'm sorry for burdening you and Maggie. I didn't know where else to go.'

Relief passed over Ellen's face. She wiped her hands on her apron and sat opposite. 'Now, that's enough of that. You've been kindness itself to my Maggie; one good turn deserves another. Mind, I'm glad you mentioned it first, lass. I can't imagine how you're fettling this morning.'

'I understand. I just . . . Lord, what am I to do?'

'You'll have to talk it through with her sooner or later. Otherwise, it'll fester inside and drive thee ruddy mad. When all's said and done, she's still your aunt.'

Sally nodded. How she'd look Grace in the face again, however . . .

'You'd best waken the babby, give him his feed. And don't you be fretting. He'll have a lovely time.'

'I feel dreadful doing this to you. You have your hands full already—'

'And love every minute. I don't know what I'd do with meself all day if not for our Maggie's two.'

Sally smiled tearfully – she was fortunate to have such wonderful friends. What she'd have done last night without them, she didn't know.

'Go on, lass. Give him his breakfast and get yourself to work. Best thing you can do is keep busy.'

Lifting him from the basket, her stomach flipped. *Jonathan.* She couldn't bear that, now. She'd bestowed the name proudly, believing . . . lies. Everything she held dear, memories she cherished – all lies. Her mind had built up her father into some virtuous saint. For years, she'd mourned a man who didn't exist.

She watched the baby suckle, her thoughts in disarray. What heartbreak her father and aunt had made her poor mother suffer. They betrayed her in the worst possible way. It had affected *her* whole life, too. But for their actions, how might life have been? Would she have married a decent man instead of a monster? Would her mother be alive? The lost possibilities were difficult to dismiss.

Thoughts of Stan, however, quashed her growing resentment. The utterance of a few words had lost him not only the father he believed to be his, but respect and trust for his mother, and a sister he'd thought was his full sibling. Moreover, the cousin he'd longed to reunite with was now his half-sister. Her pain paled in comparison.

Sally squeezed her eyes shut at the memory of his devastation. Everyone he'd ever loved had concealed what he'd a right to know. Would he forgive her? Gaining a sibling was an almighty shock to *her*, yet was growing on her. Whether he'd warm to it, she didn't know.

Holding her now-fed son against her shoulder, she rubbed his back. She tried to focus on the twins' voices beyond the door, desperate for her thoughts not to switch to Grace, but it was useless. Despite the agony of betrayal, she ached for the woman she'd come to love as a mother, yearned for her comforting hug, her soft voice. Attempting to deny the hurt Grace undoubtedly felt was impossible.

Last night, she'd simply snatched up the basket and fled. Her friends insisted she must stay as long as she needed but she couldn't impose on them for long. Ellen was right. However painful, she must give Grace the chance to explain.

Sighing, she rose from the pallet. She couldn't be late today. Pru had already allowed her time off; it would seem she was taking advantage of her kind nature. Donning her shawl, she thanked Ellen and left.

The twins, sitting cross-legged on the flagstones stroking Shield, waved as she passed. She returned the waves, shook her head when the dog made to rise, and hurried on. Turning the corner, she collided with her friend.

'Mind where you're going, you clumsy— Oh, it's thee.' Maggie laughed then her eyes softened. 'I'm glad I caught you afore you left. How you fettling?'

'I'm unsure. Hurt, confused . . . It's such a mess.'

'Eeh, love. 'Ere, let me take these in to Mam and I'll walk with you.' Maggie motioned to the pot of dripping and bundle of kindling she held. 'She'll be wondering where I've got to; it took an age persuading him in t' shop for a bit more on the slate. It's a good thing you've done, finding me that position, lass. We'd be facing destitution but for it. Eeh, listen to me prattling on; I'll finish up making you late. I'll not be a moment.' Flashing a grin, she scurried off.

Sally smiled fondly. Maggie was a good woman. She was so glad Pru had agreed to her working in the shop; Saturday would be here soon enough.

That she'd helped this family yet was at a loss how to repair her own didn't go unnoticed, but she pushed it from her mind. To get through the day without breaking down, she couldn't dwell on it.

Maggie rejoined her. Sally linked her arm through hers and they set off. Arriving at the pawnshop, her friend peeped through the window.

'Eeh, a few more days – I can't wait! It'll be great after all the years in t' mills.'

Maggie's excitement warmed Sally's heart. 'Why don't I introduce you to Miss Sharp while you're here?'

'Won't she mind?'

'Of course not. She's lovely, Maggie.'

Pru glanced around at the tinkling bell but before Sally could beckon Maggie – and to her utter dismay – Pru lowered her head without so much as a smile. Heart sinking, she joined her friend outside.

'Actually, Maggie, Miss Sharp's rather busy. Introducing yourself on Saturday would be wiser.'

Unaware anything was other than it seemed, Maggie nodded. 'I don't want to set a bad impression by disturbing her work. Go on, you'd best get in. I'll see thee at dinnertime, lass.'

Guilt gnawing at her, Sally bid her goodbye. If her suspicions proved correct, should she have let Maggie see?

Knowing her friend would be curious about Pru's injuries, she'd casually remarked days earlier that Pru had taken a tumble on a patch of ice. She'd hated lying but didn't feel it was her place to reveal the Sharps' business. As did most, Maggie knew about Agnes's previous employee but wasn't concerned. As she pointed out, she'd be working in the shop, not upstairs.

Nevertheless, concealing goings-on beneath this roof much longer was hopeless; the evidence would be right under her nose. Whether customers believed

Pru's excuses, she didn't know, but Maggie deserved the truth.

As she re-entered the shop, unease twisted her stomach when Pru didn't look up. She crossed to the counter and squeezed her shoulder gently. 'She's done it again, hasn't she? Miss Sharp, let me see.'

Bruising from the previous attack had faded. But this split lip was clearly a more recent assault.

'*Why* does she *do* it?'

'It looks worse than it is. Would you like a cup of tea, dear?'

Sally heaved a sigh of frustration, pity, helplessness. 'You cannot continue like this. You cannot keep excusing her wretched behaviour and brushing this aside as if it doesn't matter. When will you realise that it isn't normal, Miss Sharp? You don't deserve to be treated this way, by anyone.'

The dull response was barely audible. 'What choice have I? I'm all she has. It's my duty.'

'Why has she done this again? You said last time—'

'And meant it. I was determined not to give her the reaction she so enjoys. I failed. She can be extremely hurtful, knows just what to say to . . . maintain my suffering. She goes on and on and I sometimes feel like . . .' Pru paused, cleared her throat. 'But she insists it's for my own good so I won't make the same mistake again.'

Sally resisted asking what mistake, why she must suffer, what in heaven was going on. When Pru deemed the time right, she'd be here. 'I don't know what to say that I haven't already said. It's your life, your mother, your business. Just please . . .' She sighed, wanting to say so much but knowing it wouldn't make a scrap of difference. 'Please. Be careful.'

Pru nodded then smiled brightly. 'Now, then. Let me get you that tea and you can tell me all about your trip to Bolton, before Mother wakes. I trust your friend is well?'

Sudden tears thickened her throat. 'As it turned out, I was unable to make the visit. My cousin passed away yesterday morning.'

'My dear! Oh, I'm so very sorry for your loss. Your poor aunt.'

'She is inconsolable. Peggy was just eleven years old.' Glancing up, she was taken aback. Tears streamed down Pru's cheeks. 'Oh, I'm sorry, I didn't mean to—'

'No, no, you have no reason to apologise,' Pru choked, wiping eyes raw with anguish. 'Please, do not be alarmed. I simply adore children. To hear of one's passing . . . It is the worst possible pain a mother could go through.'

A frown touched Sally's brow. 'Yes, I'm sure it must be.'

Hand fluttering to her throat, Pru's tortured stare intensified. 'Sally, I—' A thud from above cut her off.

She nodded encouragingly. 'Yes, Miss Sharp?'

'I . . . I . . .'

She held her breath but to her dismay Pru's shoulders sagged. It was clear by her next words that the moment had passed.

'I believe Mother wants her tea. You won't mention . . . will you, dear?'

Taking a last look at the swollen mouth, Sally shook her head. Concealing truths was all her life consisted of lately and she was heartily fed up with it.

Making her way upstairs, her footsteps followed the beat of the mocking mantra tormenting her mind: *Secrets and lies. Secrets and lies. Secrets and lies* . . .

*

As before, Agnes showed no sign in word or action of occurrences in Sally's absence. Neither did she mention Tuesday's disturbing mood and talk of unwanted babies. Her unpredictability was unnerving. How Pru bore her, Sally didn't know.

The day rolled along as usual and after bidding Pru goodbye, she left with a thankful sigh. Work *had* taken her mind off her family, but worry for Pru's had replaced it.

Weary workers trudged in all directions but she barely noticed. Her thoughts were on the old woman's deplorable ability to act as if nothing had happened. Agnes must know she'd seen Pru's injuries, and was possibly aware how they got there, yet didn't seem concerned in the slightest.

Whatever her past, poor Pru didn't deserve this treatment. She herself knew better than most how it was to live awaiting the next blow. Imprisoned by such poison, day in, day out, was unbearable. How long before Pru's patience burned out, as had hers? What the outcome when it did?

Deep in thought, it wasn't until reaching the entry that Sally realised her error. Her heart sank to her boots. She'd made for Grace's instead of Maggie's.

Turning for Davies Street, her tear-scorched eyes flicked to her aunt's. They fixed on a figure and she jolted to a halt. Pressing against the wall, she peered at him. *Her brother.*

He stood stock-still, cap low over his face. When he raised his head to look at the door, the pain in his eyes brought fresh tears to hers. He continued staring but instead of entering, thrust his hands into his pockets and rested his chin on his chest.

At the sorry sight of him, lost and alone in the darkening street, Sally's arms ached for him. She pushed herself from the wall but didn't go. Despite her breaking heart, her feet refused to budge and, moments later, Stan slipped inside.

She gazed at the door for an age. Then with a sob, she turned on her heel for Maggie's.

Chapter 20

'YOUR AUNT'S FRIEND came to see thee at work? What did she say, lass?'

'Mrs Knox was very understanding. She came to tell me . . .' Sally blinked as tears welled up. 'Peggy's funeral is on Sunday. She said my aunt's in a bad way. She's not eating or sleeping. She's dreading the funeral and . . . she's pining for me. She wants me home.'

'What will you do?' Maggie asked softly.

It was Friday night and peaceful in the small kitchen. The twins were in bed, Jonathan asleep in his basket. Shield lay by the fire and, for a long moment, his gentle snores were the only sound.

'I shall have to go and see her. Despite everything, I feel dreadful for leaving, what with Peggy . . . However difficult seeing my aunt and Stan will be, I cannot miss the funeral. I couldn't do that to Aunt Grace. It's too cruel.'

Ellen nodded. 'Mebbe after, you can talk through matters. It needs airing, lass. Summat needs to give.'

'What will I say? How can I look her in the face knowing she . . . they . . . ?'

No one had the answer. Sipping their tea, they jumped when a knock sounded.

'Who the divil's that at this time?'

Maggie went to see. When she revealed the visitor, Sally gasped.

'Con? What are you doing here?' His smile brought a lump to her throat. She crossed the room and fell into his arms.

'Easy now, acushla,' he murmured, holding her close.

Resting her head on his chest, Sally closed her eyes. 'Have you been to my aunt's? Did she tell you I was here?' Feeling him nod, she sighed. 'How is she?'

'You and your friend sit yourselfs down. I'll brew a fresh pot.'

Ellen's words brought heat to Sally's cheeks. She disentangled herself from him. 'I'm sorry, I don't know what came over me. This is Con, a dear friend.'

'You're upset, lass, no apologies needed. Come and sit down. And you, lad. You're more than welcome.'

Inwardly cringing, Sally resumed her seat. She hadn't thought twice about embracing him – she had missed him since their last meeting. Fleeing here the other night, she'd half expected to see him, having grown accustomed to him appearing when she was in trouble. Of course, he hadn't, but he was here now.

Though glad to see him, she couldn't help worrying what Maggie and Ellen thought. She'd told them a little about her marriage; would they believe her to be loose, a wedded woman throwing herself at another man?

Thankful when Ellen handed back her refilled cup with her usual smile, she stole a glance at Maggie. Her friend raised an eyebrow, twinkling eyes flicking to the Irishman, and Sally blinked. Maggie wasn't disapproving. She was smitten!

For the next hour, they talked quietly. Con expressed regret at Peggy's passing and each of them shed a tear when, from his jacket pocket, he produced a pale-green ribbon, purchased for her that morning.

Gradually, the mood lightened and Con, Maggie and Ellen chatted easily. Only half listening, Sally fingered the silky strip, which she'd promised to give Grace on Sunday. She smiled when Maggie laughed at something Con had said. Why couldn't others resist his charms yet she wanted only friendship? Why didn't her feelings run deeper? Was something wrong with her? Had Joseph's evil tainted any chance at love?

Tommy slipped into her mind and she quivered. She must visit Bolton, soon. She had to see that Ivy was well. And, however hard she tried denying it, she had to see Tommy, too.

Girlish giggles dragged her from her thoughts. Watching Con lean closer to Maggie, she sensed something between them; their laughter melted but their gazes lingered. Her chest swelled with pleasure. Then, to her disappointment, Con turned to *her* with his slow smile and the moment between him and Maggie was broken.

As Sally predicted, Pru and Maggie hit it off right away.

Throughout the day, laughter filtered upstairs and Agnes would cock an ear and frown. She was still unaware that Pru had employed her, and Sally would hold her breath, worried that she'd demand to be told what was going on, but she didn't. Whether Agnes took the extra voice to be a customer's, Sally didn't know. She was certain, however, that Pru couldn't conceal Maggie much longer.

It was minutes from finishing time. Preparing to leave, Sally sighed inwardly at the muffled laughter.

It had evoked mixed feelings all day. And the reason wasn't entirely due to Agnes.

Since Con's departure last night, she'd sensed a cooling in Maggie. Walking to work, she'd been giddy about her friend's first day and, though not snubbing her excited chatter, Maggie's short responses and tight smiles were out of character.

The journey to and from home at dinner wasn't much better. And whenever she'd ventured downstairs to fulfil Agnes's requests, Maggie would find a way to busy herself as an excuse not to talk. Something was wrong. She sounded her usual self with Pru.

Did Maggie suspect there was something between her and Con? she brooded, descending the stairs. Her friend had clearly taken to the handsome Irishman; was she perhaps jealous?

Bidding Pru goodnight, they drew their shawls tightly against the cutting wind and hurried home through the gloomy streets. Sally tried making conversation twice, and received short responses. After the third, she'd had enough. She forced her to a halt.

'Maggie, have I done something to upset you?'

Her friend's colour rose instantly. She lowered her eyes to the ground. 'Nay, course not.'

'Then what? I must have done something. You've been your cheery self all day with Miss Sharp.'

'I'm sorry. You're not to blame for, for what I . . . I made a fool of meself last night, didn't I?'

Sally sighed. She'd known this was about Con. Was Maggie embarrassed at showing a liking for him because she believed he and *she* . . . ? Linking her arm, she squeezed. 'There's nothing between Con and me. He's a good friend, nothing more.'

'Oh, lass, I know that! I never thought that forra second. Eeh, I'm sorry.' Maggie turned her gaze to the leaden sky. 'My late husband, my Danny, were the only man I ever had eyes for. His passing near killed me. Without a shadow of a doubt, if not for Mam and the little 'uns, I'd not be here. Last night, making cow eyes . . . I don't know what the divil came over me.'

Sally smothered a chuckle with her hand. 'I'm sorry. I'm simply relieved. I thought I'd upset you. Oh, Maggie, don't berate yourself for being human. You're a young woman with your life ahead of you. As for Con, my aunt swears he could charm the birds from the trees. Don't be embarrassed nor harbour guilt towards your husband's memory. Surely, he'd want you to be happy?'

'Aye. Eeh, I am sorry, Sally. I couldn't look thee in t' eye, I were that ashamed.'

Sally squeezed her arm again, a wicked smile spreading across her face. 'Lord, he *is* handsome, though, isn't he?'

Maggie clicked her tongue but soon she too was grinning. 'By, he is that!'

And as they hurried on, their giggles rang along the street.

As with her arrival in Manchester, the following morning Sally hesitated at her aunt's door. She breathed deeply. Was it only three weeks ago she'd stood here, as uncertain of the outcome? So much had happened that it was difficult to believe.

She glanced inside the basket. A posy of snowdrops purchased on Carruthers Street lay by Jonathan's feet. The flower seller, hearing what they were for, had added sprigs of baby's breath at no extra charge and

Sally sighed, wishing she were giving them in different circumstances.

Bringing a baby to a funeral wasn't ideal but not knowing what today held, she'd declined Maggie's offer of minding him. She'd need to be close by to feed him. And she knew Grace would be missing him.

Another deep breath did nothing to calm her as she knocked. In those seconds, the emotional storm, which had plagued her throughout the sleepless night, returned. How would she feel, seeing Grace? How would Stan react? She pushed her worries aside. Today was about Peggy. And whatever Grace had done, she needed her support. She'd soon have to bury her child. No woman deserved that.

Footsteps within sounded and the door creaked open.

'Hello, Uncle Ed.'

His weary gaze widened. He leaned across the step and embraced her.

When they parted, she glanced over his shoulder. 'Uncle Ed, I—'

'I know, lass,' he murmured. 'Ta for coming. It'll mean the world to your aunt.'

Grace's eyes tore Sally's heart. Agony had sucked her soul from their depths. As Sally crossed the kitchen, Grace lowered her head. Staring down at the slumped frame, her heart thumped but no anger arose. She felt nothing but heavy sadness.

She was relieved and dismayed that Stan wasn't there. Part of her dreaded seeing him, yet she longed to. Spying him Thursday evening haunted her. She just prayed that time apart had diminished his anger and sense of betrayal towards her.

When her gaze rested on the cheap coffin in the corner, loss and regret almost broke her heart. She'd barely got to know the girl lying cold within. Why was life so cruel? she raged inwardly, screwing her eyes to block the sight. And imagining this mother's pain, the last vestige of animosity faded. She stooped and put her arms around her.

Grace's shoulders heaved. Her arms flew around Sally's waist and she held on tightly, as though afraid if she let go, she'd take flight.

'I love you, Aunt Grace.'

The low cry was of sheer relief. 'Eeh, I'm that glad you're here. I'll get through this day a little easier with you by my side. Oh, I have missed you, love. I wanted to tell you . . . But I were frickened to death of losing you. My wickedness lost me my Rose. I couldn't lose thee, an' all. Not again. I couldn't, lass.'

Sally wiped Grace's tears. 'Let's not talk about that. I'll not make this day harder for you. I cannot begin to imagine what you're going through.'

'What's *she* doing here?'

They turned to find Stan in the doorway.

Ed rose from the table. 'Now then, lad—'

'You should've stopped away. In fact, you should've never returned to Manchester. We were all right till you turned up like a bad penny.'

The degree of resentment cut Sally to the quick. She moved towards him and frowned sadly when he stepped back. 'Don't hate me, Stan. I never meant to hurt you. It wasn't my place to tell you. Please try to understand.'

His eyes flared with pain. 'I thought we were friends.'

'Oh, Stan.' She took another hesitant step, heart fluttering with hope when he didn't move. 'What we've learned . . . To discover I have a brother – that *you* are my brother . . . I'm as shocked and confused as you. But let me tell you something: I will not allow this to come between us. The moment I arrived, I liked you. Since then, as with Peggy, I've grown to love you. I've lost her, Stan. I won't lose you, too.'

The room was still, all of them awaiting his response. When his lower lip trembled, she forced herself not to go to him. She must let him decide in his own time, his way.

A lone tear splashed to his cheek. He turned and left the room.

She stared at the door for a long moment then closed her eyes in despair.

Until this day, Sally wouldn't have believed it possible for a body to shed the tears her aunt had. Her level of grief was distressing to witness. When Peggy disappeared into the ground her mother's beast-like cries drew sobs from everyone.

They hadn't seen Stan again until leaving for Christ Church on Every Street. He'd slipped into the kitchen at the last moment without a word to anyone. Sally had felt his eyes from the doorway as, tears streaming, she laid Thunder beside her cousin. She'd then produced Con's ribbon and Grace tied it in Peggy's hair.

When Ed secured the lid and drove the nails through, shutting away their daughter for ever, Grace had wept herself hoarse. He'd held his wife tightly and Stan had screwed up his face in anguish. Sally made to comfort him but he turned away, and she'd had no choice but to leave him be.

Now, as Ed and Grace clung to each other by the graveside, Stan stood alone. Tears dripped from his chin on to the cap he clutched to his chest and Sally gripped the basket's handle, aching to go to him. However, he'd made his feelings clear. She must respect his decision.

The mourners drifted across the churchyard to allow the family private goodbyes. Sally said a silent prayer and dropped the delicate white flowers beside the small wreath atop the coffin.

'How you bearing up, lass?' asked Winnie when she came to stand beside her.

'My heart breaks for them. And Stan . . . I don't know what to do. He detests me.'

'The lad's just looking for someone to blame. He lost a sister and gained another in t' same day. He's hurt, confused, but he'll bear it, somehow. Give him time. He'll come round.'

Shortly afterwards, the small procession meandered back to Boslam Street. Sally walked in front with her aunt and uncle, Stan following with Winnie and the rest. Reaching the entry, she felt a tap on her shoulder. She thought it was Stan but, turning, had to swallow her disappointment.

Winnie drew her aside. 'Can you lend a hand with summat, lass?'

'Of course. What is it, Mrs Knox?'

Grace's friend explained how in the days following Peggy's death, she'd knocked at every house and, as the poor did in times of need, neighbours gave what coppers they could spare. After purchasing the wreath, she'd spent the remainder on the funeral tea, which she'd prepared at home last night.

Within minutes, they had carried the meagre spread to Grace's. As they placed the last dish on the table, gratitude and shame filled Sally. She fumbled inside the basket then pressed coins into Winnie's hand.

'What's this?'

'My belated contribution. With all that had happened, I . . . I feel dreadful. You're an angel to my family, Mrs Knox.'

'Now, don't be daft. What you've had to deal with, it's no wonder. Eeh, try and talk with Grace, won't you? You'll both feel better for it. She made a mistake but in my opinion, she's paid for it a hundred times over. Go on, lass. I'll mind the babby.'

Glancing across, Sally frowned. Could she bear it?

'The wench needs her family round her, now more than ever.'

She nodded. Brushing this under the mat wouldn't solve anything. Whatever the outcome, she must try, for all their sakes.

When she slipped into the chair opposite her aunt, she knew foreboding shone from her eyes – Grace's dimmed in response. A thousand questions whirred in her mind but her tongue stuck to the roof of her dry mouth.

'You ready to hear it, lass?'

Raw pain behind the words made Sally look away. 'I'm sorry, it can wait. I promised I wouldn't upset you with this today—'

'I want to. I've explained to Stan; I need you to understand, too. I know nowt can excuse what went on but if you hear it, you might just find it in your heart to forgive me. And your father. He weren't a bad man, love.' Grace rose and motioned for her to follow.

Passing Ed, Sally was struck by the tender look he gave his wife. If nothing else, this sorry mess had united her aunt and uncle.

Grace led the way to the backyard. She leaned against the crumbling wall and folded her arms. 'I know this is selfish but I feel nowt but relief. My wickedness, it's been a black shadow, allus there, following me through the years wherever I went. It'll be a blessing to shift some of it.'

Sally went cold with dread but Grace clearly needed this release. 'I'll admit the thought of hearing this makes me shudder. However, if it will help you heal a little . . . I don't know how I'll feel afterwards but shall try my best to understand.'

'It's probably the owdest excuse in t' book but in our case, it really is true – we never planned it. At the time, I still dwelled with Father. Mam had cleared off years afore with the tripe dresser down the road. Did you know about that, lass?'

'I didn't. I don't remember my grandparents.'

'Aye, you'll not. Mam scarpered long afore you were born, and Father . . . Well, Rose didn't see much of him after she wed.'

'No?'

'Nay. She didn't know how lucky she were.'

Frowning, Sally waited for Grace to continue but she remained silent, as though lost in thought. 'Aunt Grace?'

'I knew what were to happen. It were the same every weekend. When I heard the door go, I shot upstairs but only got halfway. Father spotted me, ordered me back. My pleading usually worked; he'd leave me be and I'd escape to bed. That night, he were having none of it.'

Sally's frown deepened. 'I don't understand.'

'When Mam scarpered, it were left to me and Rose to look after him. I did the donkey's share to save her the burden; she were nowt but a babby. Father weren't mithered so long as the house were clean and a meal were on t' table of an evening.

'Anyroad, eventually, she met Jonathan. Father were dead set against them courting. He didn't want her marrying, same as he didn't me. He were frightened of being alone, you see, with no one to wash his clothes, clean his house and fill his belly. I begged him to give permission, promised him I'd never wed, would look after him all his days if he let her.

'She were smitten and I loved her more than owt in t' world. I'd have done anything for my Rose. Well, he agreed. I were that happy for her, lass, I can't tell thee. Eeh, but it were lonely in that house, after. Father's drinking were as bad as ever and she kept her distance. I can't say I blamed her. He'd never been a good 'un, really. His needs allus come afore owt else.'

'What happened, Aunt Grace?' she asked gently. 'What did your father do after ordering you downstairs?'

'He'd harp on summat shocking when at the drink. He'd shout and curse till the early hours, convinced I planned to run away with some fella or other. I'd promise I'd not leave, plead with him to stop, but nowt worked. I'd cry with relief when he finally passed out.' Grace's eyes burned with the pain of remembrance. 'I thought he'd go on as usual, thought I knew what were coming. Not that night.

'I could see in his eyes summat were different. I'd reached the bottom stair when the first blow came. Honest to God, lass, my head near left my shoulders. There weren't no pain at first; the shock, you know? His sniping I were used to but he'd never struck me afore. He dragged me across the room by my hair and like a man possessed, beat me black and blue.

'Someone had told him about Ed. We'd met the month afore. He'd started work at the tobacconist's where I went for Father's bacca. I knew he'd be furious but I fell for your uncle at first sight. I thought we'd been careful but some swine must've spotted us.'

Sally tore away her gaze. To think her grandfather . . . He'd been no better than Joseph. 'And *my* father?' she asked tentatively.

A red hue covered Grace's face. 'He were homeward bound from the tavern, been forra dram of brandy for Rose's toothache. Passing ours, he heard my screams. Next thing I knew, he were dragging Father off me. Well, they argued and Father staggered to bed threatening he'd never let me marry, would murder Ed if I saw him again.

'Jonathan sat me by the fire and, while he brewed tea, I prayed. I prayed Father wouldn't return to the kitchen. I prayed for strength. Most of all, I prayed for God's help to endure life without Ed. Anyroad, Jonathan adds some brandy to the tea for my nerves. Whether that . . . Nay, I'm making excuses.

'Brandy or no . . . He tried comforting me and I . . . Oh, Sally, I'm the wicked 'un. I threw meself at him, desperate forra bit of love. I thought I'd lost my Ed, were destined forra life of misery with Father. It's no excuse, I know. I don't know what I were thinking. I just, I just . . .' She burst into sobs. 'I begged him to stay awhile. I seduced him, lass. How could I do that to my Rosie?'

Hugging herself, Sally stared at nothing. 'What followed?'

'I disobeyed Father and continued courting Ed. When I realised I were with child, I went fair daft with fear but told Ed straight away. To my amazement, he vowed to stand by me. We told Father together and Ed made out the child were his. I were scared sick but besides shouting, then getting blind drunk, there weren't much Father could do. He'd not have wanted a bastard beneath his roof.

'We promised to dwell with him after we wed, save him being alone.' Grace's face contorted in pain. 'Rose were over the moon for me. I tried putting the betrayal to the back of my mind, but Jonathan were a wreck. He wanted to tell her but I pleaded with him. I knew it'd kill her, that she'd never forgive me. I were right on both counts.'

Sally closed her eyes. 'How did she discover the truth?'

'Jonathan, lass, confessed on his deathbed. As with me, it'd haunted him; he were never the same. He lived and breathed for Rose. That one act of weakness fair sucked the soul from him.' Glancing up, Grace winced. 'Your expression . . . It's like stepping back in time.

'Rose begged me to say it weren't true. And looking at her, widowhood but an hour old, I'd have given owt to. The lie were on my tongue – I were this close to uttering it.' She held thumb and forefinger an inch apart. 'But I couldn't. I looked down to our Stan, the result of my wickedness, near full-grown, and knew the time for honesty had come. She deserved the truth and I deserved to pay for my sin.

'My punishment were losing the best sister a body could wish. She swore she'd never forgive me, and she didn't. In the space of an hour, she lost not only her husband but her only sibling, for when them words left me, I were dead to her, an' all.'

Tears streamed down Sally's face. 'Was that the last time you saw her?'

'I plucked up courage and went round weeks later, but my knock went unanswered. Looking through the window, I wanted to die. Norra soul nor stick of furniture remained. You'd gone, taking my heart with youse.'

'Did she realise who fathered Stan?'

'I don't know, lass, and that's the truth. If she'd asked, I'd have had to tell her. She didn't. Whether she put two and two together, later, I can't say.' Through hooded eyes, Grace peered at her. 'There's nowt more to add but sorry. I'm so sorry, lass. Please tell me you forgive me, that things will be well betwixt us.'

Uneasy silence descended.

Part of Sally wanted to scream no, everything wouldn't be well. Her mother had been unable to forgive the sister she loved – would her doing so be betraying her? Would it make a mockery of all she'd suffered?

Yet anger and bitterness couldn't quell another emotion. She loved this woman. Grace had bent over backwards for her. She'd put a roof over their heads, food in their stomachs. She'd been a shoulder to cry on, her kindness knowing no bounds, despite her own burdens. Moreover, why must she carry the blame? Her father was as much at fault.

Could she cut from her life one of the precious few she had left, as had her mother? She couldn't deny the answer.

'I forgive you,' she heard herself say.

Slowly, Grace's expression melted into one of sheer serenity. As she heaved a long sigh, years of grief seemed to rise from her. She opened her arms.

Without hesitation, Sally walked into them.

Winnie was seeing out the last neighbour when Grace and Sally emerged from the backyard. Her eyebrows rose in trepidation. 'All well?'

Grace nodded. She turned to smile at Ed but catching Stan's eye, it slipped from her face. 'Don't look at me like that, son. Can't we put this behind us, start afresh?'

Sally looked away. Today had sucked all energy from her. She didn't have the strength to fight.

'Stan,' Ed prompted. 'Your mam's right. We shouldn't be tearing each other to bits. This day should be about those lost and those still here. We're a family, lad, and families stick together. For better or worse,' he finished to Grace, eyes gentle.

Stan rubbed the fine stubble on his chin. He ignored Winnie's encouraging smile and Ed's nod, also his mother's pleading stare. When his gaze rested on Sally, emotion flickered across his face then vanished as quickly. He shook his head.

Grace raised her eyes to the ceiling. '*Please*, son.'

'I can't. Can't . . . even *look* at her! It weren't meant to be like this. She were my cousin, not my . . .' He leapt to his feet. 'Peggy were my sister, not her. I don't want her as a sister. And I don't want her here. Either she leaves or I do.'

Grace and Ed made to protest but shaking her head, Sally stopped them. Returning Winnie's sad smile, she took the basket from her.

'Goodbye, Mrs Knox.' Stan's glare bore into her as she crossed the room. 'Goodbye, Aunt Grace, Uncle Ed.' Their looks of helplessness and despair cut her to the bone. As she opened the door, her step faltered. Unable to stop herself, she rushed to Stan and kissed his cheek. 'Goodbye, Stan. I love you – always remember that.' She turned and ran from the house, Grace's weeping ringing in her ears.

Blinded by tears, she passed through the maze of streets in a daze. Once again, she'd lost her family. Years of yearning, her efforts to find them, countless emotions she'd endured to maintain a relationship and for what? To have it all snatched away within weeks?

Was it worth it? Was her love for them enough for such upset, worry, pain of rejection? She didn't need to think about it – of course it was. What she carried in her breast for those people was beyond measure.

But what do I do? she asked herself.

Stan wouldn't come round, she realised that, now. He'd said he couldn't bear to so much as look at her. She dashed away fresh tears with the back of her hand. She understood, despite the pain it brought. His anger was a natural response, she accepted this. But as far as she could see, she'd had no choice. She'd promised Grace.

Should she have broken her vow? she agonised, walking on aimlessly. Deep down, she knew she'd made the right decision. However much she believed Stan deserved the truth, she couldn't have gone back on her word.

As she and Grace had resolved matters, her despondency diminished somewhat. They had eked one positive thing from this dreadful day at least.

Passing through Bradford Road, she glanced to the pawnshop and heaved a sigh. She seemed to roll on a continuum of worry and uncertainty. Complications followed her everywhere. Was a simple life too much to ask? Escaping, she'd craved calmness, security. The beatings were in the past but her future was as precarious as ever.

Drawing level, she looked up to Agnes's window. An unexpected sight chased away her troubles: Pru stood motionless, staring back.

She raised a hand and when Pru nodded slightly, then disappeared, she shrugged. Though surprised – Pru steered clear of Agnes whenever possible – at this moment, whatever the reason, Sally neither knew nor cared. She couldn't deal with further worries today.

None the less, heading for Maggie's, guilt spiked and she resolved to make it up to Pru tomorrow. Whatever was amiss, she'd bet her life Agnes was at the centre. She would set off early; they'd talk before work. She'd think up some reason to leave before Maggie. She just wished she didn't have to.

She couldn't continue lying. She'd learned a harsh lesson this week. Hiding truths had lost her Stan. She wouldn't lose Maggie, too.

Tommy flicked his wrist. The stone skimmed the water several times before sinking to the riverbed. Watching the ripples left behind, he heard footsteps approaching. He smiled as Dolly, curls poking from her bonnet and bouncing about her shoulders, rushed towards him.

'I didn't think you'd show,' she breathed, pink-faced with pleasure.

He pulled lightly on a curl. Released, it sprang back into shape and he smiled again. 'I promised, didn't I?'

She nodded and he kissed her plump cheek. She smelt of fresh butter and cream and when she slipped her hand in his, it was soft and warm. She was a lovely lass, too good for him. He'd treated her shockingly the past weeks. He didn't deserve her.

As though sensing his despair, she frowned. 'What's wrong, Tommy? Is it your mam? Has summat else occurred?'

He looked away, guilt rising. He wondered what would happen if he told her he was thinking of someone else entirely. Someone who, for the life of him, he couldn't forget. A woman who, if she returned tomorrow and declared *her* love for *him*, he'd drop Dolly for in a heartbeat.

He knew what. Dolly wasn't like other lasses. She wouldn't scream and curse or claw his face, much as he'd deserve it. She'd let him go without much fuss because she'd want him to be happy, even if that meant with someone else. She loved him, always had. Why couldn't he share that devotion? Why wasn't she enough any more?

He imagined the boot on the other foot – how would *he* feel if she admitted loving another man? The answer was like a blow to the stomach. He'd feel only relief.

'What is it? Has that divil been back?'

Letting her hand go, he ran his through his hair. 'He'd not dare. We searched for him Tuesday night but—' Her horrified gasp interrupted him. 'Nay, lass, don't fret. He's no match for us. Anyroad, we couldn't find him.' He didn't mention that he and his father wouldn't rest until they did, however long it took. 'And Mam's on t' mend. Tough as they come, she is.'

'Thank the Lord for that – and not just about Ivy. He's dangerous, he is.'

Tommy crossed to the knoll by the river. He patted the stubbly grass and when she sat beside him, asked, 'Dolly, are you happy?'

She cocked her head, considered this. 'Aye. Some folk are far worse off. I've a steady job, a good family and my health. And I have thee.' She smiled, slipping her hand in his. 'I'd say I've plenty to be happy about.'

'I want to say sorry.' She made to speak but he shook his head. 'Hear me out, lass. I've been cruel standing you up of a Sunday. I've had . . . matters on my mind, is all.' Sighing, he drew her towards him. She rested her head on his shoulder and he smiled sadly, gaze sweeping the meadows beyond. 'You're special to me. You know that, don't you?' He felt her nod. 'I never thanked you proper on Monday, were too angry to think straight. I am grateful, Dolly. But for you—'

'Don't dwell on that,' she cut in softly.

'Tha fair saved Mam's life. If I tried every day for the rest of mine, I couldn't thank you enough.' She curled into him. Her hand travelled up his chest, around his neck. Fingers played at his nape and he closed his eyes. 'Dolly, I, I must—'

'Shhh.' She tilted her head to gaze at him. 'Being with thee's all the thanks I could want.'

Shame so acute it brought bile to his throat, stabbed. He tore up a handful of grass. She loved him so much, yet he . . . Chestnut hair tumbling around slender shoulders burned in his memory. He blinked furiously, longing and self-reproach giving way to resentment. He must stop this!

His arm tightened around Dolly. This was where his future lay; had all along. She wasn't to blame for his mind turning. She wouldn't suffer a second longer for his lapse in loyalty and common sense.

He didn't realise he'd squeezed his eyes shut until he felt pressure on his lips. Opening them, the expression he saw in Dolly's took him aback. They shone with love so true, it stole his breath. He read her thoughts in the liquid depths, knew she sensed something in him, that he was slipping from her. That she'd do anything to prevent it.

Here, entwined by the secluded river, innocent love he'd once held for her, unquestionably, stirred. The tip of her tongue tasted his lips hesitantly and his heartbeat quickened. Raised with high morals, they had always shown restraint; he'd never pushed his advances.

'You're happy, an' all, ain't you, Tommy?'

Fear tinged the gentle tone and all he desired was to reassure her, make her happy – free himself of the guilt consuming him from the inside out. He nodded.

There was an urgency to her kiss he'd never known. Fire low in his stomach smouldered and spread and when the swell of her breasts pushed against him, he could hold back no longer. He fumbled at the ribbon tied beneath her chin and tossed her bonnet to the grass. Burying his hands in her hair, he kissed her hungrily.

In that moment, he was powerless to resist. To feel wanted completely and loved so intensely was what his battered heart yearned for.

Chapter 21

'I DON'T MIND setting off early with thee. Mam will see to the children.'

Draping her shawl around her shoulders, Sally shook her head quickly. 'No, no. It's fine, Maggie.'

'If you're sure? Aye, as you say, a brisk walk will do the trick. I'll see you later.'

Wincing at her sympathetic smile, Sally mumbled goodbye and left. She *loathed* doing that. The deceit itself, that she needed to walk off a headache before work, was bad enough; Maggie's concern only added to her guilt.

She quickened her step. Pru at Agnes's window had stayed with her throughout the night. She just hoped there hadn't been further conflict over the weekend.

Sudden thoughts of her own family brought now-familiar pain and she forced her mind elsewhere. The issue with Stan was out of her hands. Her only option was to pray that one day, he'd forgive her.

Despite her inner turmoil, she couldn't help smiling as, repositioning her shawl, she glimpsed the garment beneath.

On returning to Maggie's yesterday, her friend told her Con had just left. He'd called to see how Sally was bearing up after the funeral, but her heart-to-heart with

Grace detained her longer than the time he could spare and she'd been saddened to have missed him by minutes. After the day she'd had, she'd have welcomed his company.

However, her dismay turned to curiosity at Maggie's soft eyes and pink cheeks – and the dove-grey blouse she held. Ellen had pointed to the twins, proudly sporting new cap and bonnet, and held up a cream-coloured blouse of her own in delight. She'd then motioned to a bundle on the table. They were gifts from Con from his market stall.

Though second-hand, everything was in sound condition and, holding the dark-blue blouse with black trim against herself, Sally had marvelled with the rest at the Irishman's generosity.

Like Maggie and her family, she'd never owned such a beautiful garment. The unfamiliar material felt strange against her skin but was a good fit, accentuating her curves to perfection.

Turning into Bradford Road, her smile deepened. He was calling again this evening. She couldn't wait to see him, to thank him. She was so fortunate to have him for a friend.

The pawnshop came into view and her smile melted as she saw a crowd huddled by the door. What on earth . . . ?

'It's locked, lass,' a perplexed customer announced. 'Been banging for ten minutes, I have. Summat's afoot. I've never known Miss Sharp be late opening.'

Sally glanced at each of them in turn. They held bundles containing Sunday-best clothes, which were pawned at the beginning of the week and redeemed on Saturday, for church the following day. It was the same week in, week out. The customer was right. For the shop to be closed at this hour, today of all days, something was indeed wrong.

Stepping into the road, she squinted at the upstairs windows. There was no sign of life this time. Curtains were drawn at each, including Agnes's. A customer banged on the door but still there was no movement beyond the panes.

'You work here, don't you? When did you last see the daughter?'

'I saw Miss Sharp at the window, there, yesterday afternoon.' As her answer hung in the air, dread crept through Sally, increasing when the customers' expressions showed they shared her concern.

At the back of the crowd, a stout woman turned to a girl beside her. 'Gertie, go and fetch the butcher, lass. This door needs kicking in. Wilf's a big beggar; he'll get it open.'

As the customers whispered amongst themselves, Sally watched the girl's spindly legs fly across the cobbles. *Please, Lord, let all be well,* she prayed. Yet deep down, she knew it wasn't. Her heartbeat quickened when Gertie emerged with Wilf. Crossing her fingers, she continued praying.

The butcher, bloodstained apron flapping in the breeze, nodded grimly at the woman's explanation. He stepped back, rolled his head side to side then ran and slammed his shoulder against the door. On the third attempt, there was the crack of splintering wood and after a final shove, it crashed open. Nodding to the subdued crowd, he motioned for them to remain outside.

Before he disappeared, Sally tugged his sleeve. 'Wait, I'm coming with you. I work here.'

He hesitated but at her determined look, nodded. 'All right, lass, but I'll lead. We could be walking into owt, here.'

A glance revealed the shop was empty. They hurried for the door behind the counter and mounted the stairs, calling Pru's name as they went, but silence greeted them.

On the landing, Wilf motioned to the closed doors. 'Which is the owd 'un's?'

Heart galloping, she pointed.

He pressed his ear to it then opened it slowly. 'Mother of God . . .' Staggering back, he hauled her away. 'Don't look, lass. Dear Lord, don't look upon that room!'

Sally heard herself scream. She pushed past and stumbled inside.

Agnes lay twisted at an odd angle in the blood-soaked bed. Emerald eyes, holding surprise, stared unseeing at the ceiling. Crimson splatters streaked her snow-white hair and beside her battered head lay her bloodied poker.

A noise like rushing water swam in Sally's ears. The room swayed and she gripped the door frame. Making to turn from the gruesome scene, she froze.

'Come away, there's nowt you can . . .' Wilf's words petered out as he followed her gaze to the window.

'I think it's Miss Sharp,' she whispered.

His voice was hesitant. 'Miss Sharp? Is that you?'

The kneeling figure lifted its head. A shaft of light from the slit in the curtains fell across the bruised face and, with a cry, Sally rushed forward. But the large knife in the woman's hand stopped her in her tracks.

Rocking slowly, a ghost of a smile touched Pru's mouth.

'Miss Sharp, it's me. Please . . . put the knife down.'

Pru stilled. A gentle frown accompanied her smile. 'Hello, dear.'

A sob caught in Sally's throat and she dropped to her knees. 'Oh, Miss Sharp, what—?'

'You must keep your voice down, dear.' Pru held a blood-smeared finger to her lips. 'Mother will be furious if we wake her.'

Wilf crouched beside Sally. 'Miss Sharp, let me have that knife, lass.'

He reached out and Sally held her breath.

Pru blinked. She gazed at the butcher, then at the knife. Then she began to laugh.

Time seemed to stand still and Sally could only watch as her friend raised her arm. Before Wilf could make a grab for it, Pru smiled softly and plunged the blade into her chest.

'Drink this. I've put in plenty of sugar for your nerves. Eeh, you poor girl. What an awful thing to witness. I can't believe it, I can't.'

'I don't understand. Miss Sharp . . . such a sweet, gentle soul . . .' Fresh tears burst from Sally. 'Her eyes . . . They were empty. Simply empty.'

Ellen sighed. 'She must've been in a dark place to do what she did but, harsh as it sounds, she's probably better off where she is now. She's at peace, lass, and she's free of her mother and all what went with it.'

'She was so thoughtful, so kind. Not once did she judge or question me regarding my marital affairs, though she must have thought it odd I never mentioned my husband. How has this happened? Perhaps I, I could have . . .'

Maggie knelt beside her. 'Sally, listen to me. Don't blame yourself for any of this. That troubled woman took her mam's life and her own. Her hands, not yours, brought about the deeds. There were nowt you could've done.'

'Drink your tea,' Ellen instructed softly. 'That constable said he'd need nowt more from you, didn't he, so when you've drunk that, you go and have a lie down. Rest is the best thing for shock.'

Minutes later, Maggie tucked Sally into her own bed. 'You'll not be disturbed. Try and get some sleep.'

'Please, stay with me awhile. Every time I close my eyes . . .'

'Eeh, course I will.' Her friend perched on the bed and shook her head. 'I should've come with thee this morning.'

'There's nothing you could have done. There's nothing anyone could have done.'

Maggie's eyes flashed with hurt. 'Why didn't you tell me sooner, Sally? I'd not have told no one. Honest, I wouldn't.'

Fear rolled through her stomach. She'd dreaded this. It was Stan all over again. Would lies and secrecy lose her her friend, too?

When she'd arrived home, leaning on the butcher for support, and revealed what had happened, their horrified cries rang through the house. They grew when she'd confessed all regarding the Sharps' relationship.

Though relieved to unburden herself of the terrible secret, she'd known their shock would dampen and she'd have some uncomfortable questions to answer. Now, trepidation overcame her. She sent up a silent prayer before attempting to explain.

'Maggie, I don't know where to begin. I strongly believed you deserved to know what went on behind those walls. Lying to you, making excuses . . . it's eaten away at me. I, I just—'

'I understand. Miss Sharp told you in confidence. It's fair wrong of me to say you should've told me. I'm just sorry I weren't there for thee, to give an ear to your worries. You must've felt wretched knowing what you did and having no one to talk to.'

Amazement slackened her mouth. 'You mean you're not angry with me? You understand my predicament? Oh, Maggie.' She threw her arms around her friend's neck. 'Thank you. Oh, thank you. I've been sick with worry at the thought of telling you. I thought you'd be furious, that you'd hate me, that you'd—'

'Eeh, course not,' Maggie soothed, rubbing her back as she would the twins'. 'I understand, lass, I do. I don't know what that there premicadent word were but think I can guess its meaning.'

Sally laughed through her tears. 'I thought you wouldn't want to see me again, like Stan. I'll never keep anything from you again. You have my word.'

Distraction tinged Maggie's smile.

'What's wrong?'

Maggie tapped her lips, eyes thoughtful. 'I've just remembered summat Miss Sharp said Saturday. I never thought nowt of it at the time . . . I were talking of the twins, how they can be imps at times, as children are. Well, she gorra bit teary. She said how she loved children, that if I ever needed a break, she'd gladly take them off my hands forra few hours. I thought it reet kind and told her so, but explained Mam helps out.'

'That was simply Miss Sharp's way. She mentioned after Peggy's passing how much she adored children.'

'Nay, that weren't all. She said how fortunate I were, that I had everything a woman could wish in life. She said to be a loving mother and *have* a loving mother were the greatest gifts a body could possess. I thought nowt of it, but . . . Eeh, lass, d'you think she were trying to tell me summat?'

Sally sighed. 'Almost every conversation we had, I felt she wanted to confide in me. But whenever I believed she was on the brink of doing so, she'd clam up. Their relationship was woven with long-held secrets and resentment. The atmosphere when they were together . . . well, it wasn't pleasant, put it that way.

'Miss Sharp admitted she couldn't bear to be in the same room as her. It's hardly surprising; I saw with my own eyes how her mother treated her. The feeling was clearly mutual. Mrs Sharp revealed she prayed for Miss Sharp's death after her birth.'

'That's wicked! How could anyone harbour such hatred for their flesh and blood?'

'I have no idea, Maggie. She once blurted she didn't know what some man or another saw in her daughter, but . . . Oh, I don't know. Whatever happened in the past seems irrelevant considering the enmity Mrs Sharp held for her before she even left the womb. There was such hatred, such a complete lack of love between them. It's so very sad.'

Maggie lowered her gaze. 'I know it's early on to mention this but, well, it needs thinking on sooner or later. We're out of a job, now, love. We need to think on what we're to do. Sorry as I am for what's occurred, I've the little 'uns and Mam to think of; as do you with the babby.'

'Do you know, I hadn't thought about that but you're right.' Sudden yearning for Breightmet, for Ivy and her family, the fields and meadows she missed so much, struck.

'We'll talk later. Try and snatch a few hours' sleep, it'll do you good.'

After Maggie left, Sally stared at the door for an age, thoughts tumbling. Recent events had taken centre stage in her mind and she felt wretched realising she'd almost forgotten about the attack at Bolton. She curled into a ball and squeezed her eyes shut. Peggy's death, discovering that Stan was her brother, the horrific incident today – all had consumed her thoughts, pushing aside the one person she owed her life to.

Shame stung and she hugged herself tighter, the urge for Spring Row rising. She didn't want to remain here any longer. The Manchester of her childhood was in a past she could never return to. There was nothing for her, here, now. Her relationship with her family was in tatters and, as Maggie pointed out, work no longer tied her.

Reliving the day's events yet again, tears burned. She could scarcely believe Pru and Agnes were gone. Pru's face at the window would haunt her for ever. What transpired over the weekend to tip her over the edge? Why, *why*, had she continued on her way yesterday when it was clear Pru needed her? Her presence was a cry for help – but selfishly, she'd walked away.

The constable had surmised that the murder occurred many hours before discovery. Had Pru already done the deed when she'd seen her?

For the remainder of her days, she'd never forget that haunted expression of someone beyond help. Agnes had provoked her, she *must* have, and after years of mental and physical torture, Pru snapped. There was no denying the old woman could be wicked beyond words.

Yet whatever Agnes's sins, she'd paid for them today and Sally hoped both were now at peace. It was just heartbreaking that it had to be in death; it clearly hadn't existed in life, for either.

These last days were the worst of her life. How much heartache could she bear?

Convulsing with sobs, she wept bitterly.

A loud rap woke Sally with a jolt. The slit of sky between the curtains was purple-black and gasping, she hauled herself up. Why had no one woken her? Feeding Jonathan her main concern, she hurried from the bedroom.

Tears she'd shed before falling into the fitful sleep had brought on a splitting headache. Reaching the kitchen, she shaded her eyes with her hand. 'It's as though my head has been trampled by a dozen horses. Why didn't you wake me?'

'There you are!'

Her head sprang up at the familiar voice and she saw Con in the doorway. Pain stabbed and she winced then shivered as the night breeze hit her.

Maggie rushed to her. 'Sit yourself by the fire, Sally. Con, come in and shut that door,' she added, then frowned to see he wasn't there. 'Where's he gone?' she asked her mother.

Ellen ceased pouring tea to look outside and almost dropped the pot when he suddenly reappeared. 'Mother of God, my heart!'

Con flashed her and Maggie a grin then winked at Sally. 'Close your eyes, acushla. I've a surprise for ye.' He returned to the street then sauntered back in, pushing a black perambulator. 'What do you think? 'Tis fit for a prince, to be sure.'

Sally gazed at the huge contraption. 'Is that for me?'

'Sure, you'd have a job squeezing in! 'Tis for your man, there.' He smiled at Jonathan. 'You didn't think I'd leave him out, did ye? I didn't bring it yesterday with the other items because I hadn't time to pick it up from my friend's stall. I collected it this afternoon. 'Tis clean,' he assured her. 'Sure, 'tis a little battered but it's solid and the wheels are sturdy. Aye, laid back in this, 'twill be grand he'll look, better than any toff.'

She forced a smile. 'You shouldn't have. Thank you; for the blouse, too. You're too kind.'

Studying her, his grin vanished. 'What's wrong?'

Maggie placed a protective arm around her shoulders. 'You've not heard?'

'Heard what, Maggie?' He sighed and rubbed his chin. 'The funeral. Jaysus, Sally, I'm sorry. Did something happen with the family? Weren't you able to be reconciled?'

Maggie bit her lip. 'It's not that. This morning . . . I don't know how you've not heard.'

'I've been out of Ancoats all day at your man's picking up this,' he said, nodding to the perambulator, 'then collecting stock for my stall. What should I have heard?' In two strides, he crossed the room and knelt before them. 'What's happened?'

'I tried telling you afore Sally came down. Con, summat terrible's happened. Miss Sharp . . . She's taken her mam's life and her own. Sally found them this morning.'

He shook his head in disbelief. Sally began to cry, Maggie's bottom lip trembled, and Con clasped them both in a hug.

Holding her friends close, deep sadness thudded through Sally's breast but she knew she must tell them. Longing for Spring Row and the Morgans was as acute as earlier. She'd made up her mind. Her friends needed to know.

She glanced at them in turn. 'I have to tell you something. I've decided to return to Bolton.' From what little she'd revealed, they were aware of her troubled marriage so she wasn't surprised when each of them protested, faces creased with concern. 'Please, I must. I'm aching to see the Morgans and . . . Well, the stark truth is, other than you all, there's nothing for me in Manchester. I barely have a relationship with my family, no position, very little money and no home.'

'You're welcome to stop here as long as you want, in't she, Mam?' Maggie cried. 'You see,' she added when Ellen nodded, 'you're a good friend, lass – the best. I don't want to lose thee.'

'Nor shall you,' she said with feeling. 'I don't know what will happen when I arrive or how long I'll be able to stay. And if I'm honest, at this moment, I don't know whether I'll return here afterwards. But I have to go. I have to, Maggie. I've left it far longer than I should. I must see Mrs Morgan is well. Whatever happens, wherever I am, I promise we'll always be friends.' Maggie lowered her head and she turned to Con. 'You'll look after her for me, won't you?'

His expression was unreadable. In answer, he squeezed Maggie's shoulder. 'When will ye go?'

'When Miss Sharp and her mother are laid to rest. I couldn't go without saying goodbye.'

He nodded curtly and strode to the door. He shot Maggie and Ellen a half-smile over his shoulder. 'I'll be away, so. Goodnight.' His gaze then flicked to her. 'Goodbye, acushla,' he murmured.

Sally hadn't time to respond. Within seconds, he'd gone, leaving her staring helplessly at the door.

Chapter 22

FOR THE SECOND time, a bounding Shield almost knocked Sally from her feet.

'Will you calm down, for goodness' sake?' she chided, steadying the basket. 'Be patient, boy.' Despite her firmness, she couldn't contain a sad smile. He'd missed Grace's as much as she.

Since leaving Maggie's, he'd seemed to sense where they headed and had leapt about like a puppy the length of the street. Wetness touched her hand and she glanced down. Tongue lolling, he stared back solemnly, as though apologising, and chuckling, she scratched his ear. However, when Boslam Street came into view, all laughter left her. As excited as Shield was, she felt nothing but anxiety. Yet visit she must. To return to Bolton, she needed her family's help.

As she opened the door, Grace's face contorted in shocked delight. 'Oh, love! Oh, come in, come in!'

Sally's arms ached to embrace her but she had to ask. 'Stan . . . ? Is he at work?'

There was a break in Grace's voice. 'Aye. Come in.'

She followed her inside. Her gaze went to the window and the empty space where Peggy's bed had been. The shelf was free of medicine bottles, the chair in which Grace had sat hunched over her dying daughter now against the wall. Averting her eyes, she placed the basket on the table.

Grace peered inside and smiled. She lifted a tiny hand and kissed it. Looking at Sally, her eyes were bright. 'I'm that glad to see you both. Aye, and you,' she added with a laugh when Shield nudged her arm. ''Ere, I heard about the owd 'un and her daughter. Shocking, in't it?'

'There was nothing we could do. The butcher made a grab for the knife but, well, it happened so fast. Oh, Aunt Grace, the blood . . . so much blood. He said in all his years as a butcher, he'd never seen so much before that day; it was like stepping into an abattoir . . . Never, for the rest of my days, will I forget that image.'

Grace slapped a hand to her mouth then grasped her niece's fingers. 'I didn't know you were there when . . . Oh, love. I wanted to come and see you at your friend's, knew you'd be upset. You'd grown close to the daughter, hadn't you? If I'd known you'd seen . . .' She looked away guiltily. 'I didn't, I mean I, I didn't know whether—'

'It's fine, Aunt Grace.' She could see helplessness etched in every line of her aunt's face. 'If Stan discovered you'd been to see me, it would have caused you no end of grief.'

'I don't know how you can be so understanding. My heart's breaking for thee day and night. I've tried talking to him . . . Me and Ed are at a loss what to do. You should be here, where you belong, with your family.'

Sally stared at their clasped hands. 'How are you coping, with . . . Peggy?' she asked, changing the subject. Grace was in an impossible situation and it didn't look as though circumstances would change soon. Raking over it was pointless.

'It's been hard, aye. But I know she's at peace and in no more pain. It helps to think on that.'

Sally nodded then said quietly, 'Aunt Grace, I wanted to ask if Uncle Ed would make arrangements for the cart. I've decided to return to Bolton once the Sharps are laid to rest.'

'Return? You mean visit?' Grace's eyes widened when Sally glanced away. 'Nay. Nay, tha can't leave for good. Tha can't, lass! He'll come round, our Stan. He will, I know it. He needs time, is all.'

'No, he won't. You know it as well as I.'

'Nay, he will! And what about that swine, Joseph? You'd not know peace with him on your doorstep. You'd allus be looking over your shoulder. Manchester's your home, lass.'

'No, Aunt Grace, it's not. Don't you see? Since the day I arrived, there's been nothing but trouble. Stan's right. I should never have come.' She shook her head as Grace made to protest. 'It's true. I've thought about this long and hard. Settling in Bolton is impossible, I realise that. I intend to visit the Morgans and afterwards . . . ?

'The only places I know, where I know *anyone*, are Bolton and here. I cannot stay in one and don't wish to stay in the other. Maybe I'll try somewhere new; Preston, perhaps, or Oldham. It will mean starting afresh, alone, but I truly believe a new beginning is what I need. I must leave. I need to see Mrs Morgan. I *need* to get away from *here*.'

Grace's eyes dulled. None the less, she nodded. 'I'll ask Ed when he gets in.'

'Thank you. I'll send word when I'm ready.'

'I'm so sorry for how things turned out. Your mam would be turning in her grave if she knew how I've let you down.'

'You haven't. Don't think that.'

As she'd done with Jonathan, Grace kissed her hand. 'Will you have a brew or must you be away?'

It was now Thursday and she planned to call at Christ Church on her return to Maggie's to enquire over the funerals. A ripple of horror had spread throughout the town; the sorry business had been on everyone's lips. She'd seen the looks whenever she ventured out, had heard the whispers. But she'd heard nothing about the burials.

Surely they would be soon? An investigation into the deaths wasn't necessary. There had been no mistaking the causes of death and no one besides the deceased was involved. She could see no reason for delay.

'I will, thank you. I have to call at Christ Church but there's no hurry.'

Busy at the fire, Grace glanced over her shoulder. 'The Roundhouse?' she asked, as locals knew it, due to its circular structure.

'I hoped to find out when the funerals will be.'

'Funerals? There will only be the one, lass.'

'One?'

'Sally love, Miss Sharp won't receive the same as the owd 'un. She committed murder and self-murder. She can't be buried in sacred ground, for the Church don't allow it.' Grace shook her head in disbelief. 'Didn't you know?'

'Mrs Sharp provoked her, she must have done! Surely the Church will understand? Surely they'll see she was as much to blame? What Miss Sharp did was dreadful, I'm not denying that, but surely . . . ?' Her words died when Grace shook her head again. 'But she doesn't deserve that! She was the kindest, gentlest person I've ever met. She deserves a decent burial. You agree, don't you, Aunt Grace?'

'It's not for me nor anyone else to say. Them's the rules. When all's said and done, she took a life. It's a mortal sin, lass, whichever way you look at it. In any case, she'd have been buried in unconsecrated ground, for if she'd lived, she'd have been hanged for murder and buried within the prison walls.'

Sally was lost for words. Maggie hadn't mentioned anything, must have assumed she'd know. How had she been so naive? Her ignorance of the world and its workings was bewildering. That's what growing up in the confines of the workhouse does, she realised. Your life is within those walls. You're blind to the outside and its conventions.

Grace pushed a cup across. 'Drink your tea, it'll calm your nerves.' She watched her, numb with shock, take tiny sips. 'You all right, love?'

'No, Aunt Grace, I'm not. This isn't right.'

'As far as the Church is concerned, she's not entitled to the comfort of religion. There's no way round it; it is how it is. Least they don't bury them at crossroads no more, like when I were a lass. Crowds would gather to watch, morbid beggars.' Grace shuddered at the memories. 'Miss Sharp will be buried in private. Be grateful for that.'

'So what will happen? Where *will* she be laid to rest?'

'In a plot away from the main churchyard.'

'She'll be tossed into the ground, just like that? No service, prayers? No mourners to utter a kind word or goodbye?'

'That's the top and bottom of it. Come on, eh, love? Don't dwell on what can't be changed.'

Despite the scorch of injustice and disgust, Sally nodded. She didn't want to spoil this meeting; she didn't know when she'd next see her aunt.

An hour later, she and Grace shared an emotional farewell on the step. Wiping her tears, she finally backed away.

'Goodbye, Aunt Grace. Please give my love to Uncle Ed. And Stan.'

Apron pressed to her mouth, Grace could only nod.

Sally tore her gaze from the crumpled face and walked away. Unlike Shield, who turned and whimpered, she didn't look back. She'd gain nothing besides more heartache. Of that, her mind and body could take no more.

Her heart screamed for Maggie and Ellen's comfort, but she didn't turn for Davies Street. Instead, she headed down Carruthers Street and on to Every Street. Passing through the gates, Grace's words echoed in her mind:

'*Them's the rules. There's no way round it; it is how it is. Don't dwell on what can't be changed.*'

She had no doubt Grace spoke truthfully. But was there *really* no way round it? Surely it was worth her trying? Covering her head with her shawl, she whispered to Shield to stay, and slipped inside the church.

The clergyman who had conducted Peggy's funeral smiled warmly. 'Good afternoon. Please, come in. I don't bite,' he added, eyes twinkling, when she hesitated.

Sally blinked in surprise. This one was certainly nothing like the preacher! Hope fluttering in her breast, she stepped forward. 'Good afternoon, Father Collins. I'd like a word, if I may?'

'Of course, my child. What is it you wish to discuss?'

A glance around showed the church was otherwise empty and she relaxed somewhat. 'It's rather a delicate issue. It's about Miss Prudence Sharp.'

His eyebrows rose, the smile vanishing. 'Oh?'

Her resolve waned at his change in demeanour but she swallowed her nerves. 'There's no easy way of asking so I may as well just say it. Miss Sharp committed a terrible sin but there were reasons, Father.

'She suffered appallingly at her mother's hands and I believe, from what I knew of her, she simply . . . snapped. A body can only bear so much. She wouldn't have planned what she did, I'd stake my life on it. Her mother beat her regularly. She treated her as no one should be treated, let alone by a parent.

'Miss Sharp's mental state at the time, well, she cannot have been of sound mind, for as God is my witness, I can truthfully say that woman would never have committed such a deed. She suffered enough in life. Please, don't make her suffer in death. Couldn't you allow her a proper burial? Couldn't you, Father? Please?'

He released his breath slowly. 'Come, Mrs . . . ?'

'Swann, Father.'

'Mrs Swann, sit down.' He motioned to a pew and sat beside her. 'I see you are grieving, my child. You cared a great deal for the late Miss Sharp?'

Tears stung. She nodded.

'You must have been a comfort to her. She often felt alone.'

'I didn't realise you knew her.'

'Oh, indeed. She used to attend mass regularly. Not to pray as such, as I recall. I believe it was sanctuary she sought. As her mother's health declined, she had less time to attend but when the opportunity arose, she would come.' His eyes softened. 'She was a troubled soul, Mrs Swann. I'm aware of the difficulties she faced with her mother, indeed I am—'

'However?' she cut in quietly. 'There is one coming, isn't there, Father?'

He gave a small sigh. 'Mrs Swann, what you are asking is quite impossible. I appreciate your feelings on the matter but, as saddened as I am by what has occurred, a conventional burial within the main churchyard is simply out of the question.'

She'd heard enough. Deep down, she'd known she was wasting her time. And to think she'd hoped he was different from that fiend, Bailey. They were all the same.

'This may bring God's wrath upon my head but to be perfectly honest, Father, I'm beyond caring. I say the Church is wrong. You're aware of Miss Sharp's suffering, you understand, and yet . . . ?' She nodded stiffly and rose. 'I'll trouble you no further and shall take my leave before I say something I may regret. Good day to you.'

'Please, sit down.'

Lifting the basket, she shook her head. 'I don't believe there's anything left to say, do you, Father? You've made your decision quite clear. Now, if you'll excuse me.'

Father Collins laid a hand on her wrist. Though he was clearly aware they were the only ones present, his eyes flicked around the church, then to the door.

'You didn't allow me to finish,' he murmured. 'A conventional burial within the main churchyard *is* out of the question. However . . . Sit down, Mrs Swann, and listen carefully.'

Tommy stared across the table. The scraping had gone on for hours and with each passing minute, his irritation mounted. Finally, he could stand it no longer.

'You don't have to do this.'

Absorbed in his creation, the tip of his tongue poking out in concentration, Shaun didn't look up. 'Eh?'

'I said you don't have to do this.' He struggled to keep an even tone. 'It's a reet nice thought, like, but . . .'

'Don't you like it, our Tommy?'

He glanced away, rubbing a hand across his eyes. 'Aye, lad, course I do. Ignore me. I'm tired, is all.'

Shaun's face spread in a smile. 'It'll look better, soon, and I want to do it, honest. This is my way of saying thanks. If it weren't for thee, I'd not have my apprenticeship. You expect your parents to want the best for you, but for your brother . . . Well, I'm grateful.'

'I did nowt. It weren't my brass made it happen.'

'Oh, aye, aye. I'm grateful to Mrs Goden, an' all.'

Tommy's jaw clenched to hear Sally's marital name but he forced a nod.

'You believed in me. You went out of your way to change my life. I'll not forget it.'

The noticeable change in his brother brought a genuine smile. The lad had grown up.

Shaun put down his knife, lifted the block of wood from the pile of shavings and studied it through narrowed eyes. He traced his fingers along two mounds, frowned as though dissatisfied and reached for the knife.

Tommy watched swift strokes add definition to a flat cap. When Shaun began scratching a bonnet's outline on the next mound, his tolerance burned out. He scraped back his chair.

Seated by the fire, his mother glanced up as he crossed to the window, then returned her attention to her darning. But his father continued watching him. Arthur's gaze strayed to Shaun then back to Tommy. He extinguished his pipe and rose.

Ivy looked up again when her husband extracted coins from his pocket and counted them. Arthur flashed her an easy smile.

'Now, wench, don't be looking at me like that.'

'Well, on a Thursday? You'll not get up in t' morning. It's murder trying to rouse you when you've had a sup the night afore.'

'I'll be up.' His father dropped the coins into his pocket and nodded to Tommy. 'Coming forra jar, lad?'

Ivy clicked her tongue. 'There better be no moaning from you, neither, the morrow. If you don't rise from your bed first time I shout, you'll get that pail of cowd water over your head,' she warned, pointing to where it stood beside the hearth. 'That goes for thee, an' all,' she told her husband.

Donning jackets and caps, they rolled their eyes at a grinning Shaun.

'Aye, I saw that! Oh go on, you pair of inebriates, afore it gets too late.'

Smiling, they left the cottage. They passed through the row in companionable silence and it wasn't until they were sitting with their tankards that they spoke.

'So what's this in aid of?' Tommy asked.

'Just fancied a jar.'

'At this hour, on a Thursday? Come on, I'm not daft.'

His father took a long draught of ale and wiped his mouth on his hand. 'I thought it were time we had that talk.'

'About what?'

'About you and that Goden lass.' He cocked an eyebrow in surprise when Tommy thumped the tabletop.

'Why won't folk stop calling her that? She's nowt to do with him any more. She's Sally. Just call her Sally.' Slowly, his face crumpled in horror. 'I'm sorry, I . . . I'm sorry.'

His father gazed at him. 'Lord above, you've got it worse than I thought. What's wrong with you, lad? You barely know her and besides owt else, she's a wedded woman!'

'D'you not think I've tried ridding her from my thoughts?'

'Try bloody harder! It's madness.'

'I went to Manchester to see her to . . . Well, I don't know. I didn't think on what I'd do when I arrived. I just . . . I had to go.'

Arthur raised his eyes to the ceiling. 'Christ's sake. And how did you plan on finding her? By tramping the lanes hoping to bump into her?'

A bitter smile touched his lips. 'Aye, as it happens. And believe it or not, I did.'

'Tha did what?'

'See her. Can you believe it, the size of that place, the amount of folk up there? What are the chances?'

His father's tankard paused midway to his mouth. 'Oh, lad. Please don't say you told her how you feel.'

'Nay, don't fret. As it turned out, she's met someone. Hanging off some fella's arm, she were. Reet ugly divil, an' all,' he lied, to soothe his ego.

'So what now?'

Averting his eyes, he took a gulp of ale. 'I'm going to ask Dolly to marry me.'

'Why?'

The question threw him. He cursed inwardly when heat crept up his neck.

'Son, I watched you with our Shaun. You couldn't bear to look at that carving of you and Dolly, could you?'

Shame and terror coursed through him. It must have shown, for Arthur frowned.

'Oh, what now? What have you done?'

Tommy crushed a fist to his mouth but couldn't contain the words. 'Sunday, by the river . . . May God forgive me, I lay with Dolly.'

'For the love of God, you bloody fool, yer!'

The innkeeper looked across and Tommy touched his father's sleeve. 'Please, calm down.'

'Calm down? *Calm bloody down?*' His voice dropped to a growl. 'You brainless young swine, d'you realise what you've done? What will her father say; not to mention your mam?' He closed his eyes. 'Lord, your mam. I'd not like to be in your boots when she hears.'

'What am I to do?'

The answer was firm. 'What tha said. Marry her.'

'But I don't love her. Well, I do, I think . . .' Tommy prodded his chest. 'It's not enough, in here. I thought it were but since Sally—'

'And what if she's with child?' A little of the anger had left his father's tone but his eyes were steely. 'You've no choice. You've deflowered the lass. No fella will want her, now. Get Sally from your mind. There's no getting out of this. You'll have to wed her.'

Emptiness filled him. 'I am fond of her. I'd not hurt her for owt.'

'You'll do the right thing?'

'Aye.'

'You know, don't you, if there were another way . . . if there were owt I could do, I would?'

A lump formed in Tommy's throat at the sincerity in the gruff words. 'Aye, I know. This is my mess and me alone must sort it. I'll not shirk my duty. I'll call on Dolly, Saturday, and if her father gives permission . . . I'll ask for her hand.'

When Arthur went to refill their tankards, Tommy covered his face with his hands. He wouldn't ruin her reputation, abandon her after having his way. He'd made his bed, he'd have to lie in it. *Beside Dolly, every night, for the rest of his life . . .*

'Sally,' he breathed. 'Dear God, what have I done?'

Chapter 23

A SUBDUED SALLY and Maggie passed through the streets. Christ Church came into view and Sally gave a half-smile of reassurance but her friend, after attempting to return it and failing, bit her lip.

'I appreciate your coming. Please, don't worry. Father Collins assured me all will run smoothly.'

Maggie nodded uncertainly. 'It's just, well, folk might wonder why we're going early. Mrs Sharp's service ain't till two; it's only just gone twelve,' she said out of the side of her mouth. 'Are you certain he's agreed to this? Happen you got it wrong.

'I've heard whispers of this sort of thing for babbies what die afore they can be baptised, but . . .' She glanced around. 'Not with folk who've committed murder or self-murder – and Miss Sharp committed both! I've not heard afore of any priest turning the other cheek to summat like this.'

'Well, now you have. He's a compassionate man. He understands the circumstances behind Miss Sharp's dreadful act.' As had Maggie, she glanced around before continuing. 'From what he hinted, it simply comes down to the humanity of individual clergymen. I'm thankful Father Collins is a sympathetic soul unafraid of defying convention.'

'He'd be in hot water if he were found out, though, wouldn't he? Mebbe us, an' all. And that'd be nowt compared with what would happen were folk to discover what we were about. A quick prayer and blessing of an innocent babby's grave is one thing; this is summat else altogether. I reckon many wouldn't approve.'

'I cannot speak for Father Collins. I don't know what the repercussions, if any, would be, but the decision was his. And I for one am grateful. I'm not concerned what people think. This is right, I'm certain.'

Re-tying string around a posy of roses, the flower seller, sensing their presence, smiled without looking up. 'Just a minute while I . . .' She made a knot and returned the bunch to her basket. 'There we are. Now, what would you like?' Recognition flickered in her eyes and her smile turned sympathetic. 'Hello, lass.'

Remembering her kindness with Peggy's flowers, Sally smiled warmly. 'Good afternoon. You were most helpful last week and regrettably, I need your advice again.'

The flower seller nodded understandingly. Many, many people, young and old alike, died daily around here. Attending more than one funeral in the same week, for some poor souls, wasn't uncommon.

'Who's being laid to rest?'

Seeing Sally hesitate, Maggie stepped forward. 'Two posies of white roses will do, ta. They're suitable for an owder lady, ain't they?'

'Aye, they are. It's important to pick summat right; flowers hold different meanings, you see. Aye, white roses – innocence, purity and reverence. A sound choice, lass.'

Sally paid with a mumbled thank-you. Once out of earshot, she glanced at her friend. 'Oh, if only she knew . . .'

Maggie sighed. 'Let's get this over with.'

Sally now knew that, away from the main churchyard, most parish churches held a marshy or overgrown plot for the interment of sinners beyond redemption.

In a remote corner beneath an ancient, bare-branched tree, Father Collins conducted a simple ceremony and, surrounded by countless unmarked graves, laid Pru Sharp to rest.

Murmuring a final goodbye, Sally placed a posy on the fresh earth then turned to the gravedigger. 'Thank you.'

The kindly faced man leaning on his spade touched his cap. He marked the sign of the cross over his chest and nodded to the priest.

Father Collins returned it. 'Thank you, Jackson.' He motioned to her and Maggie. 'Come, let us pray.'

They walked back to the church in silence.

Sally couldn't suppress a bitter smile as Father Collins' clear voice committed Agnes to the ground. No hushed tones, here. No glancing around before blessing the grave. No secrecy.

In her eyes, this woman had sinned far more than the one condemned to lie for eternity as far from the church as possible. Pru's resting place would remain unmarked by stone or cross; no inscription, no lasting reminder of someone more sinned against than sinner. Yet despite the years of misery she'd inflicted, Agnes would lie peacefully in the Lord's garden. It didn't make sense.

Father Collins closed his bible. 'I will leave you to say your final words.'

Alone with Maggie, Sally swallowed the pain of injustice and laid the second posy on the soil. She replaced the heartfelt apology whispered at Pru's graveside with one question: 'Why?'

Maggie reached for her hand. 'That's summat we'll never know. They've carried their secrets to their graves. Dwelling on it'll do you no good.'

Despite Agnes's entitlement to a conventional funeral, it was as lonely an affair as her daughter's, and as Maggie steered Sally away, sadness for both women overcame her. They'd had only each other. What-ifs haunted her but Maggie was right. Dwelling on what she couldn't change was useless.

Father Collins stood waiting by the church doors and she clasped his hand. 'I cannot express my gratitude for what you've done today. I'll never forget your kindness, Father.'

Eyes soft, he inclined his head. 'Have strength, my child. Remember, the Lord's house is always open.'

Maggie took her arm. 'Let's get you home.'

Those words were music to her. She yearned to sit in Maggie and Ellen's cosy kitchen and hold Jonathan close.

As they passed through the church gates, a gentleman collided with them. He struggled to keep hold of the sheaf of papers he carried and they rushed to assist him.

'Thank you, thank you, I'm most terribly sorry,' he mumbled, eyes flicking behind them to the church. 'May I ask, is Father Collins still present?'

Sally nodded. 'Yes, he's—'

'Thank goodness. Good day.'

'Clumsy beggar,' grumbled Maggie when he'd gone. 'He near knocked us flying, then.'

Looking back, Sally frowned. 'He was in quite a hurry. I wonder what was so important?'

'Lord knows. Come on, lass, I hear our teapot calling.'

A beshawled figure watched the women turn into Junction Street.

When they disappeared from view, she emerged from the shelter of the branches. Wary eyes darting, she hurried to a fresh grave. She dropped to her knees and ran her fingers over the earth. She mouthed words then dipped her chin to her chest, lips still. She straightened the roses, caressed the soil once more then rose. Quickly, noiselessly, she scurried back to the trees.

Reappearing at the opposite end of the churchyard, she drew her shawl lower over her face. She flitted between the gravestones, eyes fixed on another dark mound up ahead. Reaching this, she didn't kneel. No gentle fingering of soil or straightening of flowers. No whisper, no emotion. Glaring down, her every pore emitted pure loathing.

She spat on the ground and was gone.

Chapter 24

MAGGIE SCOWLED AT the elderly man atop the cart and despite her own heartache, Sally chuckled. She pulled her into a hug.

'Don't blame him, Maggie.'

'Well, I still reckon he's a blighter, taking you away from me.'

Sally kissed her cheek and held her at arm's length. 'Look after yourself and remember, this isn't for ever. I don't know when . . . but we will see each other again, you have my word. Goodbye. Thank you, for everything.'

Lowering her head, Maggie's tears dripped to the cobbles. 'Goodbye, love.'

Guilt thumping, she turned to Ellen, who was holding a solemn-looking twin under each arm. 'Goodbye. Thank you for all you've done for me. Goodbye, Harry, Flo. Be good for your mother and grandmother, won't you?'

The children broke free and ran to her, and Ellen covered her face with her apron, unable to watch the daughter and grandchildren she adored upset.

Small arms wrapped around Sally's waist. She stooped and kissed the bewildered faces. 'Shield shall miss you both very much. Would you like to give him a hug before we leave?'

They nodded and threw their arms around his neck. 'Bye, Shield,' they said in unison. He licked their faces, and giggling, they ran back to their grandmother.

Sally climbed aboard, Shield clambered beside her and she set the canvas bag and basket by her feet. Too large for the cart, the perambulator still stood beneath Maggie's kitchen window. She hoped leaving it behind wouldn't offend Con.

Thoughts of him brought an ache to her stomach. She'd seen nothing of him since revealing she was leaving. He'd been upset, it showed on his face, but still . . . Hurt stabbed again as she scanned the street. She'd hoped to see him, say goodbye, thank him for everything. She'd miss him greatly.

Swallowing disappointment when it became clear he wouldn't show, she held out a hand to Maggie, who gripped it. 'When you see Con, tell him . . . Tell him I'll be forever thankful for his friendship.' She squeezed her hand then glanced to Ed's friend. 'I'm ready, now, Mr Lynch.'

At his command, the large bay set off. She waved to her lovely friends, tears running down her face. Only when the cart turned and they were out of sight did she look away.

Drowning in conflicting emotions, she gazed around at the fetid homes and the tall chimneys invading the skyline.

'Goodbye, Manchester,' she whispered.

Maggie was certain afterwards that if the cart had departed a mere minute later, her friend would still be here.

As it happened, Sally didn't see Father Collins passing down Davies Street in the opposite direction. She didn't see him halt beside Maggie, or catch his words. Neither did she see Maggie's hand fly to her mouth, nor hear her hopeless cry of, 'Sally, wait! You'll never believe . . . Sally, come back!'

Ivy leaned towards the bubbling pot and sniffed appreciatively. After stirring the broth, she turned to the table. She'd already laid out the pretty crockery and she nodded, satisfied with her efforts. Today was important and she'd worked hard, cleaning and cooking since dawn. It looked queer seeing five places set again. Queer but nice, she admitted.

'All right, wench?'

She glanced up as Arthur entered the kitchen. 'I were just thinking, it's queer seeing the table set for one more again, in't it?'

Her fixed smile didn't fool him. He took her in his arms. 'Tha had to let go some time.'

'I had a feeling it were coming. Even Martha did, said all what's happened would bring them closer, but . . .'

'I know. It's a big deal forra mother, losing her son to another wench. I remember what you were like with our James's betrothal.' She smiled crookedly and he chuckled. 'Be happy for him, eh? I know you've a soft spot for the lad but he's a grown man. It's time to let him go.'

'Aye, I know. I just want him to be happy. I've only ever wanted all of them to be happy.'

'And they are. You've done a sound job, Ivy, better than any mother could've. Anyroad, you'll not lose him right away. It'll take them months to save for the wedding and afterwards, they'll be dwelling here till they find their own cottage.'

She pulled away when footsteps sounded on the stairs. Fixing on a smile, she turned to look at her sons.

Having scrubbed the half-day's work from their skin and hair, they stood stiffly in their best clothes. Tommy glanced from the table to her. He flashed a smile but didn't speak. Shaun, on the other hand, grumbled to himself, wriggling on the spot.

'Mam, must we wear this lot? This shirt's itching summat awful. Dolly won't mither if we're not in our best.'

Her temper rose to the fore. 'Give over grousing, Shaun. This here's an important day. I'll not have the lass here and us favouring a bunch of vagrants. She might think twice about accepting and run a mile at the thought of wedding into a family of ragbags. Stop your fidgeting and go and fill the pail at the well.' When he'd gone, she turned to Tommy. 'I were only pulling his leg. I've not worried thee, have I? Me and my big bloody mouth, saying things like that on a day like today.'

'Nay, Mam.'

'Good. Anyroad, the lass would need her head looking at, wouldn't she, Arthur? He's a good catch, our Tommy, in't he?' At his nod, she smiled proudly. 'Nay, she's fair smitten. Have no fear, lad.'

When his mother turned back to her cooking, Tommy shot his father a look. 'Nay, she'll not turn me down.'

Dull acceptance in his tone brought a sigh to Arthur. They stared at each other helplessly.

Unaware of the silent message passing between them, Ivy nodded to Shaun as he re-entered, lugging the heavy pail. 'Put it by the hearth, lad.'

'Wind's picking up out there. Oh, and I've just seen Dolly turn into the row.'

'What? And you didn't think to mention it as soon as you come in? You put the pail back and even remarked on t' bloody weather afore telling us! She's bleedin' early,' she muttered, patting her hair. 'And you remember what I said earlier, Shaun. Don't you go letting owt slip afore our Tommy's had chance to ask her. He got Nat Jenkins's permission yesterday but she knows nowt of it. Think on, d'you hear?'

'Aye, Mam.'

Arthur went to stand beside her and she squeezed his hand. 'You all right, Tommy?' she asked, glancing across.

'Mam, I . . .' His breaths came in short gasps. 'I don't think . . .'

She frowned. 'Son?'

Glimpsing the warning in his father's eyes, he swallowed hard, forcing a smile. 'I, I don't think there's a mam in t' whole of Bolton better than thee. Thank you. You've done me proud.'

'Eeh, Tommy.' Love thickened her voice but when her bottom lip wobbled, she quelled it with laughter. 'Ay, you soppy bugger, there's no need—' Knocking silenced her. She breathed deeply. 'Good luck, lad.'

The walk to the door was like stepping to the gallows.

Luck? A damn miracle couldn't save him.

The journey hadn't been a comfortable one. Hours of bumping through ditches and potholes, squashed by Shield's bulk, all the while struggling to placate the grizzling baby, had left Sally stiff and weary.

All the way, her emotions had swung dizzily. Excitement at meeting Ivy turned to dread with thoughts of her being the woman attacked. Throbbing anticipation at seeing Tommy, she'd forced away. Indulging in the memory of him was becoming impossible to suppress; it was almost an obsession.

Frequently, thoughts of Joseph had replaced them, bringing a churning sickness. Yet whilst her feelings for Tommy strengthened in her absence, anxiety over Joseph had blessedly diminished. The prospect of seeing him still sent fingers of fear up her spine – that would never leave her completely – but it wasn't the all-consuming, gut-wrenching terror she once knew.

She'd noticed the shift over the weeks. So much had happened since leaving. She felt a different woman. She was stronger, clearer of mind. She was in control. Never again would that monster hurt her.

Her shawl, lying loose across her shoulders, she involuntarily drew over her head when grey-brown Deansgate appeared. Eyes flicking around, her hand tightened on the basket. She released her breath when they passed and, after peeking back, just to be sure, lowered her shawl.

Eventually, the clogged air grew clear. Green strips winked on the horizon and her heartbeat quickened.

'Please, Lord, don't let Joseph discover my return,' she prayed. 'Please let Mrs Morgan be well.' Swallowed by the rumble of cart wheels and thudding hooves, her quiet pleas went unheard by the driver. 'And please, *please*, give me strength to act naturally upon seeing Tommy,' she added, flushing with shame.

At the turning of Spring Row, she signalled to the driver and with his assistance stepped from the cart. Shield sniffed the air and whined, as though sad to be back.

'It's all right, boy. You have me, now,' she told him.

From beneath Jonathan's covers, she lifted the pouch containing what little money she possessed. She'd given Maggie several shillings to see her through until she found work and had calculated that, after paying

Mr Lynch, she'd enough to keep herself for a few weeks. She just hoped she'd soon find employment, wherever she decided upon, following this visit.

'Thank you, Mr Lynch. I'm most grateful. I'll be fine from here.'

'Nay, lass, keep your brass. You owe me nowt.'

'But of course I do!'

'Nay, you don't, for your aunt and uncle paid me last night, said as how you're to keep your money for yourself and the babby. You've a sound family back there. Don't leave it too long, eh, for Grace's sake.'

She took the basket and canvas bag from him, eyes misty. 'I don't know what to say. Please thank them for me.'

He tapped his cap. 'Take care, lass.'

Heart overflowing with love, she sent up a prayer that, one day, her relationship with them – all of them – would be repaired. Shield trotting alongside, she entered the row.

She avoided looking at her cottage and fixed her gaze on the Morgans'. Nearing the gate, she saw their front door ajar and her heart leapt. Worry they might be absent had niggled at her throughout the journey. Not really knowing another soul, what to do would have stumped her.

Picking up scents of his former home, Shield wandered off. He turned when she halted and she flapped a hand.

'It's all right, Shield. Go and explore,' she told him, and off he went to visit his old haunts.

When she was midway up the path, a voice drifted from the cottage. Tommy. *Tommy.* Heady heat quivered through her. She forced herself forward, knocked then peeped around the door.

Gazing upon the scene, her smile froze. She barely noticed Ivy, Arthur and Shaun. It was the objects of their attention which struck her dumb and made her want to turn tail and flee.

Sitting with her back to the door was a woman. And on bended knee at her feet, holding a ring aloft, was Tommy.

Shock hit her like a slap to the face. In those seconds, streams of memories swamped her. His soothing voice, how he'd cradled her in his strong arms . . . Their time together after retrieving the money, his smile, his laughter, how he'd sweep back his hair . . . Hopes she'd harboured for weeks, countless nights she'd lain awake thinking of him . . .

She'd never felt as foolish, ashamed, confused. What had she been thinking? Had she really believed he felt anything for her? She was a married woman; nothing could have come of it . . . Such wild imaginings . . . What in God's name was wrong with her?

In the same moment that Ivy spotted her, the woman threw herself at Tommy, crying, 'Oh! Course I'll marry thee!'

'Sally? Is that you? I don't believe it!' Ivy's words surprised everybody. As one, they turned to the door.

The sight of the older woman dragged Sally to the present. She sagged with relief. Her dear friend was all right! It wasn't Ivy who had been attacked! She laughed brokenly. 'Hello, Mrs Morgan.'

'Oh, lass!' Ivy rushed forward and drew her into her arms. 'What the divil are you doing here?'

'I heard that a woman from Spring Row . . . Oh, Mrs Morgan, thank goodness you're well.'

Ivy half smiled and looked away, and Sally turned her attention to the others. Shaun was smiling, as was the woman. Though Arthur flashed a smile, he wore an expression she couldn't fathom. Yet she forgot everything when her eyes locked with Tommy's.

He rose slowly. At his intense stare, blood rushed to her cheeks. To her surprise, the woman stepped forward.

'Hello, Sally. It's nice to meet thee at last. I'm Dolly Jenkins, soon to be Morgan.' She gave a tinkling laugh. 'Eeh, it sounds lovely saying that!'

Hurt and envy crashed back. 'Please accept my apologies for interrupting.'

'It's all right, you weren't to know.' She looked adoringly at Tommy. 'Anyroad, nowt could've spoiled that.'

Sally glanced over Dolly's shoulder. 'Congratulations, Tommy.' His eyes creased but he didn't speak. To her horror, she felt tears prick.

''Ere, I've not congratulated youse yet, have I? Come here, lad.' Ivy caught him in a hug. 'And you, lass. Welcome to the family.'

As Dolly joined the embrace, Sally tore her gaze away. Catching Arthur's eye, she squeezed out a smile. 'Hello, Mr Morgan.'

It was a moment before he returned it. 'Sit yourself down, lass. Have you just come from Manchester? Did all go well with your aunt?'

'There's time aplenty for questions, Arthur. Why don't youse lot fetch a jug from Ma Thompson's to toast the happy occasion? Take your time,' Ivy added, shooting him a look. 'There's no rush back.'

'Aye. A walk will do us good after that feast.' Shaun and Dolly followed him to the door but Tommy remained motionless.

Sally gazed into the grey-blue pools. She sensed Arthur watching but couldn't tear her eyes away.

Tommy broke the spell. He sighed softly and followed them out.

She stared after him. The way he'd looked at her . . . It was as though he'd wanted to say something. Was he angry she'd interrupted his special moment? She'd have to apologise, later, however uncomfortable it would be.

'You shouldn't have come, lass. It ain't safe.'

The seriousness of Ivy's tone took her aback. 'It's quite all right, Mrs Morgan. I made sure to cover my head while passing Deansgate. I had to come, to see . . . Mrs Morgan? What is it?'

Ivy's hand strayed to her throat. 'You need to return to Manchester. You need to get far from here and never come back.'

'Mrs Morgan, you're scaring me. What . . . ?' She shook her head as realisation dawned. 'It *was* you, wasn't it? Joseph . . .'

'The bastard sneaked in when the men were at work. He wanted to know where you'd gone and did this when I'd not tell him.' Ivy lifted her chin, revealing angry welts, adding, at Sally's horrified whimper, 'It's all right, lass, he didn't do much damage. Dolly interrupted and he scarpered.

'Nay, you can't stay. As lovely as it is seeing thee, it don't bear thinking of if he got his hands on you. Please, for me, go back to Manchester. You're not safe.'

Sally dropped to her knees at Ivy's feet, her guilt akin to nothing she'd ever known. 'I've brought this on, all of it. Oh, Mrs Morgan, how can you ever forgive me?' She crumpled, gasping with sobs.

Tears glistened on Ivy's lashes but her voice was firm. 'Now you listen to me, this ain't your fault. You've nowt to be sorry for and I'll not hear another word like that, d'you understand?'

'I brought this trouble to your door. It's all my fault.'

'Nay, it's bloody well not. No one's to blame but him. Sally, look at me. Are you listening? It's not your fault, lass.'

As they clung to each other, her blood boiled with rage. 'I loathe him with every fibre of my being. Why won't he just *die*, Mrs Morgan?'

'He'll not get away with it, have no fear. Arthur and Tommy went looking for him at that sister's of his. He weren't there but wherever he's footed it, they'll sniff him out. He'll pay for what he did – to me and to thee. I just pray they'll not go too far, however much the bastard deserves it.'

Sally cringed, her shame overwhelming. That she'd dragged this lovely family into her mess . . . It was little wonder the men hadn't seemed themselves. They resented her bringing trouble to their door, and rightly so.

'I'm so very sorry, to all of you.'

A cry broke the silence and Ivy's face brightened. She lifted Jonathan from the basket. 'He's bloody huge, lass!'

Sally allowed herself a proud smile.

'Eeh, I have missed you,' Ivy cooed, brushing her nose against his. 'It were nice having a babby in t' house again. It weren't half quiet when you'd gone.'

Though it pained her, Sally kept an even tone. 'I dare say you'll be hearing the patter of tiny feet, shortly. I must apologise for interrupting. The door was ajar . . . I did knock.'

'Nay, don't be daft, you weren't to know. I left it open, for it were stuffy after cooking. Ay, I can't believe my Tommy's to wed. Her face were a picture when he asked her; fair brought a tear to my eye, it did, soppy bugger that I am.'

'You must be very happy.'

'Aye. But it's hard letting one of your own go. You'll see when this fella's owder.' Ivy's expression turned serious. 'Sally, I've thought of what I'd say if I saw you again but now the time's come, well, I don't know how to put into words . . .'

'Mrs Morgan?'

'Thank you,' she said simply. 'That brass for our Shaun – thank you, from the bottom of my heart. You've freed him from the pit, lass. He's gorra place with a carpenter. He's doing what he loves, what he were born to. What you did . . . You're an angel, that's what you are.'

'Oh, I am pleased! I so wanted to repay you a little for all you did for me.'

'Nay, it's more than a little. You've changed that lad's life. It'll not be forgotten, not by none of us.' Ivy cleared her throat of emotion. 'Anyroad, what's been happening with thee? Did all go well with your aunt? How you faring at that Manchester? 'Ere, I hope you've kept that carving safe; be worth some money, that will, when our Shaun's a world-known carpenter,' she teased.

At the mention of Thunder, tears sprang to Sally's eyes.

'Eeh, lass, what's wrong?'

'Oh, Mrs Morgan, it's been dreadful, simply dreadful. I cannot go back.'

She told her the whole, sorry lot. Afterwards, Ivy sat back, stunned.

'Word spread here of that murder but not forra second did I think it had owt to do with you. How could so much happen in a few short weeks? How the bleedin' hell haven't you turned stark, staring mad, lass?'

'I've come close. Do you see, I cannot go back? All of it . . . I've had enough.'

'What will you do? You know I'd have you back here in a heartbeat, but Joseph . . .'

'I know. As of yet, I've no idea. I'd fare better in one of the larger towns; there would be more chance of securing employment. I just have to decide which.'

'Well, you're stopping here the night, at least. You can think on what to do the morrow.'

Thoughts of spending all night beneath the same roof as Tommy had Sally shaking her head but before she could think up an excuse, the cottage door opened. Arthur, his sons and a giggling Dolly entered and her stomach dropped. But with Ivy waiting for her response, she had no choice but to accept.

One night, she told herself. *Smile, act naturally for one night, and tomorrow I can be on my way and it will all be over.*

She glanced at Tommy and her heart missed a beat to see him staring back. She dropped her gaze. Knowing he didn't share her feelings was painful enough. That he now hated her for Joseph's actions hurt far, far more.

It was going to be a long night.

Alice was ready to do battle when the knock came. The previous performance caught them off guard. Not this time.

She jerked her head to Joseph and when he disappeared upstairs, pointed a warning to the children. It wasn't necessary; she'd threatened what would happen if they slipped up. Still, it was best to remind them.

She wrenched open the door, all set to vent her fury, but before she knew what was happening, the visitor pushed her aside and rushed in.

'Oh no you don't, not again— Oh, it's you.' Her anger turned to surprise then swiftly back. 'What's tha doing here? I told our Joseph from the off, I'll not have whores in my home. Whatever he chooses to do is his business but I'll have no carryings-on under my roof. Go on, sling your hook and wait for him at Nellie's as you usually do, afore I scrag you out.'

Bent double, hands on her thighs, Nancy fought to catch her breath. 'Is my Joseph back from Manchester?'

Alice frowned at her wide-eyed desperation. 'Aye. He went yesterday morning but it were a waste of time. He found nowt out and were back by nightfall. Been in a right soddin' mood since, an' all. Why, what's afoot?'

'I saw her. She's back.' Nancy's eyes darted to the stairs as footsteps thundered down. 'Oh, love, you're there. Eeh, I ain't half missed you, lad.'

Joseph took the last few stairs slowly. 'Did I hear you say you've seen Sally?' At Nancy's nod, he ran a hand across his mouth. 'You better not be mistaken or I'll—'

'I'm not, love, honest. I saw her pass my father's an hour or so since and disappear inside the Morgans'. I came straight here; ran most of the way, I did.'

Alice shook her head at her brother. 'Well, I don't believe it. Fancy you traipsing there yesterday and she winds up coming back of her own accord. Mind, why would she?'

With a hoot of glee, he slapped his leg. 'Lord knows but I'll tell you summat, this time, she'll not be leaving. By God, she'll not.'

'You're a lucky beggar, you are, our Joseph. You were stumped what to do not half a minute since and now, she's fallen into your lap.'

He grabbed Nancy's arm. 'Come on.'

'But how will you get to her with Arthur and that son of his?'

'I'll figure that out when we arrive. Now for God's sake, get moving. I'll not let her get away this time. The things I'll do to that whore . . . She'll hurt in more ways than she can imagine.'

Alice grinned. 'Go on, lad. Go get the rotten bitch.'

As she hurried down the alley after Joseph, a sickly feeling rose in Nancy at the sheer venom in his voice.

She'd been numb with shock when discovering what he'd done to Ivy. She thought he'd meant to frighten the woman, not throttle her to within an inch of her life. Afterwards, she'd expressed her terror at what would have become of him. He'd laughed in her face, insisting if he had finished the old bitch off, he wouldn't have swung. Alice would have given him an alibi.

What he was capable of frightened her. She couldn't lose him. She'd sooner die than live without him.

Now, as he strode down Deansgate, she caught up and grabbed his sleeve. Peering into his jet-black eyes, she hesitated to ask the burning question tormenting her, petrified to think what his answer would be. But now was the time. If he gave the right one, whatever he planned this night, she'd support him all the way.

'Joseph, you do love me, don't you?'

Irritation flared in his eyes. He pushed her into a doorway, cupped her breasts and rubbed his palms over her nipples. She moaned and he smirked. Biting her lower lip, he stared deep into her eyes. 'I can't do this without you. You want the bitch gone, don't you?'

His smooth tone brought a flush of pleasure to her cheeks. 'Aye, course I do. It's just . . .'

'What?'

'Well, just . . . This *is* for us, in't it? You want us to be together, proper like, don't you? Once she's gone, we'll be free to wed, won't we?'

He nodded.

'Oh, love. Then whatever it takes, I'll understand. I don't want to know what you're planning but, well, whatever you must do . . . do it. Just be careful, eh, lad? Please, be careful. I can't lose thee.'

With a twisted smile, he squeezed her buttocks. 'Let's get the bitch. If I need your help, you be a good girl and do as I say, d'you hear?' At her nod, his smirk returned. His fondling intensified then he pulled away, leaving her panting against the wall. 'Come on.'

She sighed in adoration. Cocooned in her conviction that he did, as she'd believed, love her, she scuttled after him, heart singing.

The fact that he hadn't actually said the words, she ignored.

Chapter 25

BY THE LIGHT of the good fire, Dolly held up her hand and, for the dozenth time, admired her ring.

'I can't believe I'm wearing this. I knew Mam were keeping it for when I wed but still, it's a dream come true.' She stroked hair from Tommy's brow. 'Did Father mention whose it once were?'

He continued gazing into the fire.

'It were my granny's. D'you know, her and my grandfather were wed over fifty year? Let's pray ours lasts as long, eh? Tommy?'

'Sorry . . . What did you say?'

Rolling her eyes, Dolly chuckled, and Sally tried to imitate Ivy's smile but it was impossible.

'Is that jug empty, Arthur?'

Puffing on his pipe, he was watching Tommy through the plumes of smoke. When his wife jabbed him in the ribs, he jumped. ''Ere, what were that in aid of?'

'Hell's teeth. What's wrong with youse two the night? I were saying, have we supped up?'

'Oh. Aye, aye. Have I to fetch another?' he asked hopefully.

Ivy's eyebrows rose to meet her hairline. 'Nay, you bleedin' well shouldn't! You and Tommy's had your fill by the looks of it. Like talking to the wall, it is. It's your beds youse need, not more ale.'

Dolly grinned. 'Aye, I'm tired; must be all the excitement. I think I'll be away home.'

For the first time, Tommy's face relaxed in a ghost of a smile. 'I'll walk thee.' He'd donned jacket and cap and was at the door before she'd reached for her bonnet.

Sally busied herself with Jonathan. She could feel Tommy's stare but didn't lift her head.

The rest of the day had been as uncomfortable as she'd feared. She'd tried her very best to appear cheerful. She'd swallowed her pain and praised Shaun when he'd shown off his latest carving. She'd managed to laugh along when Ivy told of the preacher discovering they'd lied to him – Ivy had feigned ignorance and he'd huffed and puffed 'like a pair of owd bellows' yet had no choice but to drop the matter.

Worst of all, she'd had to endure Dolly's adoring looks to Tommy and hear about their future, which the pretty bride-to-be had evidently planned long ago.

Throughout, his presence overrode everything. Like a moth to a flame, she was powerless to resist him. When her defiant eyes flicked to him, his grey-blue ones met them every time and she'd looked away, afraid she'd reveal her feelings. His, however, didn't waver.

Now, as evening turned to night, she was at breaking point. He resented her being in his home, had only refrained from speaking out for Ivy's sake. Why else was he unable to take his penetrating gaze off her?

That everyone was avoiding the attack wasn't helping. Whether it was to spare her embarrassment, so as not to upset Ivy, or they were too enraged, she didn't know. It hung over them, clogging the air like smoke.

She couldn't leave without voicing it. Whether the men accepted her apology remained to be seen, but apologise she must. She liked Arthur a great deal. And Tommy . . . However sharp the pain of unrequited love, she'd sooner have him as a friend than nothing.

She tucked the blankets around the baby and stole a look across the room. Misery clenched her stomach to see him still watching her. His anger must be eating away at him and understandably so. But dear God, it *hurt.*

As Dolly trilled goodbyes, Tommy turned the knob and she screeched when the door burst inwards. A black shape threw itself at him, knocking him to the floor.

Shaun collapsed in fits of laughter. Tommy glared at him and his guffaws grew, smothering Sally's gasp.

'Shield! Come away at once!' She rushed forward, face ablaze. 'I'm sorry, I completely forgot about him. He's been outside this whole time and . . . Shield, will you get off!' To her surprise, Tommy chuckled.

'Ay, cabbage breath, how are you? Tha frightened me half to death, then. Come on, let me up.' With a struggle, he pushed the dog off, stood and, for the first time since her arrival, smiled at her. 'Gorra thing for me, ain't he?'

Relief like no other washed through her. That he wasn't angry, was *smiling* at her . . . She laughed softly. 'It seems so.'

Something akin to pain appeared behind his eyes. 'It's been nice seeing thee, Sally.'

Her tone was just as gentle. 'You too, Tommy.'

'Time's running on, lad. Dolly wants to be home.'

Arthur's words shattered the moment and Tommy went a dull pink.

Sally stood rooted to the spot. The way he'd looked at her . . . almost as if . . . No. Her cruel mind was playing with her. He was in love with Dolly, was *marrying* Dolly. Why wouldn't these wicked imaginings leave her?

Head bowed, Tommy exited the cottage but instead of following, Dolly turned. Her expression was blank and when she smiled, it didn't reach her eyes. 'Goodbye, Sally.'

Before she could respond, Dolly was gone. She blinked, dazed. Dolly sensed her feelings for her beloved. She knew. *Dear God, she knew . . .*

Shaun yawned. 'I'm away to bed. Goodnight.'

Along with his mother and father, Sally mumbled goodnight to him. At first, she thought it was her imagination but no – definite tension had filled the kitchen. Ivy and Arthur looked decidedly uncomfortable, eyes flitting anywhere but at her.

Lord above, *they* didn't know, too? Was it so obvious?

The agonising silence grew and in desperation she blurted the first thing to enter her head: 'May Shield sleep inside, tonight, Mrs Morgan? He'll be no trouble.' She almost cringed at the inanity, but it seemed to work.

Ivy smiled her usual smile. 'Aye, he can kip by the fire. Now, I'll brew a fresh pot and make up a plate of bread and butter then we'd best get some shut-eye, or we'll be fit for nowt come the morrow.'

She needed to be alone, to make sense of these whirling emotions. As soon as she could, she'd make her excuses and retire, she vowed. She just hoped she'd escape before Tommy returned. She couldn't see him again tonight, didn't trust herself, for surely he'd sense her longing. He was bound to, if everyone else had. The shame of that really would be too much.

Sipping her tea, her eyes strayed to the door continually, heart banging. The moment her cup was empty, she lifted the basket.

'You off to get some kip, lass?'

'Yes. The travelling has worn me out,' she lied. She bid them goodnight, stroked Shield, then escaped to the familiar room next door.

She undressed and slipped beneath the blanket on the sofa. Today had been a disaster. What did tomorrow hold? Where would she go? Her future was as uncertain as the last time she'd lain beneath this roof. However, at least then she'd had an idea of her intentions. All she faced now was stark emptiness.

Yet again, Tommy crept into her mind and she moaned softly. *Had* Dolly, Ivy and Arthur sensed her burning love? She'd been such a stupid, naive fool . . .

She heard the sound of the cottage door opening. Murmurs followed, intermingled with Ivy banking down the fire. Two sets of feet ascended the stairs, then silence.

Fine hairs on Sally's arms stood to attention. Tommy was still in the kitchen; somehow, she could feel his presence. She listened intently. Footsteps sounded and she waited for his tread on the stairs, but they drew nearer. Through the gap beneath the door, two shadows appeared.

She held her breath, her body, to her shame, tingling. Suddenly, the feet disappeared. Moments later, they mounted the stairs.

Throughout the lonely night, confusion and longing were constant companions. Whys and what-ifs tormented her. Should she have gone to the door, asked what he wanted? What would he have answered?

When sleep did claim her, she woke frequently. Stirring again as dawn broke, she threw back the blanket in defeat, dressed and went to the window. Slivers of silver-white sliced the indigo sky. Distant birdsong had replaced owls' hoots. A wispy mist caressed the hilltops beyond, adding to the ethereal scene, and calmness enveloped her.

She loved it here. Despite the terrible memories, Spring Row would always hold a special place in her heart. She'd give anything to remain, to raise her son amidst the sweeping greenness and clear air. But it was an impossible dream she couldn't fulfil. Shortly, they would leave once more. And they would never return.

Scratching sounded at the door. She opened it a crack and Shield's tongue poked through, making her smile. She led him back through the kitchen, opened the cottage door and watched him trot down the row.

The sky had lightened further and, folding her arms, she gazed about. She took deep breaths of sharp air. She knew wherever she went today would be rife with factories and cotton mills' belching chimneys, and closed her eyes, savouring every lungful.

At first, she didn't sense anything amiss. No sound penetrated the stillness. It was an icy shiver the length of her spine that made her open her eyes.

The shock was so overwhelming, not a muscle moved. Her only reaction was the widening of her eyes.

'Hello, whore.'

The hissed words acted like a hammer blow. Her mouth opened but before the scream reached her lips, Joseph's fist slammed into her face.

She knew a split second of intense pain. Then the world faded.

It had been too good an opportunity to miss.

Joseph caught Sally as her legs buckled. Her weight no encumbrance to his powerful strength, he threw her over his shoulder with ease. At the feel of her, droplets of sweat sprang at his temples and blood pumped furiously through his veins. He sprinted to the hedgerow he and Nancy had spent last night hiding behind.

He couldn't afford to hang around. The consequences would be dire if Arthur and his son discovered him.

He hadn't planned it to be like this, wanted to take his time, get it just right. But seeing her standing there . . . He'd been unable to hold back. He could scarcely believe he had the bitch at last.

Stiffness from hours of crouching, he now forgot; the wait had been worth it. Not once had his narrowed gaze, trained on the Morgans' door, shifted. Despite his dew-drenched clothes, he hadn't noticed the cold; adrenaline, coupled with the flask of whisky he'd brought, kept him warm.

He couldn't say the same for Nancy. She'd done nothing but gripe and he'd used the back of his hand numerous times to shut her up. Eventually, she'd fallen silent and he was able to keep watch in peace.

Shaking in anticipation of catching a glimpse of Sally, he'd waited. His excitement reached fever pitch when, at one point, the door opened. But it turned to deep frustration when the Morgan son and a young woman appeared. Then a massive great dog launched itself at the son, knocking him flying, and Sally's voice had sounded. His mouth had twisted in glee.

Knowing she was definitely there, he found the waiting easier; she had to leave some time and he'd be ready. The son had left with the woman, returned alone and soon afterwards, light at the cottage window went out. Realising he wouldn't see Sally that night, he'd prepared himself for the long hours stretching ahead.

Now, he grinned, thrilled his perseverance had paid off. The sight of her had struck him dumb. The terror in her eyes' blue depths . . . He'd missed that. All those weeks of sleepless nights and drink-sodden stupors her absence induced, his futile meeting with the workhouse master and hours tramping Manchester, and now . . .

He could barely breathe. He had her. And by God, she wouldn't escape again.

He flung her to the damp grass, fell to his knees and gazed in awe.

Nancy, too, gazed at the woman she'd come to loathe. She was even prettier up close, she saw with scorching envy.

The wife. The one legally bound to Joseph. *Her* Joseph. Suddenly, the prick of doubt she felt when overhearing customers' conversations in the shop, of how Sally had suffered at his hands, returned. But as always, she forced it away. Vicious lies, that's all they were. Spread by this bitch.

He wasn't the monster they thought. They didn't know him like her. He loved her and she loved him. They were meant to be together. And once he'd dealt with Sally, they would. Soon, *she'd* bear the name Mrs Goden.

'I've got thee. I've finally got thee,' Joseph murmured, his tone laced with menace. Eyes travelling the length of her, he licked his lips. Her figure was more rounded. She was fuller of breast and hip. Motherhood suited her.

This evoked, for the first time, faint curiosity for the child he'd spawned and he glanced to the Morgans'. Yet as swiftly, it vanished. Children were nothing but a trial. Like bloodthirsty leeches, they drained your soul. They sucked and sucked long after you were bone dry, left you potless, bitter and old before your time. You'd only to look at Alice for proof.

Turning his attention back to his wife, his pulse raced with thoughts of her naked body. Christ, what he'd do to it when he got her alone . . . Feeling Nancy's jealous watch, he tore away his gaze with a frustrated growl. He couldn't risk Nancy flouncing off. The old whore had almost served her purpose. Almost.

He threw Sally over his shoulder again, shot a smirk at the Morgans' and signalled to Nancy to follow. Passing the dog that lay beside a ditch, a pool of blood spreading beneath its head, he smiled proudly. He'd taken care of it before making his move on Sally; after its attack on the stationmaster, he wasn't taking any chances. When it wandered by the hedgerow, he'd smashed its head with a thick branch. It dropped without a sound.

He set off across a tree-lined field. Sally's arms bumped limply against his back and he smiled again, her touch comforting.

'Where we going, love?'

His face melted in a snarl. 'Just get a move on. Folk will be up and about, soon. We'll be all right if we stick to the fields but happen we do pass someone, and they ask what's up with her, I'll do the talking. You say nowt, d'you hear? When we reach the end of the next field, you slip through the fence and cut across O'Brady's farm. It'll bring you out near your house. You stay put today, right?'

Nancy nodded and he strode on, mind on the fun he'd soon have with Sally.

'*You have my permission and gladly. I know you'll look after her, make her happy.*'

Staring at the ceiling, Tommy let his thoughts run. He didn't have the strength to fight them, had given up trying hours ago.

'*She's a good lass and like her mother afore her, will make a fine wife.*'

The speech echoed on.

'*You're the only fella our Dolly's ever wanted. It does my owd heart good to know you feel the same.*'

Knowing what came next, he squeezed his eyes shut.

'*You're a sound lad, Tommy, a sound lad.*'

Dolly's father couldn't have been more wrong if he'd tried. A sound lad? It was almost laughable. Maybe, once. Not any more.

He swung his legs out of bed, pulled on his trousers and paced the room. Glancing at his sleeping brother, envy churned in his breast. What he wouldn't give to be him, without a worry in the world.

He'd thought the day couldn't get worse. Knelt in proposal to a woman he'd all but ruined and didn't truly love was soul-destroying enough. What occurred next . . . Dear God, he'd never known shock like it, had to stop himself crying out. *Sally. His Sally* . . . A blade of grass could have felled him. In that moment, everything, *everything*, turned on its head.

Remembering what he'd almost done last night, his step faltered. He'd been a hair's breadth from entering her room, declaring his love, insisting the proposal was a mistake. Where he found the strength to desist, he didn't know, but was glad he had. He'd made enough of a fool of himself gawping at her all day – until, to his mortification, she'd avoided eye contact.

And there was Dolly. He must marry Dolly.

Standing before Nat Jenkins, Tommy had almost hoped he'd refuse permission. Of course, he hadn't. He was well aware of Dolly's long-held wish to become Mrs Morgan. But he hadn't consented purely out of love for his daughter. He sincerely believed his future son-in-law a sound man.

That bred within Tommy a tumour of shame that grew still. It was ruined, all of it. He'd made a mess of everything.

Time alone, to gather his thoughts before his family roused, was crucial. Mindful of the creaky spots, he descended the stairs. A bitter breeze met his bare arms and chest midway and his gaze went to the cottage door. He frowned to see it wide open.

He glanced to the fire and, seeing Shield absent, swallowed hard. *Sally was awake.* She must have taken the dog out to relieve itself. Despite his brain telling him to return to his room, avoid her for sanity's sake, his legs refused. Disgusted at his weakness, he made for the door.

Eyes hungry for a glimpse of her swept the row, but it was deserted. Maybe she'd taken a walk with Shield; but to leave the door wide . . . ? A sense that something wasn't right stirred in him and he headed for the front room.

He knocked, heart banging. What if she answered, had merely let Shield out and forgotten to close the door? he thought suddenly. What on earth would he say? But all that greeted him was silence and the sliver of dread returned. He turned the knob.

At first glance, the room appeared empty. Catching sight of the basket, his worry abated. Sally couldn't be far. She wouldn't leave the child unattended for long.

He returned to the cottage door and scanned the row again. Still there was no sign and, despite his reasoning, unease resurfaced. Joseph's snarling face crashed through his mind and fear clutched his heart. Surely to God, no . . .

He slapped the wall in fury and raced upstairs.

Chapter 26

FLASHES OF BLACK came and went, came and went, merging with the grey. Sally blinked drowsily then winced as agony scorched the length of her face. She was aware of a jolting sensation and nausea was rising.

From beneath lids lead-heavy, she glimpsed the shapes again. They appeared then disappeared, appeared and disappeared, blending with the greyness until everything swirled together. Another wave of sickness swooped and she closed her eyes.

A steady drum of noise grew and her fog-filled brain counted: one, two, one, two, one, two. When she opened her eyes, her vision was clearer. The blur receded and she saw the grey was cobblestones. She squinted at the flashes of black – one, two, one, two. The sound was coming from them.

They were feet.

The answer came suddenly. They were the backs of someone's clogs, appearing then disappearing with each step. At once, her mind snapped into shape. Snippets of memory . . . standing at Ivy's door, Joseph, pain . . .

Clarity brought fear so overwhelming, she gagged. Rearing back, she screamed at the top of her lungs. His hold tightened and she thrashed wildly. They reached a door and, realising he was taking her within, she gripped the frame but he prised her fingers away and hauled her, kicking and screaming, inside.

He slammed the door and threw her to the floor, the impact knocking the breath from her. She gasped for air then grimaced when a fetid stench hit the back of her throat. A long ago memory . . . That smell was unmistakable. *Dear God, no!* A familiar cackle sounded; hesitantly, she turned.

Alice sat grinning by the fire. 'Well, look what we have here. And where the divil have you been, you loose young bitch? All go well?' she added to Joseph.

'Aye.'

'Tha weren't seen? How about just now? I heard her screams from here.'

'Nay. Folk will still be kipping off last night's ale. A farmer asked what we were about when I were crossing his field, but I told him she were half-slat from last night.' Crossing his eyes, he made drinking motions with his hand then laughed. 'He swallowed it, said his wife liked a tipple too much herself, gormless shit.'

'Harold left at first light in search of a day's graft – as if the useless swine will find owt – and what children come home last night have gone out. Where's anyone's guess; probably on t' thieve somewhere, bloody wastrels. I'll take meself to Nellie's, leave youse two alone.' She grinned at Sally, donned her shawl and left.

Seeing Alice, bile had risen in Sally's stomach. However, the fear her sister-in-law evoked was nothing compared to the sight of Joseph. Their gazes locked and the room swayed.

His eyes bulged from his stubbled face, as though he couldn't quite believe what he saw. He stepped towards her. 'Well? Ain't you gorra welcome kiss for your husband?'

Her heart banged but hot anger was growing. The faded welts along Ivy's neck flashed into her mind and her fury boiled over. Of its own accord, her chin rose.

'Don't you *dare* come any closer. I'm not afraid of you. The days of my putting up with you are over. Take one more step and I'm warning you, Joseph, I'll—'

'You'll what?' He lunged and grabbed her throat. 'Grown some backbone since you've been away, ain't you?' He leaned in until their noses touched. 'Well, don't fret, my girl, for I'll soon have you back to the snivelling wreck you've allus been.' Shaking his head slowly, he curled his lips in a snarl. 'You're one sneaky, thieving young whore – what are you?

'Think you could hide for ever, did you? Did you?' he roared. 'You've ruined me good and proper, lost me my home, job, my good name, everything. I've nowt left to lose, now. I warned what would happen if you opened that mouth of yourn.' His grip tightened. 'Have a fine ol' time in Manchester, did you?'

Her eyes showed her surprise; he smiled. 'Oh aye, I know where you've been. A rat allus returns to its hole. Well, I hope you enjoyed your jaunt, my girl, for I promise you summat, you'll not escape me a second time. For the rest of your days you'll suffer for what you've done, you little bitch.'

She'd forced her anger down and listened to his rant without resistance. Years of torture had taught her well. She knew how to respond so as to receive the least pain possible.

She'd almost reacted when his hand tightened but willed herself to remain impassive. Incurring his wrath further wasn't an option whilst he squeezed her throat; he'd rendered her unconscious that way more times than she could remember. She needed a clear head, must play this right if she were to escape alive.

Relief that Jonathan was safe at Ivy's flooded through her. Dear Lord, if he'd discovered him . . . The notion was horrifying. He'd do anything to hurt her, and would have no qualms about using their son to do so, she was certain.

Surely, soon, the Morgans would notice her missing and come looking? Please God. She just hoped that until then she'd have the strength to endure the inevitable abuse to come. What further injuries he'd inflict, she dreaded to imagine. Her face was ablaze, her nose likely broken. But she knew better than to show it. He'd only strike it again for the enjoyment of seeing her suffer.

'Undress,' Joseph barked suddenly, unfastening his belt with his free hand.

Trying desperately to remain calm, she shook her head.

'I *said* undress.'

'No.' The word had barely left her when, to her horror, he grabbed her blouse and tore it open.

Her breasts spilled into his waiting hands and, despite her terror, fury charged through her feeling those all-too-familiar fingers on her flesh. She smacked them away fiercely and covered herself with her arms but before she could jump to her feet, a slap sent her sprawling. Her head hit the flags, blurring her vision, and moments later, his hands were on her thighs.

When he threw her skirts over her head and ripped away her undergarments, she kicked out, but he caught and spread her legs. He growled with pleasure and her panic reached fever pitch. His jerking member prodded and a scream tore from her.

Bucking wildly, she lashed out with nails and fists. He caught her wrists in an iron-like grip and wrenched them above her head.

'Go on, whore, fight it. I love it when you scream and struggle, makes it all the more enjoyable,' he panted, forcing her legs wider with his knee and positioning himself between.

'Please, don't do this.' She knew begging was useless but crippling desperation chased away logic. 'Beat me, do whatever you want, but not this. *Please. Not this!*'

Joseph looked deep into her eyes and uttered two words she knew would haunt her the rest of her life:

'Welcome home.'

A scream froze on her lips as he savagely thrust inside her.

Ivy held Jonathan against her chest and, making soothing noises, rocked him. His cries merely grew and her gaze strayed back to the window.

With each minute, her anxiety had mounted. Her husband and sons were out scouring the lanes and with all her heart she hoped they would find the lass safe and well.

Arthur had insisted they would prove her worries unfounded, that Sally had likely taken a walk with Shield and lost track of time. But she knew he was wrong. Sally doted on Jonathan, would never leave him alone.

She returned her attention to him, desperate for distraction. His hungry screams intensified and she began praying again for his mother's safe return. Suddenly, the cottage door burst open and she whipped around.

Arthur and Shaun, faces drawn, entered. Tommy followed, holding a black mass.

'Oh, dear God, is Sally—?'

'We didn't find her,' Arthur cut in. 'We found the dog in a ditch but there's no sign of the lass.'

Tommy laid Shield on the rag rug. 'It's had a nasty blow to the head but it's alive. Goden's done this, I'd stake my life on it. He's been back and Sally . . . I *knew* we should've checked that cottage of his sister's last time. I'll *kill* the evil bastard when I get my hands on him.'

'Dear God, if he's got her . . . if he could do what he did to me, that poor lass . . .' Ivy's words were lost in Jonathan's cries. She swallowed her feelings and turned to Shaun. 'Fetch Mrs Oakes, will you, lad? She'll wet-nurse this poor beggar, I'm sure. Let's pray we'll not need her long. Mother of God, if Sally . . .'

Arthur drew her into his arms. 'We'll find her, wench. We'll fetch her back, don't you fret.'

With increasing anger, Tommy watched his mother gulp down tears. She'd changed since the attack, wasn't the stoic woman they knew and loved. That bastard had knocked out of her a little of the fight they had always admired. Lord, when they found him . . . 'We're wasting time. We need to go,' he said abruptly.

Face as though set in stone, his father nodded. He kissed Ivy and strode to the door.

'Find Sally, fetch her back but please, be careful,' she begged him.

'Don't fret, wench. We'll not swing for him.'

Leading the way, Tommy left the cottage. Reaching the gate, he saw Shaun and Mrs Oakes hurrying up the row. 'Look after the dog while we're gone, lad,' he called. 'If it'll let thee, tend to that gash on its head, see what the damage is.'

'And call on Martha Smith,' added his father, 'ask her to sit with your mam till we return.'

Spurred on by worry and fury – and eager to give Joseph the beating of his life – they made good headway and in no time were nearing Bolton town. When Deansgate came into view, Arthur slowed his pace.

'Wait up, lad. I've summat to say.'

'Can't it wait?'

'Nay, it can't. Last night—'

'I know what you're about to say, but—'

'You couldn't keep your bloody eyes off the lass! How your mam didn't notice, I don't know. And raging as you were when we returned with the dog . . . Folk will start questioning your intentions if you don't keep a rein on that tongue of yourn.'

'We'll talk about this later, we're wasting—'

'You'll hear me out, first,' ordered his father. 'Son, this has to stop. You're betrothed to Dolly, now. She's a nice lass with enough love for the pair of you to make your marriage work. You could be happy with her but you've got to meet her halfway. For God's sake, get whatever designs you have on Sally from that head of yourn and start thinking on your future.'

He sighed helplessly at the raw pain Tommy knew shone from his eyes. 'If we find her, whatever's happened, whatever state she might be in . . . for the love of God, don't let your emotions get the better of thee. Don't go making no declarations nor saying summat you'll regret. Please, for all your sakes. Promise me.'

Heavy silence hung between them.

'I promise,' Tommy murmured without an ounce of self-conviction.

'Right. Come on.'

As they drew level with Deansgate, there came a rumble of wheels in the distance and they saw a cart approaching along a dirt road. His father didn't give it a second glance. But Tommy stopped dead in his tracks. *Surely not . . .*

'What's wrong?' Arthur followed his gaze back to the cart but clearly saw nothing that could have caused his face to pale, as Tommy knew it had. 'Lad?'

His eyes flicked to the female passenger then again rested on the man beside her. 'That fella on t' cart, there, don't half favour . . .' *It couldn't be him. It wasn't. It was merely his mind playing tricks.* 'Never mind.'

Falling back into step, his father frowned. 'Who did he look like?'

'It doesn't matter,' Tommy muttered, and was thankful when Arthur didn't press him.

On reaching Chapel Alley, his father made to hammer on number thirteen, but he shook his head. 'We'll not be knocking this time. Children or no, Sally's life could be at risk. They'll not get chance to cover their tracks this time.'

At his first kick, the rotten frame splintered and the door flew open.

The kitchen proved empty and they rushed to search the other rooms – his father making for the stairs, Tommy the front room. Within seconds, they were back in the kitchen.

'Nowt?'

Tommy shook his head.

'There's no one upstairs, neither.'

'Did you check everywhere? Happen he's hiding or, or he might—'

'The place's empty, lad.'

Kicking over a stool in frustration, he raked his hands through his hair. 'What do we do? The bastard's got her, I know it.'

His father headed for the door. 'We'll ask on the neighbours either side. Happen someone's seen or heard summat.'

'And if not? What then?'

'We keep looking. I gave your mam my word we'd fetch the lass back, and we will.'

Alice watched Joseph as he drank. When he placed his empty tankard on the table and motioned to Nellie for a refill, she shook her head.

'You've gorra problem with the ale, Joseph. You want to mind you don't finish up like our old man.'

He wiped a dribble of ale from his chin. 'Don't start, Alice, for Christ's sake. I'm celebrating, ain't I? Anyroad, you've room to talk. You've never been one to turn your nose up at a drop of gin.'

'Aye, mebbe, but you're supping like there's a shortage. Look, look how your hands are shaking. You've dragged her over here to fill your belly with ale; you should be lying low in case them fellas come looking. Start slowing down, for you'll need your wits about you if you're to keep a grip of that one.' She glanced to the corner. 'Slippery little bitch, she is. Turn your back forra second and she'll be away, you mark my words.'

But Joseph's attention was on the counter. 'Nellie, where's that ale?' he barked. 'Fetch another gin for our Alice while you're about it. Nancy will clear it, later.'

Nellie's serving girl glanced across the inn, frowned at the curled-up figure then lowered her head. Poking her nose into customers' business would earn her a thick ear or, worse, dismissal. Though she hated the position, she needed the brass.

None the less, she couldn't help sneaking another look to the corner. Pity filled her but she knew she couldn't intervene. Dropping her gaze, she continued to the door.

Stepping outside, she emptied a pail of slops on to the cobbles and was about to turn back when two men blocked her path. The elder smiled but the strikingly handsome one remained stiff-faced.

'Can I help thee with summat, mister?'

'I hope so, lass. We're looking forra fella, name of Goden, what's lodging round here with his sister. You don't know of him, d'you, or where he could be? We've asked at the cottages hereabouts but no one knows owt. There'd be some coppers in it for thee.'

She bit her lip for a long moment then through the side of her mouth, whispered, 'Is anyone watching me?'

The elder man looked to the inn door. 'Nay, lass.'

'How about the window? Look in t' window. My mistress ain't watching?'

Again, he looked behind her. 'Oh, aye, I see her. Have no fear, she's busy at the counter. Have you summat to tell us? D'you know Goden?'

She hesitated. But remembering the desperate state of the woman in Joseph and Alice's company, she nodded. 'Aye, I know him. He's in here all the time. In fact, he . . .' Her words trailed off as glancing to the window she saw Nellie staring back, face scarlet with fury. 'Oh Lord, I must go!'

The handsome one caught her arm. 'Wait, what were you about to say? In fact what?'

'Leave go! She'll flay me alive if I don't get back.' She tried tugging free but his grip tightened. 'Please, mister!'

'Tell us, lass, please. Has tha seen him today? Has he . . . ?' His questions died, his hold with them. 'He's here now, ain't he?'

Without waiting for confirmation, he pushed past her and charged into the inn.

'Well, look who's here.' Hot on Tommy's heels, his father stared in distaste at the lone customer. 'Right, where is he? And don't bother lying for the bastard, for it won't wash. Not this time.'

Joseph's sister took a slow sip of her gin, then another. 'Back again? Well, you've had another wasted journey, for I ain't seen nowt of our Joseph since last time you asked. Go on, sling your hook. Or have you a mind to belt me one as you did my husband?'

In all his life, Tommy had never laid his hands on a woman, hadn't come close. At this moment, however, he struggled not to lunge at this sickeningly smug one. 'Liar. Where is he? Where's Sally?'

'How the divil should I know where that whore is? What right have youse interfering in other folks' marriages, anyroad?'

'I'm warning you, woman.'

Her smile deepened. 'Tell them, Nellie. Our Joseph ain't been here for weeks, has he?'

Without hesitation, she shook her head. 'Nay, Alice. I've not seen him forra while.'

Tommy shot her a disgusted look then glanced at the serving girl's bowed head. 'Lass, if tha knows owt, please—'

'She don't, for there's nowt to tell. Is there?' Nellie asked with a dig to her ribs.

The girl's response was barely audible. 'There's nowt to tell. He's not been in for weeks.'

Tommy made to protest but his father stopped him. 'Save your breath, son, they'll not talk.' He jerked his head to a door behind the ale-splattered counter. 'Mind, if they've nowt to hide, they'll not bother about us searching the place.'

Nellie's mouth dropped open. ''Ere, you've no right going through there! Them's my own private quarters.' She tried blocking their path but they shoved her aside. 'Get out of my inn, now, the pair of you.'

'Oh, let them look,' called Alice. 'We know they'll find nowt, but if they've time to waste . . .' She grinned at them. 'Go on, have a good look. You'll not find him.'

As the men's footsteps thundered upstairs, Nellie shook her head at a now-worried Alice. 'Well, they called your bluff! If they find him—'

'Keep your voice down,' she hissed. 'Joseph ain't daft. He'll have found somewhere to hide.'

'If they find him,' Nellie repeated, 'you take yourselfs off, the lot of you, and battle it out elsewhere. I'll not have trouble here, don't want no police sniffing about my inn.'

'Shurrup, they're coming.'

They re-entered, grim-faced and seething.

'See, what did I tell youse?' Relief tinged Alice's gloating smile. 'He's not here, just as I said. Now go on, bugger off and don't come back.'

'We're going nowhere.' Despite their rage, the younger one spoke calmly. 'We'll bed down outside yon cottage the night if we must but I promise thee, we'll not leave till we've found Sally and made that evil bastard pay. One way or t' other, we'll find him.'

When the inn door slammed shut behind them, she hurried to the window. They crossed the road to her door and she shook her head. He'd been true to his word; it didn't look as though they were going anywhere.

'They gone?'

She turned and breathed out slowly. 'Aye. That were a close 'un, eh? How didn't they find thee, Joseph?'

Face void of colour, he peeked about. 'They definitely gone?'

'The sods have made themselfs comfortable outside the cottage. What will you do? There's no chance of leaving without them—' A noise like the cracking of a whip cut her speech. She nodded in satisfaction to see the serving girl in a heap on the floor, one side of her face livid red.

'Don't fret,' said Nellie. 'She'll get more of the same, later, loose-tongued little bitch that she is.'

Amusement creased Joseph's eyes. 'Ta for the warning, Nellie. How did you—?'

'Know they were after thee? I didn't. But by the look of that one, it's clear summat's up.' She jerked her head to Sally's limp form under his arm.

'I owe thee.'

'Aye, tha does. I'll not ask what's afoot, for I don't want to know. Just don't make a habit of what's occurred today, d'you hear?'

He nodded, but even Alice knew that if the time came again, Nellie would help him out. He – well, Nancy – spent a good deal of money here. She wouldn't risk them finding another watering hole.

Alice returned to the window. 'What will you do, our Joseph?' she asked over her shoulder. 'They're not for shifting.'

As though discarding a piece of rubbish, he threw Sally back into the corner and dragged a hand through his hair. 'Keep a lookout while I think. There's gorra be a way.'

Uneasy silence filled the inn. For several minutes, the only sounds were those of the serving girl going about her duties.

'Oh, for Christ's . . . That's all we need.'

He was ready to snatch up Sally in a heartbeat. 'What, Alice? They coming back?'

'Nay, our Lily's just rounded the corner. She knows not to say owt, they all do. Mind, you never know with that one, sneaky bitch that she is.'

His face contorted in utter fury. 'See the trouble you've stirred up, you filthy slut? By God, you'll spend the rest of your days paying for this, you see if you don't.' He delivered savage kicks to Sally. 'I'll not lose thee again, I'll not,' he muttered over and over. 'You'll not escape me a second time. With my bare hands, I'll kill you first.'

After getting in several kicks herself, Alice headed for the door. 'Stay on your toes, lad. I'll be back in a minute.'

The dead cat had been horrible, all bloated belly and gooey eyes. Lily shuddered at the memory.

The twins had cajoled her into seeing it, had made it sound like a smashing trip, something she'd be real daft to miss.

'I bet she screams,' sniggered Sid, rolling his eyes at girls' soft ways.

But she didn't. As she wrinkled her nose at the smelly heap of fur, a small grey lump, then another, had caught her eye. The first was unmarked, looked to be asleep, but the other, squashed and bloody, had had a nail driven through its eye. Her brothers had left their find to poke her offspring but Lily grabbed their sticks.

'Don't, they're only babbies.'

'They're dead, our Lil,' Joey scoffed. 'They can't feel nowt.'

Ignoring his laughter, she'd scooped them up and laid them by their mother's battered head. 'Let's leave them, now, eh?' she'd begged. 'It's a shame, it is.'

'Aye, come on, our Sid. The stink's getting worse.'

Planning their day in whispers, they slunk away. It was then she'd seen it: movement by the mother. A muffled cry followed and a tiny head had appeared between her paws.

Now, heading home with the survivor nestled in her arms, Lily frowned. What should she name it? It must be special, she decided, nodding. It was very lucky to have been spared. One foot in the gutter, she plodded on, lost in thought.

Suddenly, her fingers stilled on the silky fur and she swore under her breath. Her mother was crossing the road towards her and didn't look best pleased. She thought about stuffing the kitten up her frock or behind her back, but it was too late. She stopped in her tracks at the demand to wait and, tears pricking, prayed *she* wouldn't make her get rid of her new friend.

Her mother glanced at the squirming bundle but, to Lily's astonishment, uttered nothing. Instead, she looked beyond her daughter, laughed for a reason Lily couldn't fathom, then motioned her to follow. Frowning, Lily obeyed. When she and her mother reached Nellie's inn, she glanced over her shoulder. Two men leaning against the wall of their cottage in Chapel Alley locked eyes with her and her mouth ran dry.

The blokes who had threatened Father! Had they returned to give him a proper thrashing? She opened her mouth to yell at them to go away and leave him alone, but her mother yanked her inside the inn before she could.

'Sit.'

Filled with confusion, she perched on a stool. 'Why are them fellas back, Mam? They'll not touch Father again, will they?'

Alice had returned to the window but hearing Lily's terrified tone she swivelled around. Nodding slowly, she crouched before her.

'Aye. They're back to finish him.' She forced a sob and hid a smile when the young face crumpled. 'Me and Uncle Joseph, we're that frickened for him. Happen you could persuade the swines to bugger off, our Lil, like last time? Tell them your uncle's not been near. Put the tears on, lass, beg them to go. It might do the trick again.'

'Aye, do as your mam tells thee,' Joseph added from the corner, leaning forward to block her view of Sally. 'Lay it on good and proper, mind, or it'll not work and they'll kill your father. You don't want him to die, d'you?'

'Nay!' Lily cried. 'Nay,' she repeated, shaking her head and sending tears spilling.

Moments later, Alice watched the skinny legs cross the cobbles.

'You reckon it'll work?' Joseph asked.

She shrugged. 'The young sneak can lie through her teeth easy enough when the mood takes her. She'll lay it on thick; she's allus been soft on that wastrel father of hers. Get thinking on what you'll do if it don't, mind. Tha can't stop here for ever, Joseph, and nor can I.'

'A few hours, that's all I need,' he muttered. 'Nancy will do my bidding. She'll get me some brass so I can be away. By the time she realises I'm taking Sally and not her, it'll be too late. We'll be away; away from here, Spring Row and the bastards what live there. A few hours. Just a few more hours.'

Groaning floated from the corner and Alice clicked her tongue. 'That one's rousing. Take her back upstairs afore she starts bleating. I'll shout a warning if owt occurs.'

Tommy and Arthur had their targets in sight. Ahead was the inn, and left and right gave a clear view of Deansgate. Goden *must* be hiding nearby. If he tried scarpering, they would spot him.

The child who defended her father last time emerged from the inn and their eyes narrowed. They had planned to question her earlier but her mother dragged her away. Now, it seemed, they would get their chance; surprisingly, she was heading towards them.

When the scared-looking bundle of rags halted, Tommy crouched to her level and smiled. 'Hello, lass. That's a bonny young thing you've got. What's his name, then?'

She blinked at the kitten then back at him. Despite his manner, he knew she was remembering their treatment of her father. *These two are slippery buggers, all right. I must be careful if I'm to keep him safe,* her stare screamed. She bit her lip until her eyes watered then gazed up, chin quivering expertly.

'Why, mister? Why have you come to kill Father?'

'Nay, lass, nay. Fancy thee thinking that. Last time were a mistake. We'd not touch him again. We're that sorry you and the other little 'uns saw that carry-on. We didn't know children were present, you see.'

His father squatted beside him. 'That's right. It's your uncle we've come for, like last time. Only to talk, mind,' he added with a disarming smile. 'You know where he is, lass?'

It was evident that she didn't believe a word. Face a picture of innocence, she shook her head. 'I don't, mister. He's been gone weeks. Please leave us be. We don't know where he is, honest we don't.'

Anger rose within Tommy. The poor mite was lying and it didn't take much to work out who had put her up to it. Of all the dirty, rotten tricks . . . using an innocent child to save your own skin. What a low and wicked depth to sink to.

She looked at the scrap of life in her arms. When she raised her head, genuine tears lit her blue eyes. Her hold tightened but she murmured, ''Ere, mister.' She held the kitten up. 'Leave us be, go on home, and you can have her. I love her, I do, but I love Father more. That's a fair deal, in't it, mister?'

He half turned and sighed. Her distress was hard to stomach. He placed a large but tender hand on her shoulder.

'Lass, listen to me. I give thee my word; we'll not touch a hair on your father's head. May the Lord strike me down, that's the 'onest truth. Your uncle . . .' He paused, chose his words carefully. 'He's been a bad man, you see. He hurt my mam and will hurt a nice lady if we don't find him. Please, lass, if you know where he is, it's important you tell us. Sally's in real danger.'

Her eyes widened. 'Sally?'

'Aye. Have you seen her? Is she here with your uncle?'

This quandary dizzied Lily. *Was* Sally the kind lady from the market who gave her food and a shilling, smiled, spoke to her softly, told her she was clever? The lady she'd prayed and prayed, every night since, had taken her with her? But why would Uncle Joseph hurt her?

He *had* wanted to find her. He'd gone off in a right old rage that day – with her precious coin, too. Had he now found her? She wasn't in the inn; though he could be hiding her . . . And what of her tiny baby? Was he in danger, too?

She'd processed these thoughts in seconds when another struck. He'd hurt another lady, she remembered. She'd heard her the other week, moaning and groaning and panting like a dog, as though she couldn't breathe. Afterwards, he'd sneaked her from the cottage. He thought no one saw, but she had. She couldn't have stopped him hurting that lady. Perhaps she could with Sally.

If she did, maybe this time she'd take her home with her. She'd try harder, beg on her knees. If she'd give a shilling and grub as nice as she had for help with a rotten old basket and blanket . . . She'd take her to live with her for sure.

But were these two truthful? Mam said . . . mind you, Mam said things aplenty that weren't true, Lily reminded herself. Still, could she risk Father getting a thrashing? Were they *really* only here for her uncle, for Sally?

She chewed her lower lip raw as she agonised over what to do. Suddenly, she ceased gnawing. There *was* a way to be sure, she recalled. Father always said when a man gave his word, he shook on it, that a vow made on a handshake was worth its weight in gold.

'What you said, about Father—'

'It's the truth. We're here for Joseph, nowt else.' Without realising, the younger man secured alliance – he held out a hand. 'You have my word, lass.'

She placed her tiny one into his and nodded solemnly. *What Mam would do when she found out . . .* Pushing the thought away, she adopted the twins' motto: Mam could eat shit, for all she cared.

Despite her cunning from years of necessity, Lily knew she'd have to use all her wits to pull this off. Her mother was clever.

But as the lady at the market told me, she remembered with a determined smile, *so am I.*

Eager-faced, the men leaned in.

'He's snidy, my uncle. Snidy and slippery as a kipper. You need to be cleverer. I'll show you how but you've gorra listen. You've gorra listen and do everything I say.'

She'd been sick again.

The last acrid dribbles ran down Sally's cheek and neck. Spears of pain faded again and she welcomed impending release with a sigh.

Oblivion was on the cusp of taking her when rough fingers chased her descent away. They lifted one of her eyelids then the other. Then they raised her head from the ground.

The now-familiar scorch worked its way down her throat and on instinct alone, she spluttered and gagged. Senses too debilitated by injury and alcohol to resist, the dreamlike state imprisoned her once more.

She floated beyond reality. Her thoughts felt weighted, impossible to process. Where was she? How long had she been here? A day? Three? A week?

Place and time didn't apply to her any more. She'd wake in fits to the fiery liquid and sporadic blows – or the searing between her legs when he took her at will.

Like now. He was doing it again.

Awareness swirled around her foggy mind. Survival lent her a spurt of life and she pushed at the looming chest. Her feeble effort produced but a guttural laugh from the demon ravaging her.

As the thrusts intensified, she slipped blissfully into the sea of nothingness.

Chapter 27

'WHAT'S HAPPENING, ALICE? Is she laying it on thick enough? Is she bawling, an' that?'

Alice stroked her chin. 'I can't tell; she's got her back to me. Them two look to be lapping up whatever she's saying, anyroad.'

Nellie's face relaxed a fraction. 'I'll not have those two causing further ructions. Folk frequent my place for its reputation of discretion, where they can conduct what business they've a mind to without fear of police lurking. I want to keep it that way.'

'The young 'un's shaking her hand. I don't know how she does it. Reet devious young swine, she is. Hold up, she's coming back. She's been bawling good and proper; her face is redder than a smacked arse,' she affirmed.

'And them two?'

'Oh, they're bloody following her!'

'For the love of Christ, not again,' Nellie snapped as Lily entered, the men right behind. 'Now look here, I'll not tell youse again—'

'We're not stopping.' The father's words brought a surprised smile to Alice. 'The lass here confirmed what you said. No child could lie that well. We'll bother youse no more.' His voice dropped. 'But for our word, there's a condition.'

'Oh aye? What condition's that, then?'

'That you send word to us at Breightmet if that brother of yourn shows up,' said his son.

Knowing it wasn't worth pushing her luck, she bit back a negative retort. 'Aye, deal. Now sod off.'

Without hesitation, they left.

'Well, I'll be buggered. You really reckon they'll not be back?' asked Nellie.

'They'll not,' Lily said quickly. 'Eeh, Mam, tha should've seen me. Laid it on good and thick, I did, just like you told me.'

Her mother's eyes narrowed. 'And they believed we'd not seen him, just like that?'

She grinned. 'Nay. They knew I were lying about that.'

'Eh? But I thought—?'

'They said they must find him because he'd got someone called Sally, the liars, so I played along. I said I'd tell them a secret if they left Father alone. I said Uncle Joseph brought her to ours this morning, got his things together and hotfooted it to Rochdale.

'I told them he's gone to live there with her; bedding down at a friend's cellar, I said they were.' Doubt was leaving her mother's face. She grinned again. 'I gave them the address, said I'd heard Uncle Joseph telling thee.'

Nellie shook her head. 'Bloody hellfire. She's a rum 'un, she is, Alice.'

Her mother, too, was grinning. 'You lying young bleeder. What address?'

'Clover Lane, number five. I begged them not to tell you I'd told, and we shook on it. They've gone straight there. I hope they get blisters apple big looking for that. They deserve it for what they did to Father.'

Nellie roared with laughter, which brought on a coughing fit. 'You rum young beggar,' she spluttered, thumping the counter. 'You'll be a force to be reckoned with when you're grown. By, you will that.'

Her mother's chuckles added to Nellie's. 'Where the bugger did you pull that from?'

'Well, five, that's my age. And Clover, after my new kitten. She's lucky, she is, like four-leaf clovers. She hid under her mam and didn't get killed.' She held her up. 'Can I keep her? Can I?'

But Alice had stopped listening. 'Wait till our Joseph hears this,' she cackled, heading for the stairs. 'He said they were gormless bastards and by God, he weren't far wrong. Pour us a sup of summat for our nerves, will you, Nellie?'

Lily's heart felt set to leap from her chest but she knew she couldn't coward out now. Footsteps sounded and her gaze swivelled up. *Was* the lady from the market up there? Her heart pounded faster. She must finish this before her mother and uncle returned.

'Can I lie my kitten by the hearth, missis? She's shivering.'

Nellie, still chuckling at the gumption of one so young, nodded. 'Give the embers a prod, see if you can't drag some life from them.'

Lily hurried to the fire, laid Clover at her feet and lifted the poker. She glanced over her shoulder. Satisfied no one was watching, she let her free hand roam. Sweat sprang above her top lip as, upping the noise with the poker, she lifted the latch on a window and opened it half an inch.

Sagging with relief, she closed her eyes. Then she took a deep breath and skipped across the room.

Standing on tiptoe, she lifted the tankard of ale and glass of gin from the counter. 'These for Mam and Uncle Joseph, missis? I'll take them to a table, shall I?'

'Aye. Don't spill them, mind.'

Lily placed them on the table directly beneath the window then perched on a stool.

She could do no more. It was up to the men, now.

At the far end of the inn, the serving girl glanced from the child to the window. Turning to resume her duties, a shadow of a smile went with her.

Tommy's jaw muscles worked furiously; his impatience to begin was at fever pitch. His father laid a hand on his shoulder.

'Deep breaths, son. Not long, now.'

He nodded but his insides smouldered with a host of emotions. If that bastard had hurt her . . . What was she going through, at this very moment, while they stood idle, blindly obeying a child's instructions? His guts twisted but he knew they couldn't act yet.

Despite her limited years, the lass had been embarrassingly right. Goden had evaded them more times than they wanted to dwell upon. He had a knack of vanishing into thin air when sniffing danger; all they had got was dizzy from going around in circles trying to find the swine. This plan just might work. For Sally's sake, they had to try.

Hearing a muffled voice, they crouched lower on the crumbling steps behind the inn and cocked their heads to the window above. It grew louder, making it obvious the speaker stood directly opposite. It was also clear who it was. Thanks to the girl's sharp thinking, the voice travelled through the partially open window perfectly.

Goden. He *knew* it. Where the devil he'd hidden earlier was anyone's guess but now, they had him. They would be on him so fast, he wouldn't have time to blink.

'What did I tell thee? That pair couldn't find a tit in a whorehouse betwixt them.'

Tommy and Arthur glanced at each other, eyes burning with fury, as Joseph's scathing quip earned him a round of laughter.

'I mean, who with half a brain goes all out to search for someone and don't bloody search?' Inflated confidence filled his tone. 'I tell youse summat, that young 'un came this close to us. He had his hand on the knob of the bedroom door we were hiding behind, for Christ's sake, and didn't think to pull it back a bit.' He drew out the last words mockingly, following them with a bellow of laughter.

Tommy's hand tightened around the clump of stone he'd prised from the tumbledown steps. Goden was behind the door with her the whole time . . . Colour born of regret and humiliation flooded his face. How had he been so foolish? *Sally, I'm so sorry . . .*

'And to top it off, they finished up outwitted by a gormless slip of a lass,' Alice added. When the laughter died down, her amused voice sounded again. 'I'll be away to the cottage. Tha best get that one back across the road, an' all. And bring some gin to keep her akip. I'm not listening to her yowling all day.'

His eyes widened and his father shook his head. *Not yet, son, not yet,* it silently instructed.

Alice's footsteps faded to the door. The innkeeper's voice, as she barked orders to her serving girl, revealed she'd returned to the counter. And a loud burp told them Joseph was still by the window, finishing his ale.

This was what they were waiting for. For it to work, they needed him alone. The least support he had in the initial seconds was vital.

They needed no words. A simultaneous nod and they were ready.

His father scurried around the side of the building. Tommy's grip tightened on the rock. He eased the fingertips of his free hand through the window and teased it up a fraction more. It obeyed silently and, smiling grimly, he continued until he'd opened it fully. Then he rose.

Joseph stood with his back to him, completely unaware of what was coming. Tommy's lip curled in hatred; his drunkenness promised only to assist the success of the element of surprise.

With Joseph blocking his view, he stooped again to check the other occupants' positions. The serving girl was busy behind the counter, Alice and Nellie talking by the door. Lily stood beside her mother. Her eyes flicked to him and he nodded. All was ready.

He leaned through the window and lifted the rock above his head. But a movement by Joseph's feet threw him. He froze, all their careful plans melting at the sight of the woman he loved beyond reason. Whom he'd die for in a heartbeat. The woman lying half dead, face battered, covered in blood and vomit.

His hand flew to his mouth, trapping a cry. However, he couldn't contain the venomous loathing for her husband as easily. Lightning fast, he threw his arm around Joseph's neck and smashed the stone into his skull.

He crumpled instantly. Tommy lowered him to the ground beside Sally.

It had happened in the blink of an eye and without a sound. Alice was still talking with Nellie, the serving girl measuring out gin into an earthenware jug, each of them unaware of what had transpired feet away. Only Lily knew her uncle now lay in a heap, but she made no noise, busying herself with the kitten.

Tommy stared, transfixed, at the man he'd just bludgeoned. His father had warned him countless times to keep his calm, do nothing but injure him. As usual, his overwhelming love for Sally overtook all logic. He'd struck him much harder than he should, than they'd discussed. Joseph Goden was dead. And Tommy Morgan would swing.

His eyes swivelled to Sally and slowly they hardened. If he was to dance at the end of a rope, so be it. What that monster had done to her, to his mother . . . He deserved this and more. Joseph could rot in hell.

That he himself would soon join Lucifer for his sin, Tommy, at that moment, didn't care. Knowing this bastard would share the scorching pit would be worth the eternal suffering.

'You're free, my love,' he whispered to Sally. 'You, at least, will suffer no more.'

Calmness settled within him. He lifted two fingers to his lips, and blew. This needed finishing. Consequences could wait.

His father burst into the inn. Alice and Nellie, having turned to the window at the shrill whistle, now whipped back around as the door crashed against the wall. Like a pair of trout gasping for want of water, they gawped left to right, dumbfounded.

'What the . . . ?' Alice managed to croak. 'Where's . . . ? Oh, my God!' She made to rush to her lifeless brother, but Arthur grabbed her and Nellie by the scruff of their necks and bundled them behind the counter.

Tommy hadn't in his life heard his father raise his voice to a woman – now, he roared a threat of such ferocity, they flinched:

'Youse two stay there or so help me, you'll regret it. Same goes for thee,' he told the serving girl. 'You stay put, d'you hear?'

Her answer surprised everyone. 'Nay, mister, not me. I want to help.'

Nellie almost choked on a gasp. 'Oh! Why, you sneaky young—!'

'Shut that fat mouth of yourn and listen to me forra change.' A quaver lurked behind her words but she stuck her chin out. 'I need my head seeing to, putting up with you as long as I have. If I never find work for the rest of my days and finish up destitute in t' gutter, I'll be happier than I've ever been slaving for thee.' She waited for a response but Nellie simply gaped. She nodded once. 'How can I help, mister?'

With a thankful smile, Arthur pointed to the door. 'Keep an eye to customers, will you, lass? Say and do what you must but don't let a soul in. Or out,' he added, looking pointedly at Alice and Nellie. He turned to Tommy. 'All right, lad?'

Having climbed through the window, Tommy had crouched beside Sally. As his father approached, he lowered his head.

Arthur halted. He glanced at the crimson-stained rock, then at the gaping wound it had inflicted. He stooped and pressed two fingers to Joseph's wrist. Without a word, he let the limp hand fall to the ground. In his eyes was a look Tommy had never seen before.

'Father . . . I . . .'

Arthur held up a hand, and Tommy closed his mouth. Words couldn't undo what he'd done. They both knew it.

Arthur checked Sally's pulse. Then he spoke softly. 'Lass? Can you hear me? Can you open your eyes?

You're safe, now. Me and Tommy's here, and my Ivy will mend thee, have no fear.' Her eyelids flickered and he nodded. 'Good lass. Goden won't hurt you again, you have my word. Let's get you home.'

Tommy walked blindly to the door. His own arms burned to hold her but he didn't speak out. He was nothing to her, never would be. And soon, he wouldn't be anything to anyone.

Not a son or brother, future husband to Dolly, father to the child she might be carrying – nothing. He'd be hanged and he'd be dead. As dead as the man by the window.

He took a last look at Joseph then opened the door.

The next seconds played out dreamlike. Two sounds opened the act. The first was the serving girl's gasp, the next a horrified Lily slapping a hand to her mouth. Frowning, he followed their stares. What he saw rendered him immobile. He gazed at the large bulk which moments before had lain lifeless on the ale-soaked ground. *And was now standing behind his father.*

In Joseph's hand was the stone he'd introduced to his head – now set to make acquaintance with Arthur's. As he drew back his arm, his lips followed suit in a terrifying grin.

'*Stop!*'

The thunderous command shattered time in its tracks. At that pivotal moment, it seemed to grasp Joseph's arm in an invisible hold. The speaker charged past Tommy, pushed Arthur aside and landed a bone-crunching punch to Joseph's face. As blood and teeth flew one way, he fell the other, crashing to the ground like a sack of rocks.

In the ensuing bedlam, as Alice rushed to her brother screeching garbled curses, Nellie squawked at them all to leave and Lily clung, sobbing, to the serving girl's skirts, Tommy and his father stared at the newcomer in stunned silence.

He flashed a quick smile, demeanour cool as a summer breeze. 'Are the two of ye all right?' he enquired in a soft brogue. Then his eyes fixed on Sally and his composure wavered. 'Sweet Jesus. Is she . . . ?'

'She's alive. Who . . . ? How did you . . . ?'

'Your wife explained everything. I got here as quickly as I could.' At Arthur's confused frown, he patted his shoulder. 'Sure, there's time enough later for explanations. We need to leave. Sally needs tending to, and fast.' He held out his arms. 'Give her to me, friend. I've a cart waiting outside.'

Tommy's senses snapped back instantly. Joseph's resurrection had struck him dumb. He'd stood by, frozen with disbelief, as the bastard prepared to attack his father. The inadequacy was crippling – more so when he knew the identity of Arthur's saviour, whom he'd recognised on that cart. The man he'd come to hate almost as much as Joseph.

Because he was different from the man whose name Sally bore. One was linked to her by a marriage she loathed – the other, looking every inch the hero of the hour . . . He'd laid claim to her heart.

Seeing him hold out his arms, the last vestige of restraint Tommy clung to, snapped. The nightmare, of this man taking Sally from him, had haunted him for weeks. He'd been unable to stop it in his dreams. It wouldn't happen in reality. He clamped a hand on his shoulder.

The Irishman turned. As they stared at each other, he seemed to read the message in Tommy's hard gaze. With the briefest nod, he stepped back.

Tommy felt his father's eyes boring into him as he took Sally, but didn't care. Neither did he care what her new man thought. This was the last time he'd hold her. This precious moment would see him through the endless years stretching ahead with Dolly. No one would deny him it.

He cradled her as though she was made of the most delicate china and everyone in the world melted away.

'What about that devil?' the Irishman asked Arthur, jerking his head to the prone figure Alice was trying to rouse. 'Sure, Sally will never be safe while he breathes. Next time—'

'There'll not be a next time.' Dragging his eyes from his son, rage swamped Arthur. In a movement that belied his years, he lunged. Alice made to claw his face but a swipe sent her sprawling. Grabbing Joseph's jaw, he lifted his bloody face to his.

'You . . . I've a good mind to kill thee here and now, you worthless lump of shit. You don't deserve to draw another breath for what you've done to that lass, to my family . . . *to my wife*. Get up. Fight me. Do to me what tha did to my Ivy. Up!' He tried to drag Joseph to his feet. 'I'll murder you, yer bastard!' All trace of the man everyone knew and respected had vanished and, like a man possessed, he landed blow after frenzied blow.

'Mr Morgan, that's enough.'

The Irishman made to take his arm but Arthur shoved him aside. Undeterred, he tried again, this time managing to prise his hand from Joseph's jaw. As Joseph slumped to the ground, Arthur made to lunge again but the Irishman wrapped his arms around his middle and hauled him to the door.

'No fellow's worth dangling at the end of a rope for, not even him. Come away, now, come away.'

The fight left Arthur and he ceased struggling. With a calmness that robbed her cheeks of colour, he pointed to Alice. 'You keep him away, d'you hear me? If he shows his face again, I swear on all I hold dear, I'll kill him.' And with every fibre of his being, he meant it.

Moments later, they were aboard the cart and the Irishman instructed the driver to get them to Spring Row as fast as he could. After a last, horrified look at the woman whom, he murmured, he'd brought here only yesterday, he gave the reins a sharp flick.

'Mister, wait!'

Two figures emerged from the inn. For the serving girl, it was undoubtedly the last time. Head bowed, she scuttled away. The other was Lily. Bare feet slapping the cobbles, she ran alongside the cart, face wet with tears.

Arthur held out a hand and she gripped it. 'Thank you, lass. We couldn't have done it without thee.'

'She'll be all right, won't she, mister? You'll nurse her well?'

'Aye. Goodbye.'

'Goodbye, mister. Goodbye, Sally,' she whispered.

The cart gained speed and the small fingers slipped from his. When she was out of sight, he glanced left. The adoration pouring from his son as he gazed at the woman in his arms was, for so many reasons, too painful to watch. With a bone-weary sigh, he closed his eyes.

This wasn't going away. He was at his wits' end with the whole bloody business. He'd have to talk to Ivy. He'd carried this burden alone for long enough.

Chapter 28

SHE'D ASKED FOR *him.*

Heavy clouds scudded, promising more snow. Occasionally, chinks of sunlight penetrated but did little to brighten the row. It remained a colourless canvas, devoid of life and beauty. The temperature had plummeted and a steady wind had taken hold, whistling around the cottages like a living thing, its haunting moan encompassing all it touched.

Hunched against the wall, arms folded, Tommy stared through the window, seeing nothing.

His physical self had separated from his mind. One stood in a small cottage in Spring Row, the other was worlds away, trapped in a darkness he doubted he'd ever break from. He was dimly aware of the hum of voices behind him but they didn't mean a thing. Nothing did. Nothing mattered. Nothing.

She'd asked for him.

Tommy had carried her from the cart, up the stairs. He'd lowered her into his own bed and dropped to his knees. Flitting figures, voices – his mother, the woman on the cart with *him* – swum on the outskirts of his awareness. Like a starving dog eyeing a bone, he'd guarded the precious being from all who surrounded her.

For a long time, Sally had lain prone, eyes closed. Suddenly, taking everyone by surprise, they sprang open. The glassy pools had fixed on a point behind Tommy then her body jolted. Pungent liquid spilled from her mouth, drenching her torn blouse. He'd lifted her head, the flow ceased and she'd continued to retch, dry heaves bending her double.

Finally, her face relaxed and he'd lowered her blindly, tears obliterating his vision. As he blinked them back, his stomach had lurched to see her staring straight at him. Her gaze was steady and when her lips moved he'd had to dip his head to catch her words. What he heard shattered his heart into a thousand pieces.

She'd asked for Con.

The name scorched his soul. His head had jerked in a shake of denial but she'd looked through him and said it again. Then *he* was there. He cupped her face, caressed her cheek with his thumb, murmured her name. Sighing, Sally had closed her eyes.

For hours, Tommy's mind had replayed the scene. Throughout, the cottage was a hive of tears and voices, yet he'd heard but that one word. His was the first face she saw upon wakening. And the Irishman was the one she'd wanted.

Deep down, he'd known the truth. She'd now confirmed it, with her own lips, and crushed his heart to pulp.

'Merciful God, release me from this living hell,' he murmured against the cold pane.

Maggie glanced in turn at the people around the table. Clasping steaming cups of tea, they conversed in subdued voices. Anger, tears, questions and explanations had dwindled. Now, they shared but one concern – Sally's best interests.

'I don't want to leave her,' Maggie said. 'That swine might come back; I'll not risk that happening. Sally speaks highly of thee, Mrs Morgan, and I don't doubt you care for her as much as we, but it's just not safe, here.'

'I've a mind to agree, but what choice is there? It'll take more than a few hours' kip to sleep off all that booze. Then there's her injuries. I dread to think what pain she'll be in when the ale's not there to take off the edge.' Ivy patted Maggie's hand. 'I've known thee only several hours but see why Sally chose you for a friend. You're a good soul, with a kind heart to match. But you can't move her, lass, not today.

'My offer still stands, mind,' she added when Maggie sighed. 'You're all welcome to bed down here the night. If Sally's up to the journey the morrow, youse can set off home in t' morning.'

Martha Smith nodded agreement, followed by Con.

'She's right, so, Maggie. Sally's in no fit state to be moved.' Catching Arthur's eye, his turned icy. 'As for her husband, if he's fool enough to show his face again—'

'Then God help him,' Arthur finished for him.

Having given Jonathan a last feed with promises to return if needed, Mrs Oakes had left shortly before. Sated, he lay in Maggie's arms. She stroked his hand and nodded. 'I'll stop the night, Mrs Morgan. Thank you.' She turned to Mr Lynch. 'Are you . . . ?'

'Nay, I can't stop. My wife would fret herself sick. I'll be back the morrow, lass.'

'Ta, Mr Lynch.'

'Nay, no thanks needed. That lass upstairs is niece to my owdest friend. I'm only happy to help. I'll call on Ed and Grace, tell them what's occurred.'

‘Play it down, will thee? There’s no point worrying them witless. There’ll be time enough for explanations the morrow, once we’ve got Sally home.’

He nodded. ‘Tha stopping, lad?’ he asked Con.

‘I . . .’ Con glanced from the stairs to the window. ‘Well, I . . .’

‘You go, Con. She’s in safe hands,’ said Maggie quietly. The concern in his eyes pained her a little and instantly, she felt ashamed. Her dearest friend lay broken and all she could think of was her own wants. She lowered her head in self-disgust yet Con, putting his finger under her chin, raised it again.

‘And you, Maggie? You’ll be all right?’ he murmured.

‘Aye.’ Stupefied, it was all she could utter. She smiled and he returned it then made for the door with Mr Lynch. They bade all goodbye and were gone.

Arthur looked to the window, gave a small sigh and went to join his younger son by the fire. The lad sat cross-legged, stroking Shield, and he crouched beside him to inspect the dog’s progress. It was sleeping, its breathing steady. Hopefully, it would recover. As with its mistress, they could only pray.

Martha poured weary-looking Ivy a fresh cup of tea then motioned to Maggie.

She shook her head absently. Con’s image burned behind her eyes and his touch lingered on her skin. Flushing with pleasure and shame, she headed upstairs.

Dawn hadn’t yet broken when Sally stirred. A distant smile lingered, half her mind still suspended in a dream.

She was with her mother and Jonathan, Shield trotting alongside. They were walking through an emerald-green field abloom with cowslip and buttercups, the air heady with love. Rose held Jonathan up and he laughed as she planted kisses on his cheek.

When he turned to look at his mother with smiling eyes of the same sapphire blue, Sally's heart swelled with pride for the fine-looking boy he'd become. They sat in the sweet-smelling grass and she lifted her face to the sun with a rush of such happiness, it stole her breath. Rose drew her close and she rested her head on her shoulder.

Her heart skipped as she caught sight of a tall, dark-haired man heading towards them across the field. His face was in shadow but she knew without question that she loved him, and that he loved her. In his muscular arms, he carried a girl with hair the colour of corn. She lifted a tiny hand and Sally waved back . . .

Dull pain and a raging thirst like nothing she'd ever known were pulling her from the beautiful scene. She heard her mother's voice, soft as a whisper on the breeze:

'*All's not over. Be strong, lass. Be strong.*'

The pain came in waves and she drifted further until her loved ones were but a blot in the distance.

'Mam? Mam, I cannot find you. Please, Mam,' she cried, fingers searching the air.

'Sally? 'Ere, lift your head, lass, take some water.'

Water. Yes, she needed water.

The room was too dark to see. Fiery fingers clawed every inch of her. Her head was lifted and she guided the hand to her mouth. Cold metal brushed her lips and for a full minute she drank. She lay back against the pillow. Footsteps sounded and streaky light flared then dipped as a candle was lit.

'How are you feeling? Oh, I've been that worried.'

'Maggie?' Her voice was scratchy and she frowned, hearing it. 'Maggie, I don't . . .'

'Shhh. Everything's going to be all right. You rest.'

Another spasm cut through her and she sucked in air sharply. 'It hurts.'

'I know, lass,' Maggie murmured, a catch behind the words. 'D'you remember . . . owt? Oh, I don't know what to . . . I'm so sorry.'

Sally's breath came in short gasps. 'Tell me . . . Please, tell me the truth. My child. Is he . . . alive?'

'Oh, love. The babby's fine. He weren't with you, remember?'

She released a sob. 'Thank God. Where . . .?' She wept when her friend placed Jonathan in her arms. Ignoring the pain, she held him close. 'I remember. Joseph, he—' Her head shot up. 'Where is he? What—?'

'Don't you fret about that divil,' cut in Maggie venomously. 'He'll not harm thee again. Mr Morgan and his son – Thomas, is it? – they found you, lass.'

'Tommy . . .'

'Aye. And Con—'

'Con? How . . . ? And *you're* here. Am I at your home? Are we in Manchester?' Her voice rose in distress. 'I, I don't understand what's happening, I—'

'Shh. Easy, now. You're at Mrs Morgan's. Con's returned to Manchester with Mr Lynch but they'll be back today. Try and sleep. I'll explain everything later.'

With a hint of her former strength, she responded firmly. 'No, Maggie, tell me now. I must understand. Please. Tell me.'

For the next hour, they talked and cried in equal measures. Maggie prompted her to begin from the earliest point she remembered and, with supportive hand squeezes, helped her give voice to her ordeal.

Frequently, her memory failed and, if able, Maggie filled in the gaps from Arthur's and Con's versions.

'That's all there is to tell. You were sick summat awful yesterday, but I think you're over the worst.'

Her friend tore her gaze away and Sally's hand strayed to her face. Inside she was on the mend; outside was clearly another matter. 'Is it so bad, Maggie?'

'We . . . Mrs Morgan, Mrs Smith and me, tended your injuries best we could. Mrs Smith set your nose well, and we bathed your bruises with gentle care, lass.'

Looking down, she saw they had replaced her torn blouse with one of Ivy's. 'Oh, Maggie. Con's lovely gift . . .'

'Eeh, don't fret on that. Aye, you look much better than you did when . . . when . . .' Sally took her hand, and her facade crumbled. 'Oh, lass, your poor face and body! It's hard believing you're the same woman we know and love. I could kill that bastard with my bare hands!'

'Don't fret, Maggie, please. They'll heal.'

'Aye, lass,' she agreed determinedly. 'You'll be back to your owd self in no time. Besides the thirst, you slept well through the night. I gave you sips of water when you wakened—' She broke off, cheeks flushing. 'I latched Jonathan on to thee when he were clemmed. I hope you don't mind, only Mrs Oakes had gone—'

'Of course not. I must remember to thank her. And you,' Sally added, lips trembling. 'You, the Morgans, Con, Mr Lynch . . . I owe you all so much.' She fell silent. Words could never portray her gratitude. 'The child, too, who helped Mr Morgan and Tommy; what was her name? Alice and Harold, they . . .' This conjured up her sister-in-law's image and Sally breathed deeply. 'They have quite a few children.'

She cast her mind back. Alice was with child when she and Joseph dwelled with them before moving to

Spring Row. She'd previously borne twins but, if Sally remembered correctly, they were boys. There was also another boy, a year or two older. She trawled her memory for the senior children.

'One was Mary. And another . . . Lizzie? Yes, Lizzie.' She nodded then frowned. 'There were more but I cannot recall their names. Was it either of those, Maggie? Mary, Lizzie?'

'I don't think so. You'll have to ask Mr Morgan.'

Sally was quiet for a moment before asking, 'Is Shield hurt badly? I know I haven't had him long but I don't know what I'd do if he died.'

'Aye,' Maggie answered truthfully. 'As I said, he's gorra terrible cut to his head. But Mrs Morgan's sons kipped down in t' kitchen so we could have their beds, so don't fret, he's not alone.'

Sally shook her head and fresh tears welled up. 'So much damage . . . He's caused so much hurt and pain. He did attack Mrs Morgan; I just knew he had. I loathe him so much I can taste it.' She gripped her friend's hand. 'He forced himself on me, Maggie. Countless times. What if I'm with child? I, I couldn't bear—'

'Oh, Sally. Oh, my poor love. Whatever happens, you're not alone, not while I draw breath.'

Sally began to weep. 'I want my mother. Oh, Maggie, I miss her so much.'

'I know, love, I know. You called for her when you wakened.'

A flash of emerald green, her mother, Jonathan . . . A man, a small child in his arms. It had been a wonderful, bittersweet dream. She sighed longingly and, from far away, heard again her mother's warning from beyond the grave.

'Remember, you'll allus have us,' Maggie was saying now. 'Me, Con, the Morgans and your family. There's no real substitute forra mother, but—'

'He hasn't finished, Maggie. All is not over.'

She spoke in such a chilling, knowing tone that Maggie paled. 'Nay, lass. By the end of the day, we'll be in Manchester—'

'And he'll find me. I'll never be free of him, don't you understand? I'll never be free.'

'Then you must go somewhere else. Get right away from here; out of England, if you must.'

'What? But—'

'However much the thought of never seeing thee again pains me . . . What your husband's capable of is clear to see. If your prediction proves right, he might not spare your life next time.'

'Where would I go? What would I do for money? It's hopeless, Maggie, hopeless.'

'Ah, but it ain't.'

She frowned. 'What do you mean? You and Con – why *are* you here? What's going on?'

'Oh, Sally . . .' Maggie's eyes shone. 'After you left, Saturday, Father Collins came to see you. I shouted but you were too far away to hear. I were beside meself, unsure what to do. Thankfully, Con visited that night and when I told him, he went to ask your aunt's advice. She said to find thee, to get Mrs Morgan's address from Mr Lynch.' She reached for her hands and squeezed. 'Oh, you'll never believe.'

'What, Maggie? What did Father Collins want?'

'You're bloomin' rich, lass. Mrs Sharp's left you money – lots of it, by all accounts. Eeh, I'm that pleased for thee!'

Sally gazed at her.

'Father Collins didn't go into detail. He needs to speak to you; urgent, like, he said.'

'I . . . Why on earth would she leave *me* money?'

'I don't know, but don't you see? This changes everything. You'll have enough brass to see you and Jonathan set for life. You can get away, away from Joseph, for ever. You're free.'

She was still dreaming, had to be. Or Maggie was mistaken.

'I'll make some tea. Will you be all right while I'm gone?'

Sally nodded. When her friend's tread on the stairs faded, she released a long breath. One thought, one tantalising possibility, consumed her.

'I'm free,' she whispered to the empty room. 'Oh, Mrs Sharp . . .'

For the dozenth time that morning, her tears flowed. Only now, they were of hopeful joy.

Having drifted off, Sally jumped awake when Maggie re-entered. Fear and confusion must have shown in her eyes, for her friend hurried over, her own soft with pity.

'It's all right, lass, it's only me.' She placed two cups beside the bed and smoothed the hair from Sally's brow. 'Could you eat? Mrs Morgan's just up and preparing breakfast for the men. Have I to fetch thee summat?'

'No, thank you. Are the men awake?'

'Aye.'

'Would you ask them to come to me? I need to speak with them.'

Maggie frowned. 'Are you sure you're up to it? You should get some rest afore Mr Lynch arrives, build up your strength.'

'I cannot leave without seeing them. I owe them my life. Please, Maggie.'

'All right. I'll fetch them.'

Gritting her teeth against the pain, she pushed herself up in bed. A light knock sounded and Arthur entered.

'Morning, lass.'

Emotion choked her reply. She held out a hand. 'Oh, Mr Morgan . . .' He made to take it but she threw her arms around his neck. He held her gently until her sobs subsided. 'I'm sorry,' she murmured when they drew apart. 'I'm simply . . . Thank you. Thank you.'

'There's no need for thanks, lass.'

'Oh, but there is, I—' She broke off as a figure appeared in the doorway. The sight of him took her breath away. Again, she held out a hand. 'Tommy, I . . . wanted to thank you—'

'As Father said, there's no need.'

He remained by the door and she lowered her hand. 'Nevertheless, thank you.'

He nodded and turned to leave, but Arthur stopped him.

'Son, wait. Wish the lass well and say your goodbyes,' he instructed him quietly. Then he bid her farewell and slipped from the room.

Sally sensed tension between the men, but the object of her attention overrode everything. He hesitated then crossed to the bed.

He perched on the edge and she held out her hand, albeit hesitantly. She thought he'd rebuff her again but he took it in both of his.

Without doubt, this was the last time she'd look upon him. This man, whom she barely knew yet felt she did completely, and he her, inside out. With whom she'd hardly spent any time and yet she felt they had shared a lifetime together already. This man, who invaded her thoughts, filled her with shame, confusion – and a need to be with him so fierce, it pained her physically. How, why, she harboured this love she was at a loss to understand. But she did. Lord, she *did.*

She'd struggled to show restraint, fought herself relentlessly. And as she curled her fingers through his, she ached anew for what might have been, what never could, never would be – and what she'd have given for it to be. Her hold tightened. She'd cherish this moment, always.

'Are you well enough to travel today?'

Fresh longing flowed through her. He'd spoken softly, almost caringly. 'I think so.'

Tommy was silent. His thumb began stroking the back of her hand.

The urge to wrap her arms around him was unbearable. 'I've been meaning to apologise,' she blurted for want of something to say. 'My arrival on Saturday, interrupting as I did . . . I'm sorry. I hope you and Dolly will be very happy together.'

He opened his mouth, then closed it. He gazed at her for an eternity. Then he sighed and lowered his head. 'I'll be late for work.'

She swallowed her pain as he rose. Their fingers were still entwined and when she squeezed, desperate for his touch a second longer, he did likewise.

'Goodbye, Sally.'

His hand slipped from hers. Gripping the bedclothes, she watched him walk from her for ever.

'Goodbye, my love,' she whispered when the door clicked shut. And deep within her breast, part of her died.

Chapter 29

AGAIN, MAGGIE CROSSED to the window. She glanced along the street, clicked her tongue and returned to the table.

Sally was the picture of composure. She sipped her tea, attention on Shield by her feet.

For days, she'd willed him to pull through, praying infection wouldn't take hold. To her blessed relief, it worked. He was more alert today and, despite a shaky start, was walking around again. Love and attention were what he needed and he had them by the shovel load. Whenever she left him to attend to Jonathan, Maggie's twins would sit with him; they, too, were desperate to have their friend back. She was confident that in time, they would.

'How you're so calm, I don't know,' Maggie marvelled, gaze straying back to the window. 'I'm on pins for thee.'

'I see no point in this meeting. I've made my decision.'

'I wish you'd think about this—'

'There's nothing to think about,' Sally cut in mildly. 'That money is tainted, Maggie. It was simply another opportunity to rub her daughter's nose in the dirt. If Mrs Sharp had died from natural means, Miss Sharp would have been virtually penniless. She chose me as beneficiary for the sole purpose of destroying her child's life. I want no part in it. No part at all.'

'And Joseph?' asked Maggie bluntly. 'I get no pleasure mentioning him but you need to think on you and that babby. All that money . . . you'd want for nowt the rest of your days. This could be a fresh beginning, away from him. Can't you put your beliefs to one side, lass? If not for thee, for Jonathan. Do it for him.'

She stared at her son, asleep by the fire. She'd been so hopeful, so happy – so selfish.

It was only afterwards, when the news sank in, that her joy had turned to disgust. Remembering her excitement had her cringing with shame. As Agnes had proved countless times, she thrived on causing Pru misery. This was no different. This parting gift had been intended to crush her daughter a final time. Well, Sally wouldn't give her the satisfaction. Not a single farthing would pass through her hands.

'Even Manchester's not altogether safe,' Maggie pressed, buoyed by her silence. 'He could track you down if he'd a mind to. I feel sick thinking on it. We only want what's best for thee. Don't do owt rash when they arrive, eh? Just think on it a while more. Even your aunt agrees you should take it.'

Despite herself, Sally couldn't contain a smile at the mention of Grace.

She cast her mind back to Monday. On Tommy's departure, her spirits had plummeted to rock bottom. If she lived to be a hundred, she'd never love another man. Not like that, with him. He'd been the first to bear proof that all men were not the same. He'd awakened that something inside her, something she hadn't thought herself capable of, following Joseph's evil.

Con's arrival had eased her inner darkness somewhat. He'd held her, soothed her. He'd admitted he hadn't been able to face saying goodbye in Manchester but was here now, and he and Maggie would take good care of her.

However, her lift in mood was short-lived – she'd sobbed to see her beautiful, gentle giant. Shield had tried to rise for her but his legs buckled and he'd whimpered, as though apologising for his failure to protect her. She'd reassured him, hugged Shaun for tending him. And saying goodbye to Ivy shattered her heart.

Ivy had fussed around the cart tucking blankets about her, asked repeatedly was she up to the journey, was her pain manageable, was she warm enough . . . Then she'd grasped her hand and begged her never to return. Despite the sorrow that agreeing brought, Sally promised.

As she'd made for the town she thought she'd seen the back of, anguish had threatened to consume her. Passing Deansgate, she'd refused to think, feel. She'd eased off her marriage band and dropped it over the side of the cart. She'd felt numb at the thought of Joseph, then, still did.

Initially, she blamed herself for what had happened. Countless obstacles scuppered her return, almost foretelling imminent doom: Peggy's death, Grace's revelation, the Sharps' deaths – like a higher power warning her not to go. Ignoring the signs nearly cost her her life. She should have left after seeing Ivy was safe. She should have *left* after witnessing the proposal – another shadow of warning, to be sure.

Yet gradually, she realised she wasn't at fault, knew that to move on from this she must put it behind her. She was used to his abuse and she'd recover, as she had many times. She refused to be broken.

On reaching Ancoats, a numbness his evil wasn't strong enough to penetrate had wrapped around her. Shoulders back, head high, she'd greeted a horrified

Ellen with dry-eyed calmness. She'd then noticed the kitchen's other occupants.

Grace had caught her in a tight embrace, crying and railing over Joseph. Ed, white with shock and rage, held her next. When he stepped aside, revealing the person behind him, Sally's mouth fell open. She'd stared, elated and terrified, unsure what to do. Stan made the decision for her. Wrapping his arms around her, he'd uttered the most precious words:

'I could've lost thee. Oh, Sally, forgive me . . .'

And those long, torturous hours of rape and abuse seemed worth it. She had her family back. She had her brother.

They had asked her to come home and she'd agreed to, soon. Despite her joy at reconciling, she had to be sure they – or more to the point, Stan – wouldn't have a change of heart. She couldn't bear things going wrong again.

Now, as Maggie returned to the window, Sally sighed. She wouldn't dwell on her future. She'd take each day as it came; it was all she could do. Her friends and family were of one mind: accept the money, build a new life for herself and Jonathan. But she couldn't. If her decision proved disastrous, she'd suffer the consequences. Yet she'd do so with a clear conscience.

'Maggie, please, sit down.'

'He said one o'clock and it's nearly two. Where the divil are they?'

'Haven't you listened to a word I've said? I won't accept it.' She'd spoken more sharply than intended and sighed again. 'I'm sorry. I don't mean to be short with you, it's just—' A knock cut her off. Maggie rose and she grasped her hand. 'Please respect my decision. I won't be dissuaded.'

Sighing herself, Maggie went to answer the door.

Father Collins entered, all smiles and apologies. Catching sight of Sally, they died. He took her hand. 'My child. I was not aware that your injuries were quite so extensive. Mrs Benson said you suffered an accident in Bolton, but . . . Are you quite well enough to receive us?'

'Yes, Father.'

He looked as if he'd ask more but when she looked away, changed his mind. He motioned to a gentleman in the doorway. 'This is Mr Stockton, of Stockton and Coburn Solicitors. Mr Stockton, may I introduce you to Mrs Swann?'

Her eyebrows rose. The short, balding man who stepped forward was no stranger. His wry smile as he removed his hat showed that he clearly remembered her, too.

If her appearance shocked him, he didn't show it. He shook her hand warmly. 'Ah! These young ladies came to my rescue last week,' he informed the priest. 'My papers were headed for the gutter but Mrs Swann and Mrs . . . ?'

'Benson, sir.'

'And Mrs Benson, mercifully averted disaster.'

'Take a seat, Mr Stockton, Father. I'll brew a fresh pot while you discuss . . . matters. Mam's out with the kiddies. You'll not be disturbed.'

Tight-lipped, Sally watched Mr Stockton extract papers from his case. *Agnes's will.* The very sight made her feel ill.

'I trust you are aware of what this meeting is about, Mrs Swann? I believe Father Collins explained to Mrs Benson that the late Mrs Agnes Sharp—'

'I know what this is about.'

His hands stilled on the documents he was sifting through. 'I see—'

'And I want no part in it whatsoever. I want nothing from that woman.'

'Mrs Swann, I don't quite—'

'Do you have children, Mr Stockton?'

'Why, yes. Two girls and a boy.'

She ignored Maggie's soft sigh. 'Tell me, sir. Have you ever caused them unnecessary pain? Do you relish seeing them upset? Would you deem it acceptable to destroy their lives?'

His mouth dropped open. 'Absolutely not!'

'Then you'll understand when I tell you I won't accept what that woman has bequeathed me.'

'Mrs Swann, I'm afraid I haven't the slightest notion what you're talking about.' He shot the priest a puzzled frown. 'Father?'

'The Sharps had . . . a tumultuous relationship, shall we say. I'm afraid at times one could only describe Mrs Sharp's treatment of her daughter as deplorable.' Father Collins looked at Sally kindly. 'I think what Mrs Swann is trying to say is that she believes this money was merely a ploy to hurt Miss Sharp.'

Mr Stockton nodded slowly. 'I see. However, Mrs Swann, you are quite wrong. Mrs Sharp has indeed bequeathed you a rather substantial sum but I'm certain it was not with the intention of hurting her daughter.'

'Then why—?'

'If I may?' He selected a folded sheet sealed with a wax stamp. 'I'm sure once you have seen this, all will become clear.'

'Whatever the contents of that will . . .'

'Will? No, no, Mrs Swann. This is no will.' He pushed it towards her. 'Are you able . . . ?'

'Quite, thank you,' she affirmed with a proud lift of her chin. The daily readings Agnes insisted upon had vastly improved her literacy skills. She broke the seal and unfolded the sheet. 'This is a letter.'

'Indeed. Apparently, it explains everything.'

At Maggie's encouraging smile, she began:

Well, girl. If you are reading this, I can be sure of two things: I am dead and my solicitor has earned his reward for a job well done.

Thus, he is not completely incompetent, despite his revolting habit of housing kipper skin in his teeth. Conversing with him is an altogether unpleasant experience, don't you agree? His cook deserves a stern talking-to for serving such unappetising fare.

Sally glanced at Mr Stockton then back to the letter. Even in death, the old woman's tongue was sharp enough to cut through steel.

I am guessing I have flummoxed you by bestowing such a generous gift. And, knowing you the little I do, I suspect you are considering rejecting this offer. I am right, aren't I? You really ought to climb down from that high horse of yours occasionally.

Indignant colour flooded her cheeks, yet the hint of a smile hovered. Shaking her head, she continued.

In a moment, Mr Stockton will hand you an envelope. Contained within is two hundred pounds. It is yours to do with as you wish. I make no demands as to how you choose to spend it. However, if you do accept, it comes with but one condition.

My request is a lifelong commitment, but one I trust you will not deem undesirable. Prudence is now alone in the world and I want you to rectify that.

You must remain with her as friend and companion. You and your child will reside with her – my room is of an adequate size, I am sure. It is also of paramount importance that you assist my daughter in running the business. The shop is her main source of income; you must ensure that standards do not slip.

This may surprise you, but I care a great deal for my daughter. Her welfare after my death has concerned me a long while. The thought of her as destitute pains me considerably. You must ensure this never happens. Should you let the customers take advantage of her good nature, the business would go under in no time.

I have made some choices in my life of which I'm not proud. This, I am certain, is not one. I see something in you which I admire. You have integrity. You also possess a pure heart. I know you will not let me, or, more importantly, Prudence, down.

I leave you to ponder my terms. A comfortable life for you and your child and more money than you will know what to do with are yours for the taking, so long as you don't allow your pride to rule your judgement. Know this and take my word as truth when I tell you I would not bestow such opportunity upon just anyone.

I did not make your position easy, yet you served me well. Take it, also, as a token of my appreciation. You have earned it, girl, thrice over.

Yours in hope and faith,
Mrs Agnes Elizabeth Sharp

The paper slipped from Sally's fingers and fluttered to the floor.

Chapter 30

FATHER COLLINS FOLDED the letter. At Sally's request, he'd read it aloud, tactfully omitting the reference to the solicitor. Before her lay the unopened envelope. They stared at it in silence.

'What will you do?' asked Maggie. 'This changes everything, surely? Mrs Sharp didn't leave it you to hurt Miss Sharp; she did it to protect her. And as it says at the end, well, she wanted you to have it for serving her well, lass, an' all. Happen it's her way of saying sorry for the way she treated you, for the burden heaped on you at finding out about the goings on betwixt the pair.

'You were a true and loyal friend to Miss Sharp. Happen she were grateful for that, an' all. Who knows what went through that head of hers? But you can be certain of one thing, now,' she added, eyes gentle. 'That money's yours. You need feel no guilt in taking it. With no ill intentions in mind, I believe she wanted thee to have it, regardless. It's there in black and white.'

Sally bit her lip. 'The shop and everything else . . . ?'

'Mrs Sharp's effects – the business, all monies and possessions – she bequeathed to her daughter,' the solicitor confirmed. 'As the beneficiary committed both murder and self-destruction, and without kinsfolk to contest entitlement of ownership, those effects revert to the Crown.' He inclined his head to the envelope. 'I received a letter from Mrs Sharp the week before her death. It was delivered to my home address, not to my office as one would expect.'

Sally closed her eyes. *The letter she'd given to the maid* – Mr Stockton's maid, she realised. She'd never have dreamed it held this.

'Inside was the envelope you see before you and the letter you have read,' he continued. 'There was a second, addressed to myself, containing instructions along with my fee. Our first meeting could have saved a considerable amount of time had I known . . . You see, the reason for my haste that day was that she instructed me to deliver this to you at her funeral. She was certain you would attend.

'Alas, unrelated matters detained me and I was running dreadfully late.' His countenance turned decidedly uncomfortable. 'Mrs Sharp insisted discretion was of the utmost importance. She touched upon your marital difficulties and was adamant that your husband should not find out. Indeed, if she'd bequeathed this in her will, by law, ownership would have passed to him.'

Sally was stunned. 'But how . . . ? I mentioned nothing to her regarding my past.'

Mr Stockton smiled. 'Who knows? Mrs Sharp was extremely astute, Mrs Swann. Maybe she guessed, or perhaps it was a mere suspicion and she decided upon this route for any eventuality.

'In any case, it was a shrewd decision. The sum is yours without record of its existence, bar our letters. Only we in this room bear knowledge of it.' His eyes softened as he studied her injuries, clearly guessing who had inflicted them. 'As for myself, you need harbour no concerns as to my discretion. Once I leave this house, it shall be as though this meeting had never taken place.'

'I second that notion,' murmured Father Collins.

Too overcome with emotion to speak, Sally nodded.

When Mr Stockton took his leave, Maggie made a fresh pot of tea and the three of them discussed the day's discoveries.

Sally prodded the envelope. 'I'm still not entirely comfortable with this. I hardly knew her. I shouldn't lay claim to her money.'

'Whatever her failings, Mrs Sharp was no fool,' Father Collins said quietly. 'Had she not wanted you to have it, that envelope would not be lying there. You may not have known them a great length of time but you clearly made an impression upon both women. Furthermore, as Mrs Benson stated, you were a true friend to Miss Sharp.'

'I could have been a better one, Father. Perhaps if—'

'Alas, hindsight is an unforgiving mistress, my child. No one could have foreseen the outcome. You went above and beyond to help Miss Sharp – in death as well as in life. I am in agreement with Mrs Sharp; I too believe you have earned this money.'

'I cannot fathom it. If she cared for her daughter as she claims, why treat her so abominably? It makes no sense.'

Father Collins steepled his fingers. 'Many years ago, Miss Sharp spoke to me of her troubles. Naturally, priests cannot repeat, to anyone, disclosures made during the sacred act of confession.' He paused. 'However, my and Miss Sharp's conversation took place not in the confessional box, but a pew by the altar.'

'Father?'

'Under Church regulations, confidentiality of disclosures depends upon whether they are made in private or in public. Anything disclosed in settings where others may reasonably overhear, as in this case, could be seen as without intent to confidentiality . . .'

'Do you have something to tell me concerning Miss Sharp?'

'Some would deem it was with confidential intention . . . However . . . in what Miss Sharp revealed, and her reasons for doing so, the intention was simply, I am certain, to rid herself of the burden she'd carried for so long. I am equally certain that, in telling you, I shall not come to regret it.

'It has no bearing on anyone connected; no harmful actions can result from the telling. It may bring you, however, if not comfort then closure. *Not* to tell you would be an unnecessary cruelty.'

Sally touched his arm. 'I give you my word it shall go no further.'

Drumming his fingers together, he met her gaze. 'Are you aware Miss Sharp had a child?'

She knew her expression was answer enough. 'Father, are you certain—?'

'Quite. What I am about to reveal may pain you. Are you sure you wish to hear it?'

She and Maggie glanced at each another then nodded.

'While growing up, Miss Sharp was close to her mother. Her father showed her little interest but it didn't unduly bother her. Love she lacked from him, her mother more than made up for.' He cleared his throat. 'Forgive me for what I am about to say. I would not do so if it were not paramount to the events which followed.'

As he sought the right words, a knot of dread formed in Sally's stomach. This must be what Pru almost confided to her . . . She fumbled for Maggie's hand.

'When Miss Sharp reached adolescence, her father became attentive, affectionate. They would take walks together or, in inclement weather, play cards by the fire. Upon discovering her love of literature, he began inviting her to his study, where they pored over books for hours. The indifferent father was gone and Miss Sharp was delighted.

'Eager to retain this new relationship, she was blind to the fact that time spent with her mother dwindled. And her pure young mind was unaware that this was what he wanted. As she and her mother's closeness decreased, her relationship with her father took on an altogether . . . different nature.' He paused, shook his head. 'Barely a month into her fourteenth year, she was with child.'

Sally screwed her eyes shut, heard Maggie mutter angrily.

'Confused and afraid, Miss Sharp withheld the truth, and Mrs Sharp failed to see who had fathered the child. She discovered, upon informing her husband. She expected him to be as devastated as she – yet instead, he took the news calmly, dismissing her suggestion that their daughter be sent away to give birth and that the infant be adopted.

'He insisted she stay, that they would raise the infant as their own. Mrs Sharp's world shattered, with the terrible realisation. He denied her accusation of incestuous acts and, threatened into silence, so too did Miss Sharp.'

'Eeh, the poor, poor lass,' Maggie murmured.

'Mrs Sharp, too,' added Sally. 'Dear God, what a dreadful thing for a mother to discover.'

'Miss Sharp said her mother was never the same. Half mad with grief, with little choice but to accept his decision, she shut herself away. Despite Miss Sharp's pleas, she refused to see her. Until, that is, her pains came and she was forced to deliver her daughter's infant.'

Sally covered her face with her hands. Her words weeks before . . .

'*Never in my life had I prayed as fervently . . . I waited, waited, watching that chest rise and fall. And as the new day dawned, I knew He would not claim her . . .*'

She wasn't referring to Pru, at all. She'd prayed not for her daughter's death, but for her release from the ill-gotten child. The secrecy, all those unanswered questions. Everything was falling into place.

'Despite her loathing for her father, Miss Sharp loved her daughter on sight. She was adamant that she would raise her and – perhaps afraid that refusal might loosen her tongue – he agreed. He devised a plan. The family would relocate and Miss Sharp, an early bloomer much older looking than her tender years, would pose as a young widow.

'The very next day, his brother in Ancoats passed away, bequeathing him everything. It was perfect timing; they left Shropshire and took ownership of the pawnbroker's. Weeks later, Mr Sharp suffered a fatal blow to the head. Police surmised he'd likely disturbed a break-in during the night. No one was ever brought to justice. Miss Sharp suspected that a break-in never occurred.'

'You mean . . . ?'

He nodded solemnly. 'She never questioned her mother. They simply erased him from their lives. However, they could not dismiss him completely. Miss Sharp bore no resemblance to her father, but her child did. As she grew, so too did the repulsion Mrs Sharp felt for this constant reminder of the husband she loathed.

'This put heavy strain upon mother and daughter's delicate relationship. The stronger her hatred grew, the more Miss Sharp defended her child. The devastating event which later occurred ensured reconciliation remained a lifelong impossibility.'

'Are you referring to the child's death?'

'Indeed. Shortly before tragedy struck, she'd asked about her father. Mrs Sharp reacted badly to the innocent question and struck her. Miss Sharp warned her mother that if she ever laid a hand to her child again, they would leave and never return. Fearful of being alone, Mrs Sharp vowed to treat her granddaughter better. She was true to her word and the child warmed to her.'

'And just when their relationship was blossoming . . . Oh, how very sad. How did she die, Father?'

'She drowned while out making purchases with Mrs Sharp. Miss Sharp had remained behind to see to the shop. Watching them leave hand-in-hand, she was hopeful, for the first time, about the future. Her dreams soon crumbled. Her mother returned in a dreadful state accompanied by a constable, who revealed the child had fallen into the canal.'

'Dear Lord, how?' Sally whispered.

'Mrs Sharp said it happened in the blink of an eye. She tried her best to save her but the child's heavy skirts sucked her under. Mrs Sharp almost suffered the same fate; the constable heard her shouts and dragged her out just in time. A party of men searched the waters to no avail. The child had vanished.

'It broke Miss Sharp completely. Her mother offered comfort but, eaten up with grief, she rebuffed her. Mrs Sharp ceased trying, became distant, embittered. The strokes, which later left her body useless, further warped her mind. Her behaviour became increasingly volatile. You are aware of the incident involving her previous employee?'

Sally nodded numbly.

'As for Miss Sharp . . . Her father, mother, child – all contributed to her mental decay. I pray she's now at peace.'

For several minutes, Sally struggled to digest the harrowing tale. Did Agnes taunt Pru the day they died? She'd the cruellest tongue when the mood took her. Perhaps she mentioned the child and Pru snapped? Or was it a remark about her father? she wondered, recalling Agnes's scathing comment:

'*What he saw in her, I will never know.*'

Sadness constricted her chest. It was as though, over the years, Agnes convinced herself that the blame lay with her daughter. Pru referred to the secret plaguing her as 'my sin', said that she'd made but one mistake; was it that of trusting her father? Did her mother convince her, too, that the fault was hers? It was such a tragic mess.

Her granddaughter's demise clearly tipped Agnes over the edge of insanity. To witness, yet be powerless to prevent, such a thing would make a lasting impact upon anyone. As for dear, sweet Pru . . . It was a miracle she remained sane as long as she did.

Sally felt an overwhelming urge to be near them, tell them she understood.

'May I walk with you, Father?' she asked when he rose. 'There's something I must do.'

'Of course, my child.'

'Aye, lass, you go,' said Maggie, guessing her intentions. 'I'll mind Jonathan.'

Drawing her shawl low to cover her injuries, she followed him out. A stirring of hope fluttered. God willing, this visit would lay her guilt to rest. Afterwards, she'd light a candle for Pru's daughter, she decided. And she'd say a prayer that all three had found peace. Each deserved nothing less.

She sighed at the thought of the envelope. Agnes's letter had swayed her somewhat, it was true, and yet . . . She was certain of only one thing: if she did accept, fortune's hand wouldn't touch her alone. Used wisely, that money could change her loved ones' lives for the better, too.

By the time she reached the church, her mind was set.

Passing through the gates, she smiled. She'd made the right decision.

Chapter 31

FROM HIS MOTHER's knee, Jonathan had a clear view of Grace, opposite. When she approached, his podgy legs kicked wildly, bringing chuckles from both women.

At four months old, he'd recently discovered the delights of solid food and would treat them to his hilarious dance each mealtime. His legs opened the show and his arms followed suit, as though performing a lively jig.

'Ready for your pobs, lad?' He answered Grace with a gummy grin and she laughed. 'Pass him here, lass, afore he has a fit.'

Watching her feed him the gloopy white mixture of mashed-up bread soaked in warm milk and sugar, Sally smiled. When she'd first taken on the new venture, she'd worried herself sick whether Grace was ready to care for him again.

Peggy's passing was still raw but the heartbroken mother had been delighted to resume the role, assuring Sally it was what she needed to take her mind off her grief. Grace loved nothing more than parading Jonathan around in his perambulator, proud to show off the bonny child.

'Goodness. He hasn't come up for air, yet!'

Grace smiled knowingly. 'Secret's in t' sugar, lass. Aye, my Peggy loved her pobs, she did, would've ate it until it came out of her ears. Ay, now, don't go starting all that nonsense about me looking after him,' she added when Sally bit her lip. 'I'd go barmy in t' house all day on my own. He's a tonic, he is. Ain't you?' she cooed, chucking him under the chin. Her tone caught Shield's attention. Tail swishing, he nudged her arm and she laughed. 'Lord, you're a jealous beggar, you are. Aye, you're a tonic, an' all,' she said, rolling her eyes.

Mercifully, Shield had made a full recovery and, as she did daily, Sally thanked God. Bar the knobbly scar on the back of his head, no one would guess he'd been attacked. *Another failing on Joseph's part,* she thought in satisfaction then swiftly evicted him from her mind. His evil had no place in her life these days.

The past months had nurtured strength in her she'd never have believed possible. She too had mended, and not just physically. Her nose, though now slightly misshapen, and the multitude of bruises had healed, but so had her mental wounds.

She'd developed a somewhat detached approach to Joseph and all he stood for. She refused to be cowed. And she refused to run away as she'd previously considered. If he discovered her, so be it. As she'd done last time, and countless times before, she'd survive. She was bone-weary of fleeing. She had friends here, family, a life. She wouldn't sacrifice those for anyone.

She'd give anything to live in peace but knew it wasn't possible while he drew breath, so simply took each day at a time, resigned to the fact that he might find her but determined to live life as best she could. If she must get back up and dust herself off a thousand times, she would. She was damned if he'd win.

When her monthly bleed arrived, she'd sobbed and it spurred the healing. Her friends and family were also instrumental to her recovery – as was the bold project she'd undertaken. *Her business, her sanctuary* . . . She could scarcely believe it.

'Eeh, it's lovely we're seeing that bonny smile of yourn more often.'

Sally sighed contentedly. The walk home after making peace with the Sharps had set her on a path of extra-ordinary adventure. 'I was just thinking . . . I wonder what became of that mother and child, Aunt Grace?'

'They're well, I'm sure, thanks to thee.'

She'd witnessed an exchange outside a lodging house between the housekeeper and a woman clutching a baby who, by a farthing, was short for a bed for the night. Despite the woman begging her to show mercy for the sake of her child, who would surely perish if he spent another freezing night without shelter, the house-keeper refused admission.

Her plight had affected Sally deeply. It could so easily have been her and Jonathan but for the wonderful people in her life. She'd taken the sobbing woman to Maggie's and from the envelope pressed several notes into her hand. Her grateful tears, and certainty they would sleep easy in a warm bed as a body deserved, touched Sally.

In that instant, she'd known what to do with the money. Not only could it benefit her loved ones, but many others, too. And so the germ of an idea formed: she'd open her own lodging house. Hers would be a refuge. She'd never turn anyone from her door.

Now, she squeezed Grace's hand, then – as she did each morning – gazed around the good-sized kitchen; her favourite room.

Pale-blue curtains hung from its two windows, lend-ing it a light and airy feel. In the centre stood a large table and, to the left, were two comfortable chairs either side of the fire.

A scullery and pantry, with shelves for dry foods and marble slab for perishables, led off to the right. By the windows, another door led to a small yard, now home to half a dozen chickens which, as well as eggs, supplied unlimited entertainment for the children.

She'd set to work making her dream a reality immediately and had discovered a run-down, two-storey house on Pollard Street. The possibility of Joseph finding out and claiming ownership had struck fear and fury in her. She'd therefore asked Uncle Ed to bear his name on the deeds. She trusted him implicitly and Joseph would be unable to prove anything; he'd never get his hands on it.

'It's a far cry from what it were, eh, lass?' said Grace, as though reading her thoughts.

She'd secured the nine-roomed property at a good price but it proved a mammoth task. However, she'd relished the challenge.

'Alive with damp and vermin . . . holes in t' roof . . . You'd never believe it were the same house.'

Sally nodded. With enough money left for supplies, the exterior's restoration had reached completion in no time. Work on the interior then began and, during their free time, Con, Ed, Stan and Mr Lynch undertook the heavy duties, replacing the odd floorboard and smashed window and whitewashing the walls.

She, Maggie, Grace and Winnie then took over, while Ellen minded the children, and for days swept and scrubbed every inch of every room until the house gleamed.

'It wouldn't have been possible, Aunt Grace, without the many helping hands. Con's market contacts, too, proved invaluable. The furniture, bedding, curtains, rugs, crockery and the million and one other necessities . . . Thanks to him, costs were minimal.'

''Ere, don't go being modest, lass. You worked harder than anyone; threw yourself into it with gusto, you did.'

A soft smile stroked Sally's lips. 'The second week of the new year, when I opened for business, do you know what I did before affixing the "Beds Vacant" sign in the window?'

'What, love?'

'I drifted from room to room and cried tears of joy.'

'Ay, Sally. You'll have me blubbing in a minute.'

'With unwavering dedication, we did it, together.'

'Aye, we did that,' murmured Grace with a watery smile.

Sally pressed her hand again then wandered from the room. The ground floor boasted three: one at the far end of the passage, one to the immediate right upon entering, and hers and Jonathan's. Humming softly, she climbed the stairs. Each of the four rooms on this floor held three beds – the two larger rooms, on the second floor above, four apiece. This enabled rest and shelter for twenty people at any one time.

She could have squeezed in more but refused to conduct her establishment as many did. She'd heard of lodging houses in appalling states, beds crammed to the rafters, maximum profit the owners' sole concern. Poor souls endured such conditions through sheer desperation; she'd been determined her guests wouldn't share that fate.

Cleaned daily by herself and Maggie, each room had a rag rug covering the bare boards, a picture or two adorning the walls and a washbowl and pitcher, with hot water available upon request. It was no surprise that business was thriving.

'I never dreamed I could be this happy,' she whispered to herself, leaning against a doorway. 'This time last year, life was as bleak as it's possible to be.'

'Aye, now look at thee. And no one deserves it more, lass.'

Sally turned to see Maggie, broom in hand. Smiling, she linked her arm. 'Come. You look fit to drop.' After leading the way to the kitchen, she poured her tea from a pretty green pot and when Maggie flopped into a chair, shook her head. 'I do wish you wouldn't tire yourself so. We're meant to perform the chores equally.'

Her friend blew at a damp curl, which had escaped from the red scarf around her head. 'And you fret too much. This is the best job I've ever had. Besides, I like keeping busy.'

'You're working yourself into the ground and there's really no need.'

Maggie lowered her head. 'I'm sorry. I'm grateful, lass, is all.'

'Oh, Maggie. I'm the one who should say sorry.'

'You? Nay, love, nay—'

'Yes, me. When I returned to Aunt Grace's at the start of the restoration . . . Well, during those weeks, this house wasn't the only thing that slowly improved – my relationship with Stan did, too. Preoccupied with the first, magical Christmas with my family, all that was going on . . . I neglected you, Maggie.'

'I'd not call assuring me a position for life once business was up and running neglect!'

'But I failed to wonder how you'd manage in the meantime. When you revealed your landlord was threatening eviction . . . I was racked with guilt.'

'Oh, lass.'

She'd made to tell Maggie she'd clear the debt but an idea had stopped her. She'd put the proposition forward – that they reside at the lodging house with her and Jonathan – and to her delight, her friend agreed. Sally's joy, when she'd assigned the largest room, between her own and the kitchen, to the family, now returned.

'You've no reason to prove your gratitude. I love having you all here and don't you ever forget it.'

Maggie sniffed, swallowed hard, sniffed again. 'Ta, love.'

They were sipping their tea in companionable silence when Grace asked, 'Where's your mam, lass?'

A grin spread across Maggie's face. 'Gone for a walk.'

'With . . . ?'

She nodded, and Sally and Grace grinned back.

'Eeh, I were horrified in t' beginning with thoughts of you all spending the nights with a houseful of strangers. You could have been robbed, attacked in your own beds, or owt. I thank the Lord that Mr Lynch provided a solution.'

'Aye, so does Mam!' said Maggie, winking, and they all chuckled.

Teddy Lynch Jr, a seaman of some thirty years, had recently left the waves behind. He hankered to settle down and, when his last ship docked, decided not to sign on for another voyage. His return, however, proved problematic. His parents' house was bursting at the seams with children and grandchildren, and he'd found the squeeze tiresome.

Mr Lynch, Uncle Ed's friend, had asked if his son could have a permanent bed at the lodging house until he found a wife, that he'd pay generously for the privilege. Sally readily agreed – having a man about would ease their concerns if trouble did arise with lodgers – and the kindly bear of a man, with a thatch of dark, curly hair and thick beard, took up residence on the first floor.

He and Ellen had hit it off immediately and all agreed wedding bells would be tolling in the not too distant future.

'Are you going to the Roundhouse today, lass?' asked Grace now, and Sally nodded.

Each Sunday, she visited the Sharps' graves. Without them, the help she'd provided to so many wouldn't have been possible. Half an hour of her time one afternoon a week to show her gratitude wasn't asking much. It also gave her the opportunity to tend little Peggy's grave.

Maggie drained her cup, and rose. 'I'll finish the rooms while you're gone – and no arguments,' she added before Sally could object.

Clicking her tongue, Sally donned her shawl. 'I shan't be long. When I return, I'll prepare a lovely dinner – and no arguments!' she said when Maggie, who usually cooked, made to protest.

Grace chuckled. 'What are you like, youse two? Bloomin' stubborn, they are, lad, the pair of them,' she told Jonathan, and Sally and Maggie grinned.

'Aye, go on. I'll do the rooms and you do dinner,' Maggie agreed, shooing her out. 'Just try not to burn the soddin' thing like last time!'

Sally was still smiling when she reached the church. Life at present was rosy. She had her family, friends, the business – what more could she want?

The answer came immediately. If within her power, she'd alter two things: Joseph's existence and the Morgans' absence from her life. Sadly, both were beyond her control and always would be. Joseph would probably live to a hundred just to spite her, and the Morgans could only ever be dear friends from afar.

As for her third, deeply concealed wish . . . That, she knew with certainty, could never be.

Her step faltered. Tommy might well be married by now. Dolly could be with child at this very moment. Her guts lurched, imagining them together, loving one another . . .

'Stop it,' she told herself. 'Be happy for him and move on.'

Immersed in thought, her mind didn't at first register the crouched figure up ahead. Doing a double take, she gasped in surprise.

On all her visits, she'd never seen any indication that someone else had been. Who on earth . . . ? Was Mr Stockton mistaken when he'd said the Sharps were without kin? If so, why didn't they attend the funeral? She was debating whether to make her presence known when suddenly the woman turned.

Sally's mouth dropped open. She knew who this was. There was no one else it could be.

Deep embarrassment replaced the woman's shocked expression. Tugging her shawl over her face, she leapt up and ran for the trees.

'Wait! Please, wait!' Sally picked up her skirts and sprinted after her. 'I mean you no harm. I simply—' To her relief, the woman halted. 'I just want to talk. Please.'

Keeping tight hold of her shawl, the woman half turned. 'Leave me be. I've nowt to say.'

'You needn't fear me, nor should you have fled. You've as much right as I to visit Miss Sharp's grave. I know who you are—'

'And I know thee. Now please, let me go. I must go.'

Despite this, she made no attempt to leave and Sally stepped closer. Tentatively, she touched her shawl. 'Please, let me see,' she said softly. The woman sighed but didn't object, and Sally eased it from her face.

'Take a good look. Take a long, hard look then get down on your knees and thank the Almighty you were spared. It could well have been you bearing this disfigurement.'

Her words sent ice down Sally's spine. Pale-pink patches stood stark against what hair remained. Further down, clumps of puckered scars marred a face that might once have been beautiful. But it was her eyes, pools of melted hazel, lucid with unspeakable sorrow, which tore at Sally. They told of a deeper suffering than her flame-ravished skin ever could.

'Was she the cause of that? Did she wield that poker at thee, an' all?' the woman asked.

Sally's fingers fluttered to her nose. 'No, no. This happened at another's hand. Mrs Sharp never . . . I saw the results of her attacks on her daughter, but she didn't attempt it with me. I loathed that poker with a passion. I once threw it through the window.' She nodded when the woman lifted an eyebrow. 'Oh yes, straight into the street. Of course, she ordered Miss Sharp to retrieve it—'

'And so sealed her own fate. And by God, she deserved nowt less.'

Silence hung between them.

'What happened? Why you? One could say I gave her cause to lash out numerous times, yet she didn't. What happened that dreadful day?'

Hugging herself, the woman's eyes strayed across the churchyard, but instead of answering the question she murmured, 'I weren't surprised when I heard. A body can only take so much, you know? Mam begged me not to come but I had to, had to tell Miss Sharp she weren't bad, that she weren't to blame. I saw you and another wench with Father Collins. I saw what he did for Miss Sharp. Did you . . . ?' At Sally's nod, she smiled faintly. 'Thank you.'

Sally held out a hand. 'I wish you'd approached, but a belated introduction is better than none. I'm Sally.'

She hesitated then shook it. 'Anna.'

'Do you visit often, Anna? I've never seen—'

'Only Miss Sharp. Never *her.* And then only when it's quiet.' She tugged her shawl self-consciously. 'I don't venture out much; the stares, you see. It's allus the stares what bother me most. The jeering and name-calling, aye, they hurt, but the silent stare . . . eyes young and owd filled with disgust . . . They're the worst. Aye, they're the worst.'

'I'm sorry.'

'Don't be. Nowt will cure folk of their ignorance. I manage as best I can. Mam's an angel from heaven; without her . . . I discovered long ago no employer wants a face like mine amongst their workforce. Mam works her fingers to the bone, takes in washing from the big houses up in Salford. A purer heart you'll not find. I pity Miss Sharp that most. She never knew a mother's love.' Her eyes hardened. 'I discovered summat she'd forgot.'

'You . . . ?'

'The day she sent me stumbling into the fire. I'd discovered summat she'd forgot.'

She held her breath. 'What, Anna?'

'A letter. Nay, norra letter as such – a receipt, I suppose you might call it. Miss Sharp had a child, a daughter.'

'Yes. She drowned.'

Anna shook her head. 'No, she didn't. Mrs Sharp had her committed to New Bridge Street Workhouse.'

Sally's mouth fell open but horror chased away a response.

'She paid the master a tidy sum to take her in. I found proof bearing his signature.'

He bought as well as sold . . . Sickness rose within her. 'I . . . don't . . . Why would she *do* such a thing? All those years, to have Miss Sharp believe . . .'

'I dropped a button while darning a nightdress and it rolled beneath the bed. Careful not to make a noise, for she were sleeping, I felt around. That's when I found it, a reticule covered in dust and cobwebs. I were curious. Happen it were wrong . . . I looked inside.'

'And Mrs Sharp—'

'Aye, wakened and caught me reading it. Happen she hadn't trusted the master, wanted in writing that he'd uphold his end of the deal in keeping his silence. She thought she'd destroyed it years afore, begged *my* silence, insisted she'd done it for her granddaughter's own good.

'Her hatred for her grew daily; she were scared she'd harm the girl, said she'd had no choice, that it were for her safety. She'd been certain Miss Sharp would get over the loss.'

'Well, she was wrong! That poor woman suffered until her dying day.'

Anna nodded, eyes steely. 'She fooled everyone, concocted the whole canal tale for her own ends, watched her daughter mourn a child very much alive.'

Sally felt light-headed, had to grasp Anna's arm for support. Had gaining the child's trust been nothing but a ploy? Was she pretending all along, so not to arouse Pru's suspicion once she put her plan into action? Realisation sickened Sally to the core. She'd forgiven Mrs Sharp, excused her behaviour as a result of mental trauma. This sin was too despicable to excuse.

'I cannot believe it. That poor, poor girl. How utterly terrified and confused she must have been.'

'I suppose you're wondering why I didn't tell Miss Sharp what I'd discovered. I wanted to, truly. I told Mrs Sharp I couldn't keep silent about summat that dreadful. She pleaded, said it were pointless, for the past couldn't be changed.

'She said she'd had word from the workhouse years afore that the child died, that revealing all to Miss Sharp would break her heart all over again. I'd not listen and as I made to leave, she turned wild with fury. She said she'd destroy me and all I held dear if I spoke out, said she had the money and means to have me locked away. Then she grabbed the poker.

'When the force of the blow had me stagger into the fire, d'you know what she did? D'you know what I heard as I fell into the flames? Laughter. She laughed, Sally, laughed as I burned. She were more evil than Satan hisself.'

'Mother of God, I cannot . . .' Words failed her.

'Keeping silent haunts me. I heard later she'd told Miss Sharp she caught me stealing and lost her temper, that my fall were an accident. I should've told her the truth.'

'And your mother? Did she advise against it?'

'Aye. She said if the child *were* dead, then I should say nowt. Better Miss Sharp remained ignorant than know the truth of her mother's actions, of her poor daughter's suffering. The pain of it would've sent her mad.'

'Anna, I have a terrible feeling . . .' She ran a shaky hand across her mouth. 'Mrs Sharp was lying, I'm certain of it. If her granddaughter's still languishing in that place . . . Mrs Sharp's money paid for my home and business. If she's alive, she's entitled to it, to everything. I could never keep it, knowing . . . I must find out.'

'Oh, Sally, d'you really think . . . ? Will you meet me here next Sunday, tell me of your findings? Dear God, if she *were* lying . . .'

'I'll be here. Her name, Anna. I must know her name.'

Backing away towards the trees, she nodded. 'Aye, it were on t' receipt. It's Isobella Dickinson.'

For a full minute, Sally stood frozen.

'Dicksy . . . !'

Her cry floated above the cold gravestones as she sank to her knees.

Chapter 32

'CON! CON!'

Two whirlwinds of fair curls and gap-toothed grins hurtled down the passage. Four small arms wrapped around his legs and sweet giggles rang through the house.

'That's a grand welcome, so it is!' Taking a twin in each arm, he swept them into the air.

Maggie smiled from the kitchen doorway. 'Let him over the step afore you pounce on him,' she called over their squeals then blushed when Con winked at her.

'How's yourself, Maggie?'

'Besides these terrors running me ragged, I'm all right.'

He flashed his slow smile. 'Sure, ye don't look a bit ragged. You look grand, so.' Carrying the children upside down, much to their delight, he crossed the passage. 'Is Sally ready?'

Flustered from the compliment, she could only nod. Self-consciously, she brushed a curl from her face and stepped aside to let him pass.

He lowered the twins into a heap at his feet and wiggled his fingers. At the threat of a tickling, they pelted for the kitchen, helpless with laughter.

Watching them go, she smiled softly. 'You're good with them. Since their father passed on, they've missed . . . Well, they enjoy your visits.'

'So do I.'

Their eyes locked. She froze as he reached out and, ever so slowly, brushed his thumb across her cheek.

'Flour.' He showed her, smiled, then stepped past her into the kitchen.

Groaning inwardly, she cursed her thumping heart and returned to her baking.

Sally nodded grimly when Con entered, glad he'd insisted he accompany her. She'd need every ounce of strength and support she could find to see this through.

Despite glimmers of spring, it was bitter out and she wrapped her shawl around herself tightly. Then she kissed Jonathan in Ellen's arms, took a deep breath and headed for the door.

'Good luck, Sally.'

'Aye, good luck, lass.'

The smile she gave Maggie and her mother was of pure gratitude. Since hearing of her meeting with Anna yesterday, both agreed she must find out whether Dicksy was still alive. They also agreed that, if so, the house and remaining money were rightfully hers.

Sally couldn't have been more thankful for their understanding. This could mean homelessness for them all, yet they understood completely her need to discover the truth, and she loved them all the more for it. As for herself, a possible reunion with her dearest friend took her breath away. She'd give anything, *everything*, in a heartbeat to have her back.

That Pru was Dicksy's mother had shocked her senseless, but now she accepted it as though she'd always known. Such gentle dispositions, caring, sweet-natured – they possessed the same qualities entirely.

Though Pru had clearly registered Dicksy's birth under a false surname to uphold the pretence of widowhood, and Dicksy didn't share her looks, she should have made the comparison earlier. On reflection, Pru's company had felt familiar, like stepping back in time.

She and Con were approaching Miller Street when panic began to churn her guts. The streets throbbed with daily life but she saw and heard little, senses gripped by the sinister-looking building ahead. She'd spent years fleeing the memories of that place. Could she really re-enter the darkness within?

'Are you sure about this, acushla?'

She gritted her teeth and nodded. For Dicksy, she'd do anything.

Gripping Con's hand, she set forth for the gates of hell.

Whatever hopes Sally harboured were shattered in less than twenty minutes.

It was true, all of it. For once, Agnes had been telling the truth. Her Dicksy was dead.

She walked blindly from the master's office, down the dreary corridors and into the weak sunshine, pushing aside anyone who was in her path. Gasping with sobs, she picked up her skirts and ran for the gates.

'Sally. Sally, wait. Sally, stop.' Con caught her in a tight embrace and she crumpled.

'It's not true, Con, it's not true! He's lying!'

'Shhh. I know it hurts but it must be; the master confirmed it. Sure, the extra money you offered would have loosened his tongue if nothing else,' he added, tone hardening. 'He wants reporting to the Board of

Governors, so he does, and will be before the week's through if I have anything to do with it.'

She buried her face in his chest. 'I thought she'd gone for ever, that she'd been sent into service. Yet she'd merely been assigned other duties and moved to another ward. All the time, she was but blocks away and I had no idea.' Her grip on his jacket tightened. 'Did she suffer? Does the typhus fever bring painful death? The truth, Con, please.'

'No, acushla. No, she didn't suffer.'

Then why had he breathed a Hail Mary before answering? For her. He'd lied for her. She raised her head to look at him. Then, stretching on tiptoe, she pressed her lips to his.

'Take me home, Con.'

From the workhouse shadows, Joseph watched them leave. When they disappeared through the gates, he snatched up the woman leaning heavily on Nancy and hissed in a voice that trembled with fury:

'Follow them.'

Sally folded her arms against the cold. Evening was drawing in, splintered rays slowly sinking beyond the rooftops.

'Go on in, you're shivering. Try to get some sleep.'

'Con, wait.'

He turned back and she closed the lodging-house door and motioned to an alleyway. He followed wordlessly.

'Thank you for accompanying me. I still cannot believe . . .' Tears thickened her voice. 'Listen, Con . . . that kiss—'

''Tis all right. You were upset.'

'Nevertheless . . .'

Leaning against the wall, he peered down at her. 'Sally, I'll not deny it was nice. And I'll not deny that I love you, because I do. Sure, I love all of you. You're as dear to me as my own family. Do you remember the day *I* kissed *you*?' She flushed and he laughed softly. 'Aye, you do. My feelings for you were like nothing I'd known. But it wasn't love, acushla, I see that now. Lust, desire, call it what you will, but it wasn't love.'

'I did try to tell you, if you recall.'

'Aye, you did. Stubborn as I am, I couldn't see it. I do now and I'm sorry.'

'Sorry?'

'For trying to force you to love me back. Sure, you must have despaired at times but you never gave up on me and for that, I thank ye. I value our friendship, Sally. There's something about you I'm drawn to, have been since the day I saw you on that platform at Bolton. You have a way about you, something within that makes folk want to care for you. And I do, always will—'

'But as a friend,' she finished for him, eyes twinkling.

He smiled. 'As a friend.'

'Con?'

'Aye?'

'Tell me to mind my own business . . . Do you have feelings for Maggie?' His embarrassed laugh brought a wicked grin to her face. 'Mr Malloy, are you blushing?'

'Does she . . . ? Has she said anything?'

'She's mad about you! Surely you've noticed?'

'Mebbe. I wasn't altogether sure.'

'Talk to her, Con,' she urged, a warm glow spreading through her. 'Tell her how you feel before another man beats you to it. She's a good woman. She won't be alone for ever.'

'Ye wouldn't mind?'

'Mind? I'd be delighted! I love you both so very much. I wish you nothing but happiness.' She smiled gently. 'Do you recall that day at the pie shop when you said that us meeting as we did was fate, that it was meant to be? Well, I agree. I believe we *were* meant to meet to enable you and *Maggie* to meet. It's a queer old world, isn't it, Con?'

'And what of you? Will you one day take your own advice?'

'What do you mean?'

'Come on, Sally, you know what I'm talking about. The Morgan fellow you've been in love with since before we met.'

'How . . . ?'

It was his turn to grin. 'Because it's obvious to anyone with eyes in their head, so it is. And what he feels for you . . . That's love, Sally. I knew whatever designs I had on you weren't, when I looked into his eyes; they shone with something I've never seen before in a man, for any woman.

'Sure, that fellow would tear out his beating heart if he thought it would make you happy. Take your own advice, tell him ye feel the same. Aye, you're married still, I know, I know – oh, to hell with it, live in sin!' He grinned when she slapped his arm, chuckling, before finishing earnestly, 'You, above anyone, deserve happiness.'

When they parted, she returned to the lodging house with mixed feelings: hope for her friends' blossoming romance and sadness at Con's blindness. He'd guessed her feelings. Yet he was as wrong as it was possible to be if he believed Tommy reciprocated them. Dolly was proof of that.

The hum of Maggie's and Ellen's voices, intermingled with Jonathan's babbles and the twins' laughter, drifted from the kitchen and she forced a smile. She'd burdened them enough with her tears for one day. She was midway down the passage when a knock came at the front door.

The woman on the step looked vaguely familiar but for the life of her, Sally couldn't think why. 'May I help you?' she asked.

'I hope so, Sally.'

That she knew her name took her aback. 'Do I know you? You do look familiar but I'm afraid . . .'

Her visitor smiled broadly. 'I'm Nancy Skinner, Percy's daughter.'

'Percy?'

'Aye, runs that little shop at Spring Row.'

Her own face creased in smile. 'Percy, yes, of course. Nancy, did you say?'

'That's right.'

'What can I do for you, Nancy? Oh, where are my manners? Please, come in.' She held the door wide but Nancy shook her head.

'Nay, I can't stop. I need thee to come with me.'

'Come with you?'

'Aye. It's Ivy.'

Her knees went weak. 'Mrs Morgan? What's happened? Is she all right?'

'I'll explain on t' way but you must come now and you must come alone.' With that, she turned and scuttled away.

'Wait, I'm coming!'

With nothing in mind but her friend, Sally hurried down the darkening street after Nancy.

Chapter 33

AFTER TEN MINUTES, Sally was still none the wiser as to the reason for Nancy's visit. Despite her pleading, Nancy said there wasn't time to explain, that all would become clear when they arrived. When Sally asked where they were going, she merely told her to hurry.

Following through the maze of tumbledown streets and alleys, mind reeling with worry for Ivy, she was brought up short when Nancy pulled her inside a dilapidated house. An unidentifiable stench burned the back of her throat and she peered around the dimly lit passage in confusion.

Before she could ask what was going on, Nancy flitted through the gloom. Battered doors lined the walls and she made for one at the far end. When Sally reached her, Nancy knocked twice and entered.

A stub of candle atop a wooden box in the centre was the only light. The weak glow quivered across Nancy's face, lending her a ghoulish look.

'Nancy, what . . . ?'

Her face was stony. Then her gaze swivelled behind Sally and she smiled.

'Tha did good, Nancy.'

Sally froze. *Surely not . . . ?* She whirled around, then staggered back in horror.

The change in Joseph was striking. The bulk of pure muscle was gone. In its place stood a withered wreck. He'd lost a considerable amount of weight. His sallow-skinned face was skull-like. Dishevelled clothes hung loose and a pungent odour wafted from him as he swayed drunkenly.

She ran for the door but his iron grip yanked her back; despite his outward frailty, he'd lost none of his strength.

'Get your hands off me!' She pushed him hard, sending him stumbling, but he pulled her along. The stench of him, as he crushed her to him, made her gag and she cried out when his erect member pressed against her. She craned her neck. 'Nancy, help me!'

Nancy arched an eyebrow and, with a curl of her lip, looked her up and down.

Terror gnawed at Sally's every nerve as, with sinking heart, realisation slammed home. Nancy had tricked her. She'd *tricked* her and lured her back to hell. 'Dear God . . . *Why?*'

'Shut your trap and sit.' Joseph pushed her into a sagging chair. Arms folded, he stared down at her, his expression oddly calm.

Nancy sidled up to him. 'You want to know why? I'll tell you why, you bitch. Because I loathe the very sight of thee.'

The hatred pouring from her was tangible. Sally shook her head in shocked confusion then gasped when Joseph struck out at Nancy.

'I warned you to keep quiet,' he snarled, revealing gaps where the teeth Con knocked out once were. 'Get and fetch some ale. And remember,' he added when she'd staggered up, 'breathe a word to anyone and I'll tear your throat out. Hurry up.'

Nursing her cheek, Nancy nodded and slipped out.

He grinned at Sally. 'The dried-up whore has her uses. Her body's norra patch on yours, mind.' Bending, he squeezed her breast then slapped her face when she tried pushing him away. 'Sit!' he roared as she made to lunge from the chair.

All's not over . . . Her mother's warning from her dream had come true. Dear God, how had she been so foolish? She'd followed Nancy blindly, never suspecting . . . She and Joseph were clearly lovers: did Nancy see her as a threat, want rid of her to have him to herself?

No one knew she was here. No one would come to her rescue this time. If she were to escape again, she'd have to do so alone.

She must think fast. Once Nancy returned, she wouldn't stand a chance; he'd immobilise her with ale like before.

At the prospect, rational thought vanished. Crippling fear of what he'd made her suffer a few short months ago sucked the breath from her lungs and in desperation she dived again. This time, a clog to her stomach killed her attempt. She doubled over, winded.

'I told you to sit.'

'What do you *want* from me?' she croaked. 'For the love of God, why can't you leave me be and let this hideous marriage die the death it deserves? You have your family, and Nancy. Forget about me, live your life. Let me live mine. Please.'

He stooped so that their faces were level. 'You're forgetting one thing: I own thee, paid for thee fair and square.' Grabbing her chin, he stared deep into her eyes. 'You've ruined me. Look at the mess of me. You've done this, you.'

'Ale has turned you into the wreck that you are, not me.'

He studied her for a moment and laughed. 'The girl I bought's long gone, ain't she? I don't know whether to admire your boldness or knock it from thee with brute force.' He grazed her cheek with his fist. 'How long?' he murmured. 'How long afore you'd be back to the wreck I made you into? Days? A week?'

'Joseph, please—'

'You can't escape me however much you run, d'you not see that by now? I'll hound you till your dying day. I want thee and I mean to have thee, one way or t' other.'

She flinched as he rose suddenly. He paced the room and she glanced to the door.

'Don't even think about it,' he said without looking at her. 'I'll kill you where you stand afore you reach it.'

She forced herself to remain seated. She didn't disbelieve his threat for a second.

'I saw you today at the workhouse.' He smirked when her head jerked up in astonishment. 'Oh aye, I saw it all. I bet that Irish gutter rat can't make you scream in bed as I can.' Eyes narrowing, he rubbed his crotch. 'Don't fret, you can have it soon. Tha must be panting for it, my girl.'

Her flesh crawled in utter disgust but she willed herself to stay calm. 'How did you know I'd be there?' she asked, desperately changing the subject before he pounced. 'The master didn't recognise me and I didn't remind him.'

'You weren't the reason I were there.'

'Then why? What could you possibly want with that place?'

His sunken face stretched in a grin. 'Same as thee. Only I succeeded.'

'Succeeded—?'

'I noticed you and that Irish filth left the way you came. Did you plan on three of youse leaving through them gates?'

Fury and disbelief, not to mention utter confusion, swamped her. How, *how* . . . ? She leapt to her feet. 'You . . . ? You got the master to lie, didn't you? She's not dead, is she?'

His grin vanished. 'She will be, you along with her, if you don't sit.'

'Mother of God—'

'Sit!'

Shaking with a sea of emotions, she obeyed.

'Tha can't beat me in nowt, don't you understand? You asked and went away empty-handed. *I* asked and . . .' He let his words trail off.

'Where is she? If you've hurt her—'

'She's safe – for now,' he growled, words heavy with threat.

Sally crossed the space and stood before him. 'Joseph, please. I'm begging you. Please, don't hurt her. I'll do anything.'

'I thought you might.' He grabbed the knot of hair at her nape and drew her face to his. 'I'll not get you away without a fight, will I, you little bitch? Not without them gullible bastards you've got fawning over you getting in t' way.' He winced suddenly and touched the back of his head. 'Willing to kill for thee, ain't they? Got them wrapped right round your finger, ain't you?

'Well, this time, I'll have the final laugh. If you want her to see another sun, you'll do as I say. D'you hear?'

She nodded without hesitation, Dicksy's safety paramount.

'Put up a fight, try alerting any of them bastards, and she's done for. Understand?'

She nodded again and he flung her across the room. 'Now sit and shut your trap till it's time.'

'Time?'

'I *said* shut it.'

'Where is she? Please, let me see her.'

He raised his fist. 'I'll not tell thee again.'

Swallowing a protest, Sally lowered her gaze. And from far away, a gentle whisper caressed her like an embrace:

'*Be strong, lass. Be strong.*'

Strong porter normally worked when the hammering set in but today it wasn't having the desired effect.

Joseph took another swig as the thumping in his skull, as though someone was trying to break free from the inside out, intensified.

'You all right, love? That pain back?'

Slamming his palm to his forehead, he squeezed his eyes shut. The blows had damaged something, he just knew it. He'd not been right since that lot got a grip of him.

'Is there owt I can do?'

'Aye, shut your trap.'

Nancy bowed her head but it sprang up again when a whimper drifted through the adjoining wall. 'Shall I—?'

'Stay put. I'll go.' Making for the door, he shot Sally a glance and his anger mounted.

He'd had to put up with the whore next door all day for that bitch. She'd done nothing but whinge since they'd fetched her from the workhouse and he was nearing the end of his tether. If he didn't need her so much, he'd have done for her hours ago.

But need her he did. Sally would kick and scream every step of the way without his human bribe. She had to come quietly. Besides anything else, he couldn't chance another beating the way his head was. Another round like the last would finish him.

Recalling Alice's pleas, he sighed inwardly. Apart from himself, she was the only person in the world he held in the slightest regard. He'd miss the fat sow, he realised with surprise.

It had taken weeks to recover from the onslaught at Nellie's but as soon as he'd felt strong enough, his quest for Sally returned with a vengeance. Alice was aghast on hearing his plans:

'I believe in t' sanctity of marriage as well as the next, but this is madness! They'll do for thee next time. Leave it be, Joseph. The whore ain't worth it!'

Of course, he'd ignored her. He'd been in this stinking rat-hole that was Manchester a fortnight, now. By God, he couldn't wait to be gone – would be by morning if Nancy agreed to what he wanted.

For her own sake, she'd be wise to comply. This time, he'd planned everything meticulously. If she thwarted it, he'd show no mercy, would snub her out in a heart-beat. And he'd enjoy it.

Now, despite saying he'd go, he heard Nancy following and forced himself not to thump her back into her seat – then thump her again for not doing as she was told.

He wasn't worried in the slightest about leaving Sally alone. She wouldn't waken from her ale-soaked slumber for a while. Even if she did, she wouldn't take advantage of the empty room to make her escape. She'd never leave without the other workhouse whore.

The stench of stale urine and faeces hit him in the face as he threw open the neighbouring door. Covering his nose, he peered towards the bed. He could just make out the curled figure and his eyes narrowed.

'You'll shut your trap if you know what's good for you. How many times d'you need telling?' She answered with a moan and, clenching his fists, he stalked towards her. '*Shut* it, I said,' he snarled, and she shrank back against the wall.

'She'll quieten down. Come back next door.'

At Nancy's voice, the woman raised her head. 'Sally?' she asked weakly.

With the toe of his clog, Joseph jabbed her in the ribs, grinning when she whimpered. Nancy winced and he snorted. 'She'll have had worse than that over the years. The master rules them with an iron rod.' He stared down coldly. 'Now think on. One more sound and I'll—'

'You *bastard*!'

He whipped around to find Sally in the doorway. 'Get back in there. Tha sees her when I say. Don't make me tell you again, my girl—'

'I'm going nowhere. Get away from her, the pair of you!' She flew to the bed and dropped to her knees. 'It's me. I'm here, I'm here. Oh, I'm so sorry . . .'

'Sally?'

'Yes, yes, it's me. I'm here, I— Oh!' She fell back with a scream. 'God, no!'

Holding out stick-thin arms, Rose Swann smiled. 'My lass. Oh, my lass . . .'

Nancy touched Joseph's sleeve. 'Leave them be; they'll try nowt. The owd 'un can barely stand.'

He glanced at mother and daughter, weeping in each other's arms, and nodded. This needed finishing. 'Leave both doors ajar so we can keep an ear out.'

Nancy followed him next door, sat at a small table and folded her arms.

'What's wrong?'

'Nowt, just . . .' She rubbed her chin agitatedly. 'What's going on, love? You mean to get shot of Sally; why fetch another into it? That's two you've gorra get rid of, now. I'd rather not know your plans, it's true, but . . . You do want us to be together, don't you, lad?'

His hands itched to hit her. 'How many times d'you need telling? I've my reasons for fetching her mam, reasons you don't need to know, right? All we have to do is stick it out here the night. At first light, we'll be away.'

'Sally . . . ? She'll be dealt with by morning?'

'Aye.'

'And we can be together? Just you, me and my little 'uns?'

He suppressed a grin. 'Aye. I've got it all worked out, found us somewhere to dwell, an' that. Once I've done for that whore in there, we'll be off.'

She clapped her hands like an excited child. 'Where is it, our new home? Nay, don't tell me, I want it to be a surprise.'

He allowed his smile to surface. 'Oh, you'll be surprised, all right.'

She giggled, then bit her lip.

'What now?' he asked.

'Father. I feel terrible leaving him, love.'

Joseph licked his lips. This was what he'd been waiting for. Slipping his hand into his trouser pocket, he fingered the small package.

'I mean, he'd not know how to peel a tatty, never mind cook hisself a meal. How he'll manage without me, I don't know.'

'He'll not have to.'

'Eh?'

Joseph placed the package on the table.

'What's that?'

'Open it.'

Frowning, Nancy obeyed. The frown deepened when she saw what she'd revealed.

'There's threepence worth there. The apothecary weren't for selling it me, said he had to know a body first, but I got round him in t' end. I gave a false name. Nowt will come back on us once he's gone.'

'Once who's gone?'

'Your father. If we're to be together, it's the only way.'

She jerked back as though he'd slapped her. 'What? Why this to be together?'

'We need money if we're to start afresh elsewhere.'

'But, but surely there's another way—'

'He must be loaded, running that shop all these years. D'you know where he keeps his brass? Well, do you?' he demanded.

'Nay, but—'

'And if he caught thee searching his cottage? Would he stand there and say nowt?'

She gave a small shake of her head.

'Nay,' Joseph went on. 'He'd shout blue murder; half the row would be there in seconds. It's the only way. A meal laced with this – he'd not suspect a thing. Or do you not love me, after all? Has tha spoken nowt but lies, is that it?'

As Nancy gazed at the small measure of arsenic, it was clear from her colour that her dinner of liver and onions, washed down with a copious amount of gin, threatened to make its escape. Her voice was firm. 'I'll not do it. I could never harm him, never.'

Joseph grabbed her hair. 'I – we – need brass, you silly bitch. How far d'you think we'll get otherwise?' Her eyes sparked with a defiance he'd never seen before and his face twisted. 'Don't try that look with me or so help me, I'll tip the contents of that there packet down *your* throat.

'You'll do this, for I tell you now, if I'm called to answer for owt, I'm dragging you down with me. You've abetted me all the way. You're in it up to your neck so just you think on.'

A burst of angry voices drifted from the street.

He darted to the window and peered at a group of men across the road. They staggered off and when their drunken shouts faded, he heaved a sigh. Christ, he must get Sally away. He turned to glare at the only obstacle standing in his way. The hammering, never gone long, struck inside his skull and he gripped his head.

'I'll do it.'

He squinted through the pain to the table. The package had gone. 'Aye?'

Nodding, she patted her pocket then held out her arms. He walked into them and she clung to him.

'You'd best be gone if you're to be back by morning,' he announced, pulling away. 'Fella next door's gorra horse and cart in his backyard; he'll give thee a lift to Bolton on t' promise of being paid well, I'm sure.' He lifted an oil lamp from a shelf. 'Here. Tell him to fetch one, an' all. They'll light your path well enough.'

'Tell me you love me. I want to hear you say it.'

Joseph swallowed an angry retort. He couldn't mess this up, now. 'I love you,' he said flatly.

Calmness filled her eyes. He clutched his head again and she nodded to the table. 'Sup your ale. It'll ease the pain.'

Then she turned and walked out.

*

Pausing at the neighbouring room, Nancy glanced to the women, still wrapped in each other's arms. Sally locked eyes with her over her mother's shoulder and, with a whisper of a smile, Nancy continued on her way.

Outside, she sucked in a lungful of cold air. And as she disappeared into the night, she wore the expression she had when she'd walked away from the man clutching his injured genitals months before.

No one disrespected her and got away with it. No one.

Chapter 34

'BITCH, GET IN here!'

Sally tore another strip from the bedsheet. She found a cracked pitcher holding several inches of murky water and dipped the rags in.

'D'you hear me, whore? In here now!'

With neither fire nor candle to light the room, she wrapped her arm around her mother's waist and guided her to a stool by the window.

'Christ, my guts . . . You bitch, wait 'til I—' Whatever threat Joseph meant to deliver was lost in a string of retches.

She tilted Rose's head and, by the full moon's glow, studied her appearance.

'Oh, oh God . . . Do as you're told, bitch!'

Her mother glanced to the door fearfully and Sally took her hand. 'It's all right, Mam. I'm going to get us out of here very soon, I promise.' Gently, she began cleaning dirt, mucus and dried blood from Rose's face.

'He struck me, lass. I needed to relieve myself and kept asking to go, for I were desperate. He struck me; it ain't half sore.'

She lowered her head. *You bastard, you bastard*, she silently screamed. She'd kill him for this. With her bare hands, she'd kill him.

'I, I'm soiled, Sally. The smell . . . I'm sorry—'

'Oh, Mam.' She dropped the rag and took her in her arms. 'Don't fret so. We'll be home soon and everything will be all right.' Avoiding her gaze for fear of breaking down completely, Sally untied the string from her mother's hair and gathered her grey-blonde locks into a tidy bun.

'I'll wring your *neck* when I get my hands on thee! Come here, I need—'

She frowned slightly when again violent retching cut Joseph's speech. She guided her mother to the bed then crossed the room.

'Nay, lass! Don't go to him!'

'It's all right, Mam. I'll be back in a moment. Rest a while.'

There wasn't an ounce of fear in her; bubbling rage blotted out all else. She thrust open the neighbouring door and charged inside.

The sight momentarily threw her.

'Dear God, don't just . . . stand there. Fetch . . . help. Now, you gormless bitch, I'm in ag—' A stream of vomit erupted from his mouth.

She stared at him coldly. Whatever ailed him, she neither knew nor cared.

Crouched in the foul-smelling fluid, arms around his middle, he squinted up. 'Fetch . . . someone. Need . . . help.'

'All those years. You had me believe my mother was dead *all those years*? I hope you burn for eternity for all you've done, you evil bastard, you.'

Pain contorted his face. He clutched his head then his stomach again. 'For the love of God, help me!'

'Help you? Help *you*?' she murmured incredulously. 'After everything you've done to me, my friends, my mother?' She crossed the small space, halting inches from his bowed head. 'You've made my life a misery for more years than I want to think, and you want me to *help* you?'

He tried lifting his head and failed. 'Please . . .'

'My mother and I are leaving. If you try to stop us, if you *ever* come near me again, I swear to God, Joseph, I'll kill you.'

'You . . . bitch.'

Kicking at his feeble attempt to grab her foot, she spat on the ground and turned.

A hacking cough sounded next door and she paused. She glanced at the tankards on the table. One was empty, the other quarter-full, and this she lifted to take to her mother.

Between retches, Joseph's voice followed her. 'Get back here. Get back . . . here!'

'It was all I could find, Mam.'

Rose held the tankard to her lips then pulled back, grimacing at the strong ale's smell.

'Drink it, it will ease your cough,' Sally encouraged her.

Yet as her mother tilted it to take a sip, Sally frowned when, in the moonlight, she glimpsed something at the bottom.

'Wait. Let me see that.' Turning the tankard this way and that, her frown deepened at the blackish substance. She sniffed the contents then set the tankard on the floor. 'Never mind that. Let's get you home. Here, put your arm around my neck. That's it, take your time.'

Slowly, Sally guided her from the room. Looking left when they entered the passage, she halted. 'I shan't be a moment. There's something I must do before we leave.'

Joseph lay on his side, eyes half closed. His corpse-grey, sweat-slicked face twisted as she approached.

'Whore. Workhouse . . . whore.'

From beneath the folds of her skirt, she extracted coins from a pouch attached to her waist by a ribbon. She selected a shilling, stooped and pressed it into her husband's hand.

'You own me no more, do you hear me?' she whispered. 'You own me no more.'

His eyes widened as she rose. 'No. No, wait. Bitch! *Bitch!*'

Without a flicker of emotion, she turned her back on the devil incarnate and walked away.

Chapter 35

THE MANCHESTER COURIER
Saturday, 25 February 1854

On Tuesday morning last, Mr Rawley, the city coroner, held an inquest on the body of Joseph Goden, aged forty-eight years, who resided until a few weeks prior to his death with his sister at Chapel Alley, Bolton.

The deceased was discovered on Monday night at a lodging house where he had boarded on Lomax Street, Manchester, by Mr Greene, the proprietor. Assistance was obtained but life was quite extinct. The deceased had taken arsenic whilst intoxicated.

Enquiries were made with several apothecaries in the vicinity as to whether the deceased had recently purchased arsenic from their premises but each, upon viewing the body, answered in the negative and could offer no clue to his identity.

However, upon questioning, a fellow lodger gave information that he had witnessed the deceased the previous evening in the Bull's Head Public House, London Road, in the company of the Master of New Bridge Street Workhouse. After viewing the body, the Master identified it as that of Joseph Goden, a resident of Bolton.

Mr Goden's sister revealed he had been much troubled in his mind and had been drinking a good deal of late.

Dr Croft, of this Borough, was present at the inquest and a post-mortem examination of the body having been made, the effects of the deadly drug were plainly visible.

The Jury returned a verdict that the deceased came to his death from poison administered by his own hand whilst in an unsound state of mind.

After reading the article several times, Sally tore the newspaper into tiny pieces and threw them on to the fire. She stared at the grey ashes for an age and closed her eyes.

In the solitude of her kitchen, she sent up a thank-you to the Almighty.

Then she issued another, to Nancy.

Chapter 36
Late May 1856

THROUGHOUT THE AFTERNOON, tension within the Malloys' kitchen had steadily mounted.

Flo and Harry sat cross-legged by the fire, half-heartedly playing with a pile of wooden bricks, and along with the adults would glance up when their mother's cries sounded. They understood what was happening, had watched Maggie's stomach grow over the months with fascination and itched to meet their new sibling.

Con prayed their wait wouldn't be much longer for an altogether different reason. Why, he didn't know, but he couldn't shake the feeling . . . No, he told himself firmly. All will be well. *Merciful Jesus, please* . . .

He glanced at Rose and Teddy Lynch, sipping tea. They'd ceased trying to distract him with conversation long ago. Another wail drifted through and Teddy laid a hand on his shoulder.

'Let me take thee forra jar, lad. There's no use you wearing the floor out. There's no place for men at times like these; best to stop out of the way, leave the wenches to it.'

Con shook his head.

'Teddy's right, love,' added Rose. 'It could be hours yet. Babbies come when they're good and ready and not afore. I'll send for thee when it's over.'

'No. I'll not leave my Maggie till I know all's well. Sure, there'll be time enough later to sup the child's health. I'll stay in case she needs me.'

Jonathan squirmed to get down from his grandmother's lap and when he'd toddled to the twins she lifted the teapot. 'I'll brew a fresh pot then go up, see how things are progressing. I'm sure—'

'Mam, we need you up here,' Sally shouted. 'Quickly, Mam.'

Blood drained from Con's face. He made to follow, but Teddy stopped him.

'Nay, lad. The wenches know what they're about.' His eyes softened when tears filled Con's. 'My Ellen won't let nowt happen to her Maggie or the babby. Tha can be sure of that, lad.'

Ten torturous minutes later, a gusty cry rang through the house. Teddy grinned, and this time nothing stopped Con from rushing to the door.

He almost collided with Sally at the foot of the stairs. 'Maggie, is she . . . ?'

'Mother and baby are fine.'

Closing his eyes, he heaved a sigh. 'Can I see them?'

'Soon. Let us make Maggie and your son presentable then they are all yours.'

A slow smile spread across his face. 'The child's a boy?'

'Yes, and he's huge.' She wrapped her arms around him. 'Congratulations, Con. I'm so very happy for you both.'

He kissed her cheek soundly and with a whoop, punched the air.

Making for the kitchen for hot water, Sally let her smile slip.

The strapping child had become stuck and blind terror had rendered her and Ellen senseless. Without her mother's intervention, events could have taken a devastating turn. Worrying Con now was pointless; glory be to God, Maggie survived. Some were not so fortunate . . .

Forcing a smile, she got on with the task in hand.

Later, the bedroom made a beautiful scene. The proud father, perched beside his wife, gazed adoringly at his son and, exhausted but smiling, Maggie lay listening to the twins' name suggestions. At the foot of the bed, Ellen wiped away happy tears and Teddy, arm around her, looked as proud as Con, his joy at being part of this lovely family evident.

After a last look around at the people she adored, Sally took leave with her mother and Jonathan. They were nearing home when she noticed Rose scrutinising her.

'What's troubling you, lass?'

To her horror, tears welled and she quickly busied herself with Jonathan.

'Sally?'

'I'm just tired. It's been an eventful day.'

'Lass, I've missed out on so much of your life but I'm here now. If owt's troubling thee, owt at all, I'm here to listen, to help.'

Guilt stabbed at Sally but saving her mother worry remained her focus. 'I know. I'm fine, Mam.'

'If you're sure . . . ?'

'I'm sure.'

'Right, well, I'll take a walk to our Grace's. I'll take Jonathan, let you rest awhile.' Rose smiled down. 'Shall we visit Aunty Grace, lad?'

He grinned and prodded his chest. 'I come! I come!'

Sally watched them go, smiling when her son turned to flap a podgy hand. She waved back then turned into Pollard Street.

Inevitably, her thoughts returned to the man never far from them. Had he been as excited as Con the day he became a father? she wondered sadly. She pictured his smiling face, grey-blue eyes alight with anticipation.

That day would have begun as the happiest he'd known. Yet fate's cruel hand turned it into the worst of his life.

Tommy's suffering had tortured her; her very soul had ached to comfort him. She'd worn a brave face for friends and family but at night cried herself to sleep for many months. She'd imagined the scene repeatedly, saw him pacing the floor, anxiously awaiting the first cry. And hearing it, rushing upstairs, giddy with joy, only to discover that his wife of barely a year hadn't survived the birth.

Dwelling upon his plight had almost consumed Sally and for sanity's sake she'd *had* to force him from her mind.

After Maggie's brush with death today, however, he'd returned with a vengeance.

She paused to regain her composure but it was useless. She may have fooled her mother but Anna saw through her immediately.

'What's wrong?' she asked the moment Sally entered the kitchen. 'Maggie, the babby . . . ?'

'We delivered her of a healthy boy. Both are well. Is there tea in the pot?'

'Aye. So what's troubling you? You look like you've lost a sovereign and found a penny.'

Sally's fragile facade crumbled. 'Oh, Anna. I'm so wretchedly ungrateful. I have so much and yet . . .'

'Yet what?'

'It's not enough,' she whispered. 'It's just not enough.'

'Eeh, lass, what's up?'

Sally dropped into a chair and held her head in her hands. 'So much has happened these last years. They have been full of highs and lows but for every negative, a positive occurred to lessen the blow. I discovered Dicksy was dead; I lost her, yet gained a new friend in you. I suffered that final encounter with Joseph, yet from it, got my mother back. Do you see, Anna? Good always follows bad.'

She nodded thoughtfully. 'Aye, I suppose it does. I cursed the day I applied for a position as Mrs Sharp's companion but if I hadn't, I'd never have met thee. Aye, Mrs Sharp's assault upon me were the bad. My appearance stopped me finding employment, yet good followed – you gave me a position. And when my dear mam passed away and I couldn't bear living alone – the bad – you offered me a home – the good.'

'You see? Good does follow bad, for everyone.'

'So what's bothering thee?'

'The balance has shifted.'

Anna frowned. 'How?'

'I've had my mother back over two years and they've been the happiest of my life.'

'That's good, surely?'

'I'm not so sure, Anna. Look.' She counted on her fingers: 'I got my mother back. Joseph died. You moved in and have been a wonderful friend. Then Maggie and Con married; as did Ellen and Teddy the following month.'

'Sally, I don't—'

'Today, I helped bring a beautiful little boy into the world. He's perfect, Anna, in every way. And moments ago, I watched my mother with Jonathan. She walks tall, now. You remember her dreadful state in the beginning. Those dark days were not easy, for any of us.'

'She came through it, though, love. You built her strength, gave her a happy home same as you did me. I cope with my looks, now. The ignorance of some can't hurt now I'm accepted by so many. Tha brought me back to life and same with your mam.'

A small smile stirred. 'Her reconciliation with Aunt Grace aided her recovery.'

'Aye. She's strong and she's happy. When did you last hear her crying in t' night? The nightmares, they've left her.'

'Yes. Yes, they have.' Sally stared into the fire and sighed.

'What's wrong, lass? This ain't like you. What's this ungrateful nonsense? What d'you mean with the balance shifting?'

'It's not enough.'

'What's not? Sally, please, you're fair worrying me—'

'How many items did I list just now? Seven, Anna. *Seven.*'

'Aye. Seven happy events—'

'Precisely. Seven good and only a single bad between.' She lowered her gaze. 'Do you recall Mrs Morgan and Mrs Smith visiting last spring?'

'Aye. Con bumped into Mrs Morgan and gave her your address, didn't he?'

'At the market, yes, when calling on his cousin at his Bolton stall. Oh Anna, it was so very lovely to see my dear friend after so long. I scarcely believed my eyes when I saw her on the step. What I told no one afterwards was, Mrs Morgan imparted something that day. Her son, Tommy . . . His wife had died the previous summer during childbirth. Their daughter survived – one small mercy – but Dolly . . . She was so young, so pretty. Such a dreadful waste of life.'

'Oh, love. Why didn't you say owt?'

After a long moment, Sally met her gaze. 'Because I love him, Anna. I love him with every part of me.' She dipped her head, cheeks burning. 'That's the first time I've said it out loud. I barely held it together while Mrs Morgan was here; I couldn't have spoken of it afterwards without breaking down and revealing my feelings.'

'Eeh, Sally. I don't know what to say.'

'I simply cannot keep this inside any longer, Anna. My God, how I've tried to forget him! I cannot. Con and Maggie today . . . I'm so happy for them, truly I am. To love and be loved . . .' Her eyes misted with longing. 'I'm so very lonely at times. And that's why I'm ungrateful. I've had a clear run of good fortune – happy, happy, happy. I have wonderful friends, family and a beautiful, healthy son. I'm free of Joseph. I have the business, a home, and still . . .'

'It ain't enough.'

'And never will be without Tommy. But he feels nothing for me, Anna, in that way. And the balance between good and bad shall, I believe, ensure he never does. Besides Dolly's tragic passing, the road has been smooth. I fear I'm set for a series of unhappy occurrences to even things. Or perhaps that one torturous truth, that the only man I'll ever love will never be mine, shall mar life instead. Yes. Just that one to even the balance.'

Anna drew her into her arms. 'Oh, Sally. Ain't there a chance? Couldn't you speak to him? Tha can't be certain otherwise. You're free to love again, as is he. The time what's passed would've eased the worst of his grief. Couldn't you visit Bolton, see how matters stand?'

'I ache to see him more than I can express. I've worried myself into terrible states, yearn to know how he's faring. But I cannot see him. Being apart is hurt enough. To be in touching distance yet unable to be with him . . . That really would be too much. I cannot do it.'

Sighing, Anna held her closer.

'It pains me greatly keeping Mrs Morgan at a distance. Joseph's death gave me freedom to see her again but I have just that once – only then because she sought me. I pray things could be different but they cannot.'

'Does anyone else know of your feelings?'

'Con guessed long ago.' She pulled back to look at her. 'You won't speak of this to anyone, will you? Please. I, I couldn't—'

'I'll not breathe a word.'

Sally wrapped her arms around her once more.

'Aye, don't fret, lass,' Anna murmured. 'Don't you fret about a thing.'

The following days brought little change to Sally's mood and by Sunday Anna was in no doubt she'd done the right thing. Seated beside Sally by the lodging house step, she glanced left frequently, awaiting the familiar figure turning the corner.

Clement weather had brought Pollard Street's residents from their dank homes, eager for the sun's touch on their pallid faces. Men lounged on corners, sleeves rolled to their elbows, talking quietly, whilst their womenfolk, having abandoned their chores, sat on stools by their doors, gossiping and drinking tea.

Barefoot children of all ages filled the narrow street, their shouts and laughter ringing across the cobbles.

Boys raced or fought with imaginary swords and girls free to indulge in games collected stones, which they used as coins to play shop or create drawings on the flagstones. Those with harassed mothers played as best they could while lugging baby brothers or sisters in their small arms. Toddlers were left to their own devices to frolic in the gutter.

Whispering and laughing, lads too old for play stole glances at elder girls sitting on windowsills and flagstones who, mindful of their mothers' inevitable clouts for loose behaviour, mostly ignored the attention and instead half-heartedly watched younger siblings for squabbles breaking out.

Sally stroked Jonathan's hair as he played quietly with Shield. She gave Anna's conversation attempts brief responses and occasionally even managed a smile. But it didn't reach her eyes and too soon her morose expression returned.

Preoccupied, watching for Con, Anna jumped when Sally touched her shoulder. 'Sorry, lass. What did you say?'

'Would you mind Jonathan while I brew some tea?'

She nodded and when Sally disappeared inside, returned her attention to the corner.

He appeared and she rose, stomach fluttering in anticipation. 'Well?' she whispered. 'Will he come?'

'He will. Is Sally inside?'

'Aye. When will he be here?'

'Soon. When he appears, I'll make my excuses and ye do the same.'

'It'll work, won't it? Does he . . . ?'

The Irishman winked. 'Oh aye. Head over heels.'

'Who is head over heels?'

Neither had heard their friend emerge. They jumped apart guiltily. Anna opened and closed her mouth but Con recovered quickly.

'Me. I'm head over heels for my Maggie, for life, for the beauty that is God's green earth!'

Sally smiled. 'Is Maggie well? Baby Brendan?'

'Both are grand.' Suddenly, someone caught his eye at the end of the street. 'Well, I'd best be away.'

'But you've just arrived.'

'Sure, 'twas just a quick stop to say hello. Maggie's expecting me.'

Anna avoided Sally's gaze. 'I'll walk with thee, Con, stretch my legs. You want to come, Jonathan?' He nodded and she took his hand. 'We'll not be long, Sally.'

'Oh, Shield and I will come. We could call in at Aunt Grace's. My mother's there; perhaps they would care to join us.'

'Nay, you can't.'

She frowned, surprised. 'Why, Anna?'

'Someone needs to be here for folk wanting beds. You stay, lass. We'll be back soon.'

Disappointment glimmered in Sally's eyes but she smiled and nodded.

When they reached the corner, they glanced back. Sally and Shield were gone, and Con gave a wink to the man across the road.

'Well, we've done all we can, Anna. 'Tis up to them, now.'

'There may be some boiled ham from yesterday. Come, let's see if we can find you some scraps.'

Shield didn't need telling twice and eagerly followed Sally down the passage. Reaching the kitchen, however, he stopped. He looked back to the front door, lifted his nose and sniffed.

'What is it?' she asked when he whined. 'Is the bitch from number twelve waiting for you? Let's find you that ham and you can go back out.'

Shield gave a last, long sniff then obeyed.

After feeding him and pouring herself tea, she stared around and sighed. The house was so quiet these days. Mercifully, her mother and Anna remained but she missed the early days when Maggie, Ellen, the twins and Teddy dwelled here. Then, the house buzzed with life and laughter.

Anna had taken over their room, and Rose, who had shared Sally's since arriving, joined her to give her daughter and grandson more space. Sally's room seemed so empty afterwards and she thanked God she had Jonathan's company. The nights would be unbearably lonely when he grew and required his own.

'Stop these self-pitying thoughts,' she scolded herself now. Her loved ones were happy. That's what mattered.

She saw Maggie and Ellen at least once a week; Aunt Grace, Uncle Ed and Stan frequently. And she had her neighbours, who had accepted her into their community from the start. Their children were company for Jonathan, the women friendly, and there were any number of men to call upon for assistance with troublesome lodgers. She was by no means alone, and had much to be thankful for.

'Yet it's not enough,' she whispered to the emptiness.

The Morgans – one in particular – were the missing piece, their absence a yawning cavern nothing could fill.

'Oh, I must stop this!' she told the dog. 'No wonder Anna didn't want me accompanying them, souring the mood. What's wrong with me, boy? Why can't I free my mind of him, however hard I try?'

Shield peered down the passage. His ears pricked and his tail wagged furiously.

Moments later, there came a knock.

Winter brought lodgers to her step in droves, yet milder months still saw a steady flow. Anna was wise in insisting she stay behind. Customers' needs must come before her own pleasures. After tidying her hair and apron, she fixed a welcoming smile and opened the door.

'Good after—' The greeting caught in her throat.

'By, it's good to see thee, Sally.'

If a feather had blown through, it could have knocked her to the ground, so absolute was her shock.

Mesmerised, she watched Tommy sweep hair from his forehead, shoulder muscles rippling beneath his shirt. When he smiled, her own lips parted and a sigh escaped.

'Can I come in?'

She motioned to the kitchen. He led and her gaze travelled the length of him in wonder. She was dreaming, must be. Fuzziness overtook her. She felt weightless, as though she might flutter away like a leaf on the breeze.

He sat at the table and she drifted to the fire for the kettle. After filling it, she busied herself with cups and saucers. All the while, she felt his stare. Her hands began to shake and, abandoning the crockery, she went to fetch the caddy. As she passed him, he caught her arm.

Her every nerve leapt. She was as powerless to break free as if he had held her vice-like. She gazed at his hand, heart racing.

'Sally, leave the tea. I don't want tea.'

'Then what do you want?'

She held her breath as his hand strayed. His fingers closed around hers and her legs threatened to buckle. This wasn't real. *This wasn't real.*

'You, Sally. I want you. I've only ever wanted you.'

He rose and she saw his mouth move to hers. His lower lip grazed her own with the softest of touches and she closed her eyes. 'Am I dreaming? Are you really here?'

'Could I do this in a dream?' He wrapped his arms around her waist. 'Or this?' he asked, brushing his lips across her throat and jawline. Slowly, slowly, they returned to hers. 'Or this?'

His kiss stole her breath.

'Yes,' she breathed. 'In my dreams, yes.'

'Oh, Sally.' Her body dissolved against his and he sat and lifted her into his lap. 'It's always been you, only you. Lord, how I love thee.'

'But . . . when did you . . . ? How . . . ?'

'Explanations can wait for later, my love.' He removed the pins from her hair. Chestnut locks cascaded over her shoulders and he buried his hands in the silken mass. 'Marry me, Sally. Be my wife and make me the happiest man on earth.'

Gazing into the grey-blue eyes of the man for whom she'd yearned with all she was for years, pain stabbed her.

'You want to marry me? But I . . . I'm spoiled, Tommy. Joseph . . . the things he's done to me . . . I'm, I'm—'

'Perfect, d'you hear? Perfect. That's over with, finished. I swear to thee, Sally, with every piece of my heart, you'll never know a moment's sadness as my wife. All I've ever wanted is to make you happy. I'd deem it an honour to spend the rest of my days doing just that. You have me, mind and soul, allus have. Please say you feel the same.'

'I feel the same and more,' she choked. 'I've never wanted anything more than to be your wife.'

Their lips found each other again and the world faded.

When he carried her to her room, she gave herself completely. He took her tenderly, with understanding, and she loved him all the more for it. Afterwards, as they lay entwined in each other's arms, their soaring hearts beating in perfect rhythm, she wept with sheer joy.

Finally, she knew how it was to be loved. And it felt wonderful.

Upon the others' return, Sally knew not a shred of shame for how she and Tommy had spent the afternoon. What they had shared was the most natural thing in the world and she regretted nothing.

She was no slip of a lass whose head had been turned with passion. She was a widow, mother, a woman who had endured more than most twice her age. She'd harbour no guilt for loving and being loved by the man she adored.

When she'd informed her mother and Anna of Tommy's proposal, and their tears and congratulations died down, she took Jonathan into another room. In terms he'd understand, she explained how the future was to be, that he'd have a new friend – Jenny, Tommy's daughter – and that they would all live together.

He thought for a moment then pointed to Shield, and when she assured him yes, him too, he clapped his little hands excitedly. And she laughed through blissful tears for her beautiful boy. For the first time in his short life, he'd know a father's love.

After the evening meal, her mother drew her aside and said she'd have Jonathan in with her tonight. A hint of embarrassment touched Sally's cheeks, then, but Rose's eyes told of her understanding, her pleasure that she'd finally found what she'd searched so long for. Sally couldn't have been more grateful or loved her more if she tried.

That night, she and Tommy talked and made love until the sun peeped over the grey rooftops.

They spoke of Dolly and Joseph, Con, their children and families. They discussed their future, hopes and wishes. They cried, laughed, kissed, their bond strengthening with each minute, hour, that floated by. And they loved as neither had nor thought possible. They were one. Their unity had made them whole.

After a lingering goodbye the following afternoon, Sally watched him walk away with a peaceful heart. Once he'd seen to business in Bolton, he'd be back. And she'd be counting the seconds.

Chapter 37

MAGGIE EXTRACTED THE poker from the fire. The heat had turned it orange-red and, after blowing off ash, she tilted Sally's head. Tongue peeking from the side of her mouth, she wrapped a length of hair around. When she unwound it, it bounced around Sally's face in a perfect curl.

Sporting new hats and matching smiles, Rose and Grace looked on, shiny-eyed with love and pride. Anna, too, wore a new hat in periwinkle blue and she lifted its short veil to wipe a happy tear.

'Hold still,' Maggie instructed when Sally shifted to glance at the clock, 'else you'll be walking down the aisle stinking of the goose fat we'd have to put on your burns. That would be too much even for Tommy, daft for thee as he is.' The women laughed and Maggie smiled. 'Not long now, lass. A few more and we're done.'

When at last she stood before them, there wasn't a dry eye. Her mother had dressed her hair and beneath the lace veil, delicate as a spider's web and studded with imitation pearls, she'd left several curls to flow. They framed a face alight with anticipation, midnight-blue eyes sparkling and cheeks, which had needed no pinching, delicate pink.

Around her throat lay a string of tiny pearls, a wedding gift from Maggie and Con, which set off the stunning, cream-coloured taffeta gown to perfection. This too had imitation pearls along the seams; she'd fallen in love with it on sight. Though initially she'd baulked at the dressmaker's quote, her mother, aunt and friends had insisted this was the one.

Sally was glad they had. It felt glorious, like a second skin – a far cry from the tattered, earth-coloured one the first time around.

Rose took her hand. 'Oh, lass. I'm so very proud of thee.'

'And me,' choked Grace. 'Eeh, tha look as pretty as a picture.'

Maggie and Anna nodded agreement.

'He's a lucky fella, he is.'

'I'm the lucky one, Aunt Grace.' She squeezed her hand, then turned to Maggie. 'How are you feeling?'

'Aye, all right.' Glancing at the bump beneath her new dress, her friend smiled ruefully. 'Little divil's been jigging all morning. Must be all the excitement.'

Falling pregnant barely a month after Brendan's birth had pleasantly surprised Maggie but was proving a trial. Aches and lethargy had replaced the sickness she'd suffered from dreadfully in the early months, and Sally had promised Con she'd ensure she didn't tire herself today.

'Well, remember, take it easy or Con will have my guts for garters.'

Maggie clicked her tongue but the twinkle in her eye for the husband she adored belied her exasperation. 'Con frets too much. I intend to enjoy myself today. Anyroad, never mind about me; how are you feeling? Tha must be sick with nerves. I know I were – both times.'

The softest smile lifted the corners of Sally's mouth. 'I feel nothing but peace. Tommy's my everything. He completes me.' Four pairs of arms enveloped her. Tears threatened and, laughing, she pulled back. 'Please, you'll have me weeping.'

Her mother caressed her cheek. 'Right, lass, you ready?'

She nodded. She'd never been more so for anything in her life.

That balmy August afternoon held no resemblance to the day of Sally's marriage to Joseph Goden. This day, she glowed with an inner light apparent to all.

Outside, a sea of loved ones hugged and kissed the new Mr and Mrs Morgan. They had filled the church to bursting; their smiles, as Sally glided down the aisle on Ed's arm, brought tears to her eyes.

On one side were seated her mother, Jonathan, Stan, Grace and Winnie; Anna, Maggie, Con and the children; Ellen, Teddy and his father, Mr Lynch. Numerous neighbours also attended. In the opposite pews she saw more dear faces, none more so than Ivy, Arthur, Shaun and little Jenny.

Tommy's elder siblings, their spouses and children, were a happy sight; Sally had met them the previous month and couldn't have been more delighted with her new in-laws. Several pit lads were present, and Martha Smith. George Turner was also there, suspiciously bleary-eyed but smiling.

They couldn't have hoped for a better turnout; even Shield had been in attendance, albeit on the church steps.

After thanking Father Collins for conducting the beautiful service, the party returned to the lodging house, where a lavish wedding tea awaited.

They didn't have to spare a thought for paying lodgers as, for the first time, there were none. Sally had freed the rooms for her Bolton guests, who would travel home the following morning.

When all were assembled in the kitchen with drinks, Tommy called for attention.

'On behalf of myself and my wife, thank you for coming today.' He and Sally raised their glasses. 'A toast, to you all.'

'To the bride and groom!' trilled the grinning guests.

He turned and raised his glass again. 'To my wife. You've made me the happiest man to ever walk the earth. Thank you.'

'And to you, my husband,' she murmured then smiled shyly at the guests' collective 'Aww'. She raised her glass once more. 'Last but by no means least, please join us in raising our glasses to absent friends.'

Two people instantly sprang to mind but she dashed them away. Absent they were, but friends they certainly were not. As far as she was concerned, despite the good that had come from the money, Agnes harmed too much in life to be remembered in death. As for Joseph . . . all she'd ever wish for him was to burn in hell for eternity.

'To Jonathan Swann who, despite everything, was a good father to me. To my dear cousin, Peggy. To my friends, Dicksy and Miss Sharp. And to Dolly,' she added, squeezing Tommy's hand.

'To absent friends,' they chorused, more than one wiping away a tear.

'Now, let's celebrate!' Tommy ordered, then kissed his wife soundly, much to their guests' delight.

And so they enjoyed themselves for all they were worth. Everyone got along brilliantly, mutual love for the bride and groom binding them in friendship. They ate, drank, laughed and sang and, thanks to the carter's accordion skills, danced for hours.

At one point, Ivy took Sally and Tommy aside and held them close. 'I'm so very happy for youse,' she said huskily. 'Me and Arthur guessed of your feelings years ago.' She smiled wryly at their sheepish expressions. 'Aye, we're not bloody blind. It's been a long time coming, has this. Now you've got each other, you hold on tight and don't let go, d'you hear?'

When they nodded, she stroked Tommy's cheek tenderly. 'Don't hold no self-reproach over Dolly. Tha were a good husband to that lass. You put her happiness first and for that, I'm proud of thee. It's time, now, to think of *your* happiness. You have Nat Jenkins's blessing. Make the most of what you've allus wanted, lad.'

He caught her in a hug. 'I love you, Mam.'

'And I you, son.' She turned to Sally and took her hand. 'You've been part of my family from the start; I can't tell thee how glad I am it's official. You've made my young lads happy, changed both their lives. You've an angel's heart. Don't let bad memories of that divil have any part in your new life. You're free of what's gone afore, lass.'

Tears spilling, Sally embraced her. Then George started up a new tune, Tommy took their hands and they laughed and danced, bringing smiles from everyone.

Later, they thanked Anna yet again for intervening, then sought out Con. When he'd shaken Tommy's hand, Sally hugged him tightly.

'Thank you,' she told him for the dozenth time. 'If you hadn't gone to Spring Row and told Tommy how I felt . . .'

'You'd have found each other eventually, regardless. True love will out, so it will. Be happy, acushla,' he added softly.

The twins' giggles rang above the noise and, turning, they saw Maggie and Ellen, helpless with laughter, dancing a lively number while Teddy, holding little Brendan, looked on with a smile.

'Mind you're not for tiring yourself, so, Maggie,' Con called and when she rolled her eyes and beckoned him to join her, grinned. 'Sure, let's show them how it's done.'

Despite her aching feet, Sally allowed the men to lead her. Others vied for a dance with the new bride until, finally escaping the floor, she flopped beside her aunt at the table.

'Look at them two, lass,' Grace murmured, nodding to her son and sister dancing together. 'Things turned out well in t' end, for us all. I can't believe I've got my Rosie back. And to see her with Stan . . . It's more than I deserve but by God, I'm happy.'

Since reuniting, the sisters had cried an ocean between them. They had righted wrongs and at long last buried the past. Rose's years in the workhouse put the precious gift that was life into perspective; she understood more than most that it was far too short to hold grudges.

Sally sighed contentedly then turned with a groan, feeling a hand on her shoulder. 'Oh, Anna, please don't ask me to dance,' she begged, laughing. 'My feet are throbbing.'

'There's no fear of that, lass. I've two left feet; you'd not get me up dancing for owt! Nay, someone's asking for you at the door. I invited her in but she refused, said she needed to talk with thee in private, like.'

'Did she give her name?'

'Nay, lass.'

Frowning, Sally slipped from the kitchen. Everyone she knew and loved were beneath this roof; who could be asking for her, and at this hour? When she reached the door, her mouth fell open.

'If you want me to leave, I'll understand.'

'What do you want?'

'To explain. To say sorry. To say thank you.'

After a long moment's deliberation, Sally stepped outside, shutting the door behind her. 'I haven't got long. I have guests to attend to.'

'Congratulations to youse both.'

Sally nodded and folded her arms. Under her steady gaze, Nancy flushed.

'Knowing you were wedding today, that you'd found happiness at last as you deserve . . . I had to come. I've put this off long enough. I'm so very sorry, Sally. I were weak with infatuation. He were evil and I couldn't see it. I couldn't *see* it.' She glanced left and right then leaned in. 'It were me. I killed him.'

'I know.'

Nancy's mouth stretched into an O.

'Joseph was too selfish to end his life. If he'd had his way, he'd have lived to a ripe age – to spite me, if nothing else.'

'Then why didn't you . . . ?'

'Shout what you did from the rooftops? That you lured me back to a man who had caused me more pain than you could imagine? That you were a murderess? That *you* slipped that lethal dose into his ale?' Sally shuddered, recalling how close her mother had come to drinking the deadly brew. 'I had my reasons.

'I didn't mention your name to anyone and my mother was in too poor a state to remember. I told my loved ones Joseph came here, threatened to hurt my mother if I refused to go with him, but that we escaped. They wanted to hunt him down but I said I couldn't recall the address.'

'Why, Sally?'

'I'd left him in a state of illness but never thought . . . or perhaps I did. Perhaps, in the back of my mind, I knew Satan was soon to collect his favourite son.'

'And if you'd told, they might've found him afore he died?'

'Precisely. I believe I wanted to avoid that.'

'But weren't they suspicious upon hearing he'd died?'

'They were simply glad he was gone. If they suspected foul play, they didn't voice it.'

Nancy nodded. Tone soft, she asked, 'Why keep silent about me? Mercifully, the housekeeper at that lodging house made no mention to the police of me or your mam having been there. Whether it slipped his ale-sodden mind or he didn't want the greater scandal of murder tarnishing his place, I don't know. And I told Alice I returned to Bolton the night afore Joseph died, pretended to be as shocked as her.

'I said he'd sometimes spoken of ending it all, never thinking he'd act on it. She didn't suspect a thing. I knew you were the only one with the power to see me swing; it were torture. Yet you kept your silence. Why?'

'You gave me back my freedom,' answered Sally thickly. 'In return, I ensured you kept yours.'

'Thank you.'

'Thank *you*. I hold no ill feeling towards you, Nancy. You were under his control as much as I. Difference is, I didn't have the courage to end his life.'

Nancy's hardness surfaced. She lifted her chin. 'I can't believe I were so blind for so long. I convinced myself he loved me. I let him strike me time and again, telling myself he didn't mean it. I neglected my children to be with him, stole from my father to please him. Everything were for him.

'The thought of losing him filled me with such terror, I were prepared to do owt. Even at the cost of your safety.' She cringed at the admission. 'I've done some terrible things and for the remainder of my days must live with the guilt. But I don't regret removing him from this earth. I don't regret that forra second.'

'What made you see him for what he was?'

'That poison were intended for my father.' Nancy nodded when Sally shook her head in horror. 'Joseph wanted him gone and his hands on his brass. His words were like a pail of icy water in my face. He didn't love me at all. I knew that, then. He never had.'

Sally frowned at the question that had niggled at her for years. 'There's one thing I don't understand. How did he find me? Manchester is vast; just happening to see me at the workhouse is too incredible a coincidence. I'm right, aren't I?' she asked when Nancy looked away.

Her eyes burned with humiliation. 'He ordered me to ask around. I sniffed about the row like a stray mongrel, desperate for scraps, desperate to please *him*. Dishing out Father's dinner one day, I heard him enquire about your health to Martha Smith. She told of the hard time you'd had, said you'd worked for that mother and daughter what were in the newspapers.

'Father never throws nowt out; I searched his owd papers for the article. It said where it occurred, so we had an idea of the area you lived. We trawled Ancoats for days and one afternoon saw two little 'uns playing with yon dog.

'We waited forra sighting of thee but the dog must've remembered Joseph's scent. It began barking, forcing us to scarper, but we knew then we had the right street. Then Joseph said we were collecting your mam. I were flummoxed but he said not to ask questions. You see, he . . . he . . .'

'He what?'

'He said he'd get shot of thee so we could be together. I didn't know his plan but God forgive me, I went along with it. I'm so sorry . . . that I'd stoop to such wickedness . . . Leaving the workhouse, we spotted you. We couldn't believe it. He had me follow to see where you dwelled, while he . . .' Sighing, she closed her eyes.

'Dragged my mother to that stinking lodging house?'

'Oh, Sally. You'll likely not believe that your mam's state and how he treated her hurt me, but it's true. How's she . . . faring?'

'She's as happy as a body could wish.'

'Lord, tha must loathe me. *I* loathe me. All I were focused on were us skipping off into the sunset, foolish bitch that I am. I realise now he collected your mam to bribe you back. If we'd not seen you at the workhouse, he'd have lain in wait in this here street till he spotted you. He'd have let me murder Father then used the money to scarper with thee.'

Sally released a long sigh. 'Put it behind you, Nancy, as I have. Forget him, live your life. Concentrate on your children, your father. Don't let his ghost consume you. Don't let him win.'

'By, you're a fine woman. I wish I had an ounce of your goodness.' Nancy shook her head in wonder then drew up her shawl. 'Goodbye, lass.'

'Goodbye, Nancy.'

Having laid to rest another demon from her past, Sally walked into Tommy's arms with a lighter heart. She could now put to him the secret wish she'd carried for so long. Only thoughts of seeing Nancy had deterred her; now, nothing stood in her way.

He wrapped his arms around her waist, saying 'I love you.'

'And I love you.' She glanced about, then took a deep breath. 'Tommy, there's something I've been meaning to speak with you about. How would you feel—' There was tugging at her skirt. Glancing down, she saw Jonathan and Jenny smiling up.

'How would I feel about what, my love?'

'Oh, it will keep.'

She took the children's hands and Tommy did likewise. And as they danced, Shield bounding between, they heard more than one guest remark that they made the most handsome family they had ever seen.

Evening turned to night and the exhausted children were put to bed. The adults continued the jollifications and it wasn't until much later that Sally and Tommy snatched a moment alone. He found her by the window, pink-cheeked but still smiling.

'Finally, I've got thee to myself,' he whispered, nuzzling her neck.

'Tommy, people are looking!'

'Let them.'

She giggled then stared at him earnestly. 'What I said earlier . . . that I wanted to speak with you . . .'

'Aye. What is it?'

'I want to return to Spring Row.'

He pulled back to gaze at her.

'Years ago, I promised myself if I had the chance, I'd leave the smoke of Manchester behind and raise Jonathan amongst Breightmet's green hills. I miss it, Tommy. I miss the freshness, the meadows, the tranquillity. I miss the people, the cottages; the row itself. Manchester holds a place in my heart and always will, but it's not home. Spring Row . . . It's like a yearning inside. Can you understand?'

'I can, but Sally . . .' He ran a hand through his hair. 'The memories, everything you've been through—'

'Cannot hurt me any more. Not now I have you.'

'But your family, friends, this place. You'd leave all this behind?'

'I'd still see them. Bolton is but a train journey away; one I'm sure I could brave with you beside me. As for this place . . . I'll explain later.' She caressed his cheek. 'You were willing to leave behind all you hold dear for me. But I know that, in your heart, you share the same love for Breightmet as I. And there's Jenny. Dolly's parents deserve to see their grandchild grow. She's all they have of their daughter. I couldn't take that from them.'

Tommy's eyes could have shone with no purer love. He kissed her tenderly. 'Dear God, I love you. More than you'll ever know.'

'I simply pray . . .'

He followed her gaze to Rose, who was chatting with Grace. 'Will she agree?'

'I do hope so. I cannot be without her, not again. Yet the thought of taking her from Aunt Grace pains me, Tommy.'

'As you said yourself, Bolton's but a train away.'

'Still . . .'

'You'll not know until you ask, love.'

Sally's heart was thumping as she took her mother aside, but she needn't have worried. Rose shared her sentiments entirely: where her daughter went, she went. Grace shed a tear upon hearing, but once Sally reassured her they would visit often, agreed she must do what made her happy.

'It's what youse both want?' asked Ivy excitedly.

Tommy nodded. 'Mind, we might have to live on here a good while,' he told Sally. 'Cottages don't come empty often.'

Ivy bit her lip. 'Nay, they don't, but . . .'

'But what, Mrs Morgan?'

'There's a young Irish couple moved in last year. The lass were telling me only yesterday they'll soon be moving on.'

Sally laughed delightedly. 'Oh, what marvellous good fortune!' Bewilderment replaced her joy, when she saw Tommy's expression. 'My love?'

He stared helplessly at Ivy, and it was she who mumbled, 'The cottage they dwell in . . . It's your owd 'un, lass.'

Sally was silent. When finally she turned to her husband, her voice was calm. 'How would you feel living there? If you're fine with it, I am.'

'But . . . the hell. The horrors you went through . . . I don't want you reliving that past every day. Surely you'd never know peace beneath that roof? I vowed today, besides the rest, to protect you. That means all of you, body *and* mind. I'll not have memories of that divil clinging to our marriage, our family, our *home* like a cancer.'

'That could only happen if we allowed it to.' She rested her palm against his chest. 'Would living there be so very difficult for *you*, my love?'

Tommy answered without hesitation: 'Truthfully? Nay. Nay, it wouldn't. My past doesn't dwell within those walls. I hold no nightmares of the place. It's not myself I'm thinking about, but you. And it's forgetting all that's been that I want to help you to do.'

'But I don't want to forget, Tommy.'

'You . . . don't—?'

'Hear the lass out, lad,' murmured Ivy, nodding slowly, and Sally knew the older woman understood.

'To forget is to pretend it didn't happen. It did. And in a way, I'm almost glad. I don't expect you to understand,' Sally told him when he frowned. 'I realise it must sound madness to you. But you see, I view life as I never would had I not encountered Joseph. I'm grateful for each day, every breath. Enduring what I did makes what I have now all the sweeter. I cherish this, with you, more than you'll ever know, *because* of him. No, I don't ever want to forget, I know that now. What I want is to accept. Accept that it happened, put it behind me, finally, and live happily. Whether in that cottage or the other side of the world makes no difference to me. None whatsoever. It truly wouldn't to you, too?'

'What you went through there, it pains me, imagining . . . I'll not deny it. But if you can face it, I can, if it's really what you want . . . ?'

'It is.'

'You're certain?'

'As long as I'm there with you then yes, I'm certain. It will be different this time. We'll make it a happy home, we six, together.' She held out a hand and smiled. 'And now, Mr Morgan, would you care to dance?'

As had Nancy, he shook his head in awe. 'Mrs Morgan, you *incredible* woman, I'd be honoured.'

Chapter 38

'SIT YOUR ARSE by the fire, you big bugger, afore you knock me south.' Ivy jerked her head across her kitchen, expression stern, but couldn't contain a smile as Shield sloped off. 'He's like a bucking hare, ain't sat still since you arrived.'

'He's excited to be back, I suspect,' said Sally, then chuckled, seeing her mother grinning at Ivy's no-nonsense way.

Ivy sat with a groan. 'Eeh, my bleedin' back. Rotten owd age, I could swing for it.'

Rose could hold back no longer and laughed. 'Oh, Ivy, you're a tonic. I sympathise, mind. My knees ain't what they were; creak like an owd barn door, they do.'

'Aye. They don't know when they're well off, these young 'uns, Rose.' She nodded to Sally. 'You wait till you're owd and grey. There'll come a day when your crumbling bones struggle to shift thee.'

'I shan't mind. I'll have my husband to carry me in his arms.'

Ivy hooted with laughter. 'Soppy bugger, yer. By, but it's good seeing you sat there, lass. Have you really no regrets? Don't you miss yon lodging house, not even a bit?'

'No,' she answered truthfully. 'It shall remain what I intended, with or without me. That's what matters. Oh, Anna's face when I handed her the keys and deeds. The woman whose money bought that house, all she suffered at her hands . . . Anna deserves it far more than I ever did.' She peered around the cosy kitchen she'd so missed. 'Oh, it's good to be back.

'Truly, it is,' she insisted when Ivy shot Rose a look. 'I feel nothing but hope, Mrs Morgan; that won't change upon Tommy's return. Do you remember my taking the carrier's cart all those moons ago?' she asked quietly.

'I do.'

'As we passed through the row, I admit, I vowed never to set foot inside there again. But it wasn't the cottage I loathed and feared, I know that now. From today, it will be what it never could under Joseph's rule. It will be a home.'

Ivy's eyes were suspiciously bright. 'Drink your tea, lass, afore it grows cowd.'

Sally and her mother shared a tender smile for this woman. Having her for a neighbour was a delight; a friend, more so. To call her family was a blessing from heaven. Their futures were all the brighter for having her.

Voices sounded beyond the door. The children burst inside, holding hands.

'Go see, Mama, go see!' said Jonathan excitedly.

'See, see!' mimicked Jenny.

Sally chucked the toddler under the chin then ruffled her son's hair. He had no idea she was no stranger to the cottage soon to be his home. And she hoped he never would. She glanced to Tommy in the doorway. He held up a key and winked, and she smiled.

'Let your mam and father look round by theirselfs,' said Ivy. 'We'll stop here, eh, and have some fruit cake.'

With her mother's encouraging hug, Sally took her husband's hand. His love lent her strength and as they passed up the familiar path, her step didn't falter.

Inside, he hung back and she was grateful for his understanding. As she'd secretly feared, past demons lingered and she knew if she was to be happy here, she alone must banish them. No one could do it for her.

She wandered through the rooms, long-ago memories flitting then disappearing. At last, she returned to Tommy, pale but calm.

'Can you face it, Sally?'

'Yes.' Though she spoke truthfully, she knew pain flickered behind her eyes.

He wrapped his arms around her. Then he took her face and kissed her.

Taking her hand, he led her to the next room. Again, he held her then kissed her softly. This, he repeated in each. They spoke no words and needed none. After holding her in the last room, his kiss was more tender still. When they drew apart, Sally knew he saw a different look: one of peace and hope.

She stared around through fresh eyes. With each embrace, each kiss, the badness had seeped away. This wasn't a house any more but a home. They had blessed it with their love.

'Happy?'

'Happy,' she answered on a sigh of serenity.

They left hand in hand. At the gate, she motioned to Ivy's. 'You go in. I'll follow in a moment.'

Alone, she gazed at her new home and smiled for the future. She envisioned family life: eating dinner together at the table, the children's laughter as they played with Shield, sipping tea with her mother by the fire on wintry nights, she and Tommy making love beneath the eaves . . .

'Hello, missis.'

Sally turned in surprise.

The child, a fluffy cat in her arms, was taller, cleaner, less pinch-faced. None the less, there was no mistaking her. 'Lily? It *is* you! Oh, how lovely to see you!'

'Please don't be angry with me.'

It was then that Sally noticed the dread in the blue eyes, the nervous biting of her lip. 'Lily, what's wrong? Why on earth would I be angry with you? I'm delighted to see you after all these years.'

'Aye?'

'Of course.' She tapped the tip of her nose. 'Why would I ever be angry with you, lass?'

'Because of Uncle Joseph.'

'Your . . . Uncle . . . ? Dear God, it was *you*? Tommy said the child who helped them was named Lily, but I never . . . never imagined . . .'

'I'm sorry, missis. I never knew you were his wife and when I saw you in fat Nellie's, and what he'd done to you, and I knew it were you from the market, I cried, and I'm sorry, and, and—'

'Shhh, Lily, it's all right. It's all right.' Sally drew her, sobbing, into her arms.

'He were wicked, he were, wicked. I thought you'd not want to be my friend if you knew he were my uncle. I thought you'd be angry, that you'd tell me to bugger off.'

'Oh, Lily. You're as innocent as a lamb. You helped the Morgans rescue me. You saved my life. You've been only brave, clever and good. I could never be angry with you, never.'

Lily wiped her nose on her sleeve. 'You mean it, missis?'

'Of course.'

The cat struggled for release. Setting it down, Lily pulled a face. 'Bleedin' heavy, that thing. I've carried her all the way. Never go nowhere without Clover, I don't.'

A slow frown creased Sally's brow. 'How did you know I was here?'

'I were at the market, earlier, saw thee and another lady and Mr Morgan's son boarding a cart. I thought my eyes were having me on.'

'The lady's my mother. And Mr Morgan's son, Tommy, he and I are married now, Lily. We left Manchester this morning.' She pointed to her cottage. 'There's our new home.'

Lily smiled. 'I saw that babby of yourn, an' all. Grown, ain't he?'

It suddenly struck her that Lily and her son were cousins. Lord, but it was a small world. 'You can come say hello to him if you like.'

'Can I, missis?'

Sally nodded, wondering how this lovely girl had come from the womb of such a terrible woman. And with thoughts of Alice, her smile melted.

'Does your mother know you're here?'

'Nay. Long gone, she is.'

'Gone?'

'Aye. Father had enough and slung her out. She's been gone this past year, thanks be to God. He'll not mind me seeing thee, for he knows you never did wrong. He couldn't stand Uncle Joseph, neither.'

'Well, I don't know what to say. And your mother's never returned?'

'Nay and I'm glad. She worsened after *he* died, began drinking more and thumping us about. She said you drove him to do away with hisself with your wicked ways. We knew she were wrong; he were the wicked 'un, not thee. Home's better, now. Father's not sad and he's gorra job. And our Lizzie's returned with her babby.'

Their conversation at the market, of Lily's sister allowing her master's son in Manchester to have his way, came back to Sally. Little had she known it was Alice's Lizzie the child was referring to. 'I'm so very glad you're happy, Lily.'

'Ta, missis.'

She held out a hand and asked, 'Shall I take you to see your cousin?'

Lily clasped it with a nod and a grin. 'Stay there, you,' she told Clover. 'The missis here's gorra dog the size of a horse. Gobble you up in one, he would.'

'If we hurry, there may be some cake left,' Sally said as they headed for Ivy's. 'Are you hungry?'

The child smiled at what she clearly still deemed a daft question. 'Do fishes have a fondness for water?'

Epilogue

BIRDSONG BROUGHT A smile to Sally. Gazing at larks swooping and gliding through the azure sky, she sighed contentedly.

She was with her mother and Jonathan, Shield trotting alongside. They were walking through an emerald-green field abloom with cowslip and buttercups, the air heady with love. Rose held Jonathan up and he laughed as she planted kisses on his cheek.

When he turned to look at his mother with smiling eyes of the same sapphire-blue, Sally's heart swelled with pride for the fine-looking boy he'd become. They sat in the sweet-smelling grass and she lifted her face to the sun with a rush of such happiness, it stole her breath. Rose drew her close and she rested her head on her shoulder.

Her heart skipped as she caught sight of a tall, dark-haired man heading towards them across the field. His face was in shadow but she knew without question that she loved him, and that he loved her. In his muscular arms, he carried a girl with hair the colour of corn. She lifted a tiny hand and Sally waved back . . .

This time, there was no pain. The beautiful scene didn't blur. As Tommy drew nearer, a long-ago whisper echoed on the breeze. And Sally smiled.

Indeed, all was not over. It was just the beginning.

Acknowledgements

To my agent, Judith Murdoch, for everything, and my editor, Francesca Best, for her sound advice and understanding. Thanks to you both.

About the Author

Thirty-two-year-old mother of three **Emma Hornby** lives on a tight-knit working-class estate in Bolton and has read sagas all her life. Before pursuing a career as a novelist she had a variety of jobs, from care assistant for the elderly, to working in a Blackpool rock factory. She was inspired to write after researching her family history; like the characters in her books, many generations of her family eked out life amidst the squalor and poverty of Lancashire's slums.

You can follow her on Twitter @EmmaHornbyBooks and on Facebook at www.facebook.com/emmahornbyauthor

As good as Dilly Court or your money back

We hope you enjoyed this book as much as we did. If, however, you don't agree with us that it is as good as Dilly Court and would like a refund, then please send your copy of the book with your original receipt, and your contact details including your full address, together with the reasons why you don't think it is as good as Dilly Court to the following address:

Emma Hornby Money-Back Offer
Marketing Department
Transworld Publishers
Penguin Random House UK
61–63 Uxbridge Road
London
W5 5SA

We will then send you a full refund plus your postage costs. Please note you have 60 days from the date of purchase to make your claim and only one claim is permitted per person. We will only use your details in compliance with the Data Protection Act and in accordance with our privacy policy. The promoter is Transworld Publishers, Penguin Random House UK, 61–63 Uxbridge Road, London W5 5SA. No retailer is responsible in any way for any refunds under this money-back offer.